A Lady of Scales and Smoke

THE AUSTEN LEGACIES: RELICS OF ASH AND AETHER

BOOK ONE

KELSIE ENGEN

LITERA SCRIPTA MANET

ISBN: 978-0-9984994-8-2

Litera Scripta Manet
PO Box 10845
Fairbanks, AK 99710

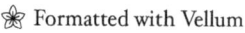 Formatted with Vellum

Dedication

FOR EVERY READER WHO HAS EVER FELT HOPELESSLY OUT OF PLACE:
YOU WERE NOT MADE IN ERROR;
YOU WERE DESIGNED FOR A TIME LIKE THIS.

"For if you remain completely silent at this time, relief and deliverance
will arise for the Jews from another place, but you and your father's
house will perish. Yet who knows whether you have come to the
kingdom for such a time as this?"
Esther 4:14

Foreword

Dear Reader,

This book has been years in the making. Originally, I intended it to be a Regency gaslamp fantasy—true to the era and a faithful ode to Jane Austen. But as the story grew, it became clear to me that Austen's stories are hers alone. What began as a close retelling with fantasy elements transformed into a series inspired by all of Austen's works, and I could not be happier with that evolution.

Within these pages, you will find echoes of *Lady Susan*. Some characters may feel familiar, as may certain actions. But if you are expecting strict Regency accuracy...please don't. Names are altered, places are renamed, and characters are reimagined. While Austen remains my inspiration, the story itself is my own.

There is one other meaningful way in which my story differs from Austen's. As she herself wrote in *Persuasion*, "Let other pens dwell on guilt and misery." I do not share that constraint. My books contain darkness—deliberately so. While I do not write explicit evil on the page, evil exists, and to ignore it does my reader a disservice, for true Light cannot shine except in the darkness. Be prepared for wrongdoing, for shadows, and for morally gray choices, for it is only through the dark that the Light can be fully seen.

With that, thank you for reading—and for giving *A Lady of Scales and Smoke* a chance.

With all sincerity,
   Kelsie

Contents

Prologue

TEN YEARS EARLIER

Blood dripped steadily into the porcelain bowl from his wife's arm, the mixture of the cloying, metallic essence and repeated plops turning his stomach. He couldn't remember the last time he had eaten.

He clutched the slight, frail hand, pale and clammy atop the bedsheets. She inhaled, raking a ragged breath across her once lush lower lip. His heart raised in hope.

Her eyelids fluttered, eyes flitting under their curtains of blush, periwinkle, and dawn.

He leaned forward in anticipation of consciousness.

Hope blossomed in his heart. But her eyes did not open; instead, she gasped, her mouth gaping open like a fish dying.

No, she was a waif, an imprint of what she had once been, a shadow of what her children had taken from her and left her with. Her white-blond, wispy hair completed the picture of life being sucked from her, one breath at a time.

After all this time since his daughter's birth, he found himself waiting for an awareness in his wife that never came. A false spring.

The floorboards of the ancient castle creaked behind him, but he did not turn. Could not reveal the rawness of his heart that he knew his face exposed.

The Healer walked to his wife's bedridden form and exchanged the brimming bowl with a fresh, clean one, this one decorated with Stormbringers stretching their wings around the rim in an endless, hopeless pursuit of freedom. The bowl caught his attention for a few moments as the dragons, enchanted by a mage with an Artistic Legacy, fought for escape from their confines. He understood their desire for escape —he'd never understood it more.

The Healer poured the blood into a vase, cursing under his breath when his hand shook and blood spilled over the rim and coursed down the outside of the etched jar.

The general felt his ire rise. Her lifeblood spilled in such a careless fashion. But this Healer was the best, a genius, according to some.

Continuing his task, the Healer emptied the saucer and set it aside on the cart. Wiping his bloody hands on a cream-colored towel and leaving streaks of red behind, he finally spoke. "General, if I may...?"

The general flicked his fingers in permission.

"Removing the ill humors may gain you a week now, but she shall not live long with her malady." When the general did not respond, the Healer added with grim hesitation, "Sir, this will be fatal."

Again, the general did not move from his position. Watching the blood pool and drip against the ravenous Stormbringers. Watching the life drain out of his wife. Watching her ragged breaths barely lift the sheets.

He willed his heart to harden, but she had always been his one weakness, his one truth, his one compass. How could he exist without her? How could they all?

Without raising his gaze or leaving his post, the general said, "You will find me a solution, Mage Healer."

His precious wife twitched at his voice, and both men paused, watching greedily for any signs of health, as though she were a delicate, priceless bud about to bloom.

But it was quickly clear that she would not bloom, that her blossoming had gone. He watched a flower dying, not budding. And slowly, the general slid his gaze to the reedy man with a long nose and robin's down hair.

"We might isolate her," the Healer said. "Isolated from all emotion, her Empath nature can no longer spark, and she *might* have years."

Isolation? The general held his breath, knowing his anger would offer precisely what she did not need. But keeping his own emotion at a distance was one thing—not feeling it at all, an entirely different beast, for his wife, the Empath, felt all emotion now whether she wished to or not.

"Sir?" the Healer questioned, the bloodied towel hanging limp between his hands.

"I will not accept your failure, Mage Healer. Isolation is failure." The general pressed his hand over the woman's to cup her limp fingers within his strong, battle-worn hands. Her arm twitched, and his gaze followed it as his emotion seemed to travel from her fingers up towards her face. He withdrew his hand. "And if she dies, so do you."

The Healer's throat quivered. "I—" he began, but quaked as his words failed under the general's stern glare.

The towel fluttered to the cart, heaping itself in front of the jar of crimson.

Only the crackling of the fire could be heard in the room.

Then, "There might be a solution," the Healer said in his bedside voice, as though he tried not to awaken his patient. "However..." He raised his brows and lifted a finger to the door.

Understanding, the general flicked his fingers towards it without removing his hands from his wife's. The Healer, at the permission, snapped his own long fingers, and the door, as if waiting for his command, snapped shut in answer.

The Healer dipped his blood-stained hands into a bowl of water. The glacier water bloomed rose pink, but the stench of blood in the room mingled with the coppery taste of anticipation on the general's tongue.

"Get on with it, man," he snapped, impatient. "You know how short her time is."

The Healer dipped his head this time, shielding his face from the icy gaze pinning him to his spot. "Yes, sir. General, sir."

The general's face betrayed his annoyance. "What. Can. We. Do?" He deliberately punctuated each word with a ringing silence behind it.

The Healer cleared his throat once. Then again. Opened his mouth. "Forgive me, sir, but have you heard of the 'Perfect Mage'?" His voice barely carried in the room, and despite himself, the general leaned forward over his wife's inert body to hear the Healer better.

"The what?" Irritation laced his voice with delicate threads. "Speak up!"

Upon the bed, his wife flinched and moaned. He softened his tone and pushed away his pain.

"Explain."

"The creation of the Perfect Mage. One who might heal such a desperate affliction as beleaguers your wife."

The general sat back. "That's ridiculous. The only Perfect Mage that has ever existed has been the First King."

The Healer leaned in. "But what if there were a way to restore Legacists—back to the way we were supposed to be, before the First King made his decision to isolate the Elements?" His eyes glittered in the candlelight, amber-hued daggers slicing through the general's heart with hope he could taste but not imagine.

The general's breath skimmed over his mustache. The backs of his hands tingled. His heart had stilled only to reawaken with the pulse of promise. "Go on." His voice was husky and low in the dim light of the sick room.

The Healer ducked his chin. "There is a myth. A myth that the bearers of the Relics might be able to combine their Relics—their Legacies—to recreate the whole."

"Take the broken parts and recombine them?" The general's eyes widened. In all of his deepest dreams of more, he had never considered such a thing. Who had dared?

"Yes, sir." The Healer clutched his still-damp hands before him, entwining his long fingers with themselves. A touch of dried blood clung under his thumbnail.

The general flicked his fingers again. "Go on. A myth is lovely, but not practical."

"Yes, sir. The myth, it says that if one can combine the four Elemental Legacies into one, then a Perfect Mage will be born."

The general set back against his chair in wonderment. "Is that... possible?"

The Healer spread his palms to the ceiling. "Imagine the possibilities. If it were. One might find themselves a mage without limit. One who might control Fire, Air, Water, and Earth...and more."

The general fixed the thin, reedy man with unsettling intensity. "Or a Healer who might work miracles."

The Healer's eyes glinted. "Indeed."

Chapter One

JOLIE'S SCHOOL FOR
LEGACY REFINEMENT
OF THE MODERN LADY

Miss Fenya Verena perched stoically as Magess Jolie outlined—in great detail—the exact sins Fenya had committed while under the magess's tutelage at Jolie's School for Legacy Refinement of the Modern Lady.

Even the name of the school made Fenya's stomach roll. Jolie's school had nothing modern or refining about it. But if it had only been her listening to this for the tenth time, Fenya could have ignored it. What made today infinitely worse than any other time was the presence of another woman in the office: her mother, Lady Magess Seraphina Verena, Rank II Order 3, the dear friend to Magess Ailyn Jolie, who had begged the magess to take Fenya at her school after her father's death.

The sprawling oak desk seemed the perfect kindling between herself and Magess Jolie—all she needed was a spark to ignite the richly lacquered wood.

No. I shouldn't even think that. Especially not with Mama sitting primly beside her, the new lace half-mourning gown fashioned out of a deep gray muslin that brought out the silvery gray of her eyes.

That's right. Papa died six months ago now.

Tears pricked her eyes as the fire snapped in the grate in sympathy, and Fenya carefully inhaled and refocused her efforts on keeping the fire at bay. There was something different today. Something with Power that Mama had brought with her.

Breathe. In. Hold. Out. Hold. Repeat. In. Hold. Ignore the fire. Out. *Ignore the fire.* Hold. In. Out. No, she was supposed to be holding her inhale. She clenched her eyes shut as the fire crackled in annoyance.

"Fenya, dear, are you listening?" The voice demanding her attention was calm on the surface, but like the fire could burn, the voice held the promise of punishment if Fenya acted wrongly.

"Yes, Mama," she answered demurely, dropping her gaze to her folded hands resting on her black skirt. Her fingers seemed to shimmer slightly, as though they were made of fire and heat shivered over them.

"Miss Verena," said a different voice, this one of Magess Jolie, the hard woman who seemed to enjoy most when Fenya failed at anything. She was just like Mama, delighting in Fenya's struggles and failures. Why were they even here talking about her like she was a child, deciding her future for her, once again? When Papa had died, Fenya had been packed up and shipped off to Jolie's school, nary a care for what she wanted.

From her position in a hard oak chair that had her shifting subtly every few minutes, Fenya did her own debating within while she watched and waited for the two women to decide her future. The only thing worse than staying here with the sanctimonious, self-seeking bullies who pestered her at Jolie's daily was returning home, a failure, with Mama.

"I've done my best, and she is worse today than when she arrived," Magess Jolie complained.

Mama inhaled almost too softly to discern. Perching on a chair, Mama flexed her hands into the folds of her skirt.

Why does she bother with appearances so much? Lady Magess Verena kept the order of mourning to the hour, and yet she had cared little for her late husband, who had made her a Relic Protector in the Verena family with Fenya as Heir as soon as she turned eighteen...or the Emberheart Relic accepted her as its next Bearer.

But there's little chance of that if I can't control Fire anyway. No Relic would accept me as its guardian if I'm uncontrollable. What a mess.

"You know how important her control is, given her future." Magess Jolie slid a gaze Fenya's direction, and Fenya stiffened but tried not to show it.

"Of course," Mama agreed, lifting her embroidered gray handkerchief to her eyes to dab away invisible tears. "If only my son had lived."

Fenya wanted to roll her eyes, to rise and scream at Mama that she wished her brother—born and dead before Fenya—had lived too. The pressure put on Fenya wouldn't exist then. Turning away from Mama so that she wouldn't speak, she fixed her attention on Magess Jolie again.

How she longed to tell Magess Jolie that she had never been helped here. That her Legacy burned with passion and Fire and begged to be released. If she hadn't kept such a hold on it as she did now, she would have destroyed the same hateful office they sat in. Magess Jolie had no idea how even a candle flame called to her. How Powerful she could become if she just gave in to the desire that never stopped tugging at her. It was an intoxicating scent, as if the mere sniff of wine made her drunk if she didn't seek fresh air. She'd skipped lessons dozens of times, just to disappear into the woods and run away from the constant attack of fire.

"We all wish for things we have not, Seraphina," Magess Jolie said softly. "But we must deal with the things we have been given."

Nodding, Mama dabbed at her nose with her handkerchief. One more thing Fenya could never measure up against: the sainted babe in heaven. Her shoulders drooped.

"Fire is one of those Legacies that must be tamed early on if it's to be tamed at all," Magess Jolie said with a disapproving wrinkle of her nose in Fenya's direction. "And she's simply not trying."

Not trying? Fenya choked back her retort.

Mama spread her gray-gloved hands over her lap. "Is it too late for her?"

"Never marry a Fire Legacist," Magess Jolie said with a wry grin, and the fire in the grate crackled with glee. The flames bent toward Magess Jolie, as though she had done it on purpose, simply to show her Power. "Or at least, marry them off early before they can reveal their true character in society."

Still behind her oak desk, Magess Jolie drew a ball of flame from the fireplace and hovered it over her hand, lifting it enough to display it fully to them. Despite herself, Fenya's eyes locked on the flame.

"You've seen Fire up close, Seraphina, much more than the average person. Elementals are common enough, but Fire is considered one of the more dangerous Legacies. Even the air is fuel for us. And thank God she's not a Spark—so much Power with such an ability would be tragic. She would be Blacklisted for certain, despite the Relic. They've done it once before, reassigning the Relic to a family that can protect it and have more children. It's already tragic that she's the last Relic Heir for the Emberheart Relic."

Fenya flinched. *Tragic?*

"No chance of your brother-in-law taking the Relic? Passing it on to one of his children?" Magess Jolie pressed.

The fire in the grate churned and gnawed at the logs, taunting Fenya like she had never known. Her heart thumped unevenly with something like hope. If she could but pass this burden on, everything would be better.

Mama sighed. "No. Before my husband died, we tried to pass the Relic to Caius." She withdrew Papa's pocket watch from her clutch and let the chain run through her fingers. It had multiple gems on it, something Fenya had thought to be surprisingly gaudy for her simple-styled father—before she knew that the largest gemstone in it, a teardrop amber gem, was the very Relic that she cursed on a daily basis. "He is not a Flame, and though his children might be, according to the Relic laws, we must first attempt to bond it to Fenya."

"Is that it?" Magess Jolie whispered, holding out a hand for it, then pulling back in sudden fear. "I can feel it. From here. I'd best not touch it."

Fenya tried to shut herself off from it. She'd felt it as soon as Mama had walked into the office. *God, why did it have to be Fire?*

Mama inhaled and turned to Fenya. "Dear girl, try again."

Fenya recoiled. "Try—the Relic—?" She flashed a look to Magess Jolie, but her expression was hungry, eyes sparking with eagerness. "Mama? Are you...?"

Mama's eyes narrowed. "Take it, *darling*, see if it claims you yet."

Fenya shivered though she was anything but cold. Instead, the office seemed to close in tight around her, the fire licking at her skin. The last time she'd touched it, before coming to Jolie's school, it had been with such hope that she would find herself claimed and her Legacy miraculously controllable. Instead, it had done nothing except make her Legacy itch daily as though it hadn't forgotten the Relic's touch and longed for it as a balm against her skin.

"Take it," Mama insisted, offering the round, silver watch with its silver chain connected by gemstones.

Holding her breath, Fenya reached out a trembling hand. Mama lifted the watch so the chain dangled above her hand, and then slowly dropped the chain into her palm, setting the watch on top.

The chain and gems were cold against her flesh, and though the Relic pulsed with its lingering Power inside the gem, nothing happened.

"Do you feel anything?" Magess Jolie asked eagerly, leaning forward.

Fenya shook her head.

Mama sighed and Magess Jolie sat back in her seat.

"Disappointed again." Mama seized the watch and slipped it into her clutch, the slight lines around her mouth appearing as she pursed her lips in annoyance.

"Perhaps in another year..." Magess Jolie trailed off. "But she can't stay here. If the Relic accepted her today, perhaps she could stay, but she's a liability here without the Relic. She's not even something to boast about having at Jolie's. She can't be married off with her risks. It would destroy my reputation. And who's to tell what she'll burn down in the next year?"

At the list of insults, Mama's face tensed, but she smoothed down her skirt and faced Magess Jolie with an expression of understanding.

"Of course, Ailyn, but you know how traumatic events affect a child. She's a bit slow, I confess, but the desire is there." Mama placed a hand to hover over Fenya's knee.

Slow? Fenya schooled her face into indifference as they talked about her as though she weren't there. The fire popped in the grate in complaint. She wanted to defend herself, to protest that she under-stood what they were asking, but neither of them had the amount of

Power that coursed through her. If she unlocked the gate, all her Power contained behind it poured out like oil spilling from a lit, broken lamp. Neither of them had ever explained how to stop it—and Papa had fallen ill and died before training her

"Unfortunately, she's a growing danger to us all here at Jolie's. She's quite incapable of going a day without claiming an accidental fire. Her traumatic past is no excuse. I've had many children here who have lost a parent and arrive still in mourning." Magess Jolie tapped a finger against her chin in thought.

Fenya raised her gaze at that, ready to speak her own defense, but Magess Jolie barged on.

"Which brings me to the others I must—we both must—think of. Many students have real fears of her burning the place down as they sleep."

"That's ridiculous. Surely you can do something..."

Magess Jolie spread her hands palm up to the ceiling before clasping them under her chin and leaning forward on the desk to speak. "I'm doing you a favor, Seraphina. If I keep her here, she will prove herself an inadequate match for any man, regardless of her Relic Bearing status. You know how rumors fly."

Am I now being accused of purposefully misusing my Legacy? In. Out. In. Hold. Hold.

"What other options do I have, Ailyn?" Mama's plea was more a whine than a question.

"If she gains some control in the next six months, I would consider taking her again next year."

"Can't she stay just another six months? Complete the year?" Mama asked, a sweetness to her tone that told Fenya Mama had plans of her own that would take those six months to complete, and she didn't wish for Fenya's interference. "Time helps with control, or so I hear. And the extra time would be useful in deflecting awkward questions."

"I trust you can deflect awkward questions without my help, Seraphina," Magess Jolie said with twinkling eyes that also brooked no argument, despite their status as friends.

Mama had already asked a favor in bringing Fenya here in the first place. They had no money anymore, the manor had been sold, and

Mama had shipped Fenya off to Jolie's as though she were an unruly dog sent to a kennel for training.

Fenya slid her gaze discreetly to the side to catch her mother's profile, but she gave nothing else away. Why would Mama demand only six months for Fenya to be gone when she could happily lock her up in an asylum and be rid of her forever? Mama had plans indeed. But were they for Mama or for Fenya?

Magess Jolie considered Mama for a moment, then swept her hand across the room and with its return drove a ball of fire from the fireplace into the center of the room. "Miss Verena, if you can manipulate the fire back to the flames without growing the fireball, then I shall give you another month."

Fenya's heart sank. She could never keep a fire small. It always grew under her control, as though her enthusiasm for it, her desire to nurture it and make it grow did just that. Maybe that was the key. Maybe she just had to think thoughts that would make it shrink. But no, she was supposed to return it to the other fire, its mother fire.

Fenya bit her lip. Magess Jolie was waiting, the flame burning happily over her palm. Mama had turned to watch Fenya perform.

Her stomach clenching in a knot, Fenya straightened and took a breath. *Hold. Out. Take control.* She stretched out her hand, palm up, inviting the flame to her. It leapt from Magess Jolie's palm to hers joyfully, the fire in the fireplace surging with excitement to have its child in *her* hand.

Fenya tensed at the fire's touch. It didn't harm her, but it was uncomfortable, like she'd stuck her hand in icy water. The air around her hand shivered in delight.

Breathe!

The reminder made her exhale sharply, and the fire surged happily, doubling in size within seconds.

The ball of fire burst in the air, showering the room with sparks.

Mama's face morphed into shock, the barest shimmer in her façade dissolving.

The sparks splashed against the wall, bounced off Magess Jolie's desk, and snuggled into her grade book.

"No!" Fenya exclaimed as they tumbled toward the ground. She couldn't set fire to the school. She'd be sent to an asylum for sure.

At her panic, a second shower erupted, spraying onto Mama, coating her skirt in tiny sparks that burrowed into the dark grey lace covering the muslin underneath.

Mama's shrieked, and Fenya jolted back to herself and covered her face with her hands, abandoning all attempts to control the fire, fighting to sever it from her touch.

Magess Jolie swept her hands through the air, catching the fire and all its sparks.

Fenya clenched her eyes shut, but each of the sparks invisibly clung to her skin. Each one that Magess Jolie captured was a hair pulled from her arm, her face, her head. Magess Jolie gathered them back together in a fireball, but the damage was done.

Fenya had failed. *Again*. What was wrong with her?

Magess Jolie returned the fireball to its mother in the grate, and the reunion revived her, a sharp contrast to the agony that burned inside her.

"I suppose that answers that." Mama stood, disappointment lacing her words as she brushed off her skirts. "You might as well go pack your things."

Fenya rose, bobbing the quickest curtsy to Magess Jolie that she could escape with, desperate to remove herself from her failure.

"Now, Ailyn," Mama began as Fenya reached the door, "let's talk expulsion versus dismissal. The consequences are very different, you know."

Fenya slipped out the door, but stopped outside, listening to the continued conversation within.

"You know how hard that will make it for my daughter to be accepted into any school except a government reform school should you expel her—and that would also make it nearly impossible to find her a suitable husband even with Emberheart. The only chance I have for the girl would be private tutors—and with having to sell Leighton House, I simply couldn't justify the expense."

There was a pause inside. It was rare for Mama to admit her lack of funds. Fenya stared at the hallway lined with paintings. Several were Animated by Legacists, and a ballerina danced in the confines of one frame, while a famous mage manipulated fire in another. She'd always tried to avoid looking too long at that one.

"Seraphina, do you honestly wish the girl married?" Magess Jolie said from her office.

"Of course! She has her duty, just like the rest of us. More so with her being the Heir. Curse my dead husband for not giving me another child." Mama's voice had lost its softness now to coat each word in bitterness. "And curse him for dying with such debts."

"Perhaps it's best to let there be no further Verena Heir to the Relic."

"What are you suggesting, Ailyn?" Mama asked coldly.

"As your friend, I suggest strongly considering whether this line of Fire Elementals is worth preserving."

There was a very pregnant pause within the room. Was Magess Jolie suggesting what Fenya thought? Her body went cold, but the fire within called to her as if trying to warm her, embracing her, reassuring her that she was not as alone as she felt. Why was she a Fire and not a Beauty like Mama? She never would be in this situation if not for her Fire.

"An asylum?" Mama said slowly. "To let her simply...burn away?"

"There are some that could contain her. Her Power will continue to grow until she is at least twenty-one. I wouldn't be surprised if she eventually tests as a Rank I Magess. And if she does not control herself, an asylum is where she will end up—to your own reputation's detriment." Magess Jolie gave a cynical chuckle. "Could you imagine her with child? The surge of Power she would have during her condition?"

"She could kill someone."

"Or herself." Magess Jolie added.

"A village..." Mama's voice almost whispered.

Another pause.

Fenya's skin shivered at the fear in both of their voices. *I'm a monster. They think me a monster.*

"But an asylum...it's a death sentence, Ailyn. And it would destroy the Relic, unless the Crown decided to transfer Power to another Flame."

Fenya stared at the wall opposite the door, trying to ground herself. Inside another frame, a pair of girls danced around a maypole, this painting Animated by a previous student, she'd been told.

"I'm not certain they would, darling," Magess Jolie said. "It's been a century since a Relic was transferred in such a way. But, better that it's destroyed. Legacies will exist outside the imbalance of the Relics. They are ancient things that never should have been created, if you ask me." Magess Jolie scoffed loudly. "Some fool of a man deciding that Legacies shouldn't be passed on whole. A house divided cannot stand— Seraphina, you must unite your house or your daughter will crumble it from within."

"Unite..." Mama murmured, "of course."

The words rattled around in her brain, assaults on her very being. Veins of fire, gold through a cave, streaked throughout her. Fenya shuddered. *Marriage, child bearing.* If it wasn't an asylum and certain death, it would be death through bearing some man's heirs. She was only suitable for a man because of her Relic anyway. The very thing that made her mother marry her father: the power of a rare family Relic that—

A snap of the fire inside Magess Jolie's room caught Fenya's attention mid-thought.

That fire contained an aether shield, delicate, holding the flames within. Magess Jolie's doing, for Fenya sensed the tie between the magess and the flames. A net of gold, protective, loving, the arms of a mother keeping something contained for its own safety.

I could break it.

The realization came abruptly to Fenya. The flames wanted her to break it. They didn't want to be safe, they wanted to consume. And so did she. She could burn this school to the ground, if she wanted. Maybe she did. She wanted to consume her mother with it—burn the Relic into the ground, free herself from this horrible Fire forever. She would be better off if she had never been born a Flame, better to be born an Ordinary than a Wylde!

She could burn it all down. The Power was within her grasp...

But she couldn't. Because she lacked the courage. Instead, she covered her ears with her hands and bolted for her rooms.

Chapter Two

WHITLAND MANOR

Running from the office had afforded her only a few minutes of reprieve. There had been no one to save her, no one to prevent her departure with her mother. And now the horse and carriage ride to Whitland Manor showed Fenya just how much money she and her mother now lacked.

If they had anything remaining from the sale of her father's birthplace and Fenya's intended inheritance, Mama would have spent it on traveling in style, fully displaying their remaining wealth in a dragon or pegasus coach that would land in some impressive display at her aunt and uncle's house, as well as making the trip take a third of the time. Instead, they bounced along on rutted roads that seemed to have more holes than even ground, all in the name of saving a few pennies.

The carriage, though private—Mama wouldn't lower herself to sharing a carriage with strangers unless absolutely destitute—stank slightly of mildew and had several threadbare patches in the purple velvet seats. Fenya liked it like that. It made her think of the hundreds of others who had ridden here before. Perhaps one hole was even a burn mark that wasn't her fault for once.

Even a dragon coach wouldn't have spared Fenya Mama's lectures and cold shoulder for hours of travel on bumpy roads that constantly elicited an annoyed huff from her mother, though it would have spared her the assault of passing flames from villages and even sheepherders trying to keep warm in today's damp cold and fog. There weren't flames in the air, after all.

Fenya sat with hands locked in her lap, staring out the thick glass window, her gaze fixed on something—anything—other than her mother. When Mama drifted off to sleep about an hour in, Fenya didn't dare relax to do the same, but instead quietly opened her satchel and pulled out her sketchbook.

For a year, she'd meticulously sketched dragons and their parts in its pages. If she was lucky when she skipped classes, she found a dragon to be her model image. It was the only thing outside of the clean air and forest that gave her peace from the fires assaulting her from all sides. Somehow, the dragons seemed to soothe her, creating comfort for the time she sketched them, or even when they were near. Sometimes, they seemed to pose for her, remaining still long enough for her to sketch their wings with precise details.

A lingering inspection of Mama showed Fenya that she was still asleep, her head lolling slightly back, beautiful even in her slumber, though it hid her bright, gray eyes. Her long, dark lashes rested on her cheeks, and her dark hair with not a single gray strand, was pulled back into a perfect braid wrapped around her head in a crown with a dark gray hat that had a half veil pulled back to expose her face.

Fenya sighed and turned away. With nothing outside the window but endless lanes of grassy fields interspersed with village houses, she shifted sideways on the carriage seat, pulled up her knees under her skirts, and dove into her sketches. She'd been having a nightmare of a time getting the angle of the Thistle Sprite fairy dragon's wings right. It should be parallel with the hip, but no matter how she tried, she couldn't get it.

Fenya lost herself in the lull of the carriage, only growing frustrated at the way the bumps jarred her pencil across her page at the most inopportune moments. For once she agreed with Mama: travel by air was much more comfortable.

When the light was growing dim in the carriage, the driver's voice called out to halt the horses, and Fenya's concentration broke. A moment later, the carriage shifted as the driver climbed down. Mama stirred, and Fenya threw her legs back down on the floor, arranging her legs so she appeared proper. She smoothed her skirts as the carriage door opened, and Mama roused herself fully.

"We're just swapping out the 'orses," said the carriage driver. "Thought you might like to stretch your legs." He nodded at Mama, his blank stare lingering on her before jolting back to Fenya. "There's places to grab a bite nearby as well, if ye like." He couldn't keep himself long from staring at Mama, so captivated by her image.

"Thank you." Mama offered him a demure smile as she shook out her skirts and accepted the driver's help in descending the carriage. She walked stiffly, as though the slumber had made her body sore. It created a strange juxtaposition for Fenya, as she knew her mother aged, but she never showed any sign of it. Perhaps the occasional wince of pain as she woke and shifted after a long time seated, but her Beauty covered all other indications of aging.

Fenya stepped to the door, but the man had escorted Mama further away from the carriage instead of waiting for her, and she suppressed a sigh. Mama constantly received that sort of attention from men, to her delight, especially when it angered other women witnesses.

Without bothering to wait for the driver to return, which was a hopeless cause, Fenya picked up her skirts and hopped down the steps to the gravel road below.

The carriage driver was called back to tend to his horses, and Fenya seized the chance to stretch her legs in the small patch of trees nearby. She breathed in the fresh air of the outdoors. Above her in a small tree, a cat-sized dragon gave an owl-like hoot. Fenya eyed it, but it remained on the branch with no indication of attacking, its yellow eyes glinting in the gaslight shining off the carriage station. Her skin itched at the recollection of the flames.

Nearby horses whinnied, and hooves clopped on brick paving stones. Making certain no one was watching, Fenya stretched her hands behind her head and bent backward, stretching her spine.

A jolt rocked through her like every nerve was electrified.

Something had sparked.

She whirled and saw the tell-tale glow of a new flame on the carriage. *Of course. It's growing dark, and the horses need light to travel the roads by, as does the driver.*

Fenya bit her bottom lip as the driver lit three more lamps so that two hung on each side of the carriage.

"One for the inside, Magess?" The driver's voice carried to Fenya where she stood shadowed, and though Fenya couldn't hear her answer, the driver lit two lamps and placed them inside the carriage so it glowed, revealing Mama as she climbed inside to wait.

Fenya inhaled slowly through her nose and held it. They should be at Whitland in only a couple more hours. She just had to make it through the rest of this day...and then...

Then...

Fenya exhaled heavily. Then there would be fires all over the manor house. Never could she let her guard down; she had to learn to keep her Fire forever suppressed. It would have been so much easier if she had been born a Beauty like Mama. When had anyone ever killed with Beauty?

"Fenya, darling," Mama called, her voice holding a sharp edge. "We must leave now."

Fenya inhaled once more, and held it as the dragon above gave another mournful hoot. Fenya peered back at it, giving it a nod to acknowledge its farewell.

Steeling herself against the burn of the lamps, she climbed back into the carriage. She leaned back on the bench, her eyes fixed on her lap. The carriage lurched forward, and the lanterns swung wildly from side to side, the flames wobbling and pulsing in their confines. Fenya couldn't keep herself from examining the one closest to her.

Only feet away. Just over arm's reach.

It was like a hot meal thrust before a starving man.

She swallowed and looked away only to find Mama staring at her.

"You'll have to resist more flames than these, you know, my darling," Mama said.

"I know," Fenya said, her tone sharper than she intended.

Mama stared at her with narrowed eyes for six swings of the lantern. "Have you considered your future? We can't afford any more failures."

"Of course," Fenya said, working to keep her tone even and soft.

"I've been considering it too. So I came up with an agreement for us..."

Fenya's stomach clenched. Agreements with Mama were akin to selling her soul to the Devil. She held her breath.

"Aren't you going to ask what it is?"

"I know you'll tell me," Fenya said, shrugging as though she didn't care. She folded her arms across her chest, hugging herself tightly. *Inhale.*

"Maybe I won't." Mama's tone was carefully controlled. "After all, I don't need you messing it up."

Fenya caught her breath. Hold. Hold. Her vision started spotting. Black dots flashed on the edges. The fire in the lantern sputtered, growing smaller. She just wanted to make her mother proud. Why was it so hard?

Mama turned her attention to her lap and opened a book sitting on it.

Fenya's heart teetered. Her gaze snuck to the bench, where her satchel sat, but her sketchbook was gone. Mama had seized the chance and taken it when Fenya wasn't there to protect it. Her stomach twisted into a Gorgon's knot as the lantern flames spat.

"I think it comes down to this, my darling," Mama said, flipping a page and pausing to consider the image. "If you can control yourself around the flames for the next few months, I'll let you marry a man who won't control you. A man who deserves a wife with a Relic like yours." She ran a finger along the page, scratching at what Fenya knew were burn marks.

Fenya held her breath. "I'm only seventeen. Papa didn't want me to marry until the Relic claimed me—"

"And growing in Power every day." Mama spoke over her and swept a hand toward the lantern swinging by the window. "Danger surrounds you at every turn, all before the Relic claims you. Or do you expect to go live as a hermit? Live on uncooked meat and fruit and vegetables?" Mama's sarcasm bit deep.

"Of course not. I plan on finding a...a tutor...or another school... one that can help with my control. There has to be someone who can help. A scholarship program perhaps. Magess Jolie mentioned a few..." Her words trailed off, her cheeks heating at the amusement dancing in Mama's eyes.

Mama stared at her for a moment before her lips curved into a pitying smile. "My dear...my darling. If your brother had lived—God bless his soul—we would have more options. But you are a woman. And soon to be a Relic Bearer at that. You know your uncle has failed to be accepted by the Relic. If you are not..." she trailed off in ominous silence.

Fenya's cheeks burned. Inhale. Hold. Exhale. Hold. If she didn't suffocate before she turned eighteen, it would be a miracle. "It might not accept me."

"You have no option other than to have it accept you." Mama leaned forward, urgency replacing her amusement. "The Verena line dies with you—"

"My uncle has children, perhaps—"

"The Relic doesn't work like that. It wants an unbroken line of Flames, and would rather choose a woman than the son of a man who is not a Fire Legacist. Your uncle, despite his wealth and large family, is not a Flame."

"But I might not need to marry..." Fenya bit her lip as the foolish words slipped from her mouth.

"An *unmarried* Relic Bearing woman?" Mama scoffed. "It cannot happen. You must marry and must bear a child."

Fenya steeled herself. "It might be different this time. Perhaps I marry a Flame who will be accepted by the Relic..."

"Or there is another option. One that forces the Crown to act."

"What's that?" Fenya asked in hesitation.

"Reform school. Or asylums," Mama added thoughtfully.

"Reform school means the Gray List. Asylums...the Black List, Mama," Fenya's words trembled, but she searched for some sort of reason to avoid such a future. "Would you do that to me *and* tarnish *your* reputation?"

"My darling." Mama tilted her head. "It's already tarnished. But at least you'd have a future then. And maybe a suitable marriage could be found. Perhaps even amongst a Relic Bearer. Can you imagine being joined to another Relic Bearer?"

Fenya scowled. "Aren't they all married?"

"Obviously not the heirs." Mama's eyes glinted. "I should be able to convince one of them that you're suitable. I am still the daughter of a count, after all, and you the granddaughter."

Suppressing a wry smile, Fenya picked at a thread on her skirt. "Well, perhaps you should marry one of them."

"You think me not young enough to bear another heir with a virile young man?" Her lower lip pouted out. "Do you think me too old to marry?"

"Mama, that's not what I meant—" Fenya began, regret coursing through her.

Mama held up a hand to stop Fenya's defense. Biting back a sigh of frustration, Fenya turned to the window, sinking back against the cushions. There was something out there...something large, watching.

Outside were dim pastures filled with white dots...sheep. Something lurked. The sheep were moving, uneasy. She narrowed her eyes and leaned forward. Then, sharp and sudden, a shadow descended.

A Nightstalker dragon the size of two horses combined grabbed a sheep with its claws and flew off into the night. The captured sheep bleated in fear and pain as the others scattered. The carriage jolted as the horses spooked at the sight.

"Oh dear Lord, save us," Mama muttered, gripping the seat.

The driver spent the next few minutes soothing the animals, and Fenya determinatively pretended the lantern flames weren't angrily hopping in their confines. Was the oil in the lantern even fueling them? Or was it Fenya's anger? She felt them as though they were a finger or a toe attached to her.

"I assume by your silence that you're thinking you'll get out of your first real decision?" Mama said sweetly, picking up their conversation as though there had been no interruption.

Fenya's attention jerked back to Mama. The confined flames leaped tall, and Fenya couldn't help but wince.

Mama smiled knowingly. "Is that a vote for the reform school?"

"No," Fenya said quickly. Reform schools were just the first step toward asylums. If she went there, she would all too soon be at an asylum. It would only take a couple of accidents for them to put her name on the Black List with the Crown, and forget Mama, *Fenya* would be forever ruined.

Regardless of where she lived, if she ended up on the Black List, she would be a criminal on the run. She would be homeless, dependent upon her own skills...which should be impressive, as one of the most Powerful Flames in Avenesse thanks to the Emberheart Relic. She'd been raised with the expectation of inheriting her father's Power upon his death. Only he'd died too soon to pour them into the Relic for safe-keeping, and her Powers had exploded. The greatest skill she had was sketching, but who could make a living as an artist when there were Legacy Artists who could literally make their images dance on the page?

But marriage? Fenya tried to swallow down the fears that locked up her throat, trying to choke her. How could she agree to marry someone her mother chose and approved? She knew Lady Magess Seraphina Verena better than anyone, and Fenya knew what she valued. She cared only for wealth, status, and Power. And if the man she chose for Fenya was anything like Mama or agreed with Mama on anything, Fenya's future looked miserable indeed.

Maybe Fenya could find a young man, one who wasn't worried only about status and wealth. One who didn't just want her for her Relic.

But with only eight known Relics in the world, it made Fenya all too eligible a young woman, even uncontrolled. She'd be far too easy for Mama to marry off to any suitable man, in other words. If only she could keep her Fire under control.

If she could...perhaps Mama would let her choose who to marry.

"What do you think, my dear? Marriage? Or would you rather go back to school?" Mama pressed, smoothing a wrinkle out of her skirt. "Once we reach Whitland, I'll make the choice for you."

"Please don't send me away to an asylum," Fenya whispered, tears pricking her eyes.

Mama's head tilted just enough to indicate her pleasure, along with the sly rise of one corner of her mouth in a smirk. "We'll see if we can marry you off then. Perhaps a few children will take the edge off your

Flames…and as soon as there is a decent heir or three, you'll probably be an Ember."

The knot in Fenya's chest loosened, but it didn't disappear. Mama had laid out her future in unerring accuracy, concealing it as a choice that wasn't a choice at all. All women married in the end—unless they were tarnished. And child-bearing often created surges or emptying of a woman's Legacy Power. Some died from Legacy Fever during pregnancy, while others had their Legacies drained by the child within them. There was no telling what would happen to her, and not knowing was as terrifying as anything else. An Ember…it was almost better than any future she could carve out alone. An Ember would be a shell of the Power she had now, and that would mean no unexpected fires. It was, unwittingly, her deepest desire that Mama had suggested.

Perhaps there was a shred of hope in marriage then. Perhaps her mother would choose wisely, and perhaps the man she would be forced to marry could actually be kind and loving.

It was nearly impossible to believe, but it was all the hope Fenya had.

Chapter Three

AUNT AND UNCLE VERENA

L
ow clouds and mist embraced Whitland Manor as the carriage rattled its way around the last bend to reveal the sprawling façade of Mage Caius Verena's home. As the second son of a Relic Bearer, he'd made his own fortune and purchased his own land, something Mama had always derided. Long ago, Fenya had concluded Mama's disdain was the reason she couldn't remember ever visiting Whitland and its estate or meeting her uncle and his family.

The land was almost flat with a slight wave to the grassy expanse, and a quaint cottage with a pond before it crouched only a short distance from the main house with a path connecting the two. She found herself automatically pulled toward it, drawn by the soothing promise of the water against the fire living in her veins.

The carriage wheels clattered against the road, jarring her, but the bumps on this road were small and repetitive, the feel of wooden wheels against brick—a welcome distraction.

"I cannot believe my life has come to this," Mama muttered, peering out the window. "To think I'm reduced to living on my brother-in-law's goodwill. I've spent so much money on your schooling and on quieting the rumors that have plagued us since your father's death." She shook her head, her lips pressed tight.

Guilt and shame made Fenya's hands clammy, and she brushed

them down her skirts. Mama hadn't offered her any new garments yet, but she'd seen fit to immediately dispose of the dress Fenya had singed and had worn two new ones in dark gray since then. Of course, Mama had to be well-dressed to remain in society, and that was the only hope of getting either of them a wealthy husband who would provide for them.

Mama smoothed her muslin skirt and eyed Fenya. "Do not mention your expulsion, Fenya, do you understand me?"

"Expulsion? But I thought—"

"Call it what you want, dearest, but it's expulsion except in name." Mama's gray eyes flashed dangerously. "You will say that you didn't have enough Fire in you to succeed at finishing school. You failed due to a lack of Legacy; you were not expelled." Mama quelled Fenya's retort with a firm look. "But we all know that everything will change when your Relic accepts you."

Fenya's cheeks burned once again. *How much shame could she take? She was to pretend that she was both a Relic Heir and nearly Powerless? That was the epitome of shame.* Fenya's eyes shifted to Mama's neck, where she had secured the Relic and Papa's watch underneath her shawl, her duty as a Relic Guardian.

There would come a time when Fenya was permitted to try again, but traditionally she was not to touch the Relic unless she were attempting to have it accept her, like she had at Jolie's. It had shown she was not ready by withholding any binding to her, so she was to wait a year to try again up until she was twenty-five, when the Relic would choose another family more worthy. Or so Papa had always said.

Of course, if and when Fenya married, her husband would assume Relic Guardian if it had yet to accept her.

And if he was a Flame, there was the possibility that the Ember-heart Relic would accept him instead. Having it was the only thing that made her such a valuable prospective wife at the moment. If only there wasn't a chance of her burning him to death before marriage.

"Fenya?" Mama's voice cut across her thoughts. "Do you understand me? You won't mention a word about being too Powerful. If you say anything, it's that you're weak. You will *not* label yourself a threat or you'll get us kicked out of your uncle's home and get yourself Black Listed before the end of the week." Mama's eyes pooled with tears as she leaned forward. "If you are Black Listed, you'll make *me* unsuitable for marriage, and *I'll* be homeless. Is that what you want?" Her gray eyes glimmered.

"No, Mama. Of course not." Fenya's heart twisted. How could she hurt Mama, who had given up so much for her?

"Then remember what you say." Mama's tears were gone, blinked away as quickly as they'd come.

Fenya shrank back against her seat. "Yes, Mama," she whispered.

"Whoa now!" The carriage driver's cry jolted as much as the lurch of the cart as the horses halted.

Mama plucked an invisible speck of fuzz from her skirt. "Don't forget."

"Yes, Mama," Fenya murmured as the carriage door swung open and an unfamiliar man was there, holding out a hand to Mama.

Mama smoothed away her irritation before the man, her expression once again implacable.

He politely delivered Mama onward, then pivoted toward Fenya. Fenya, surprised at the unexpected attention when Mama was present, accepted his support as she descended. Mama's brow furrowed as she cast a glance back at him, clearly disconcerted at not having the usual reaction at her appearance.

"Ah, Seraphina," said a familiar voice. "As beautiful as ever, I see."

Heart lurching, Fenya looked up at the sound of her father's voice, only to see an unfamiliar face in the speaker.

The man had similar features to her father, a shade of hair darker, a shade of blue eyes darker, the nose a touch wider, and the jaw a bit rounder, but it was reminiscent of a face Fenya hadn't expected to see again. Even Mama's smile tightened around the edges as she accepted Uncle Caius's kiss on each cheek.

"You've met my wife, I believe," Uncle Caius said, waving a hand behind him.

Aunt Cali, a pretty woman who looked less than ten years older than Fenya herself, offered Mama a stiff smile. Mama didn't seem to notice, smiling her prettiest smile and bowing her head just enough to indicate that she would pay the barest amount of respect to the woman of the house.

"And this must be my niece," Uncle Caius said so loudly that Fenya jumped as he turned his attention to her.

"Yes, sir," she answered, bobbing a curtsy.

"Ah, impeccable manners, just like your mother," he said with a smile. "I've never seen her set a foot wrong."

Mama smirked as Aunt Cali's eyes narrowed upon her.

Aunt Cali was quite pretty in her own right, with her olive-colored gown highlighting the pale blue of her eyes under her golden blond hair that was twisted into a crown similar to Mama's. She wore modest jewelry, with an emerald the size of a pea resting on her chest and a matching set of earrings and a wedding band of plain gold on her finger.

"Come in, won't you?" Aunt Cali said in a soft voice that made Mama jealous, judging by the tightening of her shoulders.

Fenya followed the others inside, her eyes raking the interior of the home. Paintings, all dancing with an Animationist's touch, graced every wall. A thick carpet spanned the middle of the grand oak stair-case with a carved wyvern at the base. Lingering behind Mama, Fenya admired the intricacies of its design.

"Miss?" a voice prompted.

Startled, Fenya turned and found a maid not more than two years older than her offering to take her shawl and satchel. "Oh." She glanced at Mama, but she was already walking with Uncle Caius down the hallway, and Aunt Cali was speaking with another servant, ordering tea.

Fenya handed over her shawl, but clutched her satchel to her. After reclaiming her sketchbook from Mama's hands, she didn't want to let it go again. She'd worked for so many hours to fill its pages, she couldn't risk it.

Still drawn by the staircase, Fenya examined the wyvern making up the last post of the oak-carved wood railing. His eyes—she could tell it was a "he" from the crest on his head—seemed to sparkle in awareness, as though he might just fly away. She reached out a hand to touch it and pulled back, afraid to damage it. Or maybe afraid she would be bitten. She smiled at the thought.

"It's beautiful, isn't it?" Aunt Cali said, stepping up beside her. "It's the Verena crest, you know."

Fenya nodded. "Yes, I just haven't seen one so intricate before. Was it carved by an Artist?"

"Yes, Caius commissioned it from a rather impressive Artist Mage when he purchased the house. Or so I'm told." She smiled. "Will you walk with me?"

Fenya gave the wyvern and its onyx eyes a last glance and fell into step beside her aunt down the hallway.

"Was your travel satisfactory?"

"It was..." Fenya answered, "long."

"Mmm, yes." Aunt Cali nodded knowingly and led her through the door into a sitting room where Uncle Caius and Mama already sat, chatting benignly about the same travel. Though she could have said much about the chosen method of their arrival, Aunt Cali said nothing more.

"It's been some time since I've traveled by horse and carriage," Uncle Caius mused as if to answer Fenya's thoughts. "Was it as awful as I recall?"

"Worse," Mama said, without missing a beat, though her eyes flashed with annoyance and, Fenya thought, a bit of embarrassment.

Uncle Caius gave a shudder. "I am sorry it's come to this. But I'm glad you're finally here."

Mama's smile tightened in such a way that only Fenya could notice. It was that tension before the storm, a cloud upon her brow that descended suddenly unless it was diverted.

"Come, Fenya," Aunt Cali said, all but pulling Fenya into the room and sitting her down on the couch with Mama as she claimed the seat beside her husband. "Tell me all about your travel. Have you ever come so far before?"

"No," Fenya answered. "This is the farthest. I have not traveled much at all, in truth."

"We'll have to introduce you around!" Aunt Cali clapped her hands together and napkins from the table flew to her lap.

Uncle Caius chuckled, and she blushed.

Fenya blinked at the objects. "You're an Animationist!"

Her cheeks still flushed, Aunt Cali nodded, twirling a finger. The napkin folded itself in the air, and with a flick of her finger, returned to the table. "I am. When I get excited, I forget myself sometimes. Caius loves to laugh at my silly excitements." She softened her words with a pat on his knee.

Caius smiled warmly at her, plucking her hand out of the air and squeezing it, bringing it to his lap, where he held it as he spoke. "I do indeed find pleasure in them. She's an expert at tying ties, let me tell you."

Aunt Cali's cheeks brightened more, but before she could respond, the door to the sitting room swung open and three children burst through. The eldest was a young girl only six or seven at the most, who almost maintained a poised attitude of control, while her brother, a couple of years younger, pushed past her in a half run so that she immediately began to walk faster in order to keep up with him. Behind them both was a third child, a little boy no more than two, who toddled after them, desperately attempting to keep up. When he let out a cry, the girl turned and swept him awkwardly into her arms, thrusting him on her slender hip like a mother might.

Fenya smiled at the three whirlwinds boldly sweeping across the room, not a care for who might see them or demand manners. She shuddered to think what would have happened if she had burst in upon one of Mama's drawing room visits at such an age.

"Mama! Papa!" babbled the youngest, drawing a smile from his sister's face.

"Oh, children," Aunt Cali said, worry pinching her brow as she cast a quick glance at Fenya and Mama. "You should have been abed an hour ago. Did you talk your governess into letting you stay up late again?"

The oldest opened her mouth to answer, but the middle child announced loudly, "We wanted to meet our family."

Caius laughed and pulled the boy up onto his knee. "You did, did you?"

The girl frowned like she battled between admitting the truth and agreeing with her brother, but finally she nodded, handing over her little brother to Aunt Cali.

"Well, here they are," Uncle Caius said. "This is your Aunt Seraphina and her daughter, Miss Fenya."

A woman appeared breathless in the doorway. "I'm so sorry, Mage, Magess, they slipped out when my back was turned."

With a wicked little grin darted at her brother, the little girl bobbed a proper curtsy to Mama, then turned to Fenya and did the same, though less pronounced, as was proper. "Nice to meet you," she murmured as her brother bowed at Mama and then Fenya in turn. "I'm Zhara. This is my brother, Yarrow."

Fenya smiled warmly. "And who is that?" She pointed to the youngest boy.

"Oh. That's my baby brother, Tobias."

"Well, it's lovely to meet you. I haven't met any cousins of mine before," Fenya said. The little girl beamed and then frowned. "Really? Do you have any others?"

"I don't believe so," Fenya answered. She knew her mother had a brother or two, but Mama was not close with her family, and they never visited.

Yarrow leapt down from his father's knee and pushed past his younger brother, bumping the table violently. The candelabra shook violently, the flames leaping on their wicks.

Fenya sucked in a breath as the fire demanded her attention.

Uncle Caius reached for a candle and caught it just as the stick tilted halfway out of its base. By such a violent motion, the flame should have gone out. Instead, it clung to the wax and reignited the wick with a flare.

"Careful!" Uncle Caius admonished, replacing the candle into its base.

The governess started forward, scooping up Tobias and chastening him.

"All right, my dears," Aunt Cali said, her gaze flickering to Mama, whose expression darkened as Fenya's breath caught, her eyes locking on the flames.

She clenched her fists into her skirts. What would have happened if the candles had fallen? Would she have been able to put it out or would she watch it grow with pleasure?

"Good night," the children chorused, curtsying and bowing their way out of the room with their governess holding a now crying Tobias.

Mama brushed her skirts off as though the children had somehow sullied them. "So tell me, Caius, are there many eligible men in the neighborhood?"

Uncle Caius's eyes twinkled. "Are you asking for yourself or for your daughter?"

Mama laughed but Fenya caught the barbs in it. "For my daughter, of course. She's almost of marrying age, you know."

"She's got several years still," Aunt Cali said protectively. "Shouldn't she claim the Relic before she marries?"

Fenya sat tall in her seat, watching the flames bob on the candles. Outside, the light of the setting sun had vanished, and a servant had finally brought in tea and sandwiches. Mama helped herself to a few pieces, and Aunt Cali motioned Fenya to do the same.

"No honey for your tea?" Aunt Cali asked as she doctored hers with a generous spoonful.

"No, I don't care for the taste," Fenya answered, her eyes on the delicate ceramic cup with wyverns engraved on the sides.

"And how did you like your last school?" Aunt Cali asked Fenya.

Fenya accidentally took a deep swig of her tea and choked as it started down the wrong way. She forced herself to swallow to avoid coughing tea everywhere, scalding her throat in the process. Coughing and clearing her throat, she dabbed the napkin to her lips. "I'm so sorry. Excuse me."

"Oh, dear, it's all right," Aunt Cali said encouragingly. "I didn't mean to spring such a question on you. It must have not been a proper fit if you were to leave before the year's end."

Fenya bit down on her lower lip. Proper fit? No. It had been miserable. But it had been better than being shadowed by Mama's constant disapproval. "I'm sorry. It was...not bad. It's a good school."

Aunt Cali's forehead creased, but she sipped her tea, seeming at a loss for how to answer or keep the conversation going.

"I've heard of Mage de Croia, of course," Mama was saying to Uncle Caius. "I had no idea he lived so close."

"He's here at least half the year," Uncle Caius said, a proud note to his voice. "The rest of the time he spends up north on his family lands."

Mama pursed her lips slightly and sipped her tea. "And Sir Milton... I've not heard of him. What do you know about him?"

"Oh, not much about him. Cali, dear? What do you know about Sir Milton?"

Aunt Cali considered her husband over her tea. "He keeps to himself, mostly," she finally said. "I've invited him over a few times, but he's as likely to arrive as not. It's quite confounding. But he seems pleasant enough."

"Is he a Mage?" Mama asked curiously.

The crease between Aunt Cali's eyebrows deepened. "I'm not certain. I've never asked."

Fenya bit her lip to keep from smiling and hastily lifted her teacup to her mouth again, staring past her nose into the dark liquid. It was a red tea, which wasn't her favorite, she much preferred the bite of a black tea. But it was something to keep her attention off her mother's unusual gaff. It was considered quite rude to ask one's Legacy in polite company. Of course, this was gossip, family gossip at that. Aunt Cali could have been considered rude to not engage in the topic, as it was typically this way that people discovered others' Legacies without asking. Unless, of course, they openly demonstrated their Legacies like Aunt Cali had accidentally done.

"So we have those two," Mama said as if making a mental note. "Are there any others?"

"Oh yes." Uncle Caius nodded. "Yes, we have several other neighbors. There's Milton, de Croia, and the Beauclercs." He curled his lip at the last one. "Oh, Garren as well."

"Garren's too old for her. Don't forget Mage and Magess Merivale though."

Uncle Caius glanced at her. "They're married."

Aunt Cali flushed. "Yes, of course. But the Beauclercs only have a daughter. Besides, I thought we were planning a party, not a group of single men to parade Fenya in front of."

Uncle Caius laughed, but Mama's eyes darkened.

"Of course not," Mama said smoothly, her voice dripping with honey. "We merely should meet those around us in the neighborhood. We'll be here for some time, after all."

Fenya chewed on her lower lip. She didn't want to meet any of them, but perhaps there would be a man who wasn't completely awful. And maybe, if there was someone suitable, she could find a man who might love her.

The room was growing darker around them, and flames flickered throughout the room. There was another in the hall, growing closer. A soft knock, then a servant came in holding a lit candle. She bobbed a silent curtsy and bustled around the room, lighting the candelabras in the corners and bringing twenty new flames into existence.

Fenya stiffened as the servant's candle's flame reached out to her, as certainly as though a dog ran up to her and jumped on her lap. The servant made a squeak and leaned back sharply as the flame flared large.

Let go! Fenya thought, and a pang twinged in her head as though she had cut a rope between her and the flame and the rope had snapped back to hit her in the head, leaving a bloody wound. She put her hand to her head.

"Are you all right, my dear?" Aunt Cali asked, reaching across the table toward Fenya. "You look like you're in pain."

Mama shifted, clearing her throat just enough for Fenya to understand that she should not attempt to claim any sort of excuse for leaving early tonight.

"It's nothing," Fenya answered, despite the throb in her head. The other flames were flaring now too, pinging at her head like unhappy sparks against a brick wall.

"You've had such a long day, my dear—"

"She's fine, Cali," Mama said sharply. "I'd love to get back to planning this ball."

Aunt Cali's lips pursed as though Mama had slapped her. She met Fenya's gaze, but Fenya didn't dare accept her sympathy or answer the question in her eyes. "Yes. Of course. But there's not much you need to do, Seraphina," Aunt Cali said with sweetness in her tone. "It's my house, after all. And Caius and I would love to introduce you to the neighbors, of course." Aunt Cali flicked her finger and her napkin resettled itself in her lap, where it had been sliding off her knee when she had leaned forward in her concern for Fenya.

Mama's smile tightened. "That would be—"

"You need not worry yourself about it," Aunt Cali continued. "I'll invite all the eligible men in a range of ages." Aunt Cali set down her teacup, her eyes glinting in mischief. "And we'll even throw in a few married couples so it doesn't appear like anyone is searching for a husband."

Fenya hid her smile in an extra large gulp of tea.

Chapter Four

THE PARTY

Fenya woke late from an uncomfortably deep sleep. At bedtime, Aunt Cali had slipped Fenya a potion to help treat her headache, and though it removed the pain, she dreamed of fires all night and awoke half thinking she had set her room on fire.

At her mother's orders, Fenya's fire had never been kindled last night, but she felt the embers in the fireplace nonetheless. She couldn't wait to go outside and numb the feeling by dipping her hands in the lake as Papa had taught her. *Always remember that water cancels out fire, Fenya...*

And in such fashion, Fenya spent the days before the ball trying to avoid both Mama and all fires—both of which were almost impossible.

She couldn't avoid the ball itself, as much as she might want, and the day quickly arrived.

The afternoon was spent in a flurry of activity that prevented Fenya from stepping out of doors even once. Mama insisted on bringing a servant to Fenya's rooms right after lunch and having her set to work bathing Fenya, drying her hair, styling her hair with a braid interlaced with flowers and gems. Mama's biggest reveal was a deep copper-colored gown.

"It isn't black?" Fenya asked in surprise.

Mama gave her one of her practiced looks. "I am still in half-mourning as under the law. You, however, are released to quarter mourning as you're the daughter and not the spouse. Certainly I haven't failed you so much that you don't even know this? And copper is one of the Flame colors, which we must advertise in the gentlest of ways."

Fenya bit down on her lip to stop the tears from stabbing at her eyes. "I'm sorry, Mama. I thought since..." she trailed off, not knowing what she could add that would appease her mother.

Mama sighed. "Darling, if you would just try a little bit harder..." For once, Mama's expression was soft as her eyes met Fenya's, as if she still held a glimmer of hope that Fenya could meet her expectations. But the moment passed too quickly, and Mama continued. "Tonight, nothing but the best for you, my dear. There will be many single men here all in want of a wife. You can be that perfect wife for them, you understand?" Mama put a hand to Fenya's cheek, raising her chin with her fingers so Fenya met her gaze. "You can do this. Pretend that you have control, and you shall find it."

Fenya bit the inside of her lip, her eyes wide. How was that possible? She had been pretending for years, and fiery accidents followed her wherever she went. If she simply pretended she didn't have Fire, then fires mocked her, bursting out of existence and climbing her skirts. It was impossible to pretend her Fire didn't exist—it was like ignoring her own shadow.

But she couldn't tell Mama that. And Mama was waiting for an answer.

"Yes, Mama, I will."

Mama nodded, a small, satisfied smile on her lips. "You look beautiful tonight," she murmured. "There might be some hope for us after all."

With those words, Mama slipped from the room to ready herself, not that she needed much help. She had her Legacy to help, which did more for her than any maid could do.

"Miss Verena?" said the maid, stepping up behind her.

Fenya looked in the mirror at the quiet young woman. "Yes?"

"Would you like anything else before I resume my other duties?"

Fenya blinked at her reflection. Her deep red hair had been twisted into a braid lined with contrasting gray-white flowers with bright yellow centers. A string of pearls had been twisted into the braid and gave her an almost princess-like appearance. Large pearl earrings hung from her ears and a matching necklace of small pearls in the back to larger pearls over her chest with a gold pendant in the shape of a wyvern.

The deep copper of her dress made her skin glow as though she were a full moon in a dark night sky.

"No, thank you. I need nothing else." She felt like a fraud.

The maid curtsied and left Fenya to herself, but before she could settle into her sketching and find any relaxation, a knock came on the door. Fenya called out to find Uncle Caius waiting in the hallway.

"You look beautiful, Fenya," he said warmly.

Fenya blushed and looked down at herself. She wasn't accustomed to the tightness of the corset she was required to wear, nor the silk slippers that peeked out from under her hem. "Thank you," she murmured to the ground.

"Ah, none of that, dear. You must raise your chin. Those downstairs wish to see your face. As beautiful as your hair is, your face is much more engaging."

A smile tugged at her lips at his fatherly way, and Fenya tilted her chin up, taking her uncle's arm as he led her through the hallway and down the stairs.

"Are you ready?" Uncle Caius asked gently when she hesitated at the top of the steps.

"I..." Fenya bit down on her lower lip again. She took a deep breath. There were many fires in the room already. The chandelier was burning with thirty-five small flames, the fireplace was roaring, smaller fires burned in small clumps—candelabras?—and a larger fire burned somewhere down below. Perhaps the kitchen. It seemed happy and well fed, just distant.

"My dear?" Uncle Caius prodded.

Fenya startled out of her thoughts. *Here I am, more concerned with the fires than the men.* She smiled at that. *Just as long as I don't make a mistake tonight...with either fire or man.* "I'm ready," she said to her uncle. "As ready as I can be."

They descended the stairs into the foyer, and Uncle Caius led Fenya into the ballroom, adjacent to the larger dining room in the house.

Fenya surveyed the sprawling room. She hadn't been in the ballroom of Uncle Caius's before tonight, and the chandelier flames glittered like stars in the sky. The ceiling looked as though it had been enchanted to sparkle, but maybe it was the reflection of the flames. She could count the flames without seeing them all, including the sconces on the sides and the fireplace burning at one end.

Paintings lined the room, some of the subjects dancing to silent music within their frames. One sitting in a chair with a book open upon his lap scowled in the direction of the guests, as though his peace was interrupted.

"Oh! He made it," Uncle Caius murmured to himself. "Miss Verena, might I introduce you to Mage de Croia?"

Fenya turned at the voice of her uncle.

"A pleasure, Miss Verena," the mage said, bending over her hand so quickly that she could barely catch sight of his face. "I've heard much of you and your family from your uncle."

Fenya glanced to her uncle, who was smiling welcomingly at the man.

"De Croia, I didn't think you'd make it, to be honest," her uncle said, shaking the mage's hand heartily. "Wasn't sure you were in town yet, actually."

"Yes," Mage de Croia said, tilting his head to the side, his expression a mixture of frustration and something deeper. Pain, perhaps? His brown hair curled around his ears, but his face was clean-shaven and smooth.

Uncle Caius leaned forward and lowered his voice. "Any news?"

"No, I'm afraid not. We thought we had a lead, but it turns out he hadn't been there after all."

"What a tragedy. And to drag on for so long." Uncle Caius tugged on the corner of his mustache. "You believe he's still...alive?"

"Yes. The reports continue to suggest so." Mage de Croia sipped his drink.

The conversation making no sense, Fenya took the chance to

inspect the other guests. Though Mama's intention had been to invite eligible young men, there were many families and women, so clearly Aunt Cali had taken it upon herself to invite more than just the unmarried, eligible men.

A flame wobbled to her right, drawing her attention to a group of older men who chatted together with familiarity. One eyed her thoughtfully, but another gazed solely at Mama, lost in her Beauty.

Fenya suppressed a shudder. If either Mama or Aunt Cali had ideas about Fenya marrying any one of them, she thought she might just run for the nearest reform school.

"Fenya, come this way," Aunt Cali said, appearing at her elbow. She touched her husband on the arm. "I'm going to introduce her around, darling."

"Right, right," Uncle Caius said, giving his full attention to Mage de Croia.

"You look beautiful, Aunt Cali," Fenya said. Her aunt was dressed in a deep moss-colored, high-waisted gown with white embroidery. Fenya noted the three stars in white and outlined in gold thread on the sleeves, and around them long tailed, curved arrows that indicated Aunt Cali's Legacy of Animation.

"Oh, thank you, dear." Aunt Cali smiled sweetly at her and pulled her across the room. "Now, this young man I want to introduce you to, he might not be thinking of marriage yet, but I think you'll like him. He's always been quite polite to me, and he's got a few brothers if he's not ready to marry, though I think one is married and one is a bit older than him."

Fenya's cheeks heated. Even Aunt Cali was trying to get her married—though to a better option than a lecherous old man.

"Rupert!" Aunt Cali called. She blinked and shook her head. "Mage Stephens!"

"Ah, Magess Verena!" a young man exclaimed cheerfully, spreading his gloved hands to give Aunt Cali an embrace and a kiss on each cheek.

He had to be about six or seven years older than Fenya, though his round, youthful face made it difficult to tell. He wore a deep blue jacket, his hair was swept back from his face and trimmed to above his ears. His wide eyes gave him a constantly startled but honest look. Fenya smiled tentatively at his enthusiasm toward Aunt Cali.

"You look lovely tonight!" he gushed. "Don't let Mama see you, or she'll pick your brain apart about where you got that fabric and who your seamstress is." He winked at her as Aunt Cali laughed.

How familiar was this man to her? He treated Aunt Cali almost like she was *his* mother or aunt.

But Aunt Cali beamed at his familiarity. "You're so sweet. I'll make sure that I only say hello to her when I have the time." She winked at Fenya as Mage Stephens laughed and bobbed his head in acknowledgement.

He motioned to Fenya with an open hand covered with a fawn-colored glove. "Is this the niece I've heard so much about?"

Aunt Cali scooped Fenya forward with an arm around her waist. "Yes, this is Miss Fenya Verena. She and her mother are visiting for some time, and we couldn't help but invite the neighbors to join us in welcoming them."

"What a delight." Mage Stephens bowed his head over Fenya's white-gloved hand and raised it toward his lips. She shivered, and he let go. "It's a pleasure to meet you. I've heard much of you from your aunt."

"Oh?" Fenya glanced at her aunt, not sure what to make of that. "I do hope it's good."

Mage Stephens chuckled, overflowing with friendliness. "Of course. I don't think I've ever heard a bad word about someone come out of Magess Verena's mouth."

Aunt Cali flushed and batted away his words. "Such a charmer. Now, I think you'll quite get along with Fenya. She simply adores wyverns. I caught her admiring the staircase when she arrived the other day."

"Oh really?" Mage Stephens fixed his startled eyes on her, arresting her and pinning her to the spot. "I spent an hour talking your aunt's ear off about that wyvern when I first saw it. It truly is a magnificent piece of work."

Fenya gulped at his attentions, feeling her cheeks pink. Was he expecting her to contribute to the conversation in a worthy way? She scrambled for something to say. "Yes, the eyes are particularly expressive."

"Indeed." Mage Stephens went on for several minutes about the beauty of the carved wyvern.

While Fenya didn't disagree, the conversation was difficult to maintain as Mage Stephens continued his gushing. Even her attention waned, and she started inspecting the other guests. Across the room, Mama chatted with an older man and Uncle Caius. The man was just her type. Attractive, dressed in a storm-gray jacket with fitted sleeves and a thick belt around his waist, clearly displaying his Air Mage Legacy with the colors and the embroidered cuffs.

"Have you ever visited Linthorne?"

Mage Stephen's question caught her by surprise, and Fenya blinked away her distraction before she hastily answered. "No. No, I'm afraid I haven't."

"I ask because there's a beautiful statue of a Berserker at the Dragon Academy Headquarters there." Mage Stephen's dark eyes gleamed as if the image danced before him.

"Are you involved in the academy?" Fenya asked.

"No, but a friend of mine over there—" he pointed to a tall man standing with a goblet of wine in one hand and his other tucked behind his back "—Mage Balderik, he's quickly climbing up the ranks, and I went to visit him one day. I mention it because that statue honestly looks as though it could turn and devour you. I consider the wyvern at the stairs a distant second to that creation." His eyes twinkled. But he raised a hand to the man across the room, and motioned him over. "I'll get Mage Balderik to describe it to you."

Mage Balderik, who looked perhaps a year or two older than Mage Stephens, came at the beckon. He looked the exact opposite of Stephens, if Fenya had to describe him. Sandy blond locks hung to his shoulders, gathered into a low ponytail, revealing blue eyes that reminded Fenya of a deep, secret-filled pond.

"Good evening, Stephens," the man said in a low, pleasant voice.

"Balderik, I was describing to Magess Verena's young niece here about the statue at the DAH in Linthorne. But my words fail me."

"Impossible," Mage Balderik said, a twinkle lighting the darkness in his eyes.

Stephens laughed as if the laugh bubbled up from his chest. "I know, I know. I can't help my enthusiasm. And Miss Verena has been a good sport. But I think you could do much more justice to the statue than I." Stephens motioned between them.

Mage Balderik turned to her and gave a little bow. "Lovely to meet you, Miss Verena."

"Thank you, you as well." Fenya glanced at Mage Stephens, whose attention had shifted back to the opposite side of the room.

"Oh! There's Merivale—I must say hello." Mage Stephens patted Balderik on the shoulder. "I'll be right back, chap." Stephens hurried in the direction of a woman with a miniature dragon, which Fenya recognized as a tiny Sparkwig Imp.

Fenya frowned at the woman's shoulder, for the Imp was known to be fire-breathing and highly mischievous, but she couldn't detect any fire from this one, even reaching out with her Legacy, for which she was grateful. Perhaps the woman had some sort of Shield enchantment around the dragon, or else she could be mistaken with the species. Her fingers itched to sketch it though and examine it closer.

Beside her, Balderik also watched his friend go, a slight crease to his brow as Fenya pulled herself back to the present company.

"I'm afraid I've been a poor conversationalist." Fenya tucked her hands into the folds of her skirts.

"It could only be a dragon that pulls that man from his conversations." Balderik shook his head. "Still, I don't believe Mage Stephens has stood in one place as long as he did to speak with you in his entire life."

Fenya flushed and sought out Stephens's back. He moved amongst the crowds, seeking a person he must have merely glimpsed.

"That's a credit to you, Miss Verena," Balderik said gently.

"Is it?" Fenya murmured, not entirely sure whether she should believe him.

"It is." Apparently uninterested in arguing her response, Balderik stood next to her with more interest in the crowd before him than her.

"Do you ride dragons?" she tried.

"I do. I am a member of the Elite Dragon Squad."

"What kind of dragon do you have?" she continued.

"A berserker. A powerful dragon breed that is well known for war performance."

"Have you ridden it to war?"

He hesitated before answering, and Fenya realized it could have been a rather personal question. But before she could withdraw it, he answered. "I have ridden him to battle. But it is my wish to avoid battles as much as possible. I much prefer rescue missions."

"Are...are dragons really as bloodthirsty as they are said to be?"

Balderik raised his eyebrow down at her. His manner was gentle, though distant, humoring her like he might a child.

"Balderik." A man's voice broke the stillness before he could answer, and Fenya turned with Balderik toward the speaker. A man around Fenya's age strode forward, confidence in his posture, hand extended in greeting.

"Pavlina." Balderik took the other man's hand with a firm shake. "I wasn't expecting to see you here. Is your family in town?"

Pavlina grimaced and tugged at his silver-white cuffs displaying the Air Legacy symbol of two curved feathers crossing in the middle of two curved lines, although his had a variation of it that Fenya wasn't familiar with, indicating some specialty within the Air Legacy. "Father and Mother are on their way back from the islands. I came ahead early." He dragged a hand through his wavy brown hair. "I begged them for some distance. But I promised my sister that I would come and request that you call on her." He rolled his eyes. "Thus, here I am, at a ball." He eyed Fenya.

"Yes, I believe this ball was thrown for the benefit of Miss Verena and her mother, here. They are staying with Mage and Magess Verena."

"Miss Verena?" Pavlina's eyebrows rose. "A relation?"

Fenya nodded. "My aunt and uncle own this home."

"Ah, I see. Staying for a while?"

"I believe so," Fenya answered.

Pavlina pursed his lips and rubbed at his chin, which was covered in a short, dark beard. He had the appearance of a well-to-do young man, his jacket sky blue instead of the dark blue of others, which gave him the appearance of a preening fairy dragon to Fenya.

"Any news from the Marclaine network?" Pavlina asked, ignoring Fenya again.

"Nothing I can share," Balderik answered mildly. "War seems inevitable at this point."

Pavlina sighed. "Again. Marclaine needs to be satisfied with their pegasi and leave us our dragons."

"I suppose we should have been satisfied with our dragons and not taken their pegasi for our uses either," Balderik answered with a cheeky glint to his blue eyes.

"True. But that wasn't this generation's fault." Pavlina grinned.

"When has society ever forgotten the past sins of another country?" Balderik raised a brow.

"But I suppose this is good for you. When do you take your promotion exam?" Pavlina asked.

Balderik shrugged. "Whenever my superiors tell me. I expect within the next few weeks, but I should find out when I return to Highmere in two days."

Fenya's attention wandered as the men began chatting about a Balderik's upcoming exam. Pavlina showed no interest in her, and Fenya wasn't about to force her attentions on someone who couldn't have cared less if Fenya existed.

Almost as though she had read her mind, Aunt Cali appeared beside Fenya. "Do forgive me, gentlemen, but I'm stealing Miss Verena away."

Balderik bowed and murmured something about it being a pleasure to meet her, while Pavlina ignored her.

Fenya bit her lip as Aunt Cali tucked her hand into her elbow.

"Pavlina's a bit droll, isn't he?" Aunt Cali said conspiratorially into Fenya's ear.

She almost burst out laughing but barely caught the laugh in time.

Aunt Cali's eyes twinkled merrily. "There's another man you might get along with. If your mother is so determined to have you married, you might as well meet all the eligible young men."

Fenya swallowed back her comment that she didn't want to meet any more men. She felt paraded, like she was on display, but Aunt Cali had clearly worked hard to make it seem as though this ball was not simply to marry her off.

"Now, you see over there?" Aunt Cali pointed discreetly with her head, tilting it just enough to indicate a group of young men. "They're all a bit young for you, honestly. I don't really agree with marrying a young man off before his final Legacy test. He should have his mage status fully tested and identified before he's ready for marriage. So we'll focus on those older than twenty-one. You've already met Mage Balderik, but he's said to have a young woman he's desperately in love with already. Did he mention her?"

Fenya shook her head, her hope deflating a bit. Balderik had been the kindest of the lot so far. Though Stephens was amusing in his own right.

"Hmm. How did you find Stephens?"

Fenya considered how she could answer the question without being indelicate.

Before she could formulate her response though, Aunt Cali read her answer and nodded sagely.

"He can be a bit enthusiastic about dragons. But I thought since you were such an amazing artist yourself, you might click."

"How did you know about my art?" Fenya asked.

"Your sketchbook was left in the sitting room the other day. It was open to a page with the most amazing sketch of the bannister. You're quite talented."

Fenya's cheeks heated, and she dropped her gaze to her toes. She'd never heard her own art described in such a way. It made her long once again to be an Artist, not a Flame. Why couldn't she have been an Artist? Or at least an Animationist like Aunt Cali, who could add life to drawings like hers.

She sighed.

"Come, this way." Aunt Cali pulled her across the room, through a few groups, which she greeted with kind hellos and bobs of her head. Then they came upon a man standing at the refreshments table, investigating the spread of meat pies and cheeses with an overwhelmed expression.

"Sir Milton," Aunt Cali called. "I must have you meet my niece."

He turned, expectation on his face. By comparison to others, he wasn't unattractive, but there was also nothing to commend him to Fenya. His eyes were pale blue, his face narrow, and his yellow-blond hair resting in soft, touchable curls upon his head. His hands gripped a delicate wine glass full of amber liquid. As his gaze slid from Aunt Cali to Fenya, a gleam of something Fenya could only describe as unusual interest spawned, and she shifted uncomfortably.

"Miss Verena," he said softly, extending a gloved hand as Aunt Cali chattered away with an introduction.

He clasped her gloved hand in his long fingers and bent over it, keeping eyes locked with hers until the last possible moment before placing his lips gently on the back of her hand. Her skin shivered, and the hairs on her arms raised as though she had a chill. *How odd, I'm never cold. Could he be a Water Legacist?*

"I've heard much about you. I met your mother just a few moments ago," Sir Milton said, rising.

"Oh...I..." Fenya couldn't formulate the proper response.

Aunt Cali swooped in. "Fenya is quite the artist. I've seen some of her sketches, and they would rival a Legacist. I am hoping she'll agree to let me Animate one some day."

Fenya's eyes widened at her aunt. "I—of course! I would love that."

Sir Milton nodded in polite interest, but his gaze lingered on her again.

The fires in the room faded slightly. She bit down on her lip. What was wrong with her? He seemed to have an effect on her...a strange effect. One where he became all she could see and feel, even in a room full of flames.

"I was sorry to hear of your father's passing," Sir Milton said with a sympathetic look.

"Oh, I...thank you." She pressed a polite smile to her lips.

"You have just arrived here in town?" he continued as though she had invited more conversation.

"Yes, recently," Fenya said as conversations flowed like rippling flames. Mage de Croia passed, speaking low and urgently with Colonel Balderik.

"And this is your first ball?" Sir Milton tugged on his sleeves, revealing a white wrist that was nearly as delicate as Fenya's. His jacket was a tad too big for him, she realized, perhaps he had been ill recently.

"Excuse me," Aunt Cali said, pressing Fenya's hand. "I must speak with Caius about something."

Her aunt disappeared into the crowd, and Fenya pulled her attention back to find Sir Milton with a charming smile. "I hear you're much like your father."

She blinked. "I...have been told that, yes," she answered carefully.

"Oh, there goes the music. Would you dance with me?"

Her heart skittered at the invite. Her head pounded. The fires pulsed in the periphery of her sight. "I...of course."

He offered his arm and led her to the dance floor. They began a swirling dance that made Fenya's head swim. His skin brushed her shoulder.

The world spun around her.

She swayed.

And the world went black.

Chapter Five

FANG

The Verena ballroom showed no evidence of the prior night's activities when Fenya crept downstairs, boots and stockings in her hands, just before dawn the next morning. The poor maids must have been up most of the night cleaning up after the late party.

She sneaked through the silent kitchen and helped herself to some leftover pastries, tucking rolls, dried meats, and cheese into a handkerchief for later in the day. The cook, Mrs. Petalwise, had agreed eagerly to leave Fenya food on the table when she had approached her about packing a lunch. Fenya silently thanked her, as she fully planned on losing herself in those woods today, since Mama wasn't here to refuse her.

The night before had ended in a blur of her head pounding, being walked to her bedroom, and put to bed by the maid, much to Mama's annoyance.

And so before Mama could wake, Fenya was sneaking out the side door and breathing in the dew-filled morning air. The wet grass caressed her bare feet, and Fenya released a long sigh, letting the water numb her fire before she sat and pulled on her stockings and boots.

She strolled through the kitchen gardens with its herbs and vegetables, into the house garden with hedges and pruned trees and flowers.

She wouldn't mind stopping to make a sketch of a particularly attractive orchid-like flower that grew in groups of several discernible colors glowing with the dawn light.

Her feet slowed, and she peered closer, hand halfway to her satchel to make a quick sketch when the bunch of flowers burst apart, taking to the air with annoyed twitters.

Fenya's heart pounded as she withheld her screech of surprise at the fairy dragons. They took to the air with angry voices, disappearing into the branches of an apple tree.

Her hands burned. She grimaced down at her satchel. New scorch marks.

She clamped onto her lower lip.

Breathe.

Slower.

Exhale. Hold. Breathe.

She couldn't start making sparks now. If Mama saw her in the garden from her rooms—Fenya would be shipped off to an asylum before the sun fully rose.

She hurried away from the bush that was now only dark green in the dim light of the garden and absent of the bright fairy dragons masquerading as flowers. Just as her body began to relax, a panicked screech split the woods.

Fenya tensed. An animal? A dragon?

Pausing at the edge of the garden, she listened for a full minute, but didn't hear it again and strode on past the wide trees and their leafy green branches. Ahead of her, the cottage was just poking out of the morning fog rising off the lake.

Fires flared to life behind her in the manor, and she hurried away from it. Servants must be waking and stoking the fires.

By contrast, the cottage was still quiet and unoccupied. Just being near the water calmed her burning hands further, and Fenya relaxed crouching at the shore of the small lake in front of the cottage, dipping her hands in to release some of her Fire. She'd often tried to release her Power into water, hoping that it could take it from her and make her feel less aflame. Father had mentioned the trick once, and she hadn't given up until she'd managed to do it semi-successfully. Once she'd even made the water around her hands bubble and steam. Then a fish had flopped up on the shore beside her, frightening a scream from her as she realized that she'd made his home too hot for him.

She'd wept then, and promised that she would only release so much again if she had to. So when her hand were no longer burning but still tingling, Fenya turned around and faced the cottage. A square building made of brick and glass, with vines crawling up the front that started green and flared red at the tips, it gave the impression of coziness.

She tried the front door. To her surprise, it opened, and she wandered through the lower rooms, including a small dining room, sitting room that overlooked the lake, a rear washroom, access to the lower kitchens, and upstairs four bedrooms, each with adjoining wash-rooms and closets.

Aunt Cali had promised that they would move into the cottage this week, much to Fenya's joy. From here, helped by the large body of water out front, she couldn't feel the hundreds of fires burning at the manor. Every candle was a pair of tweezers pulling on one of her hairs, locked onto her with a painful burn into her flesh. Here, was peace.

She stared out of the back bedroom window. A path that she had never noticed before led from the back of the cottage directly into the woods, and Fenya smiled. There's where she would spend her afternoon.

As she stepped outside, another screech split the air, but this time a flash of red burst in the air. Fire? No; she couldn't feel it.

Curious, Fenya lifted up her skirts and sidestepped a small puddle in the path, marching toward the trees.

The subtle path that led into the woods suggested someone walked here regularly, even if it was just a game trail.

Then the sound came again, closer this time, followed by wings hitting metal.

Cautiously, Fenya crept toward it.

She followed the sound until the edge of a wire cage peeked out from around a leafy bush and something red-orange flailed against the bars.

"Well, hello," Fenya said softly.

A rare flame wyvern peered dolefully up at her, her amber eyes dark with caution as she crouched against the back corner of the cage. The small tuft of feathers around her ears suggested her gender, for the pictures of males that Fenya had seen all had larger tufts of feathers and a more pronounced brow over their eyes.

"You poor thing." Fenya inspected the cage without getting too close. Flame wyverns were notoriously dangerous for a noxious liquid they could spray at predators when threatened, a flammable liquid.

A loud sound in the woods, a bigger dragon, perhaps, startled the wyvern so she flew toward Fenya at the cage's door.

Fenya stumbled backward, looking toward the sound, but to her relief it faded and no telltale rustling through the trees followed.

"I think we're all right," she murmured to the wyvern, who huddled beside the door now.

Slowly, Fenya crouched down beside the cage, keeping her side to it as to appear less threatening, regarding the wyvern throughout all her movements. "I'd like to let you out, but I don't want to injure you—or be injured myself," Fenya added thoughtfully. "Do you think I could do that?"

The dragon cocked her head at Fenya as though considering the offer. Then she inched herself away from the door of the cage.

"Oh, thank you," Fenya said.

The wyvern was only the size of a house cat but covered in pearly red scales that had an orangish sheen. The wings were the span of a crow's, and Fenya estimated the wyvern to be young, perhaps only a hatchling based on her feathered head and the talons on the claws that looked short and paler than an adult's. Wyvern hatchlings often became semi-independent within a few months of hatching, so it wasn't unusual for her to be alone, maybe seeking her own territory away from nesting wyverns larger than her.

"If you just stay in place, I'll be able to free you." Fenya reached for the gate on the cage, cautious to not frighten the dragon. "I hate to see you caught. You must be more careful. I've heard that traps like these are set up and the captured dragon is sold in markets or killed for its scales, talons, and even its blood." She suppressed a shudder and slipped the reluctant latch open. "So you'd best come out now and disappear." She smiled at the little wyvern, who tentatively crawled out, using her taloned wings as a second pair of feet to duck out of the cage.

Fenya shut the cage behind it. "There. Now you can't go back in, even if you wanted." Inside the cage were remnants of blood, the lure that had enticed the dragon into the trap.

The wyvern nosed Fenya's satchel and gave a tiny chirrup.

"Are you still hungry then?" Fenya clucked her tongue.

She reached into her satchel and pulled out the dried meat that she'd wrapped in her handkerchief. "You can have this." She held out the round of salami and the wyvern tentatively sniffed it and took a bite. In less than a minute, she'd consumed the entire two strips of dried meat and was sitting on top of Fenya's knee as she chewed on the last bite.

Fenya couldn't keep the smile off her face as she watched. "You're quite beautiful."

The wyvern's scales rippled at the compliment, almost as if she could understand every word Fenya spoke.

"Do you understand me?"

The dragon gave a snort, like the question was insulting.

"Of course you understand," she answered for the little animal. "But you need a name then. Shadow? Night? Hero?"

The wyvern showed her teeth, and Fenya chuckled.

"Fang?"

The intelligent eyes brightened, and her head cocked.

"Fang then?"

Her mouth opened in what Fenya could only describe as a gaping smile, much like a dog or cat might smile. Fenya returned it and offered a finger for the wyvern to sniff. Fang's delicate, serpentine tongue snaked out to lick at her finger.

"You taste meat, don't you?" Fenya reached back into her satchel and withdrew the rest of her food. "Hmm. No more meat. But some cheese and pastries." She offered the dragon a small piece of hard cheese, and Fang gobbled it down, but turned her nose up at a pastry.

With an index finger, Fenya reached for the dragon, then hesitated. "May I?" It felt only right to ask for permission to pet the wyvern, but

Fang ignored her and continued to eat, unconcerned, trusting. So Fenya brushed a finger down her neck toward her chest.

Fang eyed her with a gleaming amber eye, but as Fenya pet her neck again, closed her eye and leaned into the touch.

It was as if everything stressful about her life—Mama, her flames, the expulsion—all drained away at Fang's touch. She'd never touched a live dragon before—they were usually wild animals, after all, and always capable of great damage. Twice, she'd stumbled across the body of a poacher's remains. They would skin the animal and remove its head, talons, and venom sacs if they had them, but leave everything else. Dragon meat wasn't good for eating, so only the scales, talons, blood, and bones remained worth selling.

"Well, Fang, my new friend, I must start walking back to the manor. I'm afraid that I would be in grave trouble should I arrive late for supper."

Without hesitation, Fang hopped off Fenya's lap.

Fenya considered her. "You are a sweet thing. I hope to see you again, Fang. Don't go in any cages again—regardless of how hungry you are."

The dragon tilted her head, flapped her wings, and flew into the lower branches of a tree.

Fenya sighed, but she felt calmer with the interaction, and with knowing that she'd saved the wyvern from the fate of a poacher.

She climbed the trail winding through the woods toward the house. Her attention focused on the rustling in the branches, where the wyvern was flying from one tree to the next, as if escorting her home. "Don't get seen," Fenya murmured as they reached the edge of the woods that opened to a pasture dotted with sheep.

A small gate led through the hedges into the pasture and to the cottage, its lake, and the woods behind it. Now, she opened the gate quietly, the hinges squeaking softly.

"Seraphina."

Mama's name, spoken through a guttural sigh, stopped Fenya in her tracks.

"You don't know what you do to me," a man's voice was saying.

Fenya's cheeks flamed. She looked around. The voices were low, a lover's whisper.

They have to be close.

Her hands tingled, her Fire jumping to life.

She had to get away...her room, perhaps. *No, fire's there. But fire is here. It's all over. It's with me!*

A growl of frustration rose inside her. *It's Mama who needs to leave!*

A yelp split the air. Fenya slapped a hand over her mouth. Had she actually made a sound? Frantically, she darted for the pathway to the house, just as a fire erupted in the gardens.

"What the devil?" a man's voice said.

Mama shrieked, then cut it off as if her sense took over to avoid detection in illicit affair.

Knowing the small fire could be put out better without her, Fenya ran for it.

As she rounded the corner, she cast a quick peek over to see the back of a tall man with dark hair as he stamped out a flame consuming a weed in the dirt path. Mama caught Fenya's stare, her Legacy slipping just enough for her expression to ripple and expose the hatred on her face.

What have I done?

She had just gotten herself on the first carriage to the nearest asylum.

Chapter Six

MILTON

After nearly setting the garden on fire, Fenya tried to stay out of her mother's way, but she was met with almost immediate failure, for that very evening, Aunt Cali announced that they would be moving to the cottage the next day. Fenya managed to escape some of Mama's attentions that night by offering to help put her cousins to bed, telling them a story of a flame wyvern who got into mischievous bits of trouble. The children begged for more, but Fenya promised more the next night.

Early the next morning, Fenya's cottage retreat was no longer quiet and absent of fires. A few servants drove Mama and Fenya's trunks down the road and delivered them to their new rooms after breakfast.

Fires were lit in the cottage, but the nearby water dulled the feel just enough for Fenya to avoid any accidental sparks, and the day passed in a flurry of unpacking, arranging, and rearranging at her mother's discretion.

That evening they were expected to dine at the manor house, and Fenya hurried away from Mama and the cottage. But the closer she drew to the manor, the more the fires revived. Her fire had slumbered, and now it stirred. As soon as she walked up to the front of the manor, Fenya knew coming had been a mistake. Sir Milton's carriage sat outside the front of the building.

Fenya bit back a groan. *What was he doing here? Why couldn't it be Balderik? Right. He's in love with someone else.*

She chewed on the inside of her cheek with nerves.

But why Milton?

She knew why, if she was honest. Sir Milton was also the only one whom she had danced with. Perhaps she had given the wrong impression of partiality. But it wasn't her fault that she had felt ill after dancing with him and unable to stand. She vaguely remembered sitting in a chair for a couple of minutes, then forcing herself up to escape the ballroom as the colors of the dresses and suits swirled around her.

Thankfully, the sitting room was empty, and Fenya sank into the couch, pushing away the tugs of the fire in the grate and the candelabra burning above her. She pulled out her sketchbook and buried herself in her sketches.

"Do I see a wyvern on your page?"

Sir Milton's voice sounded so close to Fenya's ear that her pencil stuttered on the paper. She nearly dropped her entire sketchbook as she leaned away from him as quickly as she could.

He laughed softly and straightened, tugging his maroon jacket into place. "I'm sorry. Did I startle you?"

Fenya ducked her head, straightening and closing her sketchbook to fold her hands over top of it.

"Do you see everything you sketch in your head? Or do you draw best when the item is before you?" He pointed at the leather cover of her book. "It was a wyvern, wasn't it?"

Fenya held her breath before answering carefully. "Yes. I like to imagine them. In my head and on paper," she added.

"I do adore wyverns. There have been rumors of a rare flame wyvern in the woods around here over the past few months."

Another jolt went through her. *Fang? Is Milton the one setting traps in the woods?* She peeked at him, tightening her grip on the edges of her sketchbook, holding her pencil underneath her palm.

"Around here?" Fenya tried to keep her voice and face impassable. *Please don't ask me if I've seen one.*

"And it looked like you were drawing one, so perhaps you've seen it. Have you? I've seen you walking through the fields."

She tried to swallow, but her mouth was dry. "Seen one? Seen me?"

"Yes." His thin lips thinned further as they curved into a smile. "My dear, you don't need to be afraid of me. I promise, I'm harmless."

She shifted on the couch to discreetly increase the distance between them.

"So have you seen one?" he pressed.

"A flame wyvern?" Her heart thumped erratically, her breath hitching. The fire bloomed in the fireplace, tendrils lunging for the rug just out of reach. She held her breath, willing the fire to calm. But her hands tingled, and her brain felt fuzzy.

"May I?" His smile tugging at one side of his mouth, he motioned for her hand.

"What?" She tightened her fists in her lap.

"You're upset. I can feel the flames responding to you. My Legacy could help." His gaze was earnest, imploring her to trust him.

Dragons. We're talking about dragons, not fire. Or Legacies. What Legacy could possibly help me? Fenya clenched her hands around her sketchbook tighter. *Breathe. Hold. Exhale. Speak.* "No, thank you. I just need a moment. We were talking about dragons?"

"Oh, yes. Have you seen a little orange wyvern around? My reports were that it was a juvenile."

She willed her mind clear of thoughts of flames and fire. *I haven't seen the dragon since I released it.* "No. I don't believe so."

He lifted a cup of wine to his lips, but his eyes held tight to Fenya's. She looked away.

"And how are you finding the woods near Whitland?" Sir Milton asked.

"Lovely," she said firmly. "They're quiet and peaceful."

"Indeed. A ride through them is a most refreshing way to spend a morning. Do you ride?"

"No, I'm afraid I don't."

"Ah, you are here, Fenya." Aunt Cali appeared in the sitting room, a frown on her forehead. "Sir Milton, you naughty boy. You shouldn't be in here alone with a young woman."

"Are we alone?" Sir Milton cast a surprised glance around, his pale brownish-blond eyebrows climbing toward his curls. "Oh dear. Miss Verena had me so captivated with her drawings that I didn't notice."

Aunt Cali shook her head, but her smile seemed amused rather than chastising now. "Dinner is ready."

Fenya stood and collected her things, trying to calm her racing thoughts. What had he meant that his Legacy could help her? What *was* his Legacy? Fenya tried to concentrate on her meal, but her attention was on the exchange with Sir Milton throughout dinner. She sat in near silence as Mama kept engaging Sir Milton in discussions about himself and his interests. He talked tirelessly of his adoration for art, his independent wealth, and his lonely status.

"Sir Milton—why isn't it Mage Milton?" Mama asked with a coy tone as she pushed her blackberry-glazed pheasant around on her plate. She sat beside Mage de Croia, who had focused solely on his food tonight, his brow furrowed and gaze distant.

"My parents died nearly a decade ago now, when I was just twenty. They were the only ones left of my family, so I never had my Legacy testing done, as running the lands was quite enough work for me." He gave a laugh as if it were a typical thing to avoid Legacy testing. "I just never needed it for my own future. Perhaps when I marry and my children need their titles..." He trailed off.

Fenya took a long sip of her Emberclear Cider, attention on the fireplace. The flames tonight were oddly dull, though the fire crackled contentedly in the grate.

"That is wise," Mama agreed. "Your children will need their titles. Don't you agree, Mage de Croia?"

"Hmm?" Mage de Croia looked up in astonishment at being addressed.

Mama repeated herself.

"Oh, yes. Both must achieve their mage titles before children, it's the only accepted way."

Heart pounding, Fenya flushed. Everyone spoke as though Fenya was as good as married to Sir Milton. Had she missed a conversation that should have included her?

"To be honest, I never thought there would be a woman worthy of my parent's estate. An accomplished woman is difficult to find in the country," Sir Milton added. "And my parents died without any guidance regarding marriage. I was away on my travels when they passed, sudden and unexpected."

"Both of them at once?" Aunt Cali asked. "That's tragic."

"Yes, it was quite a blow. And I poured myself into the running of the estate after that." Sir Milton paused as the servant took away the main course.

Dessert was brought, a tray of candied nuts and dried fruits, and the Emberclear Cider was replaced with Starfire Mead that glinted as the servant poured it into each glass.

Conversation rippled with the addition of the mead. Uncle Caius flirted with Aunt Cali, and Mama encouraged Sir Milton to speak more about himself. Only Mage de Croia remained quiet and withdrawn.

When the men retired to the study, the women retired to the drawing room, and Fenya pulled out her sketchbook as Mama ambled around the room, dragging a finger along a surface here and there as if to remark on Aunt Cali's housekeeping. Aunt Cali pulled out her sewing basket and set to work on an embroidered wyvern that she'd shown Fenya a few nights before.

Absorbed in her sketching, Fenya only noticed the men joining them when the fire jumped at their appearance. Frowning, Aunt Cali cast a glance between Fenya and the fire before resuming her stitching, the frown moving to her forehead. A maid approached Aunt Cali behind the men, curtsied before her and murmured something that had Aunt Cali excusing herself and hurrying from the room.

"Ah, Sir Milton, Caius," Mama said, walking across the room toward them, her hips swaying gracefully under her skirts as she did. "Mage de Croia." She batted her lashes at Mage de Croia as she spoke, and he surveyed her with a considering expression.

As Sir Milton's eyes met Fenya's, a soft smile played on his lips, giving her the impression that he was attempting to gain her trust. Why didn't he get caught up in Mama's Beauty like other men? She bit back a confused sigh. She couldn't determine what to think about him, whether he was eccentric, kind, or just awkward.

He leaned against the fireplace mantle, setting an elbow on the mantle, holding a fresh cup of mead with his free hand. Still subdued compared to the others, Mage de Croia joined Uncle Caius at the tea cart and poured the older man a finger of Crestfall Bourbon, a liquor that Avenesse was well-known for.

"Miss Verena," Sir Milton said with a nod, "can I get you a drink?"

"No, thank you," she answered. *The last thing I need is something to loosen my control on the fire.*

"Sir Milton, I'd appreciate a glass of Elderleaf Digestif, if you could muster one up," Mama said in a sweet tone. "I assume you have that, Caius? Every well-stocked bar contains at least one Sarravinian Herbal."

Uncle Caius laughed heartily. "Of course, of course. One of the best parts of being allies with Sarravine."

"Undoubtedly," Sir Milton agreed, abandoning the fireplace and joining the men at the tea cart to doctor up Mama's drink.

Eyes on her page, Fenya focused on holding her pencil gently, not squeezing it so hard that it might snap under her fingers. But she counted her breaths, determined to calm herself.

Finally, she focused on the sketch of the wyvern and flipped to a new page, frustrated with her first attempt at capturing Fang. Trying to shield the sketchbook from others' view, she bent her head over it. She shouldn't be sketching the flame wyvern with Milton here if he was searching for her.

But Sir Milton stood next to Mama beside the fire, his head tilted as he listened, while Mage de Croia and Uncle Caius laughed over something else beside the tea cart. Uncle Caius must have had several drinks already, for his cheeks were flushed and his voice louder than normal. She hoped it would be a short night because of it.

Her attention drifted back to the fireplace, where she lost herself in the crackles of fiery fingers that reached for the chimney. Mama laughed softly and put a hand on Sir Milton's arm. The aether shivered between them. Something about the intimacy of their expressions and the pleasure on Mama's face as she spoke to Sir Milton made Fenya's stomach twist in unease.

Reentering the drawing room, Aunt Cali took in the room with a quick glance, frowned, then sat down beside Fenya, her expression weary. "Do you mind if I join you?"

"Of course not." Fenya smiled and scooted over a bit so that Aunt Cali had enough room.

"I should have invited more people tonight to keep everyone occupied, but I just couldn't imagine a repeat of the other night." Aunt Cali stifled a yawn. "I still haven't recovered."

Mama's twittering laugh carried across the room. She'd sat down in a chair by the fire while Sir Milton took the second matching chair and pulled it close. But to Fenya's surprise, Uncle Caius stood beside Sir Milton.

"What are they talking about?" Fenya asked Aunt Cali.

"Oh, I don't know." Aunt Cali put a hand on her stomach and leaned her head back against the chair. "I think I might have eaten too much tonight."

"Can I get you something? Some tea?" She was half out of her chair when Aunt Cali waved her concern away.

"No, no. It will pass."

Fenya sank back down in her chair. "How did you know you wanted to marry, Aunt Cali?" Fenya clapped her fingertips over her mouth. She hadn't meant to say that out loud.

Aunt Cali's face betrayed her surprise at the unexpected question. "I... Do you mean how did I know I wanted to marry your uncle?"

Fenya bit her lip and entwined her fingers in her lap. She hadn't quite been asking that. It was almost more important to know how to know if she wanted to marry at all. If she could even have a choice.

"Ah." Aunt Cali straightened up and pulled at the waist of her dress. "That's a different question, isn't it?"

Fenya pressed the fold of her skirt together, pushing the crease back into its place. She had such a hard time fitting into her own place. Why couldn't she just be ironed and rearranged like her skirt fold? What made it so impossible for her to go just one night without a fiery accident? Even now, her hands twitched, begging to call the fire from the grate to her palms simply so she could hold it.

"Marriage is not to be entered into lightly, Fenya," Aunt Cali was saying softly. "I was a couple of years older than you, twenty, when I first seriously began to consider it. Though I always knew I wanted to marry and have a family, I wasn't sure what choice I had. These days there are more options for women, you know. I considered becoming a governess, but...well, then I met your uncle. And he was kind and made me feel important. He treated me with respect and didn't speak down to me like so many of the other men I had met before. It was he who made me consider, for the first time, that marriage might not be an evil." She found Uncle Caius with her gaze from across the room, a fond smile playing on her lips, as though she recollected sweet, private memories.

Sir Milton leaned back in his seat as Mama continued speaking. Fenya wished she could read lips. It would tell her what they were speaking about. Was it her?

"Your uncle had convinced me...and I wanted to marry him. But his family needed some convincing," Aunt Cali continued.

Uncle Caius's family? Father? Or Grandpapa and Grandmama? But as her aunt's gaze bore into Mama, Fenya understood exactly who it was that hadn't been pleased with Aunt Cali joining the family. And she could imagine the animosity between them given Mama's attempt to prevent the marriage. When Aunt Cali had first seen Mama at their arrival, the air had seemed to ice over.

"They were less than approving given my lack of connections. I would be as discerning for my own children, of course, as a wise match is important. But I wouldn't wish you to be subject to such scrutiny as I was, Fenya." Aunt Cali took her hand in her own and placed her other over Fenya's. "There are times when a young woman must take the opportunity set before her."

"You...think I should accept if he asks?" Fenya whispered, barely forcing the words past her dry throat. The idea of marriage in itself was terrifying, but to marry Sir Milton? There was something about him that made her wish Colonel Balderik or even Mage Stephens stood here instead.

Aunt Cali squeezed her hand. "I think you must make your choice as wisely as possible. Sometimes the best choice is the one you don't truly see right away."

Fenya met Aunt Cali's pale hazel gaze. "I'm afraid I'm going to choose wrong."

The chatter by the fireplace intensified, and Fenya's heart squeezed in her chest. In response, the fire leapt high, sparking off the lower part of the chimney. Mama shot it a glare as if it were to blame, even though she had to know that it was Fenya.

"I'm always around to listen, Fenya," Aunt Cali said softly. "If you need someone to speak to before you make a decision."

Tears pricked Fenya's eyes. "Thank you."

Mama rose and shook out her skirts. Fenya's heart stuttered at the steeliness in Mama's gray eyes, and the fire burned higher, fueled by her own fear. "I'm exhausted. Fenya, darling? Are you ready?"

The panic building in Fenya's chest lessened. "Ready? Yes, Mama. Of course." Aunt Cali had released Fenya's hand without her noticing, and she shoved her sketchbook back into her satchel and her pencils back into the case to follow it. The fire fluttered in the grate, Fenya's hands shaking in the thrill of escaping early.

"Cali, I could use your advice." Mama seized Cali's arm and the two drifted away toward the door. Fenya hurried to follow before Mama changed her mind, but her satchel refused to accept the sketchbook, snagging on the opening.

"Miss Verena," Sir Milton's voice stopped her short.

"Yes?" The word came out more like a squeak than a refined response as she finally fastened her satchel only to find Sir Milton standing before her. How had he appeared so quietly?

"I am taking my leave as well." He offered her his hand, waiting for hers.

She pretended not to see it, half turning toward the door, but he shifted and blocked her between the coffee table and the couch.

His hand hovered in the air, and Fenya exhaled in a whisper. She hesitated again, but his hand didn't move, expectation on his face. *He will be insulted if I refuse.* Without waiting any longer, she held her breath, steeled herself, and placed her hand ever so lightly in his.

Smiling, he leaned in and gave her exposed hand a light kiss on the back.

Wincing, she slid her hand from his as soon as he began to straighten. Her hand burned where his lips had touched her skin, and the tingle spread out toward her fingers and wrist. She pulled her hand free and slipped between the gap he'd left between himself and the couch. "Good night," she murmured hastily.

Mama was waiting at the door when Fenya arrived. Aunt Cali's brow was home to several creases, and she seemed to want to speak, but Mama ushered Fenya out of the door ahead of her.

"Come, we have to walk home," Mama said.

Fenya curtsied to her aunt and stepped outside behind a servant carrying a torch.

In tense silence, Fenya fell into step behind Mama. Fenya focused on the lake up ahead, not that she could feel it, but the idea of it calmed the fire within her and made her feel less out of control. It kept the fire more even, less jittery.

Mama hummed to herself as they walked, as though something had gone well tonight. But Fenya didn't want to ask. Anything that made Mama happy was sure to cause her strife. What if she'd made arrangements for Fenya to go to an asylum?

"Here you are, magess," the servant said with a bow of his head as he opened the door for Mama and Fenya to walk into the cottage.

"Thank you," Fenya murmured, trying to escape up to her room quickly, where the fireplace would be empty and cold, per her mother's demands.

"Fenya," Mama said as Fenya's foot touched the bottom step. "Wait."

Heart thumping unevenly, Fenya obeyed. In the nearby drawing room, the banked fire sparked.

The maidservant took Mama's cloak and hurried off to stow it as though she wished to avoid Mama's detection as much as possible.

"Come in here." Mama pointed to the drawing room and led the way inside. Mama's shoulders shuddered, and she pulled her shawl more tightly around her bare neck.

Fenya didn't dare ask what Mama wanted to speak to her about, but stopped a few steps inside the sparsely decorated room. A pair of small couches perched squatly on a carpet that was several years outdated, while a timeless oak mantelpiece carved with wyverns made it seem as though the mismatch was deliberate.

"Shut the door," Mama said without looking over her shoulder.

Fenya obeyed, her heartbeat erratic in her ears. *What have I done this time?*

Mama stared into the coals of the fire for a long moment, her shoulders tight. Finally, she turned and faced Fenya. "I have good news for you." Mama's lips twitched slightly. "Though whether you accept it as such remains to be seen."

Fenya's stomach clenched in dread. She doubted much of what Mama considered "good news" would feel like good news to her.

"Sir Jett Milton has made an offer of marriage to you. And I have accepted on your behalf."

Fenya's eyes widened. She bolted forward a few steps, as if drawn by the fire, and her hands roared with pain. "No!"

"So dramatic." Mama sighed and lifted her eyes to the heavens. "For once, do not argue with me. It's as good as done."

"Please! Don't make me..."

"Fenya, I'm your mother."

"Yes! And as my mother, you should know that I want a choice! Why didn't he ask *me*?"

"Lower your voice this instant," Mama hissed. "If the servants were to overhear you—"

"I don't care!" Fenya exclaimed, her heart a sharp staccato in her chest. "I can't marry him, Mama. Please...there's something...strange about him."

Mama rolled her eyes. "Don't be hysterical. It's an advantageous match, and it wouldn't happen until next year at the earliest. You're seventeen, darling, and you can't be expected to attend academy like I did or to find a better match soon."

Fenya clenched her fists. "Please, Mama, please. Don't make me marry him. I—"

"You don't understand how advantageous this is," Mama said, lowering her voice. "You are out of control—as we saw in the—" Mama stopped, her cheeks slightly pink, and cleared her throat. "You are a Relic Heir, Fenya! Not to mention nearing a Wylde Relic Heir! Should even half of what you've done emerge, you would be completely unsuitable for marriage. Completely. You would be registered as a Dangerous Legacist should it be known. Does that not frighten you?"

"No." Fenya's stomach squirmed at the dishonesty.

"It should. I managed to pass off the event in the garden as a rare instance of the sun starting a fire through a windowpane, but had I told the truth, you would already be in an asylum. Mage—he—I—we would be forced to report what happened. About the mere possibility of you being a Spark," she whispered the last word as though it were filthy.

Fenya's heart stuttered in her chest. "Mama...I'm not though..."

"Is that what you want?" Mama asked, ignoring her protest. "To be in a Bradley Asylum, trapped with the mad and infirm? To ruin us both?" Mama's eyes filled with tears that did not seem forced for once.

Fenya bit down on her lip. To go to any asylum...her friend at Jolie's had once said an asylum was a shame upon more than just the person there. Fenya would bring shame on Mama, too. *And I'd never get out. Go to an asylum, die in one. And Bradley...that was often joked about as a graveyard of living skeletons.*

Mama sniffed. "If you marry a man like Sir Milton, a Well, he offers you one of the only hopes you have of living a normal life."

"That's what he is?" Fenya gasped. "A Well?"

"Yes. He is the perfect match for you in this situation—I couldn't have asked for a better one." Mama nodded in satisfaction. "He can absorb your excess Power, make you safe to be around. He could even help you learn to control yourself."

"I *know* what a Well does, Mama," Fenya muttered. "And they *are* Black Listed. How can marrying such a mage possibly *help* us? Besides, I've been around him far too much for my liking already. He won't help me."

Mama narrowed her eyes. "You haven't given him a chance. You will. For your sake, and for mine. He doesn't need a formal rank to be Powerful—and help control you."

"Mama, please." Tears stung at Fenya's eyes, her body shrinking in despair. "I promise I'll control myself, I'll learn control. I'll practice every day...find me a tutor, Mama, please, I—"

"No. People are already talking about why you left Jolie's."

"They are?"

"Of course they are," Mama hissed. "They don't seem to believe that you don't have enough Legacy, given your father's Power and my own rank. I've had to tell them it was additionally for financial reasons that we left. But the longer you remain unmarried and out of control, the harder your expulsion will be to conceal."

"I'm sorry, Mama." Guilt tugged at Fenya's shoulders. She twisted her hands together in front of her. *Why can't I do anything right?*

"I will do what's best for you, even if you think me a horrid mother." Mama strode past her to the door. "And so you shall make a good marriage if it's the last thing I do. You shall marry even better than I did."

The door swung shut between them.

I can't marry him.

She wanted to call Mama back, but her courage failed.

Desperate to gain control, Fenya breathed in slowly and released the breath even slower. The banked fire sparked, a flame appearing in the middle of the fireplace. She stared at it warily.

A sensation like flames tickling down her hand and arm greeted her.

It was enjoyable. It was right. How could something that felt normal be wrong?

No! I can't give into it. I can't...it is wrong. Controlling fire is wrong. It's dangerous.

The flames grew higher.

It caressed her, bringing heat that consumed her. Surrounded her.

Fenya closed her eyes.

Put it away. Close it off.

How?

The flames grew higher around her, within her. It caressed her. She adored it. She wanted it.

How can anyone ever say that fire is bad? Humans can't live without fire.

Her heart raced.

This time when she opened her eyes, the fire wasn't just in the grate.

It licked the dragon claw foot of the couch. It rippled along the carpets. And stretched for the drapes.

Chapter Seven

FIRE

"No!" she whispered.

Frantically she stared at the rapidly expanding fire. She had done that. And it was too big to snuff out.

Her body hummed with heat. Awareness of the flames and their welcoming tendrils wrapped around her.

Thirteen fires.

This was just one. The other twelve grates in Whitland Cottage had leapt to life, including her formerly ice-cold fireplace.

They grasped for the fuel that had been so cruelly kept away from them. Toward the barriers that kept humans safe.

But it was the cook's fire that Fenya's Fire loved most of all. If all the fires were handsome gentlemen, the cook's fire was a handsome gentleman with ten thousand pounds to his name.

She turned her back on the drawing room fire. Took a step toward the door.

It called to her. Calling her name, begging her to come and help it grow.

It *needed* her.

She took another step, smiling.

A shout split the air.

Fenya jolted. *Humans.*

Wait...I am a human. And Mama...

And the servants—they were here too.

A scream split the air.

Mrs. Rawlins!

Fenya turned on her heel and raced toward the screams.

The kitchen was ablaze. The cook was dumping a pot of water onto the flames, but they spat and hissed and lunged for her.

"Get out!" Fenya cried. "Leave it—it's too late."

The cook turned, panic on her face. "But the house—"

"Get the others and get out," Fenya rasped. "Hurry!"

Mrs. Rawlins nodded, threw another panicked look over her shoulder and then picked up her skirts and raced from the room.

The fire skated across the kitchen table, skipping over a glass of water and scorching its surface before leaping for a towel hanging on the wall.

With Mrs. Rawlins clearing the servant's quarters, Fenya fisted her skirts and raced for her mother's rooms.

"Mama!" she cried as she ran up the stairs.

The last things she had said to Mama were that she would refuse to obey her—and now Mama's bedroom was burning.

As she reached the top, the acrid smell of smoke filled her lungs, and she coughed. Panic stabbed through her.

Thirteen warriors, reaching for each other, joining forces to destroy.

Destroy. Eat. Consume.

It was as if the fires were alive. A monster that would wolf down anything in its path. A hungry dragon, insatiable. Uncontrollable.

Fenya slammed into her mother's door. "Mama!"

She wrenched on the handle. It held firm.

She pounded on the door. "Mama! Open the door!"

The room remained silent.

"Fire!"

The scream wrenched its way out of her lungs. An admission of guilt, of intention, of something Fenya couldn't name.

"Fire, Mama," she sobbed. "Please. You have to come out."

The door burst open, and Fenya stumbled forward at Mama's feet.

Her expression was thunderous, but her bearing elegant. Her most expensive dressing robe clung to her body over her shifts, and her fur shawl trembled over her shoulders as she shook herself free of Fenya's clutching hands, walked past her and into the hallway. In her arms she held a large traveling bag, and Fenya glimpsed a glitter of jewelry and fabric inside the half-secured bag.

"How dare you lose control?" Mama hissed. "I knew you would do this. You didn't even have the decency to gather your belongings before you ran." Mama's eyes hardened. "Get yourself outside. And pretend that you were not at fault or you'll be on the next carriage to Bradley Asylum."

Fenya blinked back her tears as her breath caught on a smoke-filled sob. "But Mama, the others—"

"They shall find their way out. I'm sure you've already seen to that, leaving me until last." Mama swept down the hallway and to the stairs, holding a bit of cloth to her face as the smoke wrapped its tentacles around her. "Come, Fenya!" Mama called sharply, ever elegant and unmoved.

Fenya tore her gaze away from Mama's outline. Smoke filled the hall behind her; Fenya coughed and held her shawl to her face. She clutched at her satchel. *My other sketchbooks!* She hadn't even thought to gather her belongings, like Mama. *Mama is right about me.*

She turned away from the path Mama had taken and raced for her rooms. There hadn't been a fire in her grate, but there was now. It licked along the empty grate, up the mantle, searching for fuel.

Avoiding it, she turned toward her travel-worn trunks. Her sketchbooks were here. She couldn't leave her years of sketches. She didn't care about any jewels or dresses, those could be replaced. But the sketchbook and pencils that Papa had given her—easily the most important thing in the world. She grabbed a handful of her filled sketchbooks and shoved them into her satchel.

Digging through her petticoats, extra slippers, and boots, Fenya sought the pencils Papa gave her, ones she had been unable to bring herself to use after his death. It was the last gift he had given her...

She flung her clothing aside in the trunks, but found nothing at the bottom except a worn pair of slippers. Fenya raced for the second, still-closed trunk, fighting with the clasp until it opened.

The cottage groaned.

Fenya paused, reaching out for the fires.

The ones along the farthest wing had melted into each other. No longer thirteen fires, but now... She searched below stairs with her Legacy.

Seven.

There had been four downstairs, two had been small and candle-sized, two large and fireplace-sized. Now there was just one. One fire stretched for the ceiling, licking at the boards that supported her.

She might be able to withstand the flames, but even she would break when the beams supporting the structure around her fell. If only she could tell if there were humans around the fires. But her Legacy didn't offer her that ability.

The Relic...

Fenya gasped, and coughing, ran to the window. Mama stood, poised, at the edge of the lake staring at the cottage with an eerie glow upon her face as the fire stretched for the windows. Even from this distance, the Emberheart Relic was visible, hanging from her neck, gleaming in the fire's cheerful blaze. Fenya released a tight breath of relief.

Around Mama was chaos. Servants had grabbed buckets and bowls, whatever was handy, to scoop water up from the pond and throw against the flames, which hissed in displeasure but surged back larger than before.

"Miss Verena!"

"Fenya!"

Distantly, Fenya heard her name being called. If she didn't emerge from the cottage soon, someone would come looking for her, worried for her safety. But she felt as though the fire wouldn't claim her...she could walk through its flames and emerge unscathed. They, coming after her, might die for her.

The smoke, a violent byproduct of her Power, clawed at her throat, thinning the air. She gasped and coughed, her breath stolen by the fire she had so lovingly made.

Hurrying out of Mama's rooms and down the steps of the cottage, Fenya tried to push away the glorious feeling of the fire consuming the old logs of the building. It was dry and ready for flames. Perfect fuel.

No. Think about other things than fire. Think about what's going to happen to you when everyone finds out what you've done!

Fenya inhaled another smoky breath and more coughs wracked her body. *If I stay, I'll be smothered. It won't be the fire that kills me, but the smoke. And to think that I nearly killed Mama.*

Fenya hurried down the last stairs. The stone entry was no longer cool to the touch. She hadn't realized until now how the constantly cool stone had always bothered her. But now, with it fire-warmed...

Fenya's feet paused, and she hesitated at the open door.

No. Keep going. Or the fire will eat you alive.

She opened her eyes and mentally pushed herself out the door.

A few steps out, and the crackle of the fire filled her ears and fresh air filled her lungs. She whirled to the cottage. Flames stretched out of the lower windows, reaching for the next floor.

"Hurry!" a voice much like Mama's cried. "Come on!"

Fenya searched the smoky darkness of the night around her, only finding shadows. She stumbled off the last of the steps to the cottage door and across a grassy lawn that seemed to shrink away from the flames.

Keep walking.

The heat on her back kept calling Fenya back.

"Call for a fire brigade!" a man's voice erupted. "Where is the fire brigade?"

"A horse! Bring me a horse!" came another cry.

A servant ran for the stables, and soon a panicked horse, shying away from the fire, raced past them.

"Back up, Magess Verena, Miss Verena, please. You are too close to the flames." Mrs. Rawlins shuffled them away from the burning cottage, concern etched on her flame-brightened face.

But the fire is so beautiful.

Mama's hand took Fenya's and clenched it tight as a dragon bite. Fenya gasped.

Fenya caught the anger glinting in Mama's eye, the Relic now tucked under her gown, but gleaming through the thin fabric. Fenya turned to Mrs. Rawlins, hoping the older woman hadn't noticed. "Did everyone make it out?"

Mrs. Rawlins nodded, pulling a shawl tight around her shoulders, her hands trembling. "Yes, everyone is accounted for. You were the last, m'dear." She winced and pulled her hand away from the shawl to reveal a large blister.

"Oh!" Fenya gasped at the injury, even as she thanked the Lord that she hadn't killed anyone. "Your hand—"

"It'll heal, m'dear," Mrs. Rawlins said with a tight, pained smile.

"What happened?" Mama asked, her hand still firm around Fenya's fingers. "How did the fire start?"

Mrs. Rawlins met Mama's unflinching, innocent gaze, searching the younger woman's face for a long moment. "I don't know. The fires in the kitchen caught. Perhaps grease. But the fire spread rapidly. Strangely quick."

Mama coughed, far more violently than usual, clearing smoke from her lungs. "Shameful," Mama managed. "That never should happen."

"The brigade!" a servant shouted. "I see the dragons coming!"

The sight did not bring Fenya relief. Instead, her heart ached for the demise of the fire. She allowed her gaze to linger upon it, tears pricking her eyes. It was such a beautiful thing, the way it curled around the rooftop, blazing through the chimneys that couldn't contain it now. They had always confined it, forced it to obey—but now it had conquered them. It was one enormous fire now. She smiled, and the tendrils climbing outside Mama's window seemed to wave back at her.

Then the air was alive with dragons—with danger.

Not fire-breathing dragons, but man-controlled dragons. Buckets hung from their bellies, and the men opened them above the house.

"No..." Fenya started forward, trying to save the fire. *It will be killed!*

Mama's hand, tight on Fenya's, held her back. Mrs. Rawlins gave Fenya an odd scrutiny.

"Fenya," Mama growled so that only Fenya could hear.

Reluctantly, Fenya caught Mama's gray eyes. They glinted with reflections of the fire as Fenya searched them, reading in them what Mama couldn't say aloud.

If you go into that fire, no one will save you—and you will ruin me. Is that what you want?

Her words were so clear that Fenya almost found them delivered into her mind Telepathically—but Mama did not have that Legacy.

Fenya stepped away from her and the cottage.

I may go to an asylum if I make it through this night. I almost orphaned myself. Almost killed several of Uncle's servants. And...even if I make out of here unscathed, undiscovered as the cause of this fire, I could get sent away.

To Bradley Asylum. The worst asylum within the borders of Avenesse.

Fenya shuddered. Once again, Mama was absolutely right.

Dragons swooped down from the sky with another delivery of horse-sized buckets filled with water.

The icy blast of the water dropped, and Fenya shuddered as though it drenched her. Perhaps it did. Was she that tied to the flames?

The house groaned under the weight of the water.

"Stand back!" a male voice cried.

"It's going to collapse!" a female servant shrieked, running for the woods.

Others followed, and Mama pulled Fenya back as Mrs. Rawlins raced away from the structure.

Fenya allowed Mama to drag her away.

I should have just agreed to marry Milton. Why did I think I could find a better solution to all this? A Well is exactly what will contain me. What I need... or deserve.

The fire hissed as another bucket of water fell upon it.

Then, with another groan and shriek, the cottage fell.

Shouts filled the air.

The fire was hot now, so hot. So...perfect.

No. I can't enjoy it. Fenya wrenched her hand from Mama's, but this time she didn't run toward the fire. She ran away, tracing the path Mrs. Rawlins had taken. She sprinted for the edge of the woods, saw a group of servants and spectators huddled there, and veered to the left. The lure of the fire faded, but not as quickly as it normally did. It was too large, too hot, too fueled to weaken its grip regardless of Fenya's flight.

At the edge of the woods, Fenya slowed and took a deep, steadying breath.

In the quiet, away from the fire's rapid crackles, Fenya heard a chirp.

"Fang?" she asked.

The chirrup repeated, and Fenya looked up to a low-hanging branch of the oak tree.

"What are you doing here?" She glanced over her shoulder and around, but the servants were huddled in a group, staring at the house, enveloped in red-orange flames, and Mama stood with someone that looked like Aunt Cali.

Fang chirruped again and leapt off the low branch to land on Fenya's shoulder. She flinched at the squeeze of the talons, but turned and the dragon reached out her beak to touch Fenya's nose with it.

The touch was soft, and relief flooded through Fenya as the hard, beak-like mouth brushed her skin.

Fenya closed her eyes and raised a hand to brush Fang's chest. The little wyvern seemed to purr. Fenya wasn't sure if dragons could purr like cats, but it certainly seemed so. And the purrs were just as soothing as a cat's.

"You're a flame wyvern, so you must understand fire, right?" Fenya said, her fingers catching on a rough scale. "My papa understood it—but he'd never talk about it with me. I miss him. He was a Flame Legacist, too, but I never saw him use his Fire. Called it dangerous and servant's business to light the fires. Then he got so ill that he couldn't, but now that he's gone, I wish he were here to tell me what to do." She continued petting the dragon, who seemed to enjoy the strokes so much that she almost glowed.

"But if anyone finds out about this fire...that I did it," Fenya whispered, "I'll never see anyone I love again. I won't see my cousins, I won't have any freedoms...I'll be sent to an asylum, Fang. And I can't live like that. Maybe I should just run away. Maybe I should have run away from school before. I'm so lucky I didn't kill someone tonight."

Fang chirruped again and leaned her head against Fenya's temple.

Tears pricked Fenya's eyes. Tears of relief and anger and sadness... the emotions spilled into her tears and down her cheeks.

84

A soft glow burned through her closed eyes.

Fenya gasped. Fang's scales were glowing.

"Fang! How—what? Did I hurt you?"

The dragon shook her head and ruffled her wings, almost slicing Fenya's cheek. She flinched back, and the dragon leapt off her shoulder and resumed her perch on the tree, but this time the scales over her heart glowed where Fenya had been petting her. Fang preened, using her beak to touch the glowing spot, but not as if she were uncomfortable, instead as if she were proud.

"Oh," Fenya realized aloud. "You're a flame wyvern. You know fire." She chuckled lightly and stretched out a hand. "Maybe that's why you like me. You are like me."

Fang tilted her head to the side and let out a decisive chirrup.

Gravel crunched a short distance away from Fenya, and she turned just as Fang took flight, seeking refuge from whomever approached.

"Miss Verena?" Mr. Thomas, the manor's butler, said. "The fire is nearly out now. A Water Legacist is coming to extinguish any embers, but Magess Verena asked that I accompany you to your aunt and uncle's if you are ready."

Fenya glanced back at the tree and followed the route in the air that Fang must have taken. But she was gone, the only evidence that she'd even been there a scale stuck to the branch, glistening in the distant fire's reflection.

Thoughtfully, Fenya plucked it from the branch and slipped it into her pocket before following Mr. Thomas out of the woods and to the manor.

Chapter Eight

DISMISSED

E ighteen fires.

No. Nineteen. Someone just lit another candle.

She was aware of each fire in Whitland Manor as though they were extensions of herself. Nineteen fingers or toes, maybe long hairs or strings like a marionette, attached to her at various places. Every bit of her body felt alive with fire. She hummed with energy and potential. She tried focusing on other things, but her mind kept returning to the cottage fire, and that drew her back to the nineteen fires.

It's going to be impossible to sleep.

She stared at the ceiling. The shadows flickered, cast by the fire in her room, taunting her, and she turned to stare at it. Burning low for the night, it lived on a fuel that wasn't supplied in the grate. It pulled at her like a clingy child, and she just barely glimpsed how she was sustaining it through one of the aether threads attached to her, but she didn't have enough energy to care or discern how exactly it worked.

I wonder if feeding it all night long will give me Legacy Fever, like Papa.

I don't think it would matter. If I do get Legacy Fever, at least my Power would be nearly empty for some time.

And erratic in the others.

And I may not live.

She scoffed to herself and returned her gaze to the ceiling. She was already erratic. And already in danger of never entering normal society.

Finally, Fenya slipped into a fitful doze, and in the five minutes she slept, she dreamed of a ball of fire separating itself from the main fire and drifting across the room. It hovered over her for a minute, then settled down upon her like a cat settling upon her chest at night, warm, comfortable, reassuring.

Wrong.

Fenya awoke with a start, and the fire, as if startled, dashed back to the mother fire in the fireplace. She gaped at it. Had she imagined the entire thing? She touched the fabric of her sleeping gown and winced.

Singed. It wasn't a dream then.

She changed into another gown, thankful that she'd forgone the covers when getting into bed. It would be more difficult to hide that damage.

She buried the sleeping gown in the bottom of the trunk and slipped into a fresh one, sitting up in her bed, hugging her knees to her chest, afraid to fall asleep, even to doze.

And so she lay awake in Whitland Manor, counting imperfections in the shadowed ceiling as the fireplace crackled low and steady. She didn't want to fall asleep again, not when the fire was so near. Not when there were twenty-seven...no, twenty-eight fires in Whitland Manor burning.

As soon as the maid came in, Fenya would ask her to put out the fire in her rooms and never start it again.

At least that might give me some peace in my sleep.

Thirty, thirty-five. Servants are up. Lighting fires.

Candles in the servant's quarters. Forty-two.

Candles in the breakfast room. Fifty-six.

Oh, there's the chandelier. Sixty- And another candelabra. Seventy-six now.

She stopped counting at one hundred. But she didn't have to count. She felt them. All one hundred and fifty-three flames. Each like a precious little pet, separate, related, but intricately formed and alive.

The morning light crept through the slit in the drapes, crawling across the floor and stretching for the bed until it finally spilled across the covers, and Fenya roused herself.

Every time she blinked, her eyelids scratched across her eyes. She smothered a yawn as she pulled open the drapes, allowing unfiltered sunlight to pour inside. In the distance, was a faint plume of smoke rising from what used to be Whitland Cottage.

She bit down on her lip. It had been a lovely cottage, too. And she'd razed it to the ground.

Wrapping her arms tightly around herself, she turned her back on the sight. A soft knock at the door roused her, and the knob turned. The maid peeked in, her eyes stopping on the bed in surprise, then traveling around the room to find Fenya.

"Miss Verena! I didn't expect you to be up." The maid entered and bobbed a curtsy. "Are you...did you sleep well?"

Fenya tightened her grip around her ribs. "Can you please put the fire out?"

"Out, miss?" Reaching for the fire iron, the maid paused to give Fenya a confused stare.

"Yes, out," Fenya said, her tone growing sharp.

"I... Yes, miss." The maid took her hand away from the poker. "Shall I help you dress first?"

"Quickly, please." Fenya itched to get out of the room. A walk in the rain would soothe the fires within her, surely.

"Yes, miss." The maid flew into motion, digging out a dress Fenya had never seen before.

In minutes, Fenya was dressed in a dark olive-green dress that was a bit too snug around the waist and a little too long. Judging by the Earth Legacy colors, it had to belong to Aunt Cali. She used one hand to lift her skirts in walking down the hall and almost tripped down the stairs on her way to the breakfast room. If she hadn't been in Whitland Manor, she would have headed straight past the carved wyvern on the bottom post of the stairs and out the front door, but she couldn't do that to Uncle Caius and Aunt Cali's hospitality.

Chewing on her lip, she turned away from escape and aimed her feet at the breakfast room. A light breakfast. That was all. Then she'd take her satchel and sketchbook, and she would head to the woods to see if she could find Fang again.

In the doorway of the breakfast room, Fenya hesitated. A spread of

Emberglass tea, and hot rolls with duskberry jam greeted her, and Aunt Cali sat at one end of the table with Uncle Caius, while Mama sat at the other, chatting softly with Sir Milton.

What is he doing here? Again?

Remembering the reason for the cottage fire, Fenya shuddered and turned to the breakfast table. Distracted, she helped herself to a small plate, for which she chose a small roll with a generous smear of jam.

"He's to arrive soon, I'm sure," Uncle Caius was saying to Sir Milton in a low voice.

"What a tragedy. You had to report it immediately, of course?" Milton said.

"Yes. Insurance has been contacted as well, and it's just such a mess," Uncle Caius said, pushing back his plate, still laden with a heaping of bacon and a half-eaten roll.

"Darling, it will all be fine. Thank the Lord there were no lives lost." Aunt Cali gave him an encouraging smile and flicked her finger at his plate, pushing it gently back toward him with her Legacy.

Silent, Fenya seated herself, but found her appetite to be like Uncle Caius's, elusive and evaporating.

"Do you know which inspector it will be?" Milton asked around a mouthful of bacon.

"No." Uncle Caius picked at a piece of his roll, wrinkling his nose in annoyance. He lifted his gaze and met Aunt Cali's solemnly. "But we must tell the truth."

"Of course," Aunt Cali agreed. "There's no other way, is there?"

The truth. That was a dangerous thing...when I'm to blame. I should just confess now. Fenya opened her mouth to speak, when Mama chose that time to enter the breakfast room, looking radiant with her hair braided in a crown of brunette tresses and a silver chain.

"Good morning," she said cheerfully. "Ah, good morning, Sir Milton. I didn't expect you here so early."

The men nodded a greeting to her, and Sir Milton gave her a private sort of smile that brought a frown to Fenya's lips.

"What's going on?" Mama asked, ignoring the plates and breakfast foods and instead opting for a cup of tea. "Why does everyone look so solemn?"

"The Crown Inspector for Fire Accidents is coming to inspect the ruins of the cottage some time today," Uncle Caius said shortly, his gaze again skipping over Fenya and locking on Mama.

Her expression faltered, and her attention shifted to Fenya, a dark look flashing in her gray eyes that let Fenya know exactly what sort of position she was in.

Fenya gazed down at her plate while Aunt Cali reached over and poured her a cup of tea. She couldn't even bring herself to acknowledge the kindness. Tears pooled on her lashes. How was she supposed to avoid Bradley Asylum *now*?

"Well, I suppose that sort of thing must happen. Insurance will want to have a legal document saying it was an accident by the housekeeper," Mama said breezily, lifting the cup to her lips.

Uncle Caius didn't seem convinced. "Who was the first to notice the fire?"

Mama held his gaze solemnly. "The housekeeper, as I told you. What's her name?"

"Mrs. Rawlins," Fenya murmured. "And she's the cook."

"Rawlins," Aunt Cali said with a tense tone. "Her conduct until now has been impeccable. Always been exemplary—first one up and last one to bed, from what I hear."

"Do you mean to say that it wasn't an accident, sir?" Sir Milton cleared his throat.

"When it spread so fast?" Uncle Caius said, eyebrows raised. "It would have had to have been extreme neglect...or else deliberately set..." He included Fenya in his gaze as Sir Milton spoke again.

Her face drained of blood.

"Fire often has a life of its own," Sir Milton said mildly. "The Crown Inspector is well versed in exploring all the possibilities."

I have to speak. I can't let someone else, especially kind Mrs. Rawlins suffer for what I've done. "I—" Fenya began.

Mama's foot found hers underneath the table and pressed down hard.

Flinching, Fenya looked at her and broke off.

Mama casually lifted a napkin to her lips. "Don't speak," she mouthed behind her napkin. "Eat up, darling," she said aloud for others to hear. "You look as though you haven't slept all night."

Fenya obediently lifted her roll to her lips only to find it tasteless and dry on her tongue.

Mr. Thomas appeared at Uncle Caius's side and gave a short bow.

"Yes?" her uncle asked, a sharp edge to the word.

"A man from the Crown Inspection Office is here to inspect the cottage, sir," he said.

Uncle Caius tossed his napkin upon his plate and took a last, long swig of his tea, wincing at the taste. *I wonder if he put something stronger in that tea today...* Fenya shook the thought away. Maybe it was just cold.

Uncle Caius rose and gave his wife a significant look that Fenya couldn't decipher. Aunt Cali nodded and took only a small bite of her neglected sausage before setting it back down.

"Sir Milton, care to join me?" Uncle Caius lifted a hand toward the door.

Sir Milton pushed back his chair. "Certainly, I'd be honored." He bowed to Aunt Cali, then Mama, and paused at Fenya's side as he passed. "I'd like to speak with you later, Miss Verena, if you would permit me."

Fenya's heart pulsed in her throat. Mama tapped her shin with her toes. "I—of course," she stammered.

He bowed and offered his gloved hand, in which she automatically placed hers. He brushed his lips against the back of her hand, and she shivered as her skin prickled. He smiled as if he knew what she had felt and left her with Mama and Aunt Cali.

Mama dabbed her napkin to her lip and poured herself a second cup of tea, seemingly unhurried. "Will you be joining the men, Cali?"

Aunt Cali almost seemed surprised that Mama had spoken to her. "I hadn't thought to. I must attend to the children. They're a bit concerned given the...situation."

Mama raised a brow. "Do they expect another accident at the manor?"

Aunt Cali met Mama's gaze solemnly. "They are children," she said stiffly. "And children have fears from such events. They will be heading to their grandparent's house soon."

Mama's lips turned down at the corners, but she didn't reply. Aunt Cali stood and bobbed her head. "If you'll excuse me then."

"Of course," Mama murmured.

Fenya kept her gaze upon her half-drunk tea as Aunt Cali left, the door snapping shut behind her. With several servants nearby, Fenya didn't dare speak freely to Mama, despite her closeness. Perhaps if they were outside...

"Dearest," Mama murmured. "Accompany me outside, please."

Apparently Mama had had the same thought.

Fenya nodded hopelessly. This was the moment where Mama reminded her that she was at fault and the only options before her were either marriage to Sir Milton or Bradley Asylum. One would subdue her, the other would shame them all. Except...she might not get a choice if the Crown Inspector determined the truth of the fire.

And she couldn't quite determine whether she was thrilled or terrified at the idea. Instead, she remained silent and waited as Mama finished her tea, called for her shawl, and finally emerged out the front door.

Mama waited until they were a hundred feet from the front door before speaking. "Don't say a word to anyone, Fenya." Her tone was hard and full of warning. "If you do..."

Fenya bit her lip, blinking away tears. Instead of the sight of the cottage up ahead around the curve and behind the pond, charred black earth reflected on the water's edge. She should have sat and sketched the cottage when she had a chance. Now, she would only have her memory.

"...it will end us all—not just me, but your uncle, your aunt, and your cousins."

Fenya's cousins. Their entire future was before them, and it had to be more promising than Fenya's. They were not cursed to Fire, but had the possibility of Uncle Caius's Air or Aunt Cali's Animation, which usually came from Earth. No Fire at all—as the Relic had rejected Uncle Caius as the next Bearer. They didn't have the burden of being a Bearer either.

"Are you listening to me?" Mama snapped.

"Yes," Fenya answered quickly. "Yes, Mama. I...I...but what happens if the Crown Inspector—"

"We will cross that bridge if and when it comes," Mama said, softening her tone. "You are to continue with the public story that your Legacy was too weak to continue at Jolie's and that your father's death left us too destitute to continue until your Legacy could grow."

Guilt and shame warred within Fenya. She was either too much or too little. She couldn't get it right. A simple loss of her temper, and she'd burned down an entire cottage. Would she ever learn control? And would the Relic help or hinder? What if it made everything worse?

"I wish you to show yourself to the Crown Inspector and then run off wherever you run off to in order to keep yourself out of trouble," Mama said. "Do you understand me?"

"Yes, Mama," Fenya whispered. She had to appear, simply to confirm that she existed and was...safe...but was she? Could she? She focused on the dulling effect of the pond ahead, on the water above in the misty clouds. She willed it to rain. Perhaps it would make the inspection more difficult. Or it would just smother her Fire.

The rest of the walk to the cottage embers passed in silence, and Fenya pushed her hands into her pockets, thankful that she had brought her satchel and sketchbooks to breakfast.

Gathered between the pond and the charred mess were a group of men, at least half a dozen, with another two strolled around the perimeter of the cottage remains, inspecting the ground. Every few steps, one or both would crouch down and point out or pick something up from the debris.

"Now that I've explained the process, I'd like to get started with my questions," a portly man with a large mustache was saying. He was dressed as though he were going to spend the entire day outside in the rain, with rubber boots and a weatherproof jacket turned up against the cold.

Is it cold? Fenya glanced at the sky again, but the sun peeked out. And yet, Mama was covered with a muted dove blue aether-coat that descended to her toes, and a shawl around her neck.

Sir Milton spotted them at the same time as the inspector and waved a hand. "Magess Verena and Miss Verena were staying at the cottage at the time of the fire."

"Witnesses?" the inspector asked, his eyebrows lifting.

Mama lifted her chin and smiled demurely. "The cottage burned shortly after I went to bed. I was still awake when the alarm rang out."

The inspector pulled out a notebook from his pocket along with a stubby pencil. "And who else was awake at the time?"

Mama met his gaze evenly, her face shimmering with her Beauty. "I had already said good night to my daughter and seen her to her room when the fires broke out. Or...when I was notified of them."

"And did you see anything unusual with your fire, magess?" the inspector asked, looking at her over his glasses, pencil poised over his pad.

Fenya paused. That was right. All the fires had erupted at the same time. No one would have been ignorant of the fires—had she panicked for nothing?

Mama shook her head, all innocence. "No. It was the screams of the cook that jarred me out of my thoughts and made me realize what was happening."

How can she lie so easily? Fenya stared at Mama, hoping her dismay didn't show on her face.

"And you, Miss?" the inspector turned his gaze on Fenya. "What did you see?"

Fenya opened her mouth but paused at the expectant faces focused on her. "I..." She swallowed and the tears threatened again.

"Miss, look at me," the inspector said.

Fenya raised her eyes to the man's, and to her surprise, his expression was gentle.

"You have nothing to worry about, miss. I am only here to find out the truth. And I doubt that a young girl like you could have burned down an entire cottage."

Mama swept her arm around Fenya's shoulders and patted her on the forearm. "Oh, of course not. She was sent home from her boarding school for lack of Legacy, in fact."

The inspector's gaze slid to Mama, and he nodded as if he agreed. "Miss? What did you see?"

"I...I just saw fire coming all over." Fenya bit her lip as tears pooled. She couldn't stop them, and they dashed over her lashes and down her cheeks as she remembered, and as the guilt attacked her. "Fire everywhere." She covered her face with her hands, her shoulders shaking as the tears fell.

"Oh, my dear," Mama said, pulling her close.

Fenya dropped her head on Mama's shoulders, remembering when she rarely comforted her as a little girl. All the emotion of the last day flooded through Fenya, emerging in racking sobs.

"I'm sorry, Magess," the inspector said. "Mage Verena, you must understand that sometimes my questions can be uncomfortable and reopen fresh wounds."

"Of course," Uncle Caius said. "It was a difficult ordeal for us all."

"Yes, miss, well, if there's nothing you can think to add," the inspector said gently, "then your mother should take you to go rest."

Mama patted Fenya's back while pushing her back subtly. "Yes, my dear, you should go and collect yourself. Take a lie down."

Fenya saw in her eyes the dismissal that Mama wanted her to take. And she did. With a bob of her head, she clutched her satchel to her stomach and raced as delicately as possible for the nearby woods.

A short time later, she found herself beside a stream with Fang hopping along the rocks. Dipping her hands into the rushing creek, Fenya felt the embers of the fire fade to her senses.

Fang chirruped, then paused, staring behind Fenya. With a quick dart of her wings, she disappeared into the woods. Fenya's heart sank. *Sorry I wasn't better company,* she thought about calling after her, but a crunching sound behind her had Fenya turning.

Sir Milton wandered the woods, hands tucked behind his back, eyes fixed on the trees.

Fenya inhaled quietly. Perhaps if she stayed still, he wouldn't see her in his distraction.

But before she could decide either to try to fade into the foliage or to stand up and walk away, his gaze fell upon her, eyes widening in shock.

"Miss Verena. I...didn't expect to see you here." He appeared as surprised as her, taking his hands to his front to clasp them together, only to reach up and scratch the back of his neck. "Are you...well?"

Fenya climbed to her feet and adjusted her skirts. "Yes, I was just... listening to the creek," she finished lamely. "I find it...soothing." She shrugged at his look of confusion. "I'm heading back to the cottage— manor now."

He smoothed his brow and nodded. "Might I escort you home?"

"I..." Fenya paused, but she couldn't think of a reason to say no. Biting her lip and glancing around the woods, she racked her brain and finally nodded. "Of course."

At least he won't be looking for Fang, if that's what he's doing here. She walked quickly, trying to close the distance between herself and the manor.

"Might I ask you something, Miss Verena?" Sir Milton asked after a minute or two of trailing her through the woods.

Fenya inhaled, her shoulders tensing. *Why am I afraid of him? Or of what he might ask me?* "Of course, Sir Milton," she said in as calm a tone as she could muster.

"I have been speaking with your mother...not just about my offer to you, but about your Legacy."

Fenya held her breath. *Is he going to demand an answer now?*

"And I have learned that your Legacy is quite out of control."

Fenya stopped short and turned to him. "She told you that?"

Sir Milton halted a few paces behind her. His lips spread into a slow smile. "No, Miss Verena. She told me nothing of the sort."

Fenya closed her eyes. *Yes, of course, he's a Well. He can feel what I am and absorb it.* "I understand, Sir Milton."

"I'm glad. I know you're quite clever, despite what anyone else might say."

Fenya frowned at the insinuation.

"And, Miss Fenya?"

She breathed in before answering. "Yes?"

"I do wish you to take as much time as you need to consider my offer of marriage."

"Thank you," she murmured, hurrying her pace. They continued walking in silence that Fenya didn't try to fill. When they came back out of the woods to the lake and cottage, the Crown Inspector was dusting off his trousers and speaking to Uncle Caius with a cheery tone.

"Sounds like that's the answer, then, sir. I would dismiss her immediately."

Fenya froze, frowning at the exchange. *Dismiss her?*

Sir Milton took her arm. "Don't worry, Miss Verena. Nothing bad shall happen to you."

Her mouth went dry, but Uncle Caius waved her away, and Sir Milton directed her toward the manor house. "Are you staying at the manor tonight?" Fenya ventured.

"Oh, no, just for the day. I thought it important to be here to support the inspection."

Fenya bit her lip. "And how...did you support it?"

Sir Milton cast her a considering glance. "Miss Verena, I am a Well, and so I can certainly direct impressions away from some conclusions..."

"But...does that mean you often do that?"

"Of course not," he answered easily. "It would be illegal."

She looked at him, not quite sure if she could believe him. "That's true," she finally agreed. "But why would you do so in this circumstance?"

He aimed a small smile her way. "I should have thought my reasons obvious."

She held her breath. Was he implying that he had feelings for her? Or was it simply her Legacy...her Relic...that he wanted?

On the rest of the walk to the manor house, Fenya couldn't decide what to ask or what to say to continue any sort of conversation. And so she simply hurried toward the manor house, eager to escape the solitude with Sir Milton.

The day passed with little chance for solitude, however, as Sir Milton followed her to the sitting room and watched her sketch in awkward silence until they all went to prepare for dinner.

Fenya had hoped that dinner would be a reprieve from Sir Milton's presence, but he was already there when she returned downstairs and he pulled out her chair for her to seat her at dinner.

The air around the table felt tense, like Uncle Caius and Aunt Cali had argued. Mama floated in late, beaming a smile over the entire table. "Good evening," she said cheerfully.

Uncle Caius grunted and turned to Aunt Cali. "She's been dismissed then?"

"Yes, dear. Both of them," Aunt Cali answered in what seemed like an attempt for a soothing tone.

"What? Who?" Fenya demanded as the first servant arrived at the table with the soup.

"Tonight's first course is Starlace Petal Broth, accompanied by Silvercrest Wine," a servant said as the bowls, brimming with a clear broth in which decorative starlace petals and a single frostleaf were set in front of them.

"Who's been dismissed?" Fenya repeated as soon as the servants left.

"Miss Rawlins and the scullery maid of the cottage," Uncle Caius barked as he picked up his spoon. "As they should have been. I'm already being inundated with messages from the farmers who claim the fire made them lose crops and frightened their sheep away. One claims to have lost an entire flock of sheep to a dragon this morning." He rolled his eyes. "Such a hassle. All because they couldn't bank the fire properly."

"Dearest, I've let them go with no recommendation, as I told you." Aunt Cali patted his hand soothingly. "It'll be all right. Of course the shepherd didn't lose a flock of sheep—we would have seen a dragon that size in the sky. It wasn't a moonlit night."

"But they'll try. Claim they saw it by the firelight." He snorted. "Irresponsible, if you ask me," he muttered and sipped his tea.

Sir Milton slurped from his spoon, smacking his lips together appreciatively and dabbing them with his napkin before speaking. "Indeed. A shame to have such a thing happen. As I was saying, if there's anything I can do to help...just ask."

Aunt Cali pressed her lips together but didn't speak.

"Dismissed without a reference?" Fenya asked. "But..." she trailed off at Mama's glare.

Sir Milton tilted his head over his glass of Silvercrest Wine.

"Maybe I could have—" Fenya clamped down on her lip.

"Darling," Mama said, quickly filling the silence. "The fire started in the kitchens. You heard the cook say that the grease caught fire. You couldn't have helped." Mama's eyes glittered, daring Fenya to disagree. As if daring her to speak and tempt Sir Milton to withdraw his still unanswered offer of marriage. "You couldn't have done anything. You know you can only feel whatever fire is in the room—Magess Jolie proved you couldn't manipulate them."

Fenya's stomach squirmed. *Right. I'm supposed to be weak. Incapable of controlling fire at all. But how long can I live this lie if I'm starting fires when I'm upset?*

"Did Miss Rawlins say that to you, Fenya?" Uncle Caius asked. "That the grease caught fire?"

Fenya clamped down on her lip. Mama's smile was dangerously edged like the blade of a knife.

"Yes, I—she did—but—" she stammered.

"See? I'm glad you got rid of her," Mama interrupted. "To think we might not have woken up if Fenya hadn't alerted us. The size of the fire must have woken her and made her aware of it more than usual."

Fenya couldn't form words.

Aunt Cali wiped at her face. "I can't imagine if we had lost any of you."

Even Uncle Caius's expression softened, and he set down his tea to take his wife's hand. "We're all safe."

A servant refilled Uncle Caius's glass of wine, and he nodded his thanks.

Aunt Cali caught her husband's eye, and a look of understanding passed between them.

Uncle Caius cleared his throat and set his glass down on the side table. "Fenya, you...you didn't feel the fires? Before they spread, I mean."

"What? Of course she didn't!" Mama exclaimed.

Uncle Caius held up a hand in Mama's direction. "I asked my niece."

Fenya's heart thudded in her chest. *How could I make Mama a liar? To openly confront her? Mama will be dismissed from the house if there are any question that I had something to do with the cottage's fire. And if they found out how much I've done, I'll go to an asylum—or be reported to the constable—or the Crown Inspector. And what would happen to Mama then? She would be poor, destitute, unsuitable for marriage. I will condemn her to living with family for the rest of her life, to be thus tainted...*

Fenya shook her head, trying to shake away her thoughts.

"You did not then?" Uncle Caius gave a sigh of relief.

Fenya stilled. In her thoughts, she'd unwittingly denied the very truth she should speak. "I...I felt them."

"But after they jumped the grate?" Uncle Caius pressed.

Fenya clamped down on her lip. "I...I always feel them, Uncle."

Aunt Cali narrowed her eyes. "Darling..." She bit her bottom lip and dabbed at her mouth with a napkin. "What he means to ask is if you might have accidentally influenced them."

Uncle Caius cleared his throat, the tips of his ears reddening. "Well, I—"

Fenya's eyes welled with tears. "I..."

"Can't you see you're terrifying her, Caius?" Mama snapped. "And in front of company? Leave the poor girl alone. The Crown Inspector did his job and determined it to be a result of negligence. *If* Fenya felt it at all, she wouldn't have been able to put out such a violent fire fed by kitchen grease that a foolish woman didn't clean up. I told you before that the kitchen was a mess at the cottage. And Fenya was the last one out of the cottage—insisted on emptying out the building by herself."

"You did?" Uncle Caius sputtered. "Fenya, I had no idea—"

Aunt Cali dabbed her nose with a napkin.

"Ys, she did." Mama was suddenly beside Fenya, pressing a hand on either of her shoulders. But far from reassuring, the fingers gripped tightly, too tight to comfort, full of warning. Mama took one hand off to blot at her face. "It's been such a stressful time."

Fenya pressed her lips together. Mama's black handkerchief, pulled out of her black pocket, reminded them all of Papa's loss, all too recent for Fenya and recent enough to keep Mama in her half-mourning clothes. Fenya knew what Mama's purpose was—and Caius caught it at once, lowering his head.

"I'm sorry, sister."

Fenya held her breath. The fire jumped in the grate, and she glanced at it, suddenly aware again of the fires in the house and disconcerted by the absence it had been to her thoughts all day. *What's wrong with me? Perhaps it was the constant drain of my fire all night, followed by the emotional toll of the inspection and talking with Milton that made her resist it?* Her gaze shifted to Milton. *Or it's him and his Well nature.*

Mama dabbed at her face with her handkerchief again as she reclaimed her seat.

"I apologize, Fenya," Uncle Caius said contritely. "Of course, we all know you're not nearly strong enough to create such a fire. The fires were banked, if improperly, as the Inspector determined. And if you could create such havoc, you never would." Offering Fenya an apologetic smile, Uncle Caius motioned to a servant, who set a delicately browned chicken pie in front of him.

Aunt Cali cleared her throat. "Fenya, I admire your concern for others, but you must realize that the consequences of our actions always come for us. When we don't take our jobs seriously and fulfill our duties, there are things that must be done, even though we hate to do them."

Fenya sank back in her chair. She couldn't speak against Mama, and she couldn't speak for Mrs. Rawlins if even Aunt Cali refused to listen. There was nothing more to do but accept her own actions.

Chapter Nine

A CONTRACT

The third day after the cottage fire, the skies opened and poured, keeping Fenya inside. She missed catching sight of Fang in the trees, of slipping her a bit of dried meat or a bit of bacon she'd saved from breakfast. The guilt plaguing her in the house wouldn't bother her before Fang, would it? She wouldn't know, as the rains were too violent to risk.

Fenya positioned herself in the pink drawing room beside the front window, as close to the rain as she could, but between the fire at her back and the rain before her gave her a strange feeling of turmoil that made relaxation impossible. But as the day waned, the rain ebbed and others joined Fenya in the room just as she was considering whether she could slip outside without notice.

Aunt Cali worked on her wyvern embroidery, occasionally asking Fenya clarifying questions regarding its appearance, and conversation flowed between Sir Milton, Mage and Magess Merivale, Uncle Caius, and Mama.

Fenya was the first both to leave and prepare for dinner and to start for the gold drawing room. But as she passed the library, voices alerted her to a presence, and she paused. Mama's voice sounded from the inside, her tone much like it had sounded in the garden.

Fenya stood in the hallway, her heart pounding. Was Mama with the same man again? If so...who was he? Did it matter? Indecision made her limbs freeze. Did she peek in the library and see who Mama was with? Or did she walk on and pretend it didn't happen?

Before she could decide, footsteps sounded, and the door moved. Fenya's heart leapt into her throat. She forced her feet to move and kept her gaze on the floor as a man stepped into the hall, adjusting his cravat.

"Oh. Miss Venera," Mage Merivale said loudly. "I—uh—good evening." He nodded sharply and hurried off the opposite direction from the sitting room.

Without acknowledging him, Fenya rushed past the library door, not daring to glance inside. She recognized her mother's voice. But what in all the Legacies in Avenesse was Mama doing with a married man?

Fenya hurried into the drawing room and claimed her usual spot in the dark corner. She buried herself in her sketchbook, sketching Fang from memory. She couldn't quite get the shape of her wings right. But she fought to focus on drawing, pushing away the anger and shame welling inside her. If Mama was to find a wealthy husband—either for Fenya or herself—and secure their future, Fenya couldn't do anything to risk it further. She was already guilty of so much. Why couldn't she just control herself and make Mama proud? Why was it so hard? And why was Mama gallivanting around with a married man if she was so worried about bringing shame on the family?

Fenya gripped her pencil so hard that her fingers turned white and her strokes heavy.

But she allowed the others trickling into the room one at a time to be her distraction. Instead of allowing her thoughts to run away, she listened as they chatted until all the men had their first drink of the night and the women sat in silence. Still, she couldn't quite keep herself from glancing at Mama, catching her frequent looks across the room to the men. Magess Merivale, a petite woman with graying hair and crow's feet around her red-rimmed eyes, kept shooting silent looks at Mama and then her husband.

When dinner was announced, Mama appeared at Fenya's side, grasping her elbow with her taloned fingers.

"What?" Fenya demanded, fear claiming her so that the fireplace snapped.

"You will not escape outside tonight after dinner," Mama hissed. "People are asking where you disappear to every day."

It's not about the library. Fenya relaxed at the accusation. "Mama, I—"

Mama held up her free hand, but her fingers tightened on Fenya's elbow, and she flinched as the others filed out of the room ahead of them. "You are running out of time to find a husband. I will not have my daughter be a humiliation, nor shall I have you raising questions regarding your Legacy!" Her words rose at the end, her cheeks rippled as her control over her own Legacy wavered. Mama paused, closing her eyes and breathing deeply as her Beauty slipped back into place as though it had never shifted.

"Yes, Mama. I'm sorry." Fenya kept her words calm, but fear leapt to life inside her, and the fire in the nearest room reached its flames far into the chimney at the taste.

Mama huffed and released Fenya's arm. "Honestly." She swept a hand over her forehead. "What am I going to do with you?"

"I'm sorry, Mama. I'll do better."

"Indeed. You will engage yourself to Sir Milton before the week is out—or I'll send you away myself, do you understand?"

Without waiting for an answer, Mama swept away follow the others out of the room.

The fire leapt across the logs, and Fenya watched it longingly before even attempting to control herself. *Cut the threads. Ignore the fire. Ignore it.*

Her chant hardly worked though. The threads were strung tight, and the fires in Whitland unhappy tonight. Rain pounded against on the windows and wind shook the shutters. She'd have to find a room that didn't have a fire or claim a headache and escape to her room after dinner. *Except Mama won't let me.*

Dinner began as an exercise in distant politeness, with Fenya answering only when spoken directly to, and the men discussing their lack of success with their wyvern traps. Soup was a smooth carrot and ginger, the spice of which made Fenya's eyes water. Ginger was even worse than honey.

"How delightful!" Sir Milton exclaimed. "What an evocative sharp bite to the carrot and ginger."

Aunt Cali offered a tight smile, but Uncle Caius had given up on responding to Milton's declarations.

Milton leaned toward Fenya, and she had to fight her automatic desire to lean far away. His breath stank of ginger, and strangely, onion. He dropped his voice to what he must have imagined to be an intimate whisper. "I must confess, that sitting beside you, Miss Fenya, a woman of such volatile brilliance is thrilling. You do things to my Legacy that I've never felt before." He wiggled his bare fingers. "Most women never affect me so strongly, even after a touch."

Fenya nearly choked on her sip of wine. *How am I to live with this man when I can barely endure dinner alongside him?*

And yet...if Mama wanted her to marry, then marry she must. Even if Sir Milton was barely tolerable. Even if he had a Black Listed Legacy. Even if he made her want to fling herself into the nearest firebreather's mouth.

"Are you finished, miss?"

Fenya jolted at the servant's question and stammered a yes, allowing him to take her three-quarter full bowl.

The course was replaced with a salmon glazed with silverleaf herb sauce, lemon zest sprinkled atop it. Fenya had three small bites before she pushed it around her plate. It wasn't unappealing, the silverleaf herb was a delicate herb harvested under the quarter moon that added a sweetness to the salmon which almost magically removed the fishy flavor. On the side were potatoes and squash dripping in butter.

"Is this silverleaf?" Mage Merivale asked, picking at the salmon.

"It is," Aunt Cali replied. "A favorite of Caius's. We try to incorporate it every month, since it's so difficult to harvest. But we have a perfect patch—"

"Don't share our secret patch, my dear!" Uncle Caius exclaimed. "I don't know what I'd do if someone else found it."

Aunt Cali laughed softly, though her mouth remained strained. Of them all, only Uncle Caius and Sir Milton finished their food, and the servants removed the meal.

Fenya followed them with her eyes to the door where they disappeared. She wished she could disappear out that door. Or that she was unburdened enough to taste the food.

The dessert was an Avenesse Apple tart with coarse sugar over the top that Fenya devoured.

"A sweet tooth, I see?" Sir Milton said from her side, smiling kindly. "Would you like mine as well?"

Fenya smiled politely. "I...I just love apples."

He nodded thoughtfully and offered her his plate again.

"No, thank you." She pushed her plate away. "I've had plenty tonight."

Fenya pushed through her mint and lavender tea, thankful that Sir Milton resumed his conversation with the men. Mama glared at her from across the table.

When dinner finally ended, Fenya slipped into place behind the others, purposefully slowing her pace as she neared the exit. The men would go to their smoking room, the women to the drawing room, and Fenya, hopefully, be allowed to beg illness soon.

At least not eating much at dinner will support that claim.

Following the women toward the drawing room, Fenya bit down on her lip as she passed over the kitchens downstairs. A large fire in the kitchen fireplace snapped and licked the iron pot hanging above it. It, at least, was happy and well-fed.

Fenya kept to herself, taking her sketchbook to a dim, candleless corner of the drawing room. Thunder rumbled outside, the rains reviving, and the fire hissed as a drop of rain slipped down the chimney upon it. She held her breath and then let it out with painstaking control.

She sank into her sketching, pushing her awareness of the fires to the edges and distracting herself with making the wyvern come alive on her page.

"Fenya?" Mama's voice beside her startled Fenya out of her consideration of the wing, and she nearly snapped her pencil in half as she looked up.

"Yes?"

"I've been calling for you, darling," she answered irritably. "Come with me. Now."

Fenya bit her lip, but sighed and stowed her pencils and sketchpad. She followed Mama and her flickering candelabra out of the drawing room and down the candle-lit hallway, biting back her questions and keeping her attention on suppressing the desire to play with the flames they passed. Each thread stretched taut as she passed, connecting her to the flames like a sticky thread of glue.

She stopped short to realize they were in the library...and not alone.

Sir Milton stood beside the fireplace, and for once, she found herself grateful for the oddly numb feeling in her body as he placed himself between her and the largest flame.

"Good evening, Miss Verena, Magess," he said with a gentle bow of his head.

Fenya's fingers tingled; she itched to reach for the fire.

Sir Milton cocked his head at her, and a warm feeling swept over her hands, a douse of warm water.

Fenya shuddered. As useful as his Well Legacy might be, she didn't like him stealing her ability from her—without permission, no less.

Is that what marriage to him will be? A constant theft of my Legacy?

"Have a seat, darling." Mama pointed to the seat beside the fire.

"I'd rather stand."

Mama's expression hardened. "Sit."

Fenya read the silent warning. Mama was not in the mood to get anything except what she wanted. And the first thing she wanted was for Fenya to obey. *Perhaps the only thing. And I've already been playing with fire since the cottage burned. Literally, in my sleep. I could have killed everyone, maybe even myself.*

Dipping her head in obedience, Fenya sank onto the couch as far from Milton and the fire as she could manage. *Whatever she's determined to do to me, I deserve it.*

Mama gracefully drifted over to the single chair beside Fenya and sat, demurely tilting her legs to one side so that her silk shoes peeked out.

"Magess, I'm grateful for you being willing to bring your daughter and listen to me today." Sir Milton turned the single chair closest to the fire and seated himself, facing them.

This is like being back in Magess Jolie's office. Am I going to be expelled again? Shame heated her cheek as she stared at her own feet.

Does he know? Does he understand just how comfortable I was in that fire? That I could've killed? But that I chose not to? She peered at him from under her lashes. He wasn't even looking at her, as if she were simply an ornament in the room that he could ignore.

"Sir Milton, I'm so pleased about our discussions." Mama squeezed her hands together in her lap with uncharacteristic nervousness.

Fenya gulped.

Sir Milton gave a thin-lipped smile that Fenya thought he meant to soothe and reassure, but she had to suppress another shudder. She returned her gaze to her lap and twisted her clasped hands together, weaving them into the fabric of her skirts discreetly so that Mama wouldn't notice.

"I am so very pleased that you trust me enough to have this discussion, Magess. I know how difficult such a situation is, but I do believe I have the perfect solution." He looked at Fenya. "A perfect solution for us all."

Mama nodded as Fenya's stomach twisted.

She tightened her grip on her skirts.

"Your suggestion was intriguing, I admit. And it may very well solve all of our problems. So tell me more and tell me how we can make the arrangements." Mama leaned toward Sir Milton.

"I've already written to my friend and received an initial reply. Her spot is available, should you accept. Within days she can be at my friend's private school learning how to reduce her Legacy."

Fenya blinked. *Reduce my Legacy?* Hope flared like a flame within her.

"But Sir Milton...the marriage..." Mama's face crumpled under the dangerous temptation to show her true feelings.

Fenya, on the other hand, froze, her features felt as though they'd been cast in wax. After everything, she was being shipped away to a school? The cottage fire had ruined everything.

Tears stung her eyes. She wanted to run away. All the fires overwhelmed her senses.

KELSIE ENGEN

"I don't understand, Sir Milton," Mama was saying. "You promised an engagement."

Sir Milton leaned across the empty space between them and reached for Mama's hand. His touch seemed to comfort her more than even Mama expected, and she didn't bother to dab at her face. "I will. In fact, I'll put it in a contract, if you would like."

Mama's face beamed under the light of her smile. Her gray eyes lit up, and her shoulders rose as though weights had been lifted from them.

Sir Milton patted Mama's hand. "Before our marriage, I will require Fenya to attend my friend's school. I have many reasons for this, but utmost is the importance of her, as a Relic Heir, being able to control the Fire that the Relic will endow her with. If she doesn't lessen her Power or learn to control it by the time she turns twenty-one, she will be in peril of having it kill her and all around her."

"Of course," Mama breathed.

How does he expect to lessen my Power? That isn't even possible.

"My friends will take excellent care of her, and at the end of the year, she will return fully in control of her reduced Power. I guarantee she'll go from an uncontrolled Rank I Magess to a Rank III or below with perfect control of her Legacy and ready to accept the Relic."

All Fenya could hear was a school run by Sir Milton's friends. *If his friends are anything like him, I'd almost rather stay here. But less Power...I don't want to be a Flame. I don't even care about being a Magess, titled or not. Mama can keep that...have another son and pass it to him. But...she can't. The Ember-heart Relic doesn't flow through Mama's blood, but mine and Uncle Caius's.*

"Yes, that's perfect. It's been my concern as well, Sir Milton," Mama whispered rapturously. "She needs less responsibility, not more. The Relic is burden enough. She doesn't need such a rank to be a Relic Bearer."

Fenya shook her head. She wasn't supposed to go to some strange school again—she was supposed to marry. She was old enough, it was the only way to stop any growing rumors that she wasn't a suitable Relic Heir, and the only way to share the Legacy Power. "I don't understand. Why do I need to attend school if you plan on marrying me anyway? Doesn't the Relic convert to the patriarchal line as soon as I marry? Wouldn't you absorb some of my Legacy as soon as I marry you?"

"Yes, that's true, my dear," answered Sir Milton. "But don't you wish to learn to control your flames without my assistance?"

Fenya bit her lip. Of course she did. But she wanted most of all to bring honor to her family—to her father and to Mama. She wanted to make them proud.

But Milton is right, isn't he? Control. That's what I need. I can control my expressions, but I'm rubbish with my Legacy. I'd love control. This is a good opportunity. So why does it feel so wrong?

Fenya glanced to Mama, who nodded and smiled as Sir Milton talked about his friend.

"He's a genius, to be true. He's the one who told me about the rules for registration as a Well and recommended that my parents get me recorded as an Ordinary," Sir Milton said gravely. "I opted to keep my privacy and avoid having the stigma of a formal declaration as a Dangerous Legacist on the Black List. Your daughter would do well to avoid the stigma as well." He motioned to Fenya but didn't look her way.

Fenya tried to keep her face expressionless. The man running the school was telling of government loopholes to avoid the Black List? Was that...wise? She didn't want to be labeled as a Dangerous Legacist, of course, but...she was. Especially if she couldn't control her Fire.

"Forgive me for being so indelicate, Sir Milton, but what is the cost?" Mama hinged forward in her eagerness, but Fenya saw the excitement flittering across her face before she controlled it.

"The cost is nothing for you, Magess." Sir Milton leaned forward toward her, pasting a comforting smile on his face.

But Mama's face rippled in concern. "It's not government school is it? Our reputation..."

"No, oh no." Chuckling, Sir Milton shook his head. "No, well, I don't wish to concern you, but it's...well, it's a very special school for young people like for her. Those who are out of control and on the verge of being a Wylde. Should she attend his school, she would be guaranteed to emerge with more control over herself. She clearly needs no practice in being well behaved—except for her Legacy." He smiled endearingly at Mama, but again left Fenya out of his inclusion. "The school I speak of has some very new and powerful techniques for controlling Wyldes. Fenya will be there with other students like her—she will not be alone."

Mamas lips pressed together. "And it's not a government school? But there's no cost to us?"

Sir Milton's lips thinned into a smile. "No cost, just my patronage and a promise. But my proposition is this: I will pay the cost to finish the schooling. On the assumption and agreement that she will consent to be my wife after completing it." He reached into his pocket and pulled out a folded piece of paper. "I recommend we sign this betrothal agreement tonight, promising marriage after her eighteenth birthday."

"Of course!" Mama exclaimed, beaming. "I want nothing more than to rid myself of this silly Relic."

Fenya's heart clenched. *I'm supposed to want this...aren't I? Papa always said it was an honor to serve King and country. And by my marriage and continuing Father's line, I serve.*

Mama beamed with joy as though Fenya had made a true love match. But betrayal coursed through Fenya's blood. She imagined a future with Sir Milton. To marry someone who could quite literally steal her Legacy from her whenever he wished. What would that mean with a Relic? What Power could he gain through her?

The fire snapped and snarled in the grate, and Sir Milton smiled at her benignly as Mama eyed the fire.

He tilted his head as if to say that she should have known better—or tried harder to hide her true feelings. He reached a hand for her, but she tucked her hands under her legs.

His lips quirked into a wider smile as he held his hand between them. For a moment she thought he was waiting for her to accept his touch, but then she felt it.

His Legacy...stirring the aether between them.

It washed over her like honey, sticking to her skin, pulling at her pores. And when he drew it back, it pulled on her every hair, every link to the fires within Whitland. It pulled until the fires faded from the front of her attention. She became aware of her body again, of the itch on her knee, of the tightness of her braid and the pins keeping it off her neck.

He stole from her. Without even touching her. And he did it with a smile.

I can't marry him.

Outwardly, Fenya remained hard as wax, gaping at Sir Milton as he held up a hand to the fire. A pin of fire went through her heart, and her connection to the fire, which had felt as thick as a braided plait of hair, thinned to a thread again.

"Miss Verena?" Sir Milton prompted.

"I... No." Fenya tried to stop the onslaught of panic and anxiety that gripped her heart. *He's taking my Legacy. Stealing it from me without even bothering to ask. How could I learn control, but shackle myself to such a man forever?*

And yet...how could she stay? If she stayed, her cousins would not be allowed to return home—not until she was in control. She'd tried her methods of control, she tried engaging with the fire, and she tried suppressing it. None of it had worked. She'd tried so hard at Jolie's school and nothing had worked. She failed miserably to control herself here and there. Every day was worse than the day before. She dreamed of flames, she dreamed of fires, and when she woke, she fixated on them. Sometimes she woke to a ball of flame hovering over her like a protective dog.

If she were discovered, or even observed in her sleep, she would ruin herself and her mother. She would be sent to Bradley Asylum— and rightly so. *It's good that my cousins have left. But what about Mama? Aunt Cali? Uncle Caius?*

Fenya was dimly aware of the conversation continuing around her. Mama and Sir Milton were discussing her options, her future, and coming to some agreement regarding it.

Shouldn't I be a part of that conversation? But this was the solution—to both problems. She had almost a year to learn control, then she would marry. This was the best of both solutions, giving her control and a suitable marriage. If any hint of her involvement in the cottage fire emerged—ever—she would be ruined. Black Listed. Sent away. And here was the perfect solution to all her problems.

And yet she remained frozen, as though her mouth wouldn't—couldn't—work to stop this arrangement. She gaped at Sir Milton, trying to muster the courage, the strength, to stop his plans for her.

He was reading from his contract, pointing with his finger as he read. "'...and after she completes the year at Wigmore, or learns control, or at the age of eighteen, we'll marry. Sir Jett Milton will assume the head of house as Relic Bearer Mage of the Emberheart Relic, and Miss Fenya Verena will be considered Relic Magess.'" He straightened and pride brightened his expression, his nose rising into the air and a smirk lifting his lips.

Mama let out a sigh of relief, covering her heart with her hand. "It's perfect, Sir Milton."

Fenya had always known, after Papa and Mama never had a son, that the Emberheart Relic would likely transfer to the man she married, if it chose, as tradition dictated a male Relic Bearer to have a strong preference by the Relic. She shuddered to hear and see Sir Milton revel in the Relic. Would he even care about her if not for the Relic?

"Even if she cannot control herself, marriage to me will be far better than an asylum for her. It's truly the best situation for us all."

Fenya's stomach turned and bile rose in her throat.

Finally, the conversation paused, and Mama turned to Fenya. "Darling, it's for the best."

As though the spell that had been cast over her broke, Fenya's seized muscles relaxed. "I can't," she burst out.

"Darling," Mama said in warning this time. "Think carefully. Think of your future...of ours."

"I'll give you a moment," Sir Milton said, a glint of annoyance darkening his blue eyes. "But keep in mind, Miss Verena, that when I return home, if Whitland's fires should suddenly surge in mischief again, that someone—or some*thing*—must be blamed." He stood and tugged down his jacket, then turned and exited the library.

He means Fang. He'll make sure that Fang is blamed—and captured and— who knows what else?

Me.

As soon as the door closed behind him, Mama's pleasant expression slipped off her face. "How dare you say such a thing?"

"But Mama, I—"

"This is the only opportunity you'll ever have, to be sure, acting as you are and after the fire. How long do you think I can hide your involvement? As soon as the truth about your Legacy is well-known, you'll be Black Listed—and my reputation will be ruined!" Mama's gray eyes sparked in the firelight. "I cannot take on the Relic, and it will pass to your Uncle Caius, whom it has rejected. So it will probably be ripped from our family, returned to the Crown in shame. Is that what you want? To burden your uncle with the Relic? Or to let the Crown reclaim it? Or even let it *die*? We would never recover from any of those shameful acts!"

"I'm sorry, Mama, but I cannot marry him." Fenya's eyes filled with tears. "Please don't make me."

Mama took a deep breath and closed her eyes. "You don't understand, Fenya. You never have. You're as insipid as your father, and you'll end up like him and drag me down along the way. When will you learn that you must obey? You'll go to Wigmore, and you'll marry him, or I'll throw you in Bradley myself." She rose and stared down at Fenya. "And from what I've heard, when a Relic dies or is severed from a living family, the Relic Heir suffers atrociously." She pointed at the table where the contract lay. "Consider that before you sign the contract."

Fenya's teeth snapped shut against any reply. Mama made it perfectly clear: Fenya had no choice at all.

Only a minute after the door to the hallway clicked closed behind Mama, Fenya reached for the quill and signed her name.

Chapter Ten

FAREWELL

Never had two days passed with such rapidity.

Fenya escaped to the forest as often as possible, returned as late as was polite, avoided her *fiancé*, and smashed down her thirst for fire at every turn through Whitland's halls.

The morning of her departure arrived, and Fenya, exhausted, slept in. She woke to her maid's arrival and threw on the first gown she could find in order to sneak down to the kitchens and outside for a last walk through the manor's gardens. The bright flowers and the fairy dragons that roosted in the bushes tantalized her. With her sketch-book and colored pencils ready in her satchel, her fingers twitched to record the gardens and their inhabitants for the last time. She would have the entire morning to lose herself in the gardens and woods she'd almost come to regard as her own.

She peeked into the kitchen, finding the cook at the long table with bowls and dough scattered all over. She scanned the corner where her morning bag of food usually sat as she stepped inside.

"Oh, not today, Miss Verena," Whitland's cook said, shaking her head and perching her floury hands on her wide hips. "You're going to go upstairs to the breakfast room and eat with everyone else. I won't have my masterful creations wasted."

"What?" Fenya blinked at the woman as she brushed her sweaty hair from her face and turned to the pot boiling over the large fire.

"Go on, then," Mrs. Petalwise said, a glint of eagerness in her green eyes.

"But—"

"They're all waiting for you."

The fire gave a leap around the pot. *They're all waiting for me? I don't want everyone to be waiting for me. I just want to go outside one last time at Whitland.* She swallowed. The corner of the table was still empty, as if saying "there's nothing left for you here."

If I don't go, it's not about Mama or Sir Milton—it's rude to Aunt Cali and Uncle Caius, who have been nothing but kind to me.

Biting back a sigh, Fenya turned and started for the door.

"Miss Verena?" Mrs. Petalwise said from behind her.

She turned. "Yes?"

"Good luck." The woman gave a sharp nod and then waved her off.

Fenya wandered her way out of the cook's domain and through the shadowed halls of the house. Light gleamed down from high windows, but it was a pale autumn light that only reminded her of the fires needed to warm the house.

The fire in the breakfast room called to Fenya when she was far from the other side of the door. But today, there was something strange about the fire in it, the thread snagging on something. *Milton.*

Fenya's stomach clenched. She'd spent the entire time since signing her name to his contract avoiding him. *I hope he doesn't go with me to Wigmore—would he?* The thought out of nowhere sent shivers down her spine, and she realized that she was standing in the hallway without any intention of walking into the room.

But she couldn't let her aunt and uncle down, not after all they'd done for her.

She forced herself to push open the door and walk inside. The fire crackled in welcome at her appearance. *Well fed, at the moment, at least.*

Conversation hushed as she faced the long breakfast table. Aunt Cali, Uncle Caius, Mage de Croia, and Sir Milton were all seated at the table, but only Aunt Cali rose to greet her. In the middle of the table was a small cake with the words, "Farewell, Fenya" written on them in icing and with nuts and dried fruits covering the top.

Aunt Cali embraced Fenya. "Happy going-away day!"

"What...what is this?" Fenya motioned to the table with its lavish cake that the cook must have referenced as her masterpiece.

"Your goodbye party, of course!" Aunt Cali kissed her cheek. "Darling, we couldn't let you go without a proper send-off."

"I..." Fenya's face burned in embarrassment as Sir Milton rose from his seat at the table, pulling out her chair for her. The fire rippled over the log as if a shiver ran over it. "I don't know what to say."

"Just a thank you will do," Uncle Caius said dryly, coming to stand beside his wife.

"I... Of course. Thank you." Fenya moved toward the seat in the center of the table that Sir Milton still stood behind. A package with her name prettily written on it sat on the plate. "What is this?"

"Open it and find out," Aunt Cali said, her smile soft but tense around the edges.

Fenya stepped toward the plate, where a brown-wrapped square was tied with a pink ribbon. She reached for it, ignoring Sir Milton's smirk. *I hope this isn't from him.*

She pulled the string, but over the rustle of the paper caught Uncle Caius whispering to Aunt Cali.

"Where is Seraphina?"

"I didn't see her come down today." Aunt Cali murmured something about Mage Merivale missing as well.

"Unbelievable," Uncle Caius muttered angrily. "Raising havoc. His wife will be here this afternoon, I promise you."

"Hush." Aunt Cali put a hand over his, but her cheeks went pink.

Is Mama so ashamed of me that she won't come down? I've tried to do everything possible to please her. Even agree to this marriage. I've done everything I could, and Mama can't even be bothered to say goodbye?

Tears pooled in her eyes, and Fenya bit down on her lip to stop them. It was no wonder after all the stress she'd caused Mama. Fenya probably didn't deserve a goodbye.

Diverting her focus, Fenya pulled a brand new sketchbook with a soft leather cover out from the package. Etched on the front was a wyvern, and Fenya gasped softly. "It's beautiful. Thank you. I can't wait to sketch something in it."

Aunt Cali smiled and left her husband's side. She bent over the sketchbook too. "It is beautiful, isn't it? Really captures the essence of the wyvern." She cast a thankful smile at Sir Milton.

Alarm growing, Fenya followed the look. *Did he pick this out?* Her stomach twisted as Sir Milton nibbled on a piece of generously buttered toast as if oblivious or uncaring. His long teeth and thin lips wrapped around the toast, and she had to turn away to hide her shudder at the thought of those lips on hers. *How can I marry him? Ever?*

Fire rippled along her spine, and a fire-breathing dragon coiled defensively in her stomach. *I won't marry him.*

"Well, Fenya, are you excited?" Uncle Caius interrupted her thoughts. "Once you graduate from Wigmore, you'll be free to claim the Relic and marry."

"I..." Fenya paused, holding her breath, and out of the corner of her eye, she found Sir Milton's intense gaze on her face. She faced her aunt and uncle, steadfastly ignoring him. She wasn't here for Milton—she was here for her family. The dragon on the sketchbook twitched its tail, adorned with spikes that sent ripples of fire through her body. "Yes, I think so. But I regret that I can't say goodbye to my cousins."

Aunt Cali smiled, pain etched in the act, but Uncle Caius frowned down at his poached egg.

"They will miss you and your stories. They already do." Aunt Cali's smile gentled. "You know that I heard all about the story of the little flame wyvern you told them? I think Zhara recited it word for word. She was utterly disappointed when I told her she'd be leaving for a few weeks."

Fenya pressed her lips together and dropped her gaze to her plate, pushing at her poached eggs with a silver fork. A wyvern with a jeweled eye glinted back at her from the handle of it, and Fenya blinked back the tears that threatened. The fire across the room leapt at the lack of her guard.

"Where is Wigmore, Sir Milton?" Fenya managed.

He tilted his head. "We are engaged—you may call me Jett, Fenya."

She bit her lip and shook her head. "Where is the school?"

"I can't tell you that, unfortunately. It's secret."

"Why?"

"Because the students there are like you—some are in hiding because they otherwise would be considered too dangerous to be educated." He seemed unconcerned with putting her in such a place, shoving another bite of egg into his mouth.

"It *is* safe?" Aunt Cali interrupted. "You said it was safe for her, Sir Milton."

"Of course it's safe. There are precautions in place." Sir Milton crunched down on a piece of bacon.

"What kind of precautions?" Aunt Cali asked for Fenya.

"Charms, wards, and aether shields," Sir Milton answered around his mouthful.

"What will I learn there? Is it like...a finishing school?" Fenya set her fork down, scrutinizing him, hoping she could tell if he were lying.

Sir Milton shook his head. "Consider it more of a health treatment and retreat location in order to allow you to heal. Sort of like one suffering from gout goes to Merryspring to bathe in the waters."

Fenya pushed a bit of egg around on her plate. It was cold. She hated cold eggs. If she had control over her Fire, she could heat it gently. But she wouldn't even attempt such a thing. "If it's so secret... will I be able to write home?"

Sir Milton hesitated. "Typically that's not permitted from the students. It's best for the students to focus entirely on their Legacy treatments during this time." He leaned forward to Fenya and smiled, a piece of pepper caught between his front teeth. "But when I come to visit, I would be delighted to take a letter home for you." He turned to Aunt Cali and Uncle Caius. "And bring presents from you, if you'd wish."

"Of course," Aunt Cali said immediately. "We'll start compiling your favorite things immediately, Fenya," she added, putting a hand on Fenya's.

Fenya's vision was blurring. Instead of making her feel better, Sir Milton's words made her hands tremble. Going to a strange place, completely cut off from everything familiar, to learn how to manage a Legacy that she didn't even want was something she couldn't do.

"Fenya will do an excellent job at Wigmore," Sir Milton announced as if noting her tears and trying to make her feel better. His hand twitched in her direction, and her heart twanged.

A moment later, her fork clattered to her plate. She scrambled to catch it and knocked her hand into her plate, sending it careening across the table, into her Emberglass Tea. "I'm sorry!" She covered her mouth with her hands. Her fingers smashed into her lips. Numb. They were numb.

"Are you quite all right, Miss Verena?" Sir Milton asked, leaning toward her as she pulled her hands from her mouth and flexed them.

"I'm sorry. My...my hands...went numb." *My whole body feels...cold. Please go away. Just go away.*

"Don't worry, miss, we'll get it cleaned up in a moment," the servant said, stepping forward to mop up the golden liquid and sweep the sodden food onto the plate and swiftly made it disappear.

"It happens, my dear," Aunt Cali said, twitching her fingers and correcting the tablecloth with her Legacy. The wrinkles smoothed out and a fresh napkin settled itself in front of Fenya.

"Thank you," she murmured, darting an uncertain glance at Sir Milton.

"Excuse me a moment," he said, dabbing his mouth with his napkin before rising and leaving the room.

Fenya turned to Aunt Cali. "I can't go."

She blinked at Fenya, her mouth agape for just a moment before answering. "Of course you can, my dear. I know it's frightening, but—"

"No. I don't—I don't want to go. I'd rather give up my Legacy entirely than go to Wigmore."

"Dear Fenya," Aunt Cali began, but she cast a look to her husband for help.

Uncle Caius cleared his throat. "Fenya, understand that there are certain things that are expected of you as a Relic Heir."

A fresh plate, filled with freshly poached eggs and a fresh roll and jam, arrived before her at the hand of another servant, but Fenya ignored it.

"But that's just it. I can't go to some mysterious school run by the government using loopholes to hide its location!" Fenya exclaimed in a whisper. "I can't even write home—what kind of place is this?"

"Dear..." Aunt Cali began, but as she spoke, she turned to Uncle Caius as if questioning herself.

"Uncle Caius, please. I've never asked for anything...but if you don't make me go, I'll give you the Relic. You are Papa's brother. I'm sure I can surrender my Legacy into the Relic as soon as it's handed to me. If I don't marry Sir Milton, if I empty my Legacy into the Relic, I can name you the Heir, right? Isn't that how it works?" She bit down on her lip to stop the desperate torrent of words from continuing over her lips.

"I'm sorry, Fenya, but it's not. You have some grievous misunderstandings of Relic lore." Uncle Caius sighed and ran a hand over his cheek. "Unfortunately, the only way the Relic would pass back to me is if you died without an heir, as I have already attempted a bond with it."

"Even if I pour my Legacy into the Relic?"

"You cannot—except upon death—do such a thing." He held up a hand to stop her words. "If you did that, not only does it take immense control, it would be sure to drain your life. Rarely is it attempted, and always fatal unless the Relic recognizes the Bearer to already be near death. That is how a dying Relic Bearer can pour their Legacy into a Relic for future Bearers to benefit from." His expression softened. "I know this isn't what you want to hear, but you are the rightful Relic Heir, and I can't change that. As soon as you marry or turn twenty-one, whichever is first, the Relic goes to you. And it will benefit you."

"And burden me," Fenya muttered, leaning back in her chair.

Aunt Cali dashed a tear away.

Sympathetically, Uncle Caius nodded. "It is a burden. Absolutely. And I wish my brother had lived to unburden you for a while longer." He spread his hands, and a rustle swept over the table. A small whirlwind swirled in his palm. "I've never controlled Fire, Fenya. To take it would be almost unheard of if the Heir lives. It would require special permission from the King to do what you're asking. And he would be sure to deny it on tradition and precedence."

"Even with me being a woman?"

"Even with you being a woman," Uncle Caius replied gently.

The fight slipped out from her. She had no option then.

"I'm sorry, Fenya," Aunt Cali whispered as the door swept open and Sir Milton rejoined them.

Behind him, an older woman entered and bobbed a curtsy before Fenya's aunt. "If you'll pardon me, Magess, but the Wigmore carriage is here."

"Already?" Aunt Cali's face paled. "But, it's hardly ten!" She shot a pleading look at Uncle Caius.

"It's a pegasus coach, Magess," the servant said, as if that explained something.

"They're just in time to join us then," Aunt Cali said, as if correcting her earlier reaction.

"They must have made good time," Uncle Caius said, patting his mouth with his napkin and tossing it on the table next to his plate. "No point in delaying. Difficult goodbyes are best done without delay."

Aunt Cali inhaled a trembling breath, and Fenya did the same.

"Miss Fenya," Sir Milton said as Aunt Cali took Uncle Caius's arm and they drifted from the room to greet the arrivals. "A moment?"

Fenya's body tightened like a log swelling with heat, reawakening the dragon inside. With a fleeting glance toward her aunt and uncle, she composed herself, and, after a pause, nodded in agreement to Sir Milton. "Of course."

"I realized that in our betrothal arrangement, I neglected something very important. So I took the time of doing it right."

Fenya blinked at him. "What?"

He smiled reassuringly and pulled something out of his pocket. "A ring, Miss Fenya. An engagement ring."

The blood drained from her cheeks.

He held out an open jewelry box, where a silver ring sat in a bed of green velvet.

Despite herself, she gasped at it. It was pretty, with delicate filigree around a large, maroon garnet surrounded by smaller diamonds. No, it wasn't pretty. It was beautiful. Something she might have picked for herself had she been asked.

"Does it satisfy?" He continued to hold the box out for her approval.

"I...I don't need a ring, Sir Milton," she murmured.

"Of course you do." He slipped the ring from the velvet and put out a hand for hers. "This is a garnet from the Lytham River that I found myself while I was in Linthorne, mudlarking years ago. One of many, but this was the largest, so I had it fashioned into a ring for my future wife."

Wincing, she allowed him to take her hand and slide on the ring. Its cold metal felt like a chain.

"Shall we then?" Sir Milton offered his arm to escort her outside.

Fenya tried to push down her anxiety, but her heart raced like hungry flames across a dry log. "Yes. Let's." She placed her left hand on the inside of his elbow, where the garnet caught the gleam of the candlelight like a blood-red flame.

Chapter Eleven

THE HEADMISTRESS

The front door perched wide open and a black carriage with sparkles like stars painted over it crouched in the middle of Whitland's circular drive, a pair of matching pegasi at the front of it.

Fenya inhaled slowly and held it. As always at any hint of emotion, her awareness of the fires intensified.

Sir Milton chatted amiably with two women, and Mama stood beside him, a delicate smile on her lips. Fenya shivered. Milton's numbing effect reached her even from here, a slight chill that settled upon her skin and crept into her bones.

She turned her attention to the horse-like creatures considered a cross between dragon and horse. All pegasi were northern breeds, warmblooded—unlike dragons—but considered so closely related to dragons that they were like cousins. Secretly, Fenya wondered whether someone had once experimented with breeding a dragon to a horse, resulting in these strange hybrids. But more manageable than dragons, since no pegasi could breathe fire, most had no horns or spikes that could injure a person, and besides the consequences of their rather scaly wings, which permitted them flight, they couldn't hurt a person much more than any horse. They were not as popular as dragons in Avenesse, but they were a much easier option to house and control.

And, they were utterly beautiful. Fenya, in her distraction at the sight of the blue pegasi shimmering in the sunlight, forgot to greet anyone. It wasn't until Mama called her name—twice—that she jerked her attention from the creatures and focused on the pair of newcomers, apology quick on her lips.

The first of the two was a thin, proper, yet no-nonsense looking woman that reminded Fenya of a vaguely disapproving grandmother, with a highcoat in iron gray wool that fitted her narrow body. She was tall, easily as tall as Sir Milton, who was much taller than Fenya.

The second was a squat woman several inches shorter than Fenya. Her dark hair was twisted into a tight, practical braid, giving her a severe, almost angry expression. She wore a slate-blue muslin dress under a washed black midcoat with tight sleeves and bone-white gloves.

The nearest pegasus shifted, its dinner-plate-sized cloven hooves clattering against the cobblestones.

"Miss Verena?" Sir Milton's voice stuttered into Fenya's thoughts.

"Sorry," she apologized again, tearing her attention from the pegasi again.

"You're Miss Verena?" said the tall, no-nonsense woman, narrowing her eyes at Fenya.

Fenya nodded, but internally shivered. *I wonder if this is what Fang felt like in that cage.*

"This is Magess Wyn," Sir Milton said, motioning to her.

Fenya bobbed a belated curtsy. "Nice to meet you."

"She's the headmistress of Wigmore Boarding School." Sir Milton's smile parted his mouth, revealing his crooked front teeth.

"You can call me Magess Wyn, Headmistress Wyn, ma'am, or just headmistress. This is Keeper Liah." The thin woman raised her nose, almost as though she expected Fenya to argue or resist.

"Yes, ma'am." Fenya nodded again, and the keeper, as she was called, dipped her chin curtly in reply.

"You'll be joining us at Wigmore, then." Headmistress Wyn made it a statement of fact, not an invitation.

Fenya glanced at Mama, who didn't meet her eye, but wiped a speck of dust from her dove blue shortcoat sleeve. "Yes, ma'am."

Aunt Cali stepped forward, putting a protective hand upon Fenya's shoulder. "Yes. We've discussed it and think it best for her situation. You come highly recommended from Sir Milton, of course." She spread a hand in his direction, and his chest puffed like the ruff of a fairy dragon trying to impress its mate.

"Excellent." Headmistress Wyn's dark gaze skimmed over Fenya in an assessing manner. "There's just one thing before we leave." Headmistress Wyn turned to Uncle Caius. "Is there a place where we could perform some quick tests? Preferably outside but secluded to avoid any fire triggers. Indoors, if well away from any fire, will work if it must."

"Tests?" Uncle Caius snapped as Aunt Cali threw Fenya a protective look and stepped toward her.

Headmistress Wyn smiled soothingly. "Nothing to be alarmed with, Mage, Magess Verena. Simply a few tests to confirm the 'strength of the Legacy diagnosis,' as we call it at Wigmore. We've performed it on every student we take."

"Ah, of course." Uncle Caius nodded.

Sir Milton grinned. "Want to confirm she is what we say, of course."

Fenya's skin shivered. "What kind of tests?"

"We find a blood test to be most accurate," Keeper Liah replied without emotion. "But as I'm a Healer, there's very little risk and healing time."

"Well planned then," Uncle Caius said rather cheerfully. "Go on then, Fenya. Might as well get it over with. There's a quaint folly, if I do say so myself, just beyond the gardens there. Or use the gardens—there are benches enough."

"The folly will do. Some protection from the elements is always best when using scientific methods." Headmistress Wyn motioned toward the carriage, where Keeper Liah stood.

"Yes, of course," Uncle Caius answered solemnly.

Keeper Liah reached into the carriage and emerged with a large wooden box, its handle gripped in her left hand, while her right carried a small bag that looked as though it had something rectangular within it.

Fenya's body shuddered. *Scientific methods? What am I, an animal to experiment on?*

Aunt Cali's arm shifted under Fenya's hold, and she drew a breath as if to steel herself. She smiled down at Fenya as Fenya had seen her smile at her own children. "Go on then, Fenya. You seem in...confident hands."

I don't want to go. The words almost ripped themselves out of her lips, but Fenya caught them just in time. *I have to. I have no other choice.* She dropped Aunt Cali's elbow then and stepped toward the head-mistress again. "I'm ready," she forced herself to say above a whisper. Still, she had to clear her throat after she spoke, fearful of betraying too much emotion.

With an appreciative nod, the headmistress motioned toward the grounds, where a few outbuildings spotted the grass amongst the trees. "Shall we get on then?"

Fenya glanced to the house, where Aunt Cali had turned and was instructing a pair of servants to carry a trunk down to the back of the carriage.

"Come, Miss Verena," Keeper Liah said, appearing suddenly at Fenya's side.

She flinched, and her hands stung as a touch of her Power begged to be released. She clenched her fists, hoping no one noticed.

But Keeper Liah tilted her head curiously and held out a hand, palm up toward Headmistress Wyn, indicating for Fenya to follow her. The shorter woman had a powerful look about her, as though she wouldn't allow others to argue with her.

"Come," the headmistress said, setting off toward the gardens. "Which way is the folly?"

Fenya pointed to the left of the gardens, where the small stone folly, just big enough for the three of them to crowd inside, stood with its rounded roof.

"Ah, of course." Headmistress Wyn marched toward it, and Fenya did her best to keep up without tripping over any stray rocks or clumps of grass.

Huffing slightly, Keeper Liah followed. When Fenya glanced at her, wondering if she should offer to help, the woman's dark eyes narrowed without any warmth, slaughtering the thought.

Fenya followed the headmistress up the six steps into the folly, and she seated herself at the headmistress's pointed glance toward the only bench inside, which provided her a view of the pastures and small hill with its lined fences and distantly dotted with sheep. At the edge of the garden was a small copse.

A clunk of the box being set upon the stone floor brought Fenya's attention back to the matter at hand.

"Your Legacy is Fire Elemental?" Slightly breathless, Keeper Liah pulled out a notebook from the bag and held her pencil poised over the paper. "And nearly Wylde, from the sound of it?"

Fenya bit her lip. "Yes," she all but whispered.

"Nothing to be ashamed of," Headmistress Wyn said shortly. "I have many a student who has made mistakes, some worse than yours."

Fenya flushed and dipped her head. *I almost killed someone. I need to be sent away. I deserve it. Who there has done worse than that?*

"So what we do at the school is first give you a sense of control," Magess Wyn said.

"How?" Fenya's heart lifted in hope, but crashed down almost as soon as it did.

The headmistress didn't seem to notice Fenya's fleeting hope. She nodded briskly and motioned to the Healer, who had set the two boxes down on the second bench shielded under the folly. "That's right, Miss Verena. You will get control back."

The squat Healer turned the boxes down on their sides and unlatched them. Tucked in the first level of the first box were two delicate silver bracelets in a bed of maroon velvet.

Fenya frowned at them. *Jewelry? They're giving me jewelry?*

"These bracelets will give you control," Headmistress Wyn said.

"I don't understand." Fenya leaned closer to inspect them.

"The headmaster designed them himself, and they're made to keep you safe," Keeper Liah said shortly. "They are a work of art, crafted to protect you from yourself."

"I won't overwhelm you with the specifics, but the bracelets suppress the aether your Power controls enough so that you can begin to learn to use it." Magess Wyn made another note in her notebook.

She's going to run out of lead soon with that amount of notes.

"The strength can be adjusted through a way you don't need to worry about, and that makes it so that we can teach you to deal with more control, just like Fledglings."

Fledgling. Fenya's heart twanged at the term for young Legacists in training. *I'm not a Fledgling. I'm not even an Ordinary. I'm practically a Wylde.*

"Not to say that you aren't already a Fledgling, of course," the headmistress said, sniffing to indicate displeasure at her own words. "But in a way, you aren't. You're gifted."

"Gifted?" Fenya managed thickly, picking at a spot of moss on the stone bench she sat on.

"Oh yes. We only accept the gifted children for our program. Which is why we need to do a quick test on you before we can take you with us." The headmistress motioned Keeper Liah forward, who carried the large box forward in her arms like one might present a gift to a monarch.

Fenya's eyes widened warily.

The headmistress seemed to understand her worry, but didn't stop. "Unfortunately, we haven't mastered a way to do it without taking a minor blood sample." She smiled. "It's why I travel with Healer Liah, of course."

Fenya searched the older woman's narrow face. She could only have been in her twenties, perhaps late twenties, but there was something in her eyes that sent shivers down Fenya's spine, raising the hairs on her arm. She rubbed down the hairs, for she saw nothing but honesty and patience in Headmistress Wyn's expression. Even though it was Mama and Sir Milton who had come together to send Fenya away, it had to be only for her good. Fenya nodded her understanding, and the women's shoulders relaxed slightly at the permission they had been waiting for.

"Excellent." Headmistress Wyn motioned the Healer over. "Let's begin."

The squat woman strode over, her dark eyes somehow giving her the appearance of halfway between refined and wild.

"Keeper Liah will now take your blood."

Fenya nodded as Keeper Liah placed her wooden box on the far end of the bench, farthest from Fenya, then sat down between Fenya and the box.

"I'll need your arm. Just extend one for me across my lap like that," Keeper Liah said without any other introduction, demonstrating how Fenya was to extend her arm across her legs.

"Tell me, Miss Verena, how much control do you think you have over your Legacy?" the headmistress asked as Keeper Liah twisted toward the box, her shoulder blocking Fenya's sight.

"Control?" Fenya asked, her voice thin. "Not as much as I would like." *Less and less this morning. I've never been so thankful that almost all the fires are out in Whitland—I can feel the cook's fire hot and well-fed. But I could help it—No!*

Another flash of light appeared behind them, and Fenya recognized the spark of a fire. *Where did that come from? Did I do that?*

Keeper Liah twisted toward the flash of light, and Fenya's gaze fell on the frighteningly large needle and a strap of linen in the woman's hands.

Fenya's skin went clammy. She swallowed thickly.

"Keeper Liah, the bracelets first, I think," Headmistress Wyn said, her voice turning sharp.

"Oh, yes, I almost forgot," the keeper agreed. She returned the other items to the box.

"Miss Verena, you must make every attempt to control yourself," the headmistress directed at her. "Deep, slow breaths."

"I...I didn't do that, I don't..." Fenya shook her head, staring at the spot where the spark had happened, tasting the remnants of the burst of fire like the aftertaste of a decadent chocolate cake.

Fenya felt a tug on her hand, fingers wrapping around her wrist, and before she could see what was happening, there was a sharp prick at the end of one finger.

"Ow!" Fenya jerked, but Keeper Liah's hand clasped around her wrist kept her in place.

Headmistress Wyn was there in a moment, taking her finger and squeezing out a drop of blood onto the open clasp of a bracelet. "Stay still," she commanded when Fenya tried to take her hand back, and Fenya squirmed in discomfort.

Another flash of light surrounded them, and all three women flinched.

"What was that?" the headmistress asked, turning accusing eyes on Fenya. "Was that you?"

Eyes wide, Fenya shook her head.

"We'll soon find out," the headmistress replied.

A chitter of annoyance sounded behind Fenya, and she dared a look behind as her as the keeper squeezed her finger a second time. "Ouch." Another pinch on her fingertip had Fenya turning forward just in time to see the keeper squeeze a second drop of blood out of Fenya's second fingertip into a crevice upon the clasp of the second silver bracelet.

Seconds ticked by and both the headmistress and keeper stared at the pair of bracelets as though waiting for them to do something. Just as Fenya was about to open her mouth and ask what they waited for, the bracelet flared as though fire had been set to it, but she could feel no flame.

A screech behind Fenya sounded.

Keeper Liah dropped the bracelets back into their box and leapt up to face the interloper.

"No!" Fenya exclaimed, jumping up also. She put a hand out just as Fang came swooping through the folly, in one side between two pillars and dangerously close to the headmistress's head with her talons extended.

Headmistress Wyn ducked and raised her hands in an offensive pose, as though she were about to use a Legacy against the dragon.

"Stop! Don't hurt her!" Fenya exclaimed.

Fang disappeared out the other side of the folly as quickly as she had arrived, and Keeper Liah sent Fenya a frown before peering out the other side of the folly after Fang. "It's gone. In the trees now," she reported to the headmistress.

Headmistress Wyn huffed in annoyance and stood over the bracelets in the box. She lifted one and brought it close to her face, squinting at the lines scratched upon it. "Hmph." She seemed displeased about something, picking up the other bracelet and inspecting it. "There's certainly something there, faded now, of course."

Keeper Liah peered at the bracelets. "Flames. For certain."

Fenya's attention shifted to the path that Fang had taken. *What was she thinking to attack these women like this? Did she think Fenya was in danger? That must have been it. Fang has become fond of me, as fond of me as I am of her.*

In Fenya's distraction, she didn't see the keeper's approach, and the older woman slapped the bracelets around her wrists before Fenya could change her mind.

Curious to see what the other women had been looking at upon the bracelets, Fenya raised her wrists to her nose, but she couldn't see anything except a scratch or two upon the pair of nearly inch-wide silver bracelets. She thought maybe she saw something shaped like flames alongside a fading image of a serpent. The metal was warm against her skin, as though she were enveloped by flames that wrapped around her hands and warmed her up to the elbow.

"Hands out, please," Headmistress Wyn said, accepting a small skeleton key from Keeper Liah.

"You lock them onto me?" Another chill settled over Fenya's skin. *Why do I have so little choice?*

"Needs must," the headmistress said matter-of-factly. "Sometimes Powerful, Legacy-deprived students decide they don't wish to remain in control. And for the safety of us all, we must make sure they're always under control."

Hesitantly, Fenya extended her wrists and the headmistress slid the key into the first bracelet.

"You might feel ill or tired, as though the beginnings of Legacy Fever are taking place, but as long as the bracelets stay in place, you'll be fine," the keeper went on. "You'll adjust in time, of course."

As the key twisted in each bracelet's lock, the bracelet flared as though lit with fire.

Fenya stilled as the bracelets heated, but neither of the magesses seemed surprised at the glow.

"Are they supposed to be doing this?"

"Not hurting you, is it?" the keeper asked. "Do you feel ill? Sometimes the first bracelet can be burned out immediately should you contain a great deal of latent Power."

"I feel fine. A bit..." She blinked slowly at the two women. "A bit sleepy, perhaps."

The headmistress smiled encouragingly at her. "That's perfectly normal."

Fenya held her arms out awkwardly in front of her as the flare around the bracelets gradually faded. The silver remained warm around her wrists, but also oddly comforting, and almost like it was a part of her.

"May I?" The keeper reached for Fenya's arm and scrutinized the bracelets, her brow furrowing so that two wrinkles formed over her nose. She pointed to the bracelet mutely, looking at Headmistress Wyn. Fenya found flames etched onto every bit of the silver around her wrists, like a fine filagree. "It's beautiful," she breathed.

"It's...informative." The headmistress looked to Fenya. "You must have been trying very hard to keep yourself under control."

"Yes...I've tried," Fenya agreed. *But I wasn't successful.*

Keeper Liah resumed her seat and motioned for Fenya's arm. "This won't feel as good," Keeper Liah warned. "But must be done. With your blood, we produce potions that mute some of your Power in order to give you control back."

Fenya bit her lip but nodded anyway. "All right."

"You're brave, Miss Verena, I like that in a student with great Power. It gives me hope that they can craft a happy future for themselves." The headmistress gave her an approving nod as she tucked the key back in her pocket. "You'll do well at Wigmore."

"A sharp pinch here," Keeper Liah said, giving her the barest warning before a burning sensation bit Fenya's arm, and she cried out in pain, jerking her arm away.

Then several things happened at once. Fang reappeared, dive-bombing the Healer with a screech and a sound like a rasp. And Fenya felt, at the same time, her Legacy answering to her defense. Fenya's wrists stung, but it was Keeper Liah's dress sleeves that began to smoke.

"Cursed dragon!" the headmistress said, too surprised to capture Fang or otherwise react.

Exclaiming in panic, Keeper Liah batted at the smoke on her arms, abandoning the needle so it clattered to the ground. "Flammable wyvern spit...it is a flame wyvern then."

Headmistress Wyn's eyes narrowed as she took Keeper Liah's hands in hers and inspected the damage Fenya had done.

"I'm so sorry." Fenya's stomach clenched as she clapped her hands over her mouth, fighting the urge to flee. *Even with the bracelets, I've hurt someone. I don't want to hurt anyone anymore! And Fang, protecting me—why?*

Magess Wyn furrowed her brow with an annoyed twist to her lips. "I wonder...with the bracelets already displaying the etchings, perhaps a second pair of bracelets would be wise, Keeper Liah."

"Yes, ma'am, I agree." Liah reached for the box, pulling out a second pair.

A swoop of wings, then rustling from the top of the folly, told the three women that Fang had landed on the roof.

"Pest of a dragon," the headmistress muttered, looking warily at the edges of the folly's roof.

Fang, please don't get me in trouble or cause trouble at Whitland anymore. Go find a new home. A safe one.

Fenya couldn't stop the thoughts from forming in her head like a prayer. Holding a bit of cloth to her bleeding arm, she stepped to the edge of the folly. More rustling, and the dragon leapt from the roof to disappear back into the forest. *Thank you.*

"Have you...befriended that dragon?" Keeper Liah asked as she pricked Fenya's fingers and primed the bracelets as she had the first time.

"Yes. She trusts me, I think." Fenya watched Fang go, ignoring the bite of the needle as Keeper Liah drew her blood. This time, no sparks, flames, or smoke appeared.

Fang was a distant orange speck swallowed in the thick green leaves of the forest when Fenya turned her attention back to the adults scrutinizing her.

"Miss Verena?" The headmistress reached for Fenya's wrists, slipping the second pair of bracelets around them and locking them in place. "How did you gain the dragon's trust?"

"I...was kind to her," Fenya finally answered. *I can't tell them I released it from a trap...perhaps I meddled in something I shouldn't have.*

"Risky to associate with wild beasts." The headmistress wiped her hands on a white towel from the bag the keeper had brought.

"I'm sorry. It's just that they're so uncommon, I found her fascinating and..." Fenya sighed and looked in the direction Fang had flown again. "I'll regret being away from her."

"It's not just uncommon," the headmistress said, a new emotion in her voice that Fenya couldn't decipher. "It's—they're quite rare."

A glint in the older woman's eyes disappeared so quickly Fenya thought she'd imagined it.

"But it answers the Spark question, doesn't it?" Keeper Liah mused, bending Fenya's arm over a scrap of fabric. "Hold it there."

"Yes, the dragon must have done it when it thought we hurt the girl," the headmistress agreed.

Fenya's stomach unclenched slightly. *Thank you, Fang. Mama doesn't want anyone to know I'm a Spark.*

"Indeed," the keeper replied.

"What a disappointment." Headmistress Wyn sighed and made another scratch in her journal.

I already know I'm a disappointment. Fenya's cheeks flushed as her gaze flit between the two women, wishing they would be less vague, before she dropped her gaze to her lap. "Am I still welcome at Wigmore though?"

"You are, Miss Verena. And the disappointment is only in..." The headmistress trailed off and her lips curved into a slightly wicked smile. "We like rare things at Wigmore, Miss Verena. And Sparks are the rarest type of Fire Elementals that exist."

"I'm not though..." Fenya protested, though the recent events had her doubting the denial. "I don't want you to take me, thinking I am. Magess Jolie said I wasn't."

Magess Wyn and the headmistress exchanged a silent look.

Then the headmistress said, "It would be extremely unusual should you be, but like I said, we like rare things at Wigmore, Miss Verena. It makes no difference. You still have more than enough Power to qualify for Wigmore."

In thinking about it, Fenya couldn't decide whether she should be pleased or disappointed that her Legacy wasn't rarer. *But maybe just having too much Legacy is rare enough. I can't imagine making sparks whenever I want. What a nightmare.*

Chapter Twelve

WIGMORE ISLAND

A *disappointment.* Fenya didn't have to worry about becoming a disappointment, she was already one. Just another uncontrolled Wylde. Some would probably call her a Feral, one who enjoyed the Wylde status and reveled in it. Imagine Mama's shame when Fenya became a homeless scamp who set fire to who knew what and ended up arrested? She'd die in an asylum for the Wyldes—and Mama would get her way, the Relic dying in a tragic manner with unknown consequence to them all. But the Relics were well-guarded and their particular identity even secret by Order of the Crown. To divulge their image even in a sketch was a crime punishable by death.

A large shadow passed above them and Fenya looked up as the blue underbelly of a Nightstalker passed over them. The carriage shuddered as though the pegasi had spooked, then took a quick dive as though the driver couldn't control them for a few seconds. A quick look of panic passed between the magesses as Liah gripped the armrest.

A minute later though, the carriage evened out in the sky and they resumed their path as though nothing had happened. Fenya worried on her lower lip. Even the flight of the pegasi, the sight of the approaching coastline she'd always wanted to visit, the ancient stone buildings dotting the cliffside below, and one that looked like a castle with several round towers couldn't distract Fenya from her thoughts or from the silver and garnet ring weighing down her finger.

Fenya shivered as the stone caught the light and cast back a bloody stain upon the inside of the carriage. She swiveled the ring around on her finger, tucking the garnet into her palm so the ring seemed to be just a silver band. *Will the other students notice? I hope not.*

When they reached the mainland's coast, and Fenya lost herself in staring down at the sea out her window. She thought she saw something large twisting in the deep. An Aether Leviathan? She hoped so. There were few dragons in the ocean that she knew of, and fairy dragons didn't like large bodies of water, so hadn't inhabited many islands. But perhaps there would be some dragons she could sketch. She twisted to look back toward the mainland, only to find it just a dot now.

Goodbye. A mixture of regret and hope twisted inside her. Everything she'd ever known was back on that pinprick of land. Below them was an expanse of water that foamed and churned like her thoughts. *What if they take my Legacy? Is that even possible? No. It can't be. It defies the laws of nature. Surely I misunderstood or Milton misspoke.*

But if he didn't?

Fenya sneaked a glance at the headmistress, who had opened her black leather journal and was thumbing through the pages. Keeper Liah had tilted her head back and was snoring softly, crooked lower teeth on full display. But Fenya's thoughts spiraled around in vicious circles, fanged with teeth that seemed as venom-coated as the Aether Leviathan's legendary barbs.

With nothing to look at out the window except the ocean, the sound of Keeper Liah's snoring broken by the wind rocking the carriage, and the gentle lull of the carriage, the bracelets did what the headmistress said. Finally safe from her own Legacy and sleepy from the bracelet's effects, keeping her eyes open proved too difficult, and she dozed in and out of a light slumber.

Through this state, she was aware of voices murmuring around her like the buzz of flitting fairy dragon wings.

"What did the test results show?" the headmistress asked. "Or is it too soon?"

"They just appeared," the keeper answered, a note of triumph in her voice. "Just as the headmaster thought. Could be a Rank I Magess if she's trained. Nearly limitless potential."

"And a descendent with a Relic. Who would have thought?" Headmistress Wyn snorted.

Keeper Liah giggled in a surprisingly girlish way.

Fenya tried not to let her confusion appear on her face. *Why is my potential Power amusing?*

"That's perfect then, isn't it?" the headmistress said. "The headmaster will be thrilled."

"What about that spark...do you think it could be...something more?" the keeper asked, almost hesitantly.

"It's possible. But the dragon interfered." The headmistress seemed confused at the reasoning.

"Perhaps the Spark Test will show more. I've never seen a Spark in real life, just heard about them. What makes them so valuable to the headmaster?"

Headmistress Wyn was slow to answer. "I believe there is a working theory about a Spark being the origin of all Fire Legacies and there is a binding property that might benefit—"

A drop of water hit Fenya's face, and she flinched, sucking in a sharp breath as the shock of cool water hissed upon her cheek.

Abruptly, the two women stopped talking, waiting for Fenya to wake. But Fenya feigned sleep and sighed, turning away from the water source, eyes securely shut.

"The headmaster is already at Wigmore?" That was Keeper Liah.

"No, Vicar Asper said he would assist with her if need be." Headmistress Wyn shifted, her boot brushing against Fenya's outstretched foot, and Fenya flinched automatically, trying to turn it into a movement that she could have made while sleeping.

There was a beat of silence.

"He is supposed to have helped proof the room as well."

Who is Vicar Asper? Is there a church at the school? I thought this was a small school, just a few students to receive personal help. Other Flames like me. And what is proofing? Fire proofing?

Another cold droplet dripped onto Fenya's cheek, jarring the questions from her head. She had so many questions about Wigmore. Why hadn't she asked them before she got in the carriage? Why hadn't she demanded Sir Milton tell her everything?

She'd been distracted by the hope he'd offered, the diminishment of a Legacy he'd promised would no longer be feared. She could finally become what she was supposed to be—the proper Relic Heir—not someone who would be better off locked in an asylum and surrendering the Relic to the Crown.

And now she sat in this carriage, two bracelets warm against each of her wrists and an engagement ring on her finger.

The carriage shuddered, and Fenya sat up with a start. Her false sleep had become real, and she opened her eyes to find both women looking unkempt, as though they, too, had been jostled awake.

"The entrance gets worse every time," Headmistress Wyn muttered. "The headmaster must take a look at the wards."

Fenya peered out the window, her view obscured by the streaks of rain. They moved through a thin cloud, and for a moment, she panicked, her hands clutching the seat as though they were falling through the air.

"Calm down," Keeper Liah said, more commanding than comforting. "It's just us going through the protections of the school."

Fenya cast her an alarmed glance. "What kind of protections?"

The headmistress picked up her bag from the floor, where it had been knocked in the bump. "All sorts. We wouldn't dare leave our... students unprotected."

"Protected against what?" Perhaps Fenya could get more information from the headmistress and keeper now that they were almost at the school.

"All things," the headmistress answered. "Weather, accidental visitors, wild dragons, and the such."

Fenya frowned at the explanation. "But why does Wigmore need protection?"

"All places for Wyldes and Fledglings have some level of protection such as this," Keeper Liah said in a clinical tone. "It's to keep the vulnerable safe from others and themselves until they can learn control."

Vulnerable. The word trickled through her mind as Fenya peered out the window at the picture emerging through the clouds outside. A small, green island, one side with cliffs that had a rocky beach underneath and a small inlet was first revealed. A spray of water coated her face again, and she flinched away as though it had been a burn. Water leaked through her window, and she turned to avoid the spray of small droplets, curiosity overpowering her dislike of the feel on her face.

"Where are we?" Fenya asked, shaking herself from her thoughts. Below them the cliffs turned into a small-pebbled beach with a few larger rocks. "I don't see any buildings." Alarm coated her words. "Where do we live?"

Headmistress Wyn chuckled. "You'll see. It's all part of the protections."

As the pegasi coach curved in the sky, readying itself to land, Fenya continued to inspect the island below through her small window. Patches of darker gray clouds hung low in the gray sky, limiting her vision. Rain pelted the window. Fenya's frown deepened. *I guess the protections we went through don't protect us from bad weather.*

She strained to see more, but all she could see was a flash of light that turned out to be the top of a lighthouse on a narrow jetty out into the sea. *I don't even know what country we're in. Are we still in Avenesse?*

Vulnerability rose in her throat, all through the whisper-quiet landing of the coach on a hard, rocky strip of land. After landing, the animals carried them a little distance on, then rolled to a stop.

The door opened and a man appeared, the driver, who helped Headmistress Wyn and Keeper Liah down before offering his hand to Fenya.

"Come on now," Liah called sharply over her shoulder to Fenya.

Hesitantly, Fenya took the offered hand, her heart thumping and wide eyes searching as she descended from the carriage into her new world.

Wind whipped up against her, and she dropped the man's hand to grab at her traveling bonnet. The swirl of air wrapped around her almost as though it welcomed her to the island, and as soon as it rose, it left. She hurried after the other women, clutching her satchel to her chest and her bonnet to her head.

Fenya cast a glance behind her at the carriage. The driver stood at the back of the carriage, pulling trunks down and stacking them on the ground.

"Miss Fenya!" Wyn called back at her, but the wind stole any words that followed.

The women were already hunched over against the wind and striding across the grass toward a small mound that was part dirt and part grass. *Where are we going?* Fenya clenched her eyes shut as a burst of wind blew dust in her face. The women simply strode on before her, and Fenya hurried to keep up.

In the span of one step, stone buildings rose up out of the grassy mounds. Halting, Fenya blinked at them, startled to see a stone castle rising into the sky at least three stories. She had heard about Illusion Legacies, but never had she seen something so spectacular. It stole her breath just as the wind had.

The arched doorway led into a courtyard of sorts where two square buildings towered high, shielding the courtyard from the low angle of the sun except for a little corner where the sun penetrated as straight as an arrow. The entire castle appeared to surround the courtyard, and directly in front of Fenya, she suspected the castle looked out over the Aether Sea.

Stepping underneath the arch, the only entrance to the courtyard, Fenya looked up. Above her head an iron gate clung to the wall, stowed, a gate that could be lowered into place if necessary. But why would it ever be needed here?

She shuddered, feeling like she walked into an impenetrable, military fortress.

"Come on," Keeper Liah urged from a few steps inside the courtyard. "We don't dilly-dally around here."

Fenya started and resumed her way into the castle's inner yard. They walked across the courtyard at an angle, toward the right, and Fenya glanced up at the windows. Bars crossed some of them, with others covered by only leaded glass.

"Why are the windows...barred?" Fenya asked.

"To protect the students—from themselves and from others." Keeper Liah scoffed as though Fenya's question was illogical.

Keeping the students safe from themselves made more sense than anything Fenya had heard yet today. As she peered back out of the castle courtyard, the pegasus carriage rattled away down the path toward a square building with what looked like a pasture for a horse to graze. Could the pegasus be let out and trusted to not fly away? Being abandoned on this island without a way to communicate with the outside world sent a cold shiver down Fenya's spine.

"Miss Fenya, if you would?" A sharp tone yanked Fenya's attention to the middle of the courtyard where Keeper Liah waited.

"Sorry." Fenya tried to forget her fears. There was no one to help her go back home. And what did she have there anyway? Could she even return without complete shame? She turned her back on the carriage and stepped into the stone castle.

"This isn't...where we live?" Fenya's stomach twisted as the door closed behind her and darkness enveloped them. Damp, stale air assailed her nostrils. Did the barred windows not open?

A torch ahead burned with a light that wasn't fire. Fenya stared at it. She turned her wrists over, inspecting the bracelets there as if they held an answer to why she couldn't feel the flames.

Headmistress Wyn was walking quickly down a two-person wide hallway made of stone. Everything was stone—except the flames that she couldn't feel. The entire thing unnerved her. Fenya followed the headmistress through a squeaky iron gate and up a set of plain stone steps built into the wall. At the top, Fenya glanced off the landing and shuddered. A fall would break an ankle or a leg.

"Come on, now," Liah said, marching on ahead, her tone growing sharp. "Don't dawdle. I can't stand one who dawdles."

"Yes, ma'am." Fenya jumped into step behind her. "Is the head-master here?"

"No," Keeper Liah answered.

"When am I going to meet him? Will he be giving me my treatments?"

"No. You'll meet him when you meet him," the keeper answered shortly.

Fenya glanced at the doors that they passed. Made of plain wood, they appeared inches thick with wrought-iron door handles and keyholes. Locks?

Fenya wasn't sure why she was so surprised. Surely the students at Wigmore were given their privacy with keys and locks on their doors. It was the third door she passed that she realized why it bothered her. The doors locked from the outside.

Another shudder traveled the length of Fenya's spine.

"This will be your room," Headmistress Wyn said, stopping at a door and unlocking it with the skeleton key hanging on a hook on the wall. "It's been fully Legacy-proofed to keep you safe."

"What does that mean?" Fenya asked, her stomach squirming as Wyn swung the door open and stepped in.

"It means that another's Legacy can't harm you."

"So I can't practice my Legacy inside the room?"

"You can—if your bracelets come off," Keeper Liah replied from inside a room filled with simple furniture and a sparsely adorned bed. "But the manipulated aether won't leave the room. It's contained within the room. There's a barrier between the room and the hall, and your window will not allow any Legacy to exit. So you could burn everything in your room, but it would stay contained to the room."

Fenya blinked at the idea. "So I'm safe from others. But not myself?" She couldn't help but chuckle at little at the idea.

Keeper Liah nodded. "Exactly. And you should be mostly impervious to your own Legacy, no?"

"I think so," Fenya agreed.

"And that's the intention. We can't protect you from yourself. But we have to protect you from others. For that reason, we'll keep you in your room for a few days to settle in, and when the bracelets have been adjusted, and we've gotten your potions and serums dosages figured out, we'll allow you bits of increasing freedom."

Still standing in the hallway, Fenya hesitated to follow either woman inside the room. Keeper Liah and Headmistress Wyn had stepped inside, checking the window and making a round in the room to inspect the items there, such as a stack of clothing lying on the bed, but Fenya's feet wouldn't move.

"Miss Fenya?" Headmistress Wyn motioned her inside.

"Sorry, I..." Fenya cast her thoughts around for some other reason to not go inside. "Why can't I feel the flame?" She pointed to the torch that the headmistress had carried into the room and placed in a holder on the wall.

Headmistress Wyn blinked at her in surprise. "It's a flameless torch. This is pure aether." She frowned. "Have you never seen one before?"

"No. Not one like that. I...small lights, yes, but..." Fenya bit her lip, feeling foolish. *Of course I should have known it was aether.* "I thought they were rare."

"They are."

"Can anyone create an aether flame?"

"No," the headmistress answered shortly.

A wave of sudden exhaustion tugged at Fenya, and she leaned against the doorway to steady herself.

"You must be feeling the effects of the bracelets," Keeper Liah said in an odd voice. "It will take some time to feel normal again. Come in, change your clothes, get situated. You have a few books here to read, paper to write home, should you wish, and plentiful blankets. There is a small washroom that is yours through here. Beware that supplies at the school are limited. We are isolated and there is little excess here."

"I thought I couldn't send letters home?" Fenya asked.

"We will attempt to send letters out periodically, but it will not be often," the headmistress said.

Fenya cast another glance down the silent, shadowed hallway. It was as dark as evening out, though it had to be only midday.

"Miss Fenya?" Headmistress Wyn said softly. "It's time to come in. There's nothing for you out there right now."

Fenya blinked at the older woman. She was only perhaps in her early thirties, still young, younger than she had first thought. Was she married? Did she have a life outside of Wigmore? Could she trust her? Hadn't she already? But she moved inside, and she allowed the headmistress to lock her inside.

The bracelets burned with ice around her wrists, heavy and cold. Foreboding. How had she ignored it before?

In the middle of the room, Fenya spread her fingers, gazing down at her hands, matching except for the ring sitting on her finger. Suddenly unable to stand it, she pulled the ring off and threw it across the room. *Curse him and his proposal.*

Fenya closed her eyes. There was nothing for it. She was here now. Trapped. The only thing to do was to step forward, willingly, into her prison and pray that she could somehow find the control she sought.

Chapter Thirteen

TREATMENTS

"I'm going mad," Fenya muttered to herself as she made another round in her room.

In her two weeks at Wigmore, each of her days had one primary activity. There were treatment days, recovery days, and healthy days, as she referred to them. On treatment days, Fenya had her blood drawn, either through the needles Keeper Liah had used before, bloodletting or, Fenya's least favorite: leeches.

Recovery days were the days where Keeper Liah stopped by to see how Fenya's injection sites or cuts had healed, help heal them if necessary with her Healer Legacy, while admonishing Fenya not to scratch them or cause an infection that would require healing on a treatment day.

"Healing treatments lead to delayed treatments," was Liah's frequent refrain as she progressed to check the bracelets and replace them if their etchings were bright. So far, Fenya had burned through a dozen pairs of bracelets, needing replacement nearly every day.

Healthy days were both Fenya's most and least favorite. She had her energy back but nothing to do. She sketched as much as she could, but without anything interesting to study, there was little to sketch but the lighthouse and coastline out her window. At least she had a lighthouse to watch, but she failed to see a need for it, as she'd never seen a ship from her window.

Every day she sketched in her new sketchbook, filling its pages with images of the lighthouse and the varying waves and tides. She sketched Fang from memory, and diagrams of her bracelets and even her engagement ring to fill the time. She used almost all the white space on her paper before using a new page.

Fenya read the books brought to her, and though they spoke of Legacies, none were about learning control, but were a rather dry rendering of the history of Legacies, laws concerning them, and a million other details which didn't seem particularly relevant to any sort of treatment or training. When she ran out of energy for sketching or reading, she often lay on her bed, pulled out the scale from Fang she had put in her satchel, and turned it over in her hand, letting it catch the light.

On her fourth healthy day, two men arrived with Keeper Liah. One wore a black cassock with a white collar, but the other wore a similar uniform to Liah's, except in trousers and jacket. They were rough material, plain and tan, utterly practical.

"Good morning, Miss Fenya," the first man said in greeting, extending a hand. "I'm Vicar Asper."

She stared at him a moment. Although her room was hardly hers yet, it felt odd to have people visiting her here, especially two men she'd never met.

She took the vicar's hand, and he clasped her fingers in a cordial greeting. He didn't quite meet her gaze with his pale, gray-blue eyes. He was attractive, with a straight nose and plump lips that curved into a smile as he greeted her. His hair, though long, had a slight wave in it and was parted on the left so that a lock fell across his forehead as he moved.

"It's a pleasure to finally meet you," Vicar Asper said, dropping her hand and wiping at the wavy bronze hair.

The other man gave her what she could only describe as a kind, but matter-of-fact smile. "Good morning, Miss Fenya. I'm Keeper Henslow. I designed the bracelets you're so happily burning through on an almost daily basis."

There was a slight teasing manner in his tone, one that immediately put her at ease far more than any other person at Wigmore had yet to do. She smiled hesitantly, even though her cheeks heated. "I am sorry about that."

"Don't be. I love a worthy challenge," Keeper Henslow answered, honesty bleeding through his words. "It's why we're all here. You and your fellow students are the rarest of rare, and that requires stretching the limits of science."

"If you don't mind?" Keeper Liah said, motioning her to the chair with a hint of impatience.

Fenya hurried to obey. *Thanks, Mama, for instilling blind obedience.* She tried to find amusement at her quickness to obey, but it was difficult, knowing the unpleasantries that were to come now. But having three people attending to her was different, so perhaps treatments would be different today. *And I'm not sure if that's good or not.*

"I'll need to check your bracelets." Keeper Henslow turned to the tea tray where a now familiar box sat that always housed a brand new set of bracelets. He lifted a metal tool from the tea cart with long fingers and brought it to Fenya.

"What is that?" She shrank back from the sharp metal object, putting a hand to her throat and following the gold chain to its lowest point, where she had reluctantly looped Milton's engagement ring through for safekeeping.

"Don't worry, Miss Fenya, it's for the bracelets. I'm a Metallurgist, you see?" He demonstrated by squinting at the sharp object and using his Legacy to bend it into a short, dull spatula, then raised an eyebrow at it and it returned to the shape it was before.

Smiling at his display, Fenya extended her arms, but it was Keeper Liah who leaned over and brought one bracelet to her nose, scrutinizing it. With a slight furrow to his brows, Keeper Henslow took her other arm and peered through his half moon glasses at the silver. His face went expressionless for a long moment, while Liah scowled over Fenya's other.

Henslow touched the sharp metal end of his tool to the clasp of her bracelet. Fenya expected it to pop open and release her, but it didn't. It simply glowed at the tip like a lit candle and then darkened again. The entire process took only a few seconds, but Henslow seemed pleased with the response.

Henslow released her first, thanking her, while Liah continued staring at Fenya's bracelets for several moments longer, peeking over at Fenya's other wrist as if hoping to see something that Henslow had missed.

Fenya pulled her hands back and clasped them in her lap. Small lines criss-crossed the silver of the bracelets, curved and giving them a flame-like appearance. Perhaps it was just that she couldn't stop thinking about flames and fire, or perhaps she just associated the bracelets with the suppression of her Legacy. Every time they were replaced, the marks flared up when her blood was dropped onto the clasp, then disappeared when secured on her wrists. Strangely, the fine lines and flame-like images almost always reappeared within the day, or at least by the time Keeper Liah removed and replaced the bracelets. *That must be what Henslow means about me burning them out every day.*

"So how are you feeling, now that you've been at Wigmore for two weeks?" Vicar Asper asked.

"Uh..." She gave Keeper Liah her other wrist to inspect. "It's been... a bit boring."

He smiled patronizingly. "Of course, but for your safety, you know? We must first learn your Legacy as well as you know it, and soon enough, we'll get you outside and mingling with the others."

Keeper Liah dropped Fenya's wrist and crossed to the desk to pick up her notebook and scribble something down.

"The bracelets..." Fenya began.

Keeper Liah eyed her over her still scratching pencil.

"They make my Legacy feel...uneven," Fenya said. "Unpredictable almost."

The vicar looked to Keeper Henslow.

"That's expected," Keeper Liah interrupted without other explanation.

"Not more so than before though?" Keeper Henslow asked in his kind tone.

"No," Fenya answered him. "It's better than before. Muted. But is it...normal...for me to feel the fires again today?"

Keeper Henslow's brows rose, and Keeper Liah's pencil paused.

"You're feeling the fires?" she asked. "Right now?"

"Yes. Just a little. I can't reach them—I couldn't influence them even if I tried, I know, but I can feel that they exist again," Fenya hurried to explain.

Liah scratched notes into her book again. "You sure it isn't the mage fire?"

"The what?" Fenya asked.

"The aether lamps," Liah said impatiently. "The lighthouse is made of one, and the lights in the hallway, remember?"

"Oh. I don't think those are the ones I feel. Do you have fires in the keeper rooms?" Fenya asked. "And the stables?"

Eyes lifting to Fenya's face, Keeper Liah's mouth fell open, her pencil stopped scratching, and her bottom jaw jutted out to the side. "Yes."

Fenya nodded. "I thought so."

"You can feel them now? Right now?"

"Yes." Fenya hurried to add, "But I can't influence them."

Keeper Liah pursed her lips.

"Might I see your bracelets again?" Keeper Henslow requested.

Fenya extended her arms. He chose her other bracelet this time, the one that Liah had spent more time inspecting. He touched the tool to its clasp, and the tip glowed. He frowned in a thoughtful manner and the tip of the metal tool rounded, absorbing the glowing tip as though it had eaten it.

"I might try something...but I'll have to run back to the laboratory for it." Keeper Henslow set his tool down on the cart, and with a distracted air, left the room. Keeper Liah continued scribbling in her journal without speaking.

"Do you mind?" Vicar Asper motioned to Fenya's bed, and when she didn't object, sat down in the middle.

"I'm sorry," Fenya said. "But what is your role here at Wigmore?"

"I'm the Potions Legacist and the parson." Vicar Asper smiled at her look of surprise. "As the parson at the church here, I'm here to support for all the students here. Should you have worries, wish to discuss things, or require comfort, simply request my presence."

Fenya darted a glance at the door. "And as the Potions Legacist?"

He smiled, revealing a crooked incisor. "I help craft the potions that you drink here, as well as the serums that help keep your Legacy controllable. It's a team effort to keep everyone healthy and safe here."

She shifted in her seat as discreetly as she could to put more distance between them. Something about the vicar made her uneasy. It seemed like he expected her to confide in him simply because of his position, but she had never confided freely in others.

Keeper Henslow returned with a box of new bracelets and set to replacing Fenya's old ones. He first pricked her finger, dropped a droplet of blood into the small hole of the clasp, then locked each on the wrist. They flared with such bright light that all of them squinted away as the seal was made.

"Interesting," Vicar Asper murmured, scooting closer as the light disappeared.

Henslow released the old bracelets and handed them to Liah, who accepted them carefully and tucked them safely into the velvet-lined box.

"Why do you care about the old bracelets so much?" Fenya asked.

Liah tensed, delivering her a look of unconcealed concern, but Henslow smiled. "You're quite observant, aren't you, Miss Fenya?" he said easily.

"Drink this." Keeper Liah poured a potion from a test tube into a chalice and handed it to Fenya.

"What is—"

"Same thing as before. Health potion." Keeper Liah made an impatient motion with her hand, and Fenya tilted the chalice back against her lips.

"So I'm going out?" Fenya handed back the chalice, her question forgotten.

Vicar Asper smiled and stood. "Well, Miss Fenya, lovely to meet you. Miss Liah, I shall catch you after my rounds."

"Yes, sir," she said briskly as he showed himself out.

"You're going to be allowed the first step of freedom on the island today," Keeper Henslow said as Keeper Liah secured the bracelet box, twisting the latch so that it couldn't fall open.

"What does that mean?" she asked, distracted by the way the flames faded on the new jewelry.

"It means you are only allowed out under Keeper Liah's supervision, and just to the library." Keeper Henslow rearranged the items on the cart, securing the loose ones so that they wouldn't fall. "I'll be off then. Enjoy your freedom today, Miss Fenya." With a kind nod, he pushed the cart out of the door and rattled down the hallway.

"Don't get any ideas about swimming off the island or something equally crazy—we've seen it all." The keeper laughed at her own joke, a high-pitched, amused laugh. "Not that you'd make it far in the attempt. The Leviathan would eat you alive."

Fenya jolted and glanced at the window. "Have you seen it?"

"Of course." Keeper Liah's expression filled with confusion and derision at once. Her drab brown hair was twisted tightly behind her head, making her appear as severe as she sometimes sounded.

"What species of Leviathan?"

Liah shrugged. "Aether, of course."

Fenya nodded, putting together bits of information about where Wigmore was located. Aether Leviathan only lived in the Aether Sea, so they had to still be near Avenesse. "I've heard of them. Any kelpies?"

"Traditionally they don't exist in salt water," Liah answered. She shrugged. "But I have my doubts about that."

"I'd like to see them. Sometime." She brushed a lock of her wavy red hair behind her ear, her new bracelet slipping down her wrist. It must have been a size larger than before. They couldn't think she'd gained weight on the sheep milk cheese, watery porridge breakfast, and mutton stew with unbuttered barley bread?

Liah snapped the lid closed on the old bracelets and secured the clasp. "I'm perfectly happy not seeing giant, man-eating dragons or kelpies, thanks." She gathered Fenya's empty cup. "Now, are you ready? Or would you like me to come back after breakfast?"

"I'd rather skip breakfast and get out of this damp room, thanks," Fenya replied, but she grabbed a roll and dipped it into the porridge.

The keeper's lips quirked into a smile. "Excellent. Save me a trip." She motioned Fenya out of the door and pointed to the right.

Fenya took a bite of the bread and snagged the single, small piece of bacon off her breakfast plate as she shoved her feet into her boots. The bread tasted as if it had been underbaked and the cook had been in a hurry, but the bacon was over crisp and dry. She gave a vague thought to wondering who the cook was and where the kitchens were. Not feeling the fires gave her an unsettled feeling.

"You're going out into the courtyard and then right to the chapel." Keeper Liah rattled out of the room with the tea cart.

"Chapel? I thought I was going to the library." Fenya took her second bite and decided against grabbing her shawl. She was never cold anymore.

"Yes. That's where the library is."

Emerging out of the building, Fenya squinted into the bright sun, but still turned her face up to greet it. She'd missed being outside, where she could fully feel the sun and wind and didn't have to smell her damp room.

"Keep going," Keeper Liah urged. "To the right, that's the chapel."

They marched all-too-quickly across the bright courtyard and hung a right toward the chapel. The only thing marking it as such was a slightly higher roof than the dorms and a cross on the front of the door.

"Inside," Keeper Liah urged, not letting Fenya stop for her eyes to adjust.

Fenya walked straight into a sanctuary of sorts, with two rows of pews and an aisle down the middle leading to a wooden pulpit. No one else was in the room, and Fenya wanted to pause and investigate, but the keeper's hand at her back kept her moving.

"See the door on the left up ahead? That's the library."

Fenya walked down the aisle, passing the hard wooden pews, her feet falling soft against the rough hewn rock floor. A large bible sat on the pulpit as she passed, and another small cross hung on the rock wall behind it.

At the door, Fenya twisted the iron handle and pushed. A girl about her age, dressed identically to Fenya but for her gown in gray turned at their entrance.

"Harker, this is Miss Fenya," Liah said, her tone all business. "We'll be joining you in the library today."

With a glance at Fenya, Harker's nose wrinkled, like she smelled something rotten.

"Hello," Fenya said, stepping inside. "Pleased to meet you."

Keeper Liah followed, seating herself in a corner and pulling out a cloth bag she'd brought with her off the tea tray. She removed a pair of socks and set about darning a hole in them.

Harker continued her silent evaluation of Fenya.

Flushing, Fenya turned to the room. The "library" was spacious but hardly seemed a library at all. A handful of books lined one of the two tall bookshelves against the stone walls, two small rickety tables graced the room, and there were several quills and stacks of paper for writing. In the corner where Harker sat, a true flame sputtered on a candle as she resumed her letter writing, but light poured through a high window, permitting the sun to bathe almost the entire room. In one corner was a staircase that went to a balcony over the top where additional books lined a quarter of the shelves. The library was much bigger then, than Fenya had first thought.

With Harker still ignoring her, and Liah working in the corner, Fenya stepped over to the books on the shelf and scanned the titles. She wasn't going to just sit in awkward silence. She needed something to do, but she had forgotten her sketchbook in the excitement of leaving her rooms for the first time. Though she could write to Mama, she didn't know what to write. About the trip here? How she hadn't been allowed out of her room for two weeks? About the endless blood draws and potions and injections? She didn't even want to think about it. And to write it down made it feel all too real.

On the shelves, Fenya found a copy of *Your Legacy and You*, a few titles that mentioned dangerous legacies, a book on dragons, and a book title *Laws and Legacies*. Fenya wrinkled her nose at the selection. Nothing seemed to hint at guiding someone to controlling their Legacies, but rather inform about them in the most boring way possible.

What kind of school is this?

After a full circle around the room, Fenya found herself in front of the books again and hesitated before pulling down the one that looked most interesting: *Myths and Reality of Avenesse Legacies.*

She seated herself at the empty table and opened the book and began to read. She had made it through a few pages of introductory material when Harker finally broke the silence.

"So you the new girl, then." The statement was neither kind nor unpleasant, but it somehow put Fenya on warning.

"I believe so," Fenya answered carefully, looking up into dark blue eyes that assessed her with guarded emotions.

Harker nodded twice. "It's been a few minutes since we 'ad a new girl. We ain't supposed to get any more."

Keeper Liah cleared her throat. Her eyes shot a warning at Harker, but she otherwise kept her face implacable.

"Are you the only other girl here?" Fenya asked Harker, drifting closer with the last book she'd been looking at in her hand.

"No."

Fenya waited for Harker to expand on her answer, but the girl bent over her writing again. Fenya hesitated, wanting to find out more, but sensing that the girl wasn't interested. Still...this was the only chance she'd gotten yet, for Keeper Liah refused to answer anything ever, just dropping food, administering treatments, and locking her back inside.

"How many others are here?" Fenya pushed.

"Girls? Just one other. Three of us here now, countin' you." Harker didn't look up from her writing except to dip her quill in a pot of ink. "Then there's the headmistress, an' Keeper Liah."

"I see. How many male students?" Fenya asked.

At this, Harker lifted her chin and tilted her head to the side, a look of concentration on her face as though she were counting. "Six... nah, maybe seven."

"Maybe?" Fenya frowned.

Harker shrugged, her attention sliding to Liah's corner. "One might've gone, or we might have gained one." She paused and swallowed. "Can't rightly say."

"How often do you get new students here?"

Harker's lips twitched as Fenya spoke, as if she found something amusing about the question.

"What is it?" Fenya asked. "I'm sorry if I'm asking a lot of questions; I haven't met any other students here yet."

"We ain't really students," she murmured, facing away from the door again.

"Excuse me?"

Harker hastily shook her head and pressed her lips shut as if she wished she hadn't said it. "They let you out when you're fixed." She shrugged. "Months, years. Longest is three years. That's Rhys."

"Oh."

"He's a Flame."

"He is? Me too."

Harker dropped her quill. "You are?" She gaped at Fenya's clothing. "You are."

"Yes. What are you?" Fenya shook her head. "I'm sorry, I shouldn't—"

With a shake of her head, Harker swept a braid off her shoulder and motioned to her olive-green dress. "I'm an Earth-based mind-talker. Only with my twin though."

"Is he here as well?"

"Yeah."

"Do we get to see the other students often?"

"See 'em now an' then...if we're all good."

"If? What..." she trailed off and darted a glance at Liah, but she was muttering to her mending.

Harker chewed on the end of her quill. "Depends on how well we all handle treatments."

"Treatments? Like the bracelets?"

"Sure," Harker muttered.

Fenya sat down near the other girl. Fenya picked up a quill and piece of paper and wrote, "What happens here?" on the page, not sure she even wanted to know, but pushed it slightly toward the other girl so she could read it. Fenya saw Harker's dark-blue gaze flick to the sheet and linger, then return to her own paper, which looked like a long letter written in sloppy penmanship to someone whose name she couldn't read.

In silence, Harker stared at her paper without writing for so long that Fenya thought she wouldn't answer. Finally, Harker spoke. "You'll find out soon enough." She set down her quill, folded her letter, and stood. She grabbed a book that Fenya hadn't noticed sitting on the other side of her candle and tucked it under her arm, slipping the letter effortlessly inside it in a swift, almost unnoticeable move.

"I'm done here today," she announced to the room.

Keeper Liah didn't bother to glance up from her darning, but Fenya watched Harker leave the room with a mixture of uncertain and uneasy thoughts churning in her head.

Chapter Fourteen

DEMPSEY AND RHYS

After two more treatments, and another three sets of burnt out bracelets, Fenya was again brought from her rooms, and this time deposited in the stone square in the middle of the castle. Several young men her age milled around, all dressed in a similar style to her, but in plain trousers and a white shirt under a solid, dark-colored jacket. Not at all the height of fashion. Mama would be disgusted at the lack of fashion here. Several adults milled around the edges of the square, as though they kept the students corralled like a flock of sheep who might wander astray.

Across the bricks, Harker stood with a small group of one girl and two boys. Fenya raised a hand in a friendly wave.

Harker's expression stilled, and she turned her back to Fenya, leaning down to touch a shorter girl on the arm. She made some motions with her hands, and the other girl peered around Harker's shoulder. Her eyes were large for her face, round and bright, icy blue. Fenya had a feeling like an ice bath passed over her. She smiled uncertainly, but the girl's lips didn't move either to welcome or dismiss. Fenya's cheeks heated.

"You must be the new student," a boy's voice said.

Fenya turned to find one of the young men about her age surveying her in interest, his head tilted. He had a pair of silver bracelets around his wrists about half the width of one of her bracelets but twice the thickness. A wind gusted through the square, blowing her hair into her face, and she brushed a curl away.

His eyes widened. "Oh! You're *that* new student. I was beginning to wonder if the rumors were true."

Fenya followed his gaze to her wrists, and she blanched, shoving her hands behind her waist. "Wha—what do you mean?"

He grinned and gave her an appreciative look. "I mean, you're the one they had to double cuff. Nice."

"Vicar Asper!" Keeper Henslow called from the boy's dorm exit. "May I speak with you?"

Vicar Asper, dressed in a dark suit with a white collar, emerged from the shadows of the church door and grimaced slightly at the summons. He caught Fenya's eye and gave a bow of his head before crossing over to Henslow, who was speaking to a boy with golden hair tucked half under a cap. He had square shoulders and was as tall as Henslow, and carried himself proudly despite wearing the student clothing. If he had been dressed in tan keeper clothing, Fenya would easily have believed him to be one of them.

"Who is that?" Fenya asked.

"Who? Vicar Asper? He's the vicar here." The young man's russet hair ruffled in the wind, and his golden eyes sparkled under its mess.

She shook her head. "No, the boy who Keeper Henslow was talking to."

The man's nose wrinkled. "Dempsey." He shrugged as if shrugging off an annoying fly. "He's another student here. A Water Elemental."

Fenya's brows rose. "Is he?"

"He'll be happy to tell you all about himself, I'm sure," he said a bit dryly. "You're upper class, aren't you?"

Fenya frowned. "And what does that matter? Aren't we all Fledglings here?"

The boy laughed, a bitter edge to the sound. "Something like that."

"And who are you?" Fenya asked. She wasn't entirely sure she liked this young man with his judgment on other students and concern about class. What did class matter? She was the granddaughter of a count and what did that get her?

"Oh, sorry. I'm Rhys. You?"

"Fenya Vere—."

"Ah ah ah!" Rhys held up a hand as she spoke her surname, though his eyes sparked in something like recognition. "Haven't you noticed? We don't use surnames here."

"What? Why not?" Fenya's cheeks heated once again at the correction.

"Oh, Miss Fenya, you have much to learn." Rhys winked at her. "We call each other by our first names because we're all each other has. And we're supposed to keep class—and—" he looked around and lowered his voice so that she leaned in to hear him over the wind, "—and Relics out of our reputations here." He winked as though they shared a grave secret between them now.

She inhaled and held it. Her skin tingled like her Legacy awoke, but the bracelets suppressed it. After a moment, she decided to ignore the plug at the Relics, tilted her head and spoke again. "And the keepers? Why do they use our first names? When we're alone with them."

He shrugged. "To keep us humble, perhaps." He leaned closer to her and lowered his voice. "Or maybe to remind us that we're isolated from society, separated even from whatever family we might imagine we have in the outside world."

Another chill snaked down her spine. Fenya bit her lip and dropped her gaze to his shoes. He wore tough brown boots like hers, but his were scuffed and scratched and discolored, as though he'd been wearing the same pair for years and taking frequent walks in them. She wasn't entirely sure she liked him and how he seemed enthralled with Wigmore. "How long have you been here?"

"Too long." He gave a soft smile. His hair, which wasn't brown at all, but rather dark red, stuck out at odd angles around his ears, as though he hadn't had a proper haircut in years and had tried to tuck the strands behind but they refused to stay.

"How long is too long?"

His gaze went distant, staring out over the square where a dozen others chatted in low enough voices that they were lost on the wind. "I'm a Fire Elemental. What are you?"

"I...I am too."

His brows rose, but seriousness infiltrated his eyes. "Interesting."

"Why so?"

Rhys shook his head, his lips pressed together, but he seemed like he didn't want to give too much away. "It's been a long time since another Flame has been here, that's all." He cleared his throat. "Did you go to church back home?"

She frowned at the change of subject. "The Church of the Aether, yes. Occasionally, but not so much with my mother, only when my father was well enough..." She blinked away the memories. As a child, she had loved going to church with her father and sitting nestled next to him.

"Why do you ask?"

Rhys just smiled.

"So, you've been here years? Do you still get treatments so often?" she pushed on, desperate for more information that the adults had yet to give.

He shrugged. "How often are you getting them? You've been here... a few weeks?"

She nodded, surprised at how much he knew about her when she knew nothing about almost anyone here. Even Harker had kept her knowledge to herself. Though Keeper Liah had sat in the corner then, keeping them from chatting freely.

"So you're getting them every...two or three days perhaps?" he added.

"Every three at the moment."

"And new bracelets every two or three days?"

"Yes...It depends." She frowned.

He seemed like he knew her answers before she gave them. "That's typical here. They have to attack strong, make sure we aren't a danger to be around before we're allowed to be around anyone." He shrugged. "Best I can figure is"—he darted a glance at the keepers and leaned closer to her again—"that the bracelets somehow contain our excess Power."

"Is that why the etchings reappear after a few hours?" She twisted her wrist to inspect her bracelets with new respect. She'd never heard of such a thing. To have such little metal things absorb her excess

Power? It was truly remarkable science. She realized Rhys was watching her and hurried to say something else. "Do you still get treatments? You're wearing bracelets, and you're here, so…" She bit her lip and shrugged. "Do the injections stop? The bloodletting?"

"Injections?" Something dark passed over him, interrupting the curiosity that had dawned. "Mm. We don't talk about those. But it's…" He wet his lips and ran a hand over the corners of his mouth. "It's different for everyone. How often do you get them?"

"Every three days so far."

He grimaced. "I got them every day at first, but now it's once a week."

"How old are you?"

"Eighteen." Rhys pulled his left bracelet halfway up his arm and did the same on his other, tucking them under his jacket sleeves.

"Are you the oldest one here too?" She blushed at his sharp, questioning look. "I mean, in addition to being the one living here the longest?"

"Oh. Uh, no, actually. Dempsey is older, but by about five months. He's only been here six months though," Rhys added with a furrowing of his brow. He sent a slivered glance toward the group of students they approached.

Six feet away from them was Harker, the younger girl, and a boy who had wavy brown-blond hair that reached his collar. He stood a few inches shorter than Harker, but there was something about his appearance that suggested he was Harker's brother. Fenya recalled that Harker had said she had a twin. Perhaps that was him, as the smaller girl didn't look at all like Harker.

Rhys's dark waves flapped over his face in the wind, and he brushed them back, his bracelet falling free from his sleeve as his arm dropped to his side. He clenched the fist as though it irritated him, but he couldn't stop it.

"C'mon," Rhys said. "I'll introduce you to the others."

She fell into step beside him, and he led her to the smaller group of students that included Harker.

"Miss Fenya," he began, his hands moving rapidly in the air, "this is Miss Harker, Miss Ivy, and Mr. Merritt."

"I've met Miss Harker," Fenya said. "But it's a pleasure to meet you."

Harker scoffed audibly.

Ivy narrowed her eyes at Fenya, her expression otherwise unreadable.

"Miss Fenya is another Flame," Rhys said, making more motions with his hands, and Ivy's eyebrows rose before she looked at Fenya and then back to Rhys. She motioned back with her hands, and Fenya suddenly realized that Ivy couldn't speak. Or perhaps hear—or both. She must be reading Rhys's hands.

Fenya watched the flurry of hand motions pass between Rhys and Ivy, and Harker joined in, smiling reassuringly and taking Ivy's hands in hers for a moment as if to soothe her. Confusion knitted Fenya's brows together. She turned to the young man introduced as Merritt. "Is something wrong? Have I done something?"

Merritt turned a dark brown stare on her, but didn't quite meet her own eyes. "No, no, it's nothing you've done. It's just...being here." His eyes flashed up to catch hers for just a moment, and she saw some sort of truth there that he seemed afraid to share.

Cheeks blazing, Fenya opened her mouth and then shut it again. It was Jolie's School all over again—people thought what they wanted about her with her Relic status being what it was.

"I'm sorry," she murmured. Tears pricking her eyes, she turned and walked away. Was she going to be able to have any conversation here without utterly embarrassing herself?

"Could you be any ruder, Merritt?" Rhys snapped as she walked away.

Fenya had hardly made it six steps across the square, her tears blurring her vision when a student out of the other group stopped her.

"Miss Fenya, is it?"

Fenya sighed and lifted her gaze to one of the most handsome men she'd ever seen. "I—" Her words died on her lips at the gray eyes accosting her. They were entirely different from her mother's angry glare; these were warm and swirling like the surf of the Aether Sea she'd been watching out of her window.

"Yes, I am," she said simply to the gray-eyed man.

"I'm Dempsey."He grinned and stuck out a hand."Let me introduce you to the rest of the students here at Wigmore."

"I know, I mean, I asked—I mean," she stammered, her face firing up again. *Lord, what's wrong with me?*

His smile widened into a large, white-toothed grin, and he extended his hand further toward her. "Dempsey, Water Elemental."

Huffing an annoyed breath at herself, Fenya took his hand with her bare fingers. "Fenya. Fire Elemental." His hand was cool and damp, as though he were made of the water he was supposed to be able to control. Her hand trembled in his, and she pulled back without thinking.

He winked. "That happens when Fire touches Water." He offered his elbow as a gentleman would at a ball, and she took it, thankful his jacket shielded their touch. "Come and meet the rest of us."

"I...all right." Her lips curved into an irresistible smile.

He brought her over to the group he'd been standing with. "Chaps, this is Miss Fenya."

A round of hellos chirruped back to her, and Fenya ducked her head a little, embarrassed by their friendly greeting compared to the others.

"Miss Fenya, this is Acyn, a Healer."

"Hiya," Acyn said with a nod of his square chin.

"Bryton, an Air Elemental."

Bryton raised a hand in silent greeting, flashing an oddly shaped red birthmark that encompassed his thumb and webbing between thumb and forefinger.

"Weston, a Water Elemental," Dempsey continued as Weston offered a crooked, closed-mouth smile, "Theodore, an Earth Elemental—"

Theodore tipped an imaginary hat at Fenya.

"—and...Pippen." Dempsey shrugged as if there was nothing more to say about the wild-eyed boy with matching wild hair that looked like it hadn't been combed in a year. "The only one not here is Remiel. He's ill today, but he's Earth, too."

Fenya nodded a greeting at all of them as they enthusiastically welcomed her to Wigmore. "What are you, Pippen?" she asked for lack of something else to say.

Dempsey laughed, but his laugh was one of appreciation, judging by the way he looked at her.

"Water. Mostly." Pippen grinned and lifted his hand. He squinted at his palm, and Fenya thought she saw a film of water cover his palm.

She nodded, forcing a smile as her forehead creased. "Mostly? What else do you have?"

"Electrokinesis," he said, tilting his head and puffing out his chest. "Fishing is pretty simple." He grinned, then amended with a shrug, "Sometimes."

She blinked. "That's the...ability to manipulate electricity, isn't it?"

He nodded proudly. "Exactly."

Dempsey chuckled. "Imagine the power to have both!"

Fenya bit her lip. "Quite the power indeed," she murmured. "You could go hunting for the Aether Leviathan, I suppose."

Pippen threw his head back and laughed. "Perhaps one day!"

"We haven't seen you out yet," Dempsey said. "Have you been permitted out before today?"

"No, only to the library," Fenya answered. "It's quite nice to see the sun not out of a barred window."

He nodded knowingly.

"Were you...kept inside for so long at first as well?" she asked.

Dempsey studied her for a long moment, then shrugged. "Yes. It's completely normal—and they have our best inter—"

"Don't lie to her." Rhys appeared suddenly at Dempsey's side.

Dempsey blinked and half stepped back. "I—I'm not."

"Yes, you are. Don't you start—"

"Don't you!" Dempsey fired back.

Fenya gaped at them. *What is going on?*

"You shouldn't act like you care about anyone here but yourself." Rhys's eyes flashed with anger.

"Rhys, come on—she ain't worth it. Neither is 'e." Harker appeared behind him, her head tilted to one side as she scowled at Fenya and then Dempsey.

Rhys stepped forward. "You don't know him, Harker, not really," he said without lifting his glare from Dempsey. "He's a pretentious worm."

Frowning at the insult, Fenya shifted half behind Dempsey as Rhys advanced.

Dempsey gave a dismissive shake of his head. "You're just jealous that your little friends in your snobby little urchin group didn't give her the welcome you wanted. Don't take that out on me."

Rhys clenched his fists at his sides, his body trembling. "You don't know half of what you think you do."

"That's all right, as long as I know more than you to correct your misinformation."

"You—" Rhys's expression darkened more, if possible, then a fiery glint flashed in his eyes a fraction of a second before he exploded, leaping at Dempsey as though he'd been bitten by a dog.

"Rhys!" Harker shrieked.

Dempsey shifted, but he was too slow, perhaps not expecting that Rhys would attack in full view of everyone.

Rhys's arm clocked back and swung through the air, connecting with Dempsey's face in a thunk of knuckles on bone.

Dempsey released a grunt of pain and staggered backward into Acyn.

Shouts erupted across the square.

Rhys didn't stop or slow, but raised his arm to strike again when it froze in place.

Fenya's breath snagged. Dempsey looked up from the ground, arm raised to protect himself, watching with wide eyes as Rhys's wrist crept backward in the air.

"That's quite enough, Mr. Rhys," calm a cool but calm voice. Keeper Henslow approached, his hand outstretched as he controlled the bracelets on Rhys's wrists, restraining him without putting a hand on him. "Get on up." The bracelets lifted him by his wrists, and Rhys clamored to his feet without the help of his hands, which remained suspended in the air with Henslow's Legacy.

Dempsey, still on the ground, rubbed his cheek.

"Are you all right, Mr. Dempsey?" Henslow asked.

"Yes, sir," he answered.

"Why don't you run off and see Keeper Liah? She can patch you up." Henslow kept his hand out toward Rhys, forcing his hands to his sides, while Rhys glared mutinously at Dempsey as he climbed to his feet.

"I'm all right, sir," Dempsey said, holding his cheek.

"If you're sure," Henslow answered mildly, walking off with Rhys and ushering him into the castle's ground floor.

Chapter Fifteen
HISTORY

The fight between Dempsey and Rhys lingered with Fenya for days, distracting her even from her least favorite treatment: leeches.

What she wouldn't give for a more permanent relief from the leeches though. She despised them. Some nights, her dreams were punctuated with them. But after meeting all the others, she found her dreams interspersed with random bits of the exchange between Dempsey and Rhys. Why were they so angry with each other? What had they experienced here that gave them such vastly different opinions of Wigmore?

A quick knock on the door disturbed her thoughts, and Keepers Henslow and Liah entered without permission. Liah brought a heartier breakfast than usual, and Henslow an extra box containing what Fenya presumed were bracelets. Her stomach knotted. *At least it isn't just Liah this morning.*

"How are you feeling today, Miss Fenya?" Henslow asked, setting the box down on her desk. He placed a pile of notebooks beside it and faced her with his calm blue eyes.

"I'm well. A bit of a headache, but nothing awful."

He nodded, his lips pursed out thoughtfully from pale stubble on his chin. Dark circles under his eyes made his pale gaze appear brighter than normal. "That should be treated with some fresh air and water, I think."

Frowning, Liah pointed to the food. "Eat first. Keep up your strength if you want to get better."

Get better? Fenya wrinkled her nose at the watery porridge. "Is this supposed to keep me healthy?"

"Well, in theory, food does help nourish the body," Henslow answered with a smile that hinged up on one side.

"Hurry up and eat." Liah rolled her eyes and turned to Henslow. "Do the bracelets need to be replaced or not?"

"Doesn't look like it today." Henslow pointed at the etchings that were just starting to appear in the silver. "We should be able to wait another day before it becomes necessary."

"You're certain?" Liah said sharply. "We don't need any more accidents on the island."

"I'll be with her anyway, Keeper Liah," he answered in his calm, even voice. "I trust that you believe I can handle any mishap? Given that she wears metal?"

Liah's scowl suggested that she didn't think so, but the two returned to their other duties, Henslow crossing the hall toward Harker's room before Liah shut and locked her door.

Fenya's skin rippled in irritation at the turning of the key. Why lock her in just for a few minutes of eating breakfast? Where did they think she was going to go? Or do?

She picked at her breakfast, eating a few spoonfuls of bland porridge before turning to the ewe's milk cheese and splitting open the barley bread roll to expose the soft insides. She smashed the cheese inside and considered it. It would be better if it were heated and the cheese were melted and gooey. Cold cheese had never been her favorite, especially the sharp ewe cheese.

Maybe I can heat it myself. She scowled at her bracelets. *Not with them on.*

Grimacing, she took a bite of the cold cheese and bread, forcing herself to eat even though it turned her stomach. Just as she finished, the door rattled and swung open.

"Ready?" Liah peered inside.

"Yes." Fenya shoved her feet into her boots and quickly laced them up as Liah hovered, huffing in annoyance when Fenya stumbled over tying the laces and accidentally knotted one, having to spend several seconds unknotting it.

"Finish up. I'm going to get the girls." Liah closed the door but didn't lock it this time, and Fenya heard the other doors jangle open.

In minutes, all three girls were standing in the hallway, Ivy looking slightly green around the edges. Was it a recovery day for her? She wanted to ask Harker, but the older girl was wrapping her arm around the Ivy and pretending Fenya didn't exist.

What have I done to be so hated by her? Fenya's shoulders slumped. *She reminds me of Mama. Hard, angry...selfish. Except when it comes to Ivy.* Fenya reexamined the little girl. She had a frail appearance, making her seem in desperate need of a protector, while Harker had a wiry frame about her that could have been built either on the streets or through hard work. *What's so special about Ivy? She's delicate, young, surely, but...we're all in the same spot here.*

"Go on out to the square," Liah commanded. "You'll be sheep counting with the others."

"Sheep counting?" Fenya raised her brows, but Liah was already disappearing back inside Fenya's room. She glanced to Harker and Ivy, but when they didn't move, Fenya began for the door, pausing to hold it open for the other girls. Ivy passed through with a cautious look at Fenya, but Harker leaned away from Fenya, sidling through as if Fenya was too dirty to touch. Fenya rolled her eyes and let the door swing shut to the dorm behind her.

Keeper Henslow already waited in the square with Dempsey, Merritt, and Bryton, and Fenya smiled at Dempsey uncertainly. Apparently only some of the students at Wigmore were assigned to sheep counting. Bryton smiled at her in greeting, and nudged Dempsey with a widening grin.

"How are you?" Dempsey sidled up to her.

Fenya started, but at his inviting smile, she found herself responding in kind. "Fine, now that I'm outside." She examined him. "You?"

His lopsided grin lit up his pale blue eyes. "I thought you'd never ask. I'm wonderful. Can I escort you on this wonderful sheep counting excursion?"

"Are we really counting sheep?" Fenya couldn't help but ask.

Dempsey laughed. "Indeed, we are."

"It's not just to keep us busy?"

His smiled widened. "No. It's a critical part of our economy here on Wigmore. We must make sure that the wards are protecting the sheep, as they also protect us. The wards, not the sheep, that is. If sheep are disappearing, it's either through their own stupidity or through a dragon snatching one for a quick meal." He twisted his lips into an expression of disgust, confusion, and annoyance.

She laughed, refusing to let Harker's glare steal the limited joy she had found on Wigmore.

"So, care to join me?" he asked with an elbow extended toward her.

"I would be delighted." She took his arm.

He winked at her and they fell into line behind the others.

She craned her head around to see who was following, but they were the last. *No Rhys today? Why? Are Dempsey and Rhys so volatile that they can't go out together?* She found Dempsey watching her with a crooked eyebrow raised. *I don't want to ask. Not yet.*

"So tell me," Fenya began, slowing her pace so that Harker and Ivy drew ahead a little, "do you get treatments all the time, too?"

Dempsey's nose wrinkled. "Too often."

"What's the worst one for you?" She realized only after she spoke that it was a rather personal question. She didn't even know his treatments, after all.

A discomfited look crossed his face, but when he turned back, his grin was back in place. "The leeches."

"Leeches!" she exclaimed with him.

"Yes!" He burst out laughing. "How can such small things be so disgusting?"

Grinning, she lost herself in their shared misery of the worst treatment as they walked out of the square and in the direction of the stables, which she had seen only when landing on Wigmore for the first time.

"Do you have family off the island?" Fenya asked after a long moment's pause.

He sidestepped a rock and paused to dig a small pebble out of his boot before he answered with a matter-of-fact shake of his head. "I'm an orphan. Do you?"

"My mother and father's brother and his family. But that's it." Fenya sighed. The others had moved ahead even farther when Dempsey had stopped to remove the pebble, and she could speak more freely with the wind whipping across them, and Harker's eavesdropping presence gone. "I wish I could have stayed with them, but my Fire was out of control. I didn't want to endanger their children any more than I already had." She bit her lip and hugged her arms around herself. "That's why I had to leave."

He nodded in understanding, shoving his hands in his navy-colored jacket pockets. "That must have been quite difficult. And brave of you to choose to leave."

They navigated the rocky soil of the island in silence. The soil crunched amongst the rock underneath their boots, the sound swept away by the wind that blew in off the water and ripped through Fenya's dark red braid. It had been difficult. It still was. But it was a relief to have someone acknowledge that. At last.

Beyond the stables, they passed a ruin of stone with its ceiling gone and black marks along the top. Vines climbed the ruins and sprawled across the ground. Behind it, small, mossy stones peeked out of short grass.

"How have you found Wigmore?" Dempsey's expression showed more genuine interest and curiosity in her feelings than anyone had yet shown her.

She smiled at him, not quite what to do with his interest. Pushing down the flutter of pleasure that it had created in her, Fenya tried to cover it with a shrug as she reminded herself fiercely that she had a fiancé—a fiancé whose ring hung around a chain on her neck, burning against her skin. She gripped the chain as if it tightened around her neck "It's strange. Not at all like the school I was at before. There I was taught to control my Legacy, even though I failed, and that's why

I'm here." Her words landed heavy, creating a silence that somehow wasn't swept away on the stiff breeze.

But when she turned to Dempsey, his open expression only encouraged her as he said, "We're all in similar positions here. They really do want to help us learn control so we can live a peaceful, healthy life."

The width of the island, which had felt large earlier, when she was locked in the building, now felt small and isolating. She remembered it from the carriage on her approach, when the entire island had been a jagged oval shape with one side ending in a cliff, a rocky outcropping with a lighthouse, and a few dots of white, which she knew now had to be sheep. And now, having crossed half the island, Fenya spotted the churning sea on the opposite side of the island from Wigmore's buildings.

"So how long does it take?" Fenya finally asked, her thoughts a churning mix like the sea.

"Take?" Dempsey frowned at her. "Take for what?"

"To lose your Legacy."

Confusion mingled with alarm knit his brow. "To lose...?" He cocked his head at her, clearly working over her words and how to answer them.

"Yes...that's what I'm here for. Aren't you?" A vague knot of unease settled in her stomach, something she couldn't quite identify. *I want to stop being confused. Get some answers.*

"Oh! *That.*" He chuckled. "Sorry, I thought...sheep..." But he didn't continue and instead ran a hand over his jaw, where light stubble lingered, making him appear older than eighteen. "It depends. There's no real answer since it's such a new...opportunity..."

"So...what are the treatments doing? For now at least?" she pushed. *I need some sort of answer. I can't do this much longer.*

"Creating equilibrium." At her answering frown, Dempsey pointed to the sky, which was scatted with bright white, wispy clouds. "Like the clouds and rain. When the water in the clouds gets too heavy, it rains. Our treatments operate on the same foundation—our bodies sometime get out of equilibrium and create storms. With Wyldes and Ferals, that's how they start—unbalanced. And the treatments here are supposed to help us regain our balance. And, eventually," he added at her questioning look, "take it away entirely *if* balance can't be regained."

"So you're not going to have yours taken away?"

He shrugged and kicked a pebble with his toe. "I...might. If the treatments fail, I suppose."

"But Rhys...you said he's almost a Wylde. Why does he still have his? Why haven't they stopped him?"

"I don't know." Dempsey's tone turned slightly bitter. "You should ask him that. I think he's got some sort of sway over the headmaster."

"'Sway over the headmaster'? Like what? He knows him? Or has special permissions? What do you mean?"

Dempsey wrinkled his nose and began walking. "I don't know. Just a feeling I get. Don't you ever get feelings you can't quite elaborate on?"

Fenya smiled wryly. "All the time, here." She followed him along the narrow, rocky path, sidestepping the largest of the rocks.

Earlier, they had followed a narrow dirt path out of the square, past the stables, and the ruins, toward the lighthouse on the other side of the island. Though small, the island sprawled before them now with rocky outcrops and patches of bushes and greenery interrupted by white dots. Fenya stumbled at a large pebble, and Dempsey grasped her elbow before she fell.

"All right?" Dempsey lifted her to her feet and didn't let go as they continued trailing in the direction the others had taken.

"Yes, thank you," Fenya replied, flushing at her own clumsiness and at the closeness of Dempsey.

"Don't mention it." He grinned at her. "Some men don't understand the role they're created to fill."

Fenya followed Dempsey's gaze forward to the others. "What role is that?"

"Protector," Dempsey said matter-of-factly. "Provider. Responsible member of society."

"I'm not sure any of us are ready for that here at Wigmore," Fenya said dryly.

Dempsey smiled down at her as she still held his arm. "Let's just say some of us are closer than others."

"We're all equal class here, aren't we? We all have at least a titled relative somewhere in our family lineage, don't we?" She thought of Harker's rough accent. Perhaps she and Merritt were bastard children, unclaimed by their noble father.

Dempsey gave a sound like a stifled laugh. "No."

"But we're all high-level magi." Fenya frowned. Since all magi descended from the elite class, in theory, everyone with a Legacy had a relative somewhere in their family line who provided their own Power. Given Harker and Merritt's supposed great Power, it seemed improbable that they would not have a close relative of equal strength.

"We're Wyldes on our way to being Ferals unless we can change ourselves here," Dempsey corrected. "That doesn't make us all equal class." His gaze darkened, shifting ahead of them again, but Fenya couldn't tell if that was because he thought less of someone ahead or if he was checking their footing. "Some of the students here have Ferals or Wyldes who gave them Powers."

"How is...how is that possible? Legacies can't be gifted...you have to be born with them." Fenya stared at him.

He shrugged. "It's not something that's talked about—or something we're to know, I suppose. But here, we learn many things we shouldn't. Except for our families." He winked. "It's strictly forbidden to discuss them."

Fenya flinched and glanced around. "I'm sorry—I didn't mean to get us in trouble."

"No, you asked if I had family, not for names. That might be borderline, but won't get us in trouble."

"But how do people get gifted Legacies? Through our lineage, right? Usually our mothers and fathers. What did you mean?"

"I just mean bastards, you know? Men and women have affairs all too often."

"Right. And surnames give away too much." She had a strange compulsion to laugh.

But at her words, Dempsey laughed darkly. "That's because some here don't have surnames worth mentioning. No surnames being mentioned is supposed to keep us on equal footing." He rolled his eyes. "But we aren't. Some people who are here have killed people with their

Legacies. Or been sent to asylums because they've attacked others. There are some here I wouldn't trust with a copper."

Fenya frowned. "Like who? Should I be avoiding anyone? I mean..." She hesitated. "Are we still dangerous even with our treatments? Is there really a reason that we're stuck in prison-like rooms for so much of the time here?"

Dempsey sighed and dragged a hand through his hair, gripping it in his long fingers for a moment before letting go. It immediately whipped back into the wind. "Shortly after Wigmore began...there was an incident that..." Dempsey wrinkled his nose, hesitating.

"Tell me?" Fenya requested softly. "Please? I need to know. I don't know anything about this place." She glanced in the direction Harker and Ivy had gone. They walked together on the northeast section of the island, pointing occasionally at what she presumed was a sheep. "No one tells me anything."

He met her gaze, sorrow darkening his. "Something happened. I don't want to name names because..."

"Because one of the ones here was involved?" Fenya murmured when he didn't continue immediately.

He looked at her sharply. "There's nothing kept from you, is there?" A wry smile twitched on his lips.

She flushed, grateful when the wind whipped her hair across her face and gave her reason to take her time and wipe it away.

"Well, yeah, you're right. And it tore everyone and everything up. Wigmore had to be completely rebuilt. And it taught the headmaster a lesson—that's why we have bracelets now. That's why Henslow is here now, and a Healer like Liah."

"That's why?" Fenya's eyes widened.

"They weren't needed before." Dempsey shrugged.

She flushed again, but felt like she had to defend her thoughts. "I guess I assumed that the bracelets were always a part of Wigmore—what made it different here."

"Originally it was just the isolation. Now it's a bit more than that." Dempsey turned his bracelet over on his wrist as if in a nervous motion. "This used to be a military compound. Years and years ago."

"That makes sense. So what's different? The treatments?"

"Yes. Hard to change if you're just isolated." He adjusted his other bracelet and scratched the skin below it.

"Well…" Fenya paused, thinking. "It has to be easier to start learning control if you're alone and don't have external pressures or others watching." Magess Jolie loomed in her mind, watching her with angry disapproval as she attempted to use her Powers.

Dempsey gave her sidelong glance as if trying to work out why she would think that.

Embarrassed at his attention, Fenya turned away, hugging her shawl around herself even though she wasn't cold in the slightest. "So what actually happened?"

"Happened?"

"Here at Wigmore? To cause the bracelets to be made?"

"Oh. An…explosion. Of sorts."

"Hurry up!"

Starting, Fenya turned at the call.

Dempsey shrugged. "I'll have to tell you another time."

Disappointed, she headed toward the others with Dempsey, the silence thick between them.

Chapter Sixteen

PRACTICE

A short distance ahead, Henslow motioned all of the students forward impatiently, scrutinizing her and Dempsey, who had fallen behind. "Let's gather together, and I'll assign you a quadrant of the island in pairs."

Fenya hurried to catch up with the others, joining the edge of the semi-circle around Henslow, stepping up beside Bryton to avoid standing next to Harker. Bryton nodded his chin at her in greeting, hooking his birthmark thumb inside of his trouser pocket as if unconsciously hiding it. Dempsey lingered on her other side, and removed one hand from his pocket to run his fingers through his golden curls mussed by the wind.

"Girls, you three take the lighthouse side of the island, and make sure to check the cave," Henslow instructed.

Fenya bit back a groan as she felt the weight of Harker's glare upon her cheek. Of course Henslow couldn't assign one female alone with the males—it was improper. She had been courting impropriety with falling back alone with Dempsey. *I didn't even think that having only three females here means we always have to stay together. And lovely how neither female seems to care a jot about me.*

"There are a few spots where sheep have gone exploring and might need help getting out," Henslow continued as Fenya tried to give him her full attention, ignoring Harker. "Check the ruins, Dempsey, and take Bryton with you."

As the burn of Harker's glare faded, Fenya shifted her gaze to Dempsey, who frowned but shrugged, as if to say he didn't have a choice in the matter.

"Boys, all of you make sure the sheep haven't huddled in the stones—they've gotten trapped there before."

Dempsey crossed his arms and rolled his eyes in Fenya's direction. "Dumb sheep," he mouthed.

She suppressed a grin.

"All right, you know where to go," Henslow said. "Girls, I'll take you toward the lighthouse. I need to check it today anyway."

Fenya held back her sigh as she turned toward Henslow, Harker, and Ivy.

They followed a narrow path, one by one, to the base of the cliffs where the coast met a rocky shore. Ivy pointed out to the sea, and Harker bent over the smaller girl, making quick motions with her hands.

Fenya scanned the choppy waves of the Aether Sea, but she didn't spot anything worth watching except the waves themselves. She'd always found the coast and the crashing waves calming—especially to her overactive Fire. Something about the salt water made her Fire ebb even without touching the water. Perhaps that's why the headmaster had chosen a place like Wigmore for someone like her.

"Girls, go ahead and check the cave. Stay together," Henslow warned.

Harker and Ivy exchanged another flurry of hand motions and hurried toward the cave. Fenya bit back a sigh and trudged along after them. It wasn't like she was going to get an invitation.

Henslow nodded his approval, standing on a flat rock which the surf crept up behind.

Fenya followed the others into the cave and paused, waiting for her eyes to adjust to the darkness. Harker pointed ahead, her one hand on Ivy's shoulder, and Fenya followed her gaze. Ahead, over a stream of seawater, was a bright white shape in the darkness.

"Is that a sheep?" Fenya asked before remembering that Harker probably wouldn't speak to her.

"What do you think it is?" Harker retorted, a hard edge to her voice.

Fenya bit back an apology.

Harker turned to her. "Don't worry, you don't have any silk slippers on Wigmore to get dirty."

Fenya glanced down at herself. "What?"

"Titles don't get you everything," she muttered ahead, stalking across the shallow water toward the now-bleating sheep.

Fenya stood for a second, shocked, then strode after her, determined to help.

"Of course they don't!" Fenya said. "And I don't have one anyway."

Harker shot her a narrow-eyed look over her shoulder. "We don't need your help."

"Too bad!" Fenya retorted, stomping across the stream of seawater to the solid ground on the other side.

A ram was caught in some soft sand. Fenya tossed her braid over her shoulder and stepped up beside it, grabbing one of his horns as Harker, not waiting, grasped the other.

"Heave together?" Fenya asked as they met gazes over the head of the ram, who bucked and thrust his body under their touch.

"Not yet," Harker said sharply. "Unless you care to rip off his hoof." Harker pointed down at Fenya's side, where the ram's back hoof was trapped under a small pile of rocks.

Fenya flushed. "Right." She reached for it.

"Stop." Harker shifted her stance, keeping one hand tight on the ram's horn so he couldn't head butt her. She raised her other hand, pointing it at the ram's foot and narrowing her eyes.

What is she doing? But almost immediately was Fenya's question answered. The rocks around the sheep's hoof shifted, tilting to the side, and as she watched, the ground shuddered, moving the ram out of the wet sand. "What—you shouldn't—" she stammered.

She isn't supposed to be able to use her Legacy with the bracelets in place. The ground shuddered beneath Fenya's feet again, then the rocks fell away from the ram's hoof, and he was standing out of the sand, and ankle-deep in water.

The ram gave a sudden jerk of his body, and he thrust Fenya backward and forward, while she gripped the horn to right herself.

"Let 'im go," Harker said through a laugh. She had stepped back and watched Fenya be tossed around.

Fenya obeyed, and a final thrust of the ram's head sent her sprawling backward into the puddle.

Harker burst out laughing while Ivy covered her mouth with both hands, and the ram bounded across the seawater and toward the cave's opening. Still chortling , Harker motioned to Ivy with her hands again.

"Ugh." The puddle had quickly soaked Fenya's skirt through to her skin. Her hands stung with annoyance as she pushed them into the water, both to calm her Legacy and remove herself from the wetness.

"Well done, Miss Harker," said a voice from the mouth of the cave. "I can see you've been practicing."

Keeper Henslow stood just outside the cave in the sunlight, a white-toothed grin splitting his face.

Harker strode toward him, her hands on her hips. "I've been working on control. Not just my Earth neither."

Fenya frowned at the other three. *Here I've been wondering about learning control and Harker just uses her Power even with her bracelets on? How is that possible? What have I missed?*

Henslow turned to Ivy. "Can you help out? Miss Fenya looks a bit damp."

Ivy tilted her head and raised a brow as if to say, "Why are you asking me something so simple?" and then squinted in Fenya's direction.

As Fenya froze on the other side of the stream, the water stopped churning and a path emerged before Fenya's feet.

Harker pointed at it and pulled her hand up, as though lifting something up, and the earth responded, creating a bridge over the stream. Ivy swept her hand through the air and the water resumed its path, this time underneath the bridge.

"Lovely teamwork," Henslow said. "Miss Fenya, do you think you could use your Fire to harden the bridge?"

Both Ivy and Harker pivoted to look at her.

"Me?" Fenya asked. "No—I—I couldn't. I don't want to hurt someone." She hid her hands behind her back as if somehow hiding them would protect everyone from her Powers.

"She couldn't anyway, Keeper Henslow," Harker said. "She's just a Flame, isn't she? And there's no fire here to manipulate."

Keeper Henslow's eyebrow lifted. "Is she?"

Harker turned an accusatory look on Fenya, as though she had lied to them. "Are you a Spark?"

"I...I don't..." Fenya didn't know how to answer. "I don't know," she finally said. "But I don't want...to hurt anyone."

Henslow smiled kindly. "Trust me when I say that we can handle whatever danger you might cause with your bracelets still in place. We've seen it all here."

Fenya slowly shook her head, remembering Dempsey's commentary about the island and the explosion. What if it had been Rhys's fire that destroyed something? "I couldn't...risk it."

Henslow's eyes narrowed slightly, but he nodded in understanding, even though his shoulders sank in disappointment. "Of course. When you're ready. I have been helping guide Miss Ivy and Miss Harker with their Legacies, but I don't wish to press you."

He reached out and turned his hand over in the air. The sandy bridge shifted.

I know he's a Metallurgist, but...is he also an Earth Legacist?

Harker started for the bridge, putting a foot on it and nodding in approval. "Nice to add some metal to harden it."

"Metal?" Fenya asked despite herself.

"I am a Metallurgist, if you recall—an Earth-based Metallurgist. The addition of metal helps to harden the ground, though I had to pull quite a bit from surrounding earth in order to support the bridge. It's more difficult than it might appear at first, and I like to replace the metals in the world where I found them, if at all possible," Henslow answered.

Harker leapt across the bridge and back to Ivy's side, but Fenya continued standing on the other side of the water, feeling more confused than ever.

"Is this how you learn control around here?" she asked. "We don't have actual classes? Or real instruction?"

Harker opened her mouth to answer, but Keeper Henslow held up a hand to quiet her. "Miss Fenya, this isn't a school like you're accustomed to. This is more of a treatment facility. But I find that practice allows the patient—or the student, whichever term you prefer—more control over their treatment. So I mentor some of the students, the ones who wish to learn control, that is." He paused to survey her. "Is that you, Miss Fenya?"

Is it? Fenya bit her lip, her heart hammering in her throat. "Yes. I want to learn control."

"Then why don't you join us in learning?"

Fenya hesitated. "I'll listen today...if that's permitted."

"Excellent idea to begin with listening. Remind me when we return to the dorms to give you a couple of books that Harker has found useful."

"Yes, sir," Fenya answered, positioning herself out of the way and watching as Henslow began to train the other girls. Under his guidance, Harker crafted a natural-looking outcropping on the inside of the cave, and Ivy diverted the eddy of the water into the cave into another area, convincing a slender line of water to travel uphill for a short ways.

From her vantage point sitting on a rock by the entrance to the cave, Fenya couldn't help but wonder if one day she could do something similar with her Fire.

Chapter Seventeen

INJURED

L istening to Henslow as he trained the other girls on Wigmore to control their Legacies gave Fenya both hope and fear. How had they overcome their bracelets? Was it possible for her to do the same?

Outside her window was a rare bright and dry day with chilled air creeping through her window, sending an itch through her to explore the island. But it was supposed to be a treatment day, so she would be stuck inside again, soon to be feeling sick to her stomach. She scratched absently at the inside of her elbow, where the last blood draw had been taken. If only she could get out of this stupid treatment. She wanted a rest from them. No more needles and leeches and cuts, just for a few days. She wanted to be outside and breathing the chill of the late autumn air, not quite crisp enough to be winter, nor so unforgiving, but invigorating. She wanted to find dragons to sketch, or perhaps sketch the coastline, ever moving and difficult to capture authentically on paper without Aunt Cali's Animation.

She grabbed the bars on the window and gave them a solid shake. Immoveable—unless she were a Metallurgist. She couldn't even climb out if she wanted. And the door—she checked—still locked.

Returning to the window, she leaned on the high stone sill and placed her chin on her arms. Birds startled off the cliff beside the lighthouse, taking to the air in swirl of blacks and whites.

A flash of red glinted in the sun atop the cliff. A figure walking along the clifftop glanced up at the birds, shielding their face from the sun. Russet hair glinted in the sunlight. Rhys. He was apparently allowed out now. Why had he picked a fight with Dempsey? She wanted to ask. And ask about the explosion on the island, too.

She sighed and paced her room, trying to work out her restless energy.

I must be bored if I'm seeking out a confrontation with Rhys about Dempsey.

Henslow had given her a couple of new books to read, which he promised to be more helpful than what she would find in the library, as these were from his personal library. When he asked her to keep them hidden from the other staff, Fenya had a strange feeling that Henslow was keeping some secrets of his own. But all he said was that "some might not approve."

Now, she scanned the books Keeper Henslow had given her for more information on Sparks. The second book that he'd given was promising, but she wasn't a fast reader, and the book was a historical account of medieval magi, thus an utter bore. Still, she forced herself through the process, hoping for information that would help her understand herself or how to control her Power.

In medieval times, the situation for magi were dire, as they were not well respected and were considered the lowest class and a danger to law and authority.

Yet when Alveston the Unifier climbed to the throne as a powerful Energy Mage, he immediately made the status of other magi greater. Thanks to his Legacy's strength, he quickly enacted laws to protect the magi and made it illegal for magi to abuse their Legacy. Both crimes were punishable by death, and many corrupt magi were tried and hanged, a true test of the King's Legacy and support.

The king proved himself a charismatic man who—

She flipped the page and frowned to find the printed text turn to neat cursive handwriting.

My dearest Honor,

I am horrified at the turn our situation has taken. I had planned a future for us where you saw our children grow, where they ran around our feet shrieking with laughter, and when they fell and scraped a knee, you were there to wipe away their tears.

Fenya frowned. *This isn't the same book. What is this?* She closed the cover, keeping her finger in the page, looked at the front and back, flipped back to the prior page, and then the page she had kept. There was another book bound within the one Henslow had given her, only to be discovered through reading the book. *But...this is like someone's diary. And it does not read like Alveston's.*

She opened back to the page she'd stopped and resumed.

Instead, my love, you are isolated to keep you safe, unable even to visit with your dear family. Hartwell grows stronger by the day. His personality seems a blend of yours and mine—the best of both. I know if you could meet him again— and when you do—you will be so impressed with how clever he is and how kind he is to his sister. Though he teases her, it seems to light her up in a way that I could not expect.

And your daughter, oh your daughter, Honor. She is just like you. In looks, in action, in temperament. I wish you could meet her. I wish that there was a future that would allow for that, but until I can heal you...I don't know how. For she has your Empathy, my dearest.

I have not told you before now, for I didn't want it to be true, and I didn't want it to be developing so very early...but it's undeniable now. If she is sad, the chandeliers tremble. If she is hurt or cries, the glass window breaks. Only Hartwell's loving, teasing, gentle manner can get through to her in a time such as that. She will calm for him and no other.

My dear, I wouldn't trade either of them for you, as I know you wouldn't want that, but trust me...I will find a way to heal you. Whether it costs me my soul or my life, I shall bring you back to us, whole, and more complete than before.

With all my love,

- G

Fenya sank back against the chair in shock. *What is this?* She turned the page and found another handwritten letter like the prior page.

My dearest Honor,

I write again to you today with nothing new other than the antics of our children. Today Everly toddled over to me, and when I took her little hand, I felt her joy. The girl is an Empath of great strength already, and I do not know how to guide her as she grows, other than to teach her control. Of course, she is so young...far too young to be in possession of such a gift. I have asked Hartwell to help me counsel her in wisdom, for he is a wise, dependable boy, and he took the charge with absolute seriousness.

Though I know in your hands she would be even more, I don't know how I could ever bring her to you. I am hopeful, however, that I one day shall be able to introduce you. I know you see your children growing in the shade of the tower. Whenever the weather is decent, I instruct their nanny to bring them outside to play on the grass. Rest assured, she does not know of your existence. You remain, in the minds of both children and society, dead and buried.

And yet, I make it well known that I shall never marry again.

You are my love, and you will remain so until the end of my days.

Dearest, loveliest Honor, I shall find a way for us to be a family again. And if I cannot find a way, I will carve one out for us. Though I might climb mountains and move mountains one shovel—or even handful—of dirt and rock at a time, nothing will stop me. I will work at a solution for you—for us—until the day my body gives out. Death will be no relief for me, and I plan to prolong it as long as possible to bring you the healing you deserve.

All my love, dearest.

- G

Fenya turned the pages again and again until the letters, all with similar sentiment from whoever "G" was to his wife, Honor, blurred in her eyes.

Why had Henslow given her this? Did he know the letters were there? Was this...

She inhaled slowly as a chill raced over her skin. Were these letters of Henslow's? Was his first name something that started with G? Perhaps it had been an accident that he had given her this tome. He was certainly guilty of creating these bracelets that drained her Legacy...what was he doing with all the extra bracelets? Was he trying to find a way to heal his dying wife?

Fenya scratched at her inner elbow and glanced out the window at a bird's caw. She had to get out of her treatment...she couldn't do this.

Couldn't allow someone to sell their own soul or life to heal one person. It was unnatural. Too close to Necromancy to even entertain.

Wait.

She inspected her skin. All her scratching had created scratches and a red scab around the needle mark. But that alone wouldn't be enough to get out of treatment.

Keeper Liah would be here any moment. How could she create an injury? Could she fake a stomachache? A headache? No. Liah would be able to tell if it was fake, wouldn't she? She had to truly injure herself in order to escape today's treatment. She couldn't burn herself—not only would she not be able to control the fire, but she would reveal that she was a Spark.

Fenya eyed her furniture. A stubbed toe might do the trick. She bit her lip. And be painful. But Liah could heal it in a few moments. It would just make it impossible to do treatments today. She had to be healthy after all...they only wanted healthy subjects to "treat."

She positioned herself in front of the foot of her bed and grabbed the bedpost. She closed her eyes, clenched her teeth shut, and kicked the post as hard as she could with her foot.

Pain radiated through her toes and a moan escaped her lips despite everything. She hobbled around to the side of the bed and sat down, holding her hand over her toes. She'd broken a toenail, and the flesh was red and throbbing. As she pressed on the toe, trying to will the pain away, a bead of blood oozed out from between her fingers and the broken nail.

Nearly an hour later, Keeper Liah found Fenya still on her bed, her toe now three times its normal size and turning an impressive shade of puce.

"What happened?" Liah demanded, pushing the tea cart into the middle of the room and marching over to Fenya.

She offered an apologetic shrug. "I stubbed my toe."

Liah cursed. "I should let you suffer for being dumb as a stunned wyvern."

Fenya blinked at the harshness of Liah's anger. "I'm sorry. It was... an accident."

"Stay still." Liah narrowed her eyes. "Or I might just make a mistake."

Fenya froze as Liah leaned over her foot. "Could you—what do you mean?"

"Of course." Liah's eyes twinkled in dark amusement. "All I have to do is spread the infection." She narrowed her eyes, holding her hand over the injured toe. "Although it's quite fresh, I must say."

Fenya's skin rippled and tingled. Her blood pulsed in her toe as if she had just injured it. She gritted her teeth at the sudden, unexpected pain, and wanted to clench her eye shut but couldn't trust Liah enough to take her eyes off the woman's face.

Her flat face with the dark eyes seemed to glow as she focused on Fenya's foot.

Her blood swirled, and her toe grew hotter, throbbing. Then as suddenly as she had stubbed it and the throbbing began, it was painless.

She blinked at it, unaccustomed to the way her nail had knit itself back together.

Brushing her palms together as though brushing off dust, Keeper Liah straightened and stepped back. "You might as well get outside. We'll do your treatment tomorrow."

Fenya barely bit back her grin of victory.

Chapter Eighteen

FAMILIAR

Within the half hour, she was walking along the clifftop with her satchel bouncing on her shoulder. Her toe was pain-free and her hair whipped out behind her. She paused at the middle of the cliff, grinning as the birds shrieked and squawked. She thought she heard a dragon cry in the midst of it, reminding her so much of Fang that homesickness stabbed her in the gut. But Fang was back at Whitland, and hopefully staying safe and keeping herself out of wire cages. At least, that was what she prayed every night.

Without any real purpose, Fenya wandered across the island, past the stables where a pegasus grazed on scrub grass, past the ruined stone building, and the odd stones behind it, until her feet brought her across the island to a large rock that sat above the lighthouse. With another surge of victory for obtaining her goal today, Fenya happily pulled out her sketchbook and pencil box.

The wind whipped across her face, tugging her hair from her braid and trying to flip her sketchbook pages as she squinted at the lighthouse. Her hand moved in quick sketches, capturing the shape of the needlelike building that reached far into the sky from its bed of rock. The top captured her attention, where the lighthouse curved outward with its railing and glass enclosure for the light. From her bedroom at night, she had often watched for the light, but she never saw it lit. When night fell, with the exception of the moon, darkness was complete at Wigmore.

The wind pulled at her skirt's hem, but she hardly noticed as she sketched, ignoring the sounds of the island, all her attention focused on the lines of the lighthouse, the shadows, and the light.

Fenya clutched her sketchbook as the wind wrenched at its pages, and dragged her skirt toward the ground.

What the—

She looked down and gasped. "Fang!"

The little flame wyvern on the ground held her left wing awkwardly off her back.

"How did you get here? What happened to you?" Fenya shoved her sketchbook and pencils aside, reaching down and scooping the little wyvern into her lap. The dragon made a chirruping sound that was half pained and half hopeful.

"Oh my poor little thing," Fenya murmured, cuddling the cold animal into her lap as though it were not a dragon but a tame cat.

The dragon curled up on Fenya's legs, but continued holding her wing out awkwardly.

"May I?" Fenya asked the dragon as if she could understand.

When the dragon just closed her eyes as though she were exhausted and choosing to trust, Fenya gently probed the dragon's wing. It seemed not to be broken, but there were small rips in the leathery portion of her wing around the hollow bones.

"I'll see what I can do. But you won't be able to fly for some time without injuring it further." Fenya glanced around. *How had she been hiding? And where?*

Her hands warmed against Fang's back. Fang arched her spiked neck and blinked amber eyes at Fenya.

"I'll do what I can, Fang, but you have to remain calm and probably not fly for at least a week or two—depending on how fast you heal." Fenya glanced around from her perch on the rock. "Where could you stay safe?"

As she contemplated, stroking the dragon's back gently, footsteps crunched directly behind her. Fenya started and twisted her head around to see Rhys approaching. He gave a crooked grin and wave of his hand at her attention.

She froze. *I can't show him Fang! How could I trust him? He attacked Dempsey without any cause—what would he do if he saw a rare flame wyvern on the island? Would he tell the keepers?*

Fenya threw her gaze around. Fang raised her head, clearly catching Fenya's distress. *I brought my cloak—where is it?*

"Shh," she whispered to Fang as she leaned far over to try and grab it. "Stay hidden." It was just outside of her finger's reach though, and though she leaned and twisted to grab it, she couldn't. Holding Fang snugly on her lap, keeping her back to Rhys, she stretched out her nearest foot and snagged the edge of the cloak. She dragged it toward her and snatched it with her fingers, pulling it over her lap moments before Rhys appeared in her vision.

"Hello," he said, his tone uncertain. He rushed his fingers through wind-swept hair.

"Hello," she replied, her hands underneath the cloak upon Fang.

"Am I...interrupting?" He bit his lip.

"Oh, no. No, I was just..." Fenya spread her hand to her abandoned sketchbook and the pencils she'd hurriedly stowed in their case. One was in the wrong spot, a skinny pencil in a thick row, and the larger pencil that fit there laying across the others. "...sketching," she finished lamely.

He raised his brows and glanced at the book. "Did you drop it? I thought I might have startled you."

"Doesn't matter." At Rhys's shocked reaction to her response, Fenya bit her lip, running her fingers absently over Fang's back. "Ouch." She flinched as her finger snagged on a sharp horn along the dragon's spine.

"What is it?" Rhys asked, his gaze skimming over her..

"Nothing." She pressed her lips together and attempted a smile. "Did you need something from me? Or are you here to pick a fight like you did with Dempsey?"

He blinked at her terse tone. "Oh, well, I..." He kicked at a small rock, watched it bounce toward the cliff a couple of times before it skittered to a halt.

She waited, pulling her hand out from under the cloak to peer at her finger. She was bleeding. Keeper Liah was going to kill her. Or heal her. One of the two. Or maybe both.

"I wanted to apologize, I suppose," Rhys said. "Well, not I suppose...I know." His cheeks went red. "I'm sorry for attacking Dempsey in front of you the other day. I should have controlled my temper. Not done it then."

She raised her brows at the half regretful apology. "Not then? How about never?"

"Yeah..." He dragged a hand through his hair, and there was a hollow exhaustion in his eyes as he met her gaze. "It's hard for me to be here. I..." He turned away to stare out at the lighthouse. "Some days I'm certain I won't be going home."

A pang of sympathy thrummed through her. Despite his feud with Dempsey, Rhys was trapped here like the rest of them—and apparently had been trapped the longest. "That can't be true. You're going to go home. You'll learn to control your Fire and..." She shrugged. "It's hard for us all. You're not alone in feeling that way."

"I've been here almost three years."

Despite her annoyance with Rhys, from his attack on Dempsey to his half-apology and his quick temper, an urge to soothe him rose within her. He had a haggard appearance that the rest of the students didn't have. A hollowness to his cheeks and sharpness to his jaw that didn't reflect a healthy person, but reminded her of her father as he suffered from Legacy Fever. "Aren't our Legacies supposed to even out by twenty-one anyway? There's no way you won't be able to go home by then."

Rhys's shoulders slumped, and he turned back to her. "You don't understand what it is to be here so long. The treatments...I've not responded well."

She brushed at a lock of hair that the wind had tugged free from her braid and lashed across her face. "Well they'll figure it out. Right?" Her mind shifted back to the letters in her room, hidden within the history book of King Alveston. "They have to," she added with a dry tone to her words. "And even if they can't do anything, time must help."

Rhys stepped toward her, shoving his hands into his trouser pockets. "I hope so, but time has been my enemy lately."

Her frown deepened. "What are you talking about?"

He kicked at a rock as if trying to screw up his courage to speak. "I...well, there's an old church on this island, did you know?"

Her heart leaped. "Yes... That overgrown ruin of rock? I noticed it as we walked across the island counting sheep. The entire island is old —clearly someone else lived here a long time ago."

Rhys nodded. "Yes, it's got a history that came before...us."

"Then why mention it?" Fenya barely resisted the urge to roll her eyes. *I should have asked Dempsey about it.*

He hesitated, perhaps catching onto her frustration. She didn't want to have a conversation with him now. She didn't trust him— couldn't trust him. He had snapped on Dempsey with no provocation.

"I...the church is important." Rhys raked his hand through his hair and gripped it behind his head in his fingers, pulling at his face so that the corners of his eyes stretched out. He grimaced. "It's old but...the church was standing two years ago, when I arrived at Wigmore."

Fenya went still. "Wait...church? So the rocks behind it...is that a graveyard?"

He met her gaze, surprise edging onto his face. "Yes. You examined them?"

"No," she admitted, her fingers tightening on her skirts around Fang. "But there looked like a lot of them."

"Yes... There was a disaster there."

"When you were here?" She inhaled slowly. *What is he trying to tell me? Is he confessing? Telling me he could do the same to me as he'd done to all those others who had been here with him? I should have listened to Dempsey and avoided Rhys more actively.*

"It was pure luck that I wasn't there. Only the headmaster and I survived."

Luck or planning, which one was it? Fenya's hair swept across her face, and she withdrew a hand from under her cloak to brush it away.

"It was horrible," Rhys continued. "I thought for sure I'd be sent home then, and I tried, but..."

Fang shifted on her lap.

"What—" Rhys's forehead creased. He pointed at her. "What's on your face? Is that blood?"

Fenya put both hands to her face. "What? Blood?"

"It's all over you—your hand." Rhys was at her side in a moment. "What did you do?"

Under her cloak, Fang's legs curled into a crouch.

"Uh... Why is your cloak moving?" Rhys leaned back. "What do you have under there?"

Fenya clamped down on her lip, knowing she was caught. *I can't answer—I can't trust him! What am I supposed to do?* Fang's muscles tensed more.

"It's fine." Rhys said, waving away his question as she continued to not answer. "But may I see your hand? Perhaps I can stop the bleeding."

Fenya hesitated, then extended her hand, keeping the other firmly on top of Fang to keep her in place and the cloak atop her.

"This is quite the cut," Rhys said conversationally. His hands hovered over hers, not quite touching her but coming close as he bent his nose close to her wound. She had sliced her finger on one of Fang's spikes, which turned out to be so razor sharp she'd hardly felt it. "Hmm." He glanced around them and then patted his pocket. "I might have a strip of fabric that we can cover that with. But you should probably get back to Keeper Liah. She can heal this in a jiff."

Fenya wrinkled her nose. "I was supposed to have a treatment day today, but I stubbed my toe. Do you think she'll be mad that I got a day out instead and then injured myself again?"

Pausing from pulling out a handkerchief from his pocket, Rhys met her gaze with a slight smile starting on his lips. "I'd say the chances are good that she'll be rather annoyed."

Fenya couldn't help but smile at his response. "I thought so." She sighed heavily and allowed him to take her hand in his. His fingers touched hers and they felt hot—a rarity. Almost always everyone else's touch felt like ice, it was odd to have a hand be hotter than her own skin. His gaze went unfocused, as though perhaps he felt it too, and he stared blankly at her finger for a long moment, then gave himself a shake and pulled the handkerchief toward her finger.

"Are you all right?" Fenya began.

His hand went tense again, clutching Fenya's fingers tightly.

"Ow, you're hurting me. Let go!" Fenya tried to pull her hand back.

At her cry, Fang burst from the cloak and flew at Rhys's face.

"Ah—!" he cried, rolling backward on his heels and falling on his bottom.

"Fang!" Fenya reached for her as Fang's strength gave out and she crumpled to the ground, her wing held out at an awkward angle. "Fang, stop! It's all right!"

"What the—?" Rhys gaped at the dragon. "What was *that* doing under your cloak?"

Fenya scooped Fang back into her arms. "*She* is injured."

"She's a flame wyvern!" Rhys retorted. "I'm lucky she didn't spew venom at me!"

"I know." Fenya shot him a sidelong look. "You aren't going to tell —are you?"

"Tell?" He picked himself up off the ground and brushed off his trousers. "Tell whom?"

"The keepers?" Her lips quirked up on the side. "Anyone?"

"No, of course not." He dusted off his hands. "But I don't know what you think you're going to do with her. She looks injured—and there are some large birds of prey around here that sometimes attack the lambs. She's not going to make it on her own."

"I need to heal her. But Liah wouldn't...and I wouldn't ask."

"Don't," Rhys agreed. "Definitely don't ever mention it to her." His eyes were dark.

Fenya cuddled Fang to her chest, running her fingers over the dragon's slippery side scales. "She followed me from home."

"Did she?" Rhys didn't get any closer, but he squinted at the wyvern with increased interest.

"Yes."

"And how did you get cut?" Rhys's eyes were eerily like Fang's amber ones as he slid his gaze from the dragon onto Fenya. "She didn't bite you, did she?"

"Oh, no, I think I sliced it on her spikes."

"Ah. Good. Because I'm reasonably certain that flame wyverns contain venom in their bites."

"Oh, well, no. She wouldn't bite me. She's...gentle." Fenya shrugged at his skeptical expression. "I rescued her from a cage." Fang squirmed in her hold.

He nodded. "Just be careful, I—" He flinched back as Fang wormed out of Fenya's grip and leapt down to her lap.

Fenya released her, holding the animal gently on her lap. "She's fine."

"She's bleeding too," Rhys said, alarm in his voice.

"Is she?" Fenya peered down at the dragon. She reached for the dragon.

"Wait, don't!" Rhys said, grabbing for her hand.

"What?" Fenya pulled away from his touch and from Fang. Fang stretched out her neck toward him and bared her teeth.

"I...I've heard that if you exchange blood with a dragon, you become forever connected with them."

Fenya frowned. "What?"

"Yeah, it's how some magi become Familiars with animals." He shrugged. "I've heard about it...it lasts forever. And ties your life to theirs."

"Forever?" Fenya murmured, taking in the dragon sitting in her lap.

"It ties you together...your health and hers become tied. I hear it gives strength to a human."

Thoughtful, Fenya narrowed her eyes. "So if I were in good health, would it heal her?"

Rhys shrugged. "I imagine so. But I wouldn't risk my life on it."

Fenya reached for the dragon again.

"Don't!" He grabbed for her hand, but Fang nipped at him, and he jerked away, looking at her with wide eyes. "I...does she understand you? Do you have Dragon Speech?"

"I think she does, actually." Fenya smiled fondly at the little wyvern. "And no, I don't."

"And she followed you from where you were living?"

"Where *she* was living. I was just visiting."

He bit down on his bottom lip as he stared at Fang. "I...take it all back. I think she's chosen you."

The dragon nestled her head against Fenya's chest as if to show her agreement.

"So what do I do?"

Rhys spread his palms to the sky. "I suppose you can either become her Familiar or not."

Fenya's heart thumped unevenly. Should she trust him? Could he trying to hurt her? Or keep her weak? Her hands tingled, like her flames were waking. "And what does that do? Having a Familiar? Just link us?"

Rhys shrugged. "That's what I've heard. I've heard rumors of some having other qualities...like speech with them. But it's only if you already have a Dragon Legacy. Do you have any Dragon Legacy?"

"No, none." Fenya shook her head. *What's the worst that could happen?* Blood still dripped off her finger, but it was slower now. Soon it would stop bleeding, and her chance would be gone. *But why should I create a deeper bond with Fang? Or maybe the question is why* shouldn't *I?*

Fang blinked trustingly up at Fenya. Her wing was still crumpled, as though she felt pain in it no matter how she moved. If Fenya bonded with her, she could help heal her. As soon as Keeper Liah healed her finger, Fang would also be healed, right? But would Keeper Liah know? Would she sense Fang? Would it be different healing Fenya now?

She bit her lip. She couldn't let the little wyvern die. But Fenya herself had very little to lose if she came off worse in this scenario. Maybe it would help them both.

She moved her dripping finger toward Fang's shoulder, where a gash was slowly dripping blood.

"Are you really going to do it?" Rhys asked in awed disbelief, but he didn't move to stop her.

"Why not?" Fenya bit her lip, held her breath, and squeezed blood out of her finger, smearing it into the dragon's wound.

Fang stayed quite still, her right eye on Fenya's face, her left on Rhys's as though she didn't trust him. *Neither do I, Fang.*

A shock of heat rushed through her like a flame that devoured fuel in a gasp. And Fenya grinned.

Chapter Nineteen

TRUST

Two days later, Fenya still felt the warmth in her skin from Fang like a healing burn. Her bracelets lasted less than a day now, and true to Rhys and Fenya's suspicions, Keeper Liah had been livid to find Fenya's finger injured and repeated her healing, leaving a thin scar behind this time as if to remind Fenya of her foolishness.

The finger injury hadn't been enough to get Fenya another day without treatment, and she endured leeches the next day. She had the odd feeling that Liah had chosen leeches because Fenya hated them so much.

No one had mentioned the wyvern yet, but Fenya still wasn't certain she could trust Rhys. How could she trust someone who attacked other people and didn't tell her the truth? For he hadn't been telling the truth, had he? He hadn't even told her the entire truth about the church...had he?

Oddly, Fenya's hunger had increased, as though her body needed more energy after being healed and her bonding with Fang. She wasn't sure if she was feeling Fang's hunger or if she just needed more energy to sustain this connection. But then, other than the odd twinges of hunger and the continued throbbing of her hand even though Liah had healed it, there was nothing that suggested Rhys had even been telling the truth. Perhaps he had been lying all along and just trying to get her to pollute herself with dragon's blood. There were all sorts of things it was supposed to be able to do, and some of them were dangerous. Maybe he'd been trying to kill her after all.

But those thoughts were impossible to prove, and Fenya tried not to focus on them. A treatment following the second day of healing in a row erased almost all thoughts of Rhys and Fang, but she felt slightly stronger coming out of her treatment, as though something was finally changing and the treatments were finally working. She wanted to return to Fang, but Liah restricted her movements after cutting herself twice in one day.

Three days after exchanging blood with Fang, Fenya was staring out the window hoping she could see Fang flying through her the sky by the lighthouse, but there was no flash of red or orange. *She's still grounded then.* Fenya needed to get out, to check on her. She had to be still alive, right? If the bonding had worked, according to Rhys, she would know if Fang were killed.

Her stomach squirmed in discomfort, an intense hunger gnawing at it. She glanced at the sun. Liah wouldn't be here for another quarter of an hour at least.

When Liah finally dropped off Fenya's breakfast with the same hard roll, the singular slice of Romano cheese made from the ewes that Fenya spotted on the island, and two links of sheep sausage, Fenya's stomach flipped over itself in excitement. Even the usual twinge of pity for the sheep she shared Wigmore Island with didn't occur today. Her stomach groaned audibly.

"Hungry?" Keeper Liah laughed, but it was a mirthless laugh that mocked Fenya.

"A bit," Fenya agreed, eyeing the mutton sausage. She could save that for Fang, if she were allowed out today. She needed to be allowed out today.

"Feeling well, are you?" Keeper Liah reached for her hand and held her wrist, performing her typical investigation of Fenya's vitals.

Fenya nodded. "Yes, actually."

"Of course you are. You'll be permitted outside then." Keeper Liah tilted her head at Fenya with eyes narrowed.

Another pang of hunger twisted her stomach. "Thank you."

"Don't get injured this time." Keeper Liah huffed, annoyance playing across her face.

"I promise I won't get injured," Fenya said.

Keeper Liah turned a glare on her.

Fenya offered a tight smile and a shrug. With a roll of her eyes, the keeper snapped the door shut on her and twisted the lock.

Fenya sighed. Wigmore was more asylum than school.

She turned to her breakfast, eyeing the bread and cheese. She'd save the sausage for Fang—who knew when she had last eaten? But the hard cheese had to be melted to be palatable. But could she manage it? Today, for the first time since being on Wigmore, she felt like trying.

She recalled Henslow teaching Harker and Ivy to wield their Powers.

Henslow had said to them, "Calm yourself with several breaths, steady your center, and breathe out, releasing a tendril of your Power... Feel the aether respond to you, and ask it to obey..."

Could she try?

She eyed her bracelets. She was starving. What did it matter if she made it more palatable?

But, what was stopping her from attempting? Sure, she'd been trying to smash down her Fire for a long time, but with the bracelets, her Power wasn't wild, it was tame, almost comfortable, like a warm blanket.

If she just tried to summon it...just asked it like Henslow had said.

Fenya closed her eyes and focused on the aether. At first, she didn't quite realize where she might pull it from, but remembering Whitland Manor when she had been attached to all the fires by a thin thread, she tried to recall where that thread had ended. It had been somewhere between her heart and her navel, and she focused on that area now.

She closed her eyes and drew on the thread, imagining it thicker than before, building in thickness, and then pulling them down through her arms and out through her fingers, closing her hands over each other and gathering the heat in her palms.

She felt her palms heat and opened her eyes, pulling her hands gently away from one another.

A grin split over her face.

A flame burned merrily in her left palm.

She picked up the bun with cheese inside and considered how best to warm it.

"I wonder," she murmured to the empty room.

When she focused on the flame, it grew. She didn't need a flame of her own to start fire, she knew that now. She was, indeed, a true, controlled Spark.

But could she direct the flame? It took nearly no Power to keep this flame going in her hand—it was like breathing. She could just do it, effortlessly.

She focused on the flame and asking it to move. It obeyed, first flickering high in her palm, then hovering further away from her palm. She grinned.

And then she simply carried the flame to the bread roll, wrapping the flame around the bread until it warmed and infiltrated the cheese.

Victory.

When the cheese had softened and begun to drip over the edge—just the way she liked it—she called the flame back to her palm and closed her fist around it, drawing the thread back inside and asking the aether to sever the connection.

So simple. How could she not have figured it out before?

The bracelets jangled on her wrists as she set about eating the warmed bread and cheese.

Of course. The bracelets withheld or absorbed her Power. It took some of it away, not permanently, but enough so that what escaped, or what she called out, might be controllable. That was how Harker and Ivy had succeeded in the cave. The bracelets were the key to understanding their own Legacies...so why...why was Henslow the only one to help guide them?

A key jangled in the lock and Fenya started, shoving her extra food in her satchel and glancing around to make sure all evidence of her fire was gone.

Keeper Liah swung open the door and motioned her out. "Come on. You're free to go outside."

Fenya leapt up and headed for the door. She needed fresh air.

"Given how prone you are to injury lately though, you're not allowed to leave the courtyard today."

"What?" Fenya's stomach plummeted. "But I...I have to." *Fang must be starving!*

"Too bad," Liah said abruptly. "You can visit the library or the courtyard. So if you want fresh air, I'd recommend the courtyard."

Fenya grit her teeth but there was no value in arguing; Liah was not one to be swayed. Perhaps there would be other students inside today. If Rhys was there, she could beg him to go feed Fang for her.

"Keeper Liah, do you know if Rhys will be out today?"

Keeper Liah paused, curiosity flickering in her dark eyes. "No...he won't."

"Oh." Her hope sank, and she shifted as she felt her stomach growl softly again.

"Why?"

Fenya shook her head. "Oh, I just had a question for him."

"What was it?"

"Nothing important." Fenya smiled and tossed down the last of her water, then returned the cup to the tray. "I'll be in the courtyard, I suppose." Without waiting for Liah to escort her, Fenya grabbed her satchel, which still held her sketchbook, but also the two books Henslow had loaned her, and marched out of her room.

Shafts of light filtered through the windows from the direction of the inner yard. Fenya glanced out a window, spotting a couple of students lingering inside and chatting. Her heart leapt and her stomach flipped to see the blond curls of Dempsey. But as she paused to watch, he waved a goodbye and started toward the gate.

Fenya leaned out of the window. "Dempsey—wait!"

He paused and looked back to Bryton, who had also turned. Then he glanced around further and resumed his walk toward the gate.

"Dempsey!" she called again.

This time, he spotted her. His confusion turned into a heart-stopping smile. He motioned to her with his hand. "Come on down."

Flushing, she grinned back and hurried down the hallway, down the stone steps, through the squeaky gate, and out into the courtyard.

Dempsey was at the bottom when she reached the last step, and she stopped short, catching her breath before smiling up at him. He offered her a bare hand, and she hardly hesitated before taking it. Chills raced up and down her arm as Water touched Fire.

"How are you?" he asked as though they'd known each other for ages.

Her body relaxed at his presence, as though his Water was a calming effect upon her nerves as well as her Fire. "Fine, fine. I just..." She rolled her eyes. "I have to stay inside the courtyard today."

"What?" Dempsey frowned, but offered his elbow to her. "Why?"

"Keeper Liah says I injure myself too often." Fenya accepted his elbow, and with a laugh, he started walking toward the gate. The sun shone from across the square to light their path, with half the stones in darkness and those they walked on bathed in light.

"How are you finding Wigmore since I last spoke with you?" he asked.

Fenya sighed. "Challenging."

He nodded. "Yes, I can see that."

"What...what is between you and Rhys?"

"Ugh." He rolled his eyes. "He thinks because he's titled and important that he gets special treatment. He arrived acting like—"

"Didn't he arrive three years ago? How long have you been here?" Fenya interrupted, ignoring the fact that he was titled. So was her mother. What had that done for either of them?

Dempsey blinked. "Yes, he did. I...I've only been here six months. But long enough to have heard the stories." He scoffed. "You know that it's sad when the keepers are still talking about his arrival years after he came. He nearly killed someone—you know that?"

Fenya bit her lip. "No. He—no one's mentioned that."

"You can't trust him. He'll tell you one thing and mean another. I don't think a true word has ever come out of his mouth."

She tugged at the end of her braid. Had he been lying about what exchanging blood with Fang would do then? Was it possible that she had injured herself in doing what he'd suggested? Why had she trusted him?

Bryton and Acyn were playing a game of marbles across the square, and she watched as Bryton made a spectacular play to capture several of the stones. From outside the marble circle, Remiel watched, his tanned face lit up in entertainment.

Fenya felt a twitch in her stomach, as though the food she had eaten for breakfast hadn't been enough.

"Are you all right?" Dempsey asked.

"Yes. Have you had to endure the leeches since we met?" Fenya asked, trying to regain an easy conversation.

Dempsey frowned, then allowed it to turn into a full grimace. "Ugh. Of course. Every treatment."

"Every time?" Fenya grimaced. "That's awful. It's only been three or four times for me."

"Well, maybe not every time, but it feels like it."

She nodded in understanding. "Absolutely. It takes me a week to forget about how they swell up when they drink my blood, then it's time for them again."

"Their teeth." Dempsey shuddered too, an echo of her own.

They walked past Bryton, Acyn, and Remiel and their marble game in silence, slowing to watch. A stab of hunger that had nothing to do with her own needs churned through her middle. An image of a rocky hiding hole, like where Fang had been, flashed before her eyes.

"Are you all right?" Dempsey's voice lowered in concern, his eyes intense upon her face.

"I..." She paused to put a hand to her forehead, but her cheeks heated at his obvious concern for her welfare. "Yes. But... What do you know about dragons?"

"Dragons?" Dempsey blinked at her in surprise. "I...don't know much, I'm afraid."

"No?"

"Not especially."

"Do you know anything about Familiars?"

His brow furrowed. He looked handsome even when confused. "No. Familiars are rare—I know that. It's impossible to become a

Familiar with anything unless you have the Legacy—Earth and Air both, I think. So it's got to be extremely rare."

Across the square, Bryton crowed in victory. He'd captured the entire set of marbles from Acyn.

"We ain't playin' for keeps!" Acyn complained, holding out a hand for his share of the marbles.

"Why do you ask about Familiars?" Dempsey asked, bringing her attention back to him.

She flipped her braid over her shoulder. "Rhys told me that if you exchanged blood with a dragon, you could become a Familiar with them."

Dempsey blinked. "When did he tell you this?"

"He found me out on the island a few days ago." She shrugged and winced at the movement. A sharp pain had sliced through her shoulder as though she'd been injured there recently. She rubbed it thoughtfully. It had been where Fang had been injured, sort of. If she accounted for no wings, that had been the side of the injured wing.

"Is something wrong?" Dempsey interrupted her thoughts again.

"I... No. But are you allowed out of the yard?" Fenya asked, the hunger pangs twisting desperately at her middle, vying for her attention.

Dempsey shrugged. "Of course. I'm just watching the boys play marbles. It's a bit windy and wet today, and I didn't feel like being blown away."

Fenya nodded, trying to ignore the pain in her stomach. So thirsty. Hadn't she just drank two cups of water? *Wait. I'm not starving because I'm hungry—it's because Fang is starving.*

"Fenya?" Dempsey said.

"I..." She closed her eyes. "Can I trust you?"

"Of course," Dempsey said without pause. "What's wrong?"

"I...have a secret."

His forehead creased. "I'm not sure how that's possible on Wigmore, but all right."

She breathed out slowly. "I...have a dragon. She followed me here."

At that his eyebrows lifted. "That's not what I expected."

"I was out the other day and found her, and she's injured. But I think she's got to be starving by now. Can you feed her for me? Liah refused to allow me out of the courtyard today."

"I..." He gave a comical tilt of his head with a confused expression. "I suppose I could. Do you have food for her or am I expected to snitch from the kitchens?"

"We have kitchens here?" she bantered.

"Of course we do." Dempsey grinned. "And storerooms. With a lot of food. We only get food delivered every six months or so."

She shrugged. "Well, then, if you have access to the storerooms, I think Fang would appreciate more food than I can offer from my breakfast scraps."

His eyes glinted in interest. "Absolutely. How big is this dragon?"

"About the size of a large cat. And she likes mutton jerky."

"Perfect. We've got a lot of dried mutton around here." He nodded to confirm. "Where is she? So I can bring her food?"

"She's tucked into a rock cluster on the cliffs. There's a large rock big enough to sit on and overlook the lighthouse. But that cluster of rocks—"

"I know it," Dempsey interrupted. "I'll find her."

The band around Fenya's chest loosened in relief. "Thank you. Tell her I sent you."

With a quizzical tilt to his head, he paused at a door near the corner to the left of the gates and glanced around. "This would be one of the storerooms."

"It is?" Fenya looked over her shoulder toward the keepers, but they were talking to each other and paying no mind to the students.

"If you just wait here, I'll be right back," Dempsey said. And within moments, he'd slipped inside the door and shut it behind him.

With him disappeared into the room, Fenya turned around, leaned against the wall and crossed her arms like she was watching Bryton and Acyn play their marble game.

Five minutes later, Dempsey cracked open the door, peeked out, and finding it clear of keepers, emerged with a grin.

"I'm good," he said as he started walking around the square again, his pockets laden with bulges that hadn't been there before. "So I'll take this to the dragon then?"

"Yes, please."

"And hope she doesn't attack me?"

Fenya smiled. "She won't. Just leave it outside the rocks. She'll be there." Fenya wasn't sure how she knew, but she knew. And somehow, the moment Fang received the food, Fenya knew that too. There was a strange little leap in her heart, first of mistrust, then as if Dempsey was able to somehow communicate with Fang, a pique of interest, and then joy and fullness. Fang was well cared for.

Chapter Twenty

BLOODLETTING

"Can I go out today?" Fenya asked as Liah checked her bracelets on her next healthy day. She'd endured a brutal session of leeches and injections, replaced bracelets, two separate injections, and day throwing up in a bucket two days prior.

She itched to return to the island, exploring its crevices with Fang. Dempsey had returned from his trip to Fang, and the hunger pains had lessened since then. Indeed, Fenya felt healthier than she had since arriving at Wigmore. Except for the morning following the last treatment—then she had felt ten times worse, but she'd recovered more quickly, and had felt almost normal by the afternoon.

Keeper Liah frowned and motioned her out of the room but pointed her to the opposite direction of the stairs. "Not today. There aren't enough keepers to keep an eye on you."

"But I'd like to get some fresh air." Fenya glanced out the window overlooking the square below. "It's been days since I've been allowed outside of the square."

Liah shrugged from behind her. "Not today. Besides, you've been injured the last time we let you out of the castle."

Fenya grimaced, but she pointed down at her floor. "I was injured in here too."

"Worse outside. I don't know what you got into, but that slice on your hand was ugly. Still is." Liah scowled at it as though the scar personally mocked her.

Fenya gaze shifted in the direction of the lighthouse, where she suspected Fang still stayed, and Fenya winced like Fang felt the chastisement too. "Well, that was an accident."

"We'd rather you not have those sorts of accidents. Especially if you want to learn to control yourself."

Liah gestured ahead to the treatment room.

Fenya groaned in awful anticipation of upcoming treatment. "This is supposed to be my healthy day!"

Liah shot her a confused look. "Your what?"

Fenya flushed. "My healthy day...the day after a recovery day, after a treatment day."

Liah's brows climbed, but she guided Fenya to a wooden chair that extended backward into a reclining bench with armrests that could be positioned outward to keep her arms in place for a bleeding.

Fenya's shoulders sank as her stomach curled in on itself.

"Well don't get used to that routine," Liah warned. "You've been here two months now, and it's time to increase your treatment."

"Increase? Is that why I was so ill after the last one?" Fenya seated herself as properly as though she'd had the chair pulled out by a gentleman at a ball. Her treatments had never made her vomit before, but a morning of violent nausea and vomiting had relegated her to bed until it passed.

"Yes. The injections might have upset your system." Liah reached for her wrist and held her fingers over Fenya's pulse. "You seem to be doing just fine. But it's important that I don't step in and heal you during those reactions. The side effects are unfortunate but necessary for the injections to work properly."

"And what is the injection supposed to do?" Fenya shifted on the uncushioned wooden chair. At least it wasn't her bed—already it was lumpy and the bedbug population was growing alarmingly large. She felt an irrational urge race back to her room and set fire to it as Liah dropped her wrist with a satisfied twitch of her lips.

"Prepare you for your next level of treatments."

"Which do what?" Fenya demanded, a hint of frustration leaking into her voice.

Liah picked up the leather strap around the armrest and fastened them around her wrist one at a time.

Fenya couldn't help but break out in a cold sweat as the bloodletting bowl was rolled toward her on the tea cart. Why couldn't tea carts just hold tea? *I will forever hear a rattling tea cart and think of blood after Wigmore. If there is an after.*

Footsteps in the hall distracted Fenya just enough as Liah made the first cut, and Keeper Henslow and Headmistress Wyn walked in together, talking in low voices.

Liah said without looking, "I've got her prepped. Making the second cut now."

"Why?" Tears stung Fenya's eyes, and she gave Henslow a desperate look. Couldn't he do something? "Why do you need to take more blood? Can't it be hair or something?"

Liah scowled at her.

"Do you need anything else?" Keeper Henslow asked. "There are two sets of bracelets in the box, as the headmaster instructed."

Fenya craned her neck, trying to see the cart and what it held. "Why do I need two sets today?"

"You don't need to concern yourself," Liah snapped. "Sit there and bleed. That's all you need to do. Keep your mouth shut."

"But—" Fenya darted a glance to Henslow, but he didn't meet her eyes, pulling his notebook out of his jacket pocket.

"Don't make Keeper Liah have to silence you," the headmistress said firmly.

Fenya pressed her lips together. It was clear that either Henslow was unable to stop whatever was happening or that he reveled in it. Since he'd given her the books, she had never been alone with him to ask about their contents, and he had not requested them back. So she sat with her head bowed, losing her battle with her tears as they dripped down her cheeks into her lap while her strength to fight slowly faded.

After three small bowls filled with her blood, Keeper Liah wheeled her back to her room on the bench and Liah and Henslow moved her to her bed, where she spent the next few hours and overnight recovering. She was brought out again in the morning, placed in a wheelchair that Liah wheeled back to the treatment room. Coldness pierced her heart, and her stomach clenched into knots. Liah hadn't bothered to heal her cuts yesterday, which were raw and angry now.

On the third day, when the same thing happened, Fenya broke down and wept openly. "How many days do I have to do this?"

Liah's expression didn't waver as she made fresh slices across Fenya's arms and positioned the bowl under her dripping blood. Henslow, however, wouldn't meet her eyes as he fixed her wrists with a pair of double-thick bracelets, using droplets of blood from her arm to activate them as he always did.

"You might be ready for the next treatment by the end of the week," Henslow finally murmured.

Fenya tilted her head back and let the tears chase each other down her face. Maybe they would move the keepers if nothing else would.

"I am sorry to distress you," he said as he packed up the old bracelets, nestling them into their velvet cushions. "It's all with the intention of giving you the Legacy you wish for—one you might command."

She rolled her head to the side to look at him. "I don't want any Legacy at all if it causes this much pain. I just want to go home and marry some Ordinary man and...and...and have a family and live my life."

Even as she spoke, Fenya wasn't sure if anything she said was true anymore. With control, she would keep her Legacy. And maybe it meant not marrying Milton—if control gave her a choice. But could it? If she kept her Legacy, he would want her for the Relic. If she didn't... he wouldn't want her at all, would he? She frowned.

Henslow nodded, separate from her thoughts and reassuring her voiced desire to have a family and live a normal life. "I know. And we'll get you there. I promise."

Liah shot him a look but kept silent as she checked Fenya's straps. When Henslow stepped outside, she followed and said in a voice just loud enough for Fenya to hear. "Don't make her promises you know you can't keep, Henslow. She very well might not make it through the Conveyance."

"Hush. I trust my science—do you trust yours?" Henslow's voice had an iron tone to it that Fenya hadn't heard before.

Liah scoffed. "Of course."

"Then return to your patient and do your job. That's to keep her alive, in case you've forgotten." His shoulder flitted half into the doorway as he spoke. "The headmaster sent word that his patron will be here for it. You should be prepared to defend your choices—including those scars on her arms."

Liah inhaled sharply, but Henslow walked off with dull, quick footsteps before she mustered a response.

Day four was the same, except that Fenya suffered through another injection and spent the entire night with her body on fire from within. Day five, Liah chose the leeches to attack Fenya with, and though it left her feeling better physically, as the leeches took less blood than the bowls, the two injections that followed made Fenya's muscles explode in pain over the night. By day six, Fenya couldn't walk on her own and had bruises under her eyes and up and down her arms, but day seven gave her a reprieve from shots, instead Henslow handed her a large cup filled with a glittering, bright blue potion. She blinked at it, wondering if she should muster the strength to ask questions or resist, but the sorrow in Henslow's eyes told her that he wouldn't be able to answer anything—even if he were permitted.

So she swallowed it as fast as she could and was returned to her rooms after a single blood draw from Liah's needle. What did they do with all her blood? They couldn't need so much for potions.

Liah checked on her throughout the day and night, so that her eyes were rimmed by circles as dark as the ones under Fenya's own eyes. Henslow also suffered, his bright eyes darkening over the week as he attended to her when Liah was not. She heard footsteps of the others students throughout the days, and the keeper's footsteps at night. When she was in the treatment room, Liah and Henslow kept flitting between the stairs that climbed up to the next floor and Fenya's room. Were they treating someone else this same way? Who?

On day eight, Fenya woke to Keepers Liah and Henslow in her room with the wheelchair.

The numbness of inevitability washed over her. Fenya didn't have the strength to cry anymore. She allowed them to move her to the wheelchair, each movement racking her body with pain. It was as though she had run around the island a dozen times and fallen in a few holes along the way. Her every muscle hurt, her head hurt, and she just wanted to sleep, but even that wasn't painless anymore.

"Another potion for you, Miss Fenya," Henslow said, handing her a lemon-colored potion this time. "It should take away some of the symptoms you're feeling right now."

She tried to lift her hand for it and failed to grasp it. Everything was too heavy.

Henslow lifted the cup to her lips and tilted it slowly, helping her drink.

True to his word, the potion dulled her pain and gave her some alertness, while also making her aware of exactly how tired and drowsy she was.

"She's ready," Henslow said softly, taking away the cup and dabbing Fenya's mouth with a napkin.

"Please," Fenya tried to whisper.

The only indication that she'd made any success was the barest flinch of agony across Henslow's face.

Henslow wheeled the chair out of her room and toward the treatment room. This time, instead of strapping her into the expandable chair, he wheeled her toward a corner of the room that she'd never paid much attention to before. But there was a wooden platform built into the wall, and heavy ropes and circular pulleys above with a crank to turn.

"I'll take her down," Liah said. "You can take the stairs."

Henslow nodded, pushing Fenya onto the platform and then stepping off so Liah could join her. "I'll crank you down." His voice still held a sorrow that seemed at odds with their goals to heal her.

The more he spoke, the worse her stomach clenched. But with the potion pulsing through her body, she felt like even if she wanted to stop something, or speak up and ask for it to stop, she couldn't. There was nothing she could do—she was as good as alone on Wigmore Island.

But she wasn't going to let them control her. If this treatment, whatever it was, didn't work, she was going to get out of here. She was going to find her control and get off Wigmore as soon as she could. She wouldn't let them be her control any longer. Fang depended on her now.

An iron grate rattled behind her chair, and Fenya half turned to see it click closed behind her. There was a moment's pause, then the floor began to lower. She sucked in a breath and tensed, but didn't have enough energy to do anything more as the floor sank beneath her chair.

A full minute later, it rattled to a stop, and Liah turned around to pull open the iron gate. She wrestled with it, forcing it back against the side of the doorway, then dragged Fenya's chair out. "Saints and scales, this foolish lift," she muttered.

Blearily, Fenya blinked at the unfamiliar room before her. The walls and room were empty except for two stretchers and a screen between them, as well as a square, wooden machine at the end of the screen.

Keeper Liah bustled her toward the empty stretcher. Feet poked out from behind the screen, feet that belonged to someone. A boy, she thought, based on his trousers. A hand peeked out from behind the screen, a hand with a birthmark that covered the pad between his thumb and pointer finger. *Bryton.*

She tried to form questions on her tongue, but it refused to obey. She squeezed her eyes shut, and then pried them open.

Keeper Liah bustled around the room, disappearing behind the screen, and adjusting items on the tray between the stretchers.

Fenya wished she could rise and walk away. She wanted to stand and walk out of this dark room with its aether lanterns. Or were they true fire? She couldn't tell anymore... They were dim lights illuminating a portion of the room to her now. Emptiness overwhelmed her mind. A sense of disconnect trickled through her veins, as if she were no longer tethered to the reality of life.

The door across the room from her opened, and Fenya squinted as a light illuminated Henslow from behind. His shoulder-length blond hair frizzed out around the edges, creating a halo effect. She blinked at him, unable to read his expression.

The next few things happened in a blur. With Henslow's help, Fenya was transported to the empty slab and strapped down. She remembered moaning a few times, but couldn't do anything as simple as raising her hand or lifting a finger.

Other people appeared in the room. Headmistress Wyn and someone—a man—she'd never seen before with an ethereal quality to him. An angel?

Keeper Liah poked her in the arm with a large needle and attached a wide tube to the needle she'd left behind in her arm. The machine between the screens began whirring. The last thing Fenya remembered thinking was that the extra man in the room must have been the elusive headmaster she'd heard about.

Then pain of such magnitude coursed through her that her body writhed in agony. The pressure built in her brain, and then blackness swallowed her, darker than the Aether Sea itself.

Chapter Twenty-One

CHANGED

Fenya lost track of time. She was in her room, her lumpy, uncomfortable bed. Bedbugs nipped at her ankles. Her dreams, when she had them, were of Fang flying over the cliffs and past the lighthouse. Her wings were strong and supple, shifting to bring her from the roof of the lighthouse over the sea, skimming down over the seawater to scoop a fish out of the surf.

Yet when Fenya's eyes finally opened, and she blinked the room into focus, she felt a surge of victory that she woke at all.

A turn of her head revealed her door wide open, with light streaming through from the inner square's windows to brighten her room and a glaring rectangle of sun that illuminated every mote of dust on her floor including the air above.

She blinked in annoyance. Her head throbbed like a pegasus had sat on top of it, and her eyes scratched as if a dragon had dripped venom in them.

A chirrup sounded from outside her window. Fang? She turned her head, but the window showed only blue skies spotted with clouds.

She wet her cracked, dry lips. *How long have I been asleep? No—unconscious. What did they do to me?*

A deep longing arose within her, yet separate from her, as if a fragment of her very soul was outside the castle. Her mind went again to

Fang. Where was she? Was she all right? Still alive? Rhys had said exchanging blood with her would kill Fenya if the dragon died. So that meant Fenya had almost killed her in return. Her eyes stung, but her body felt too shriveled to cry.

Trying to lift herself from bed, she groaned at the needles of pain stabbing her body. She was too thirsty to lie still though.

"Ah, you're awake," Keeper Liah's voice sounded like she spoke through a long tunnel.

Fenya blinked scratchy eyes at the keeper.

"How are you feeling?"

"Rotten," Fenya managed through dry lips and what felt like an even drier tongue. "Thirsty."

"Naturally. You've been asleep two days."

Fenya squinted at her. "Water?" she managed.

As Keeper Liah ambled across the room, Fenya managed to roll to her side, drag her feet off the bed, and push herself into a sitting position. Liah took hold of Fenya's wrist, her fingers groping for her pulse, and raised Fenya's bracelet almost to the end of her pudgy nose. What she saw seemed to please her, for she smiled before managing to suppress it.

Fenya shifted, and another involuntary groan escaped her lips. "Water?" she prompted.

"Mmm, right," Liah answered, the smile still playing on her lips.

Her body was weak, but something about sitting upright made her feel more controlled, more able, more alive. She had a strange sensation of drifting through the air, kept aloft by the aether around her.

Liah brought her a cup of water, holding it to Fenya's lips with a hint of curious disdain in the crease of her brow. "Drink up."

Fenya did, swallowing the entire cup of water and asking for more. As Liah returned to the pitcher to comply, Fenya asked, "Why can't you heal me from all this pain?"

"I could," Liah answered with her back turned still to Fenya. She lifted the pitcher and water gurgled out into the cup.

"Why don't you then?" Her eyes locked on the water. Every molecule of the water had absorbed into her mouth, leaving her just as dry as before.

Liah glanced back over her shoulder as she replaced the pitcher. "I've been instructed not to."

"Was that extra man...there...during my treatment...was that the headmaster?"

Facing her, Liah paused, the water cup held in her hand with concern crafting a line down between her brows. "I...didn't know you still were conscious when he walked in."

"I remember being strapped to the table. I remember the needle. The tubing." Fenya wet her lips, wishing Liah would just bring her the water. "And..."

"And?" Liah prompted when Fenya didn't continue.

"Bryton. Groaning. Screams." She shivered at the memory.

Liah handed Fenya the cup, and she took it with trembling fingers, raised it to her lips, closed her eyes and swallowed the cup's contents in two gulps. Liah watched her, then as Fenya showed no sign of leaving any behind, turned and picked up the water pitcher and held it ready to refill the cup again.

Fenya met her gaze as she poured more water into the cup.

"I'm glad you're healing," Liah said with unexpected warmth. "I'll return later with some food to see if you can keep it down."

"That's it?" The words burst from Fenya's mouth without permission.

Liah half turned in the doorway, her hand already on the handle to pull it shut behind her. "That's it," she confirmed coldly.

As the door shut and the lock clicked behind Liah, Fire crackled within her. But without any energy, and thirst abated, she lay down on her lumpy, bedbug-infested matress and fell asleep again.

When she woke, it was to see Liah drop off food as though in a dream. She rolled over and returned to sleep, uninterested in the food, for sleep sounded more appealing. But when she woke the next time, her stomach was turning in on itself and growling angry mewls of hunger.

She sat up, her head surprisingly clear, her body hydrated.

"Ah, Miss Fenya," came a voice from the corner of her room.

She jolted in surprise, not only at the presence of another, but of the voice being male. "Keeper Henslow," she murmured. "How long have you been there?"

He smiled kindly. "It's my shift. Keeper Liah was concerned when you didn't eat your breakfast." He motioned to the tea cart holding a teapot, and a plate covered by a silver dome.

"Oh, I...I was still tired."

He rose and pushed the cart toward her. "I'd encourage you to eat now."

"Thank you." She reached for the napkin on the tray.

"Are you feeling better then?" His tone was one of genuine interest, as opposed to Liah's superficial self-interest.

"Yes, I think so." She lifted the dome off the plate and saw a generous spread of rye bread, crackers, sausage, and the typical hard sheep's cheese, but also a pat of butter and what looked like a soft cheese with rind. "I guess extra treatments earn extra food."

Henslow's face flinched at her words but smooth the action with a smile. "I think, given your lack of food intake over the last two days, you might proceed slowly. But if your stomach feels up to it, I would encourage you to eat it all."

Fenya nodded and reached for the knife, cutting off a slice of butter and smearing it on the first roll, devouring it like Fang might, hardly tasting it.

Henslow reclaimed his chair in the corner of her room, watching her politely from a distance. After a moment, he picked up what looked like one of his journals from the desk beside him.

"What were the books you left me?" she asked, her curiosity taking advantage of the opportunity.

He raised an eyebrow at her over his journal. "Merely history books from the library. Did you find them interesting?"

She examined him for a moment. *Can he not speak freely? Should I not speak freely?* "I did," she said slowly. "Fascinating."

"Good. I'll bring some more next time then." Henslow returned to his journal.

She resumed her meal, chewing the tasteless food one bite at a time. "So am I cured now?" Fenya ventured after finishing the second half of the first roll.

"Cured?" He looked up from his reading.

"My...Sir Milton said I would be cured here. Wasn't that treatment intended to cure me?"

A shadow of fear passed over Henslow's face. "I don't understand."

Something cold settled in Fenya's stomach. She set down the knife on the edge of her ceramic plate and focused on Henslow. "My fiancé said that I would be cured coming here. That my Legacy would be removed, and I wouldn't suffer from it anymore."

Henslow's face was almost unreadable this time, but his eyes swirled mysteriously.

Fenya swallowed the lump in her throat. "I *am* going to be cured... right?"

He inhaled slowly and deliberately, holding his place in his journal with his thumb as he leaned forward and replied softly, "We can't make promises like that here, Miss Fenya. But I assure you that we will do our best to give you what you need."

Fenya sat immobile, trying to calm her panic. "But he promised," she managed.

"And perhaps we can," Henslow said. He set his journal down on top of a stack of the books on the desk. "And while you continue your recovery, I suggest you read up on Legacies and living with one. Miss Fenya, though the others might not know here, and I don't recommend you tell them, you are a Relic Heir. There is additional responsibility in being a Relic Heir that you may not understand. And which you must be equipped to deal with."

Without expanding on his words, he rose and left the room. But silently, at the door, he held a finger to his lips and pointed to the stack of books he'd left behind.

Fenya looked at it, seeing amidst the stack of books with clear titles on the spine, one of Henslow's journals. She frowned at it, but when she turned back to Henslow, he had slipped from the room and the lock turned in the key.

He had requested her silence before pointing to it. Was he trying to pass her a message? To not tell anyone?

She finished her sausage in two final bites, then toddled on still-shaky legs across the room to the books. Contemplating a moment, throwing a gaze at the door, she grabbed the entire stack of four books. Their weight was almost too much for her arms, and she deposited them a little more roughly than intended at the foot of her lumpy mattress. A few bedbugs flew into the air and back down.

Out of the stack slipped a sheet of paper, something that certainly hadn't been there before. Scrawled on top of the page was her name. She sank down beside the books and opened the paper.

Dear Miss Fenya,

I wish I could tell you more about this process, but I ask only that you trust me. You might experience some awful things here at Wigmore, while I deeply hope and pray that you do not. Know that I am trying to protect you, and I, like you, have your best interests at heart. Please do not despair, but know that you can trust me.

Read these books, take note of how to control your Legacy, and practice. Practice control whenever you can. You must not delay in learning to control yourself. Practice your Fire within the cave, standing in water, with or without your bracelets, and you shall find yourself rapidly able to control your flames. Trust yourself. Allow the flames to become a part of you and stop fighting them. Through fighting your Legacy, you create instability inside yourself. Denying your flames will only deny a large part of yourself, and eventually it will break free from your chains. Even your bracelets, which I crafted, will not stop your Fire forever.

H.W.

P.S. Do not speak of this aloud.

A frown creasing her forehead, Fenya turned to the other books, picking through them and finding the journal. Why couldn't she speak of it, at least in private to him? The only explanation was that there was some sort of monitoring in place. Perhaps an Exaudio, a Legacist who could hear at great distances through walls and even stone walls like that of her chambers. She'd heard that some Powerful Exaudio magi could even hear whispered conversations miles away.

Who though? Asper? Liah—no, she was a Healer of some strength. The headmistress? It had to be. She had yet to show any other Legacy.

She opened the journal and pulled it onto her lap, her mind still racing in thoughts.

If there was an Exaudio, then any further conversation she had about secrets going on here at Wigmore would have to be in writing and destroyed afterward. Or else with a very noisy background. Like the ocean with its waves and wind. Was that why Henslow had taught the others within the cave near the lighthouse? To make it harder to overhear?

Fenya turned her attention to the words on the page. She'd opened it to the middle, hoping to find some sort of in-depth explanation of what he'd written without any preamble, but nothing made sense—it was written in sort of code.

With a small pounding beginning in her left temple, she flipped to the beginning of the book and shifted the page toward the fading light streaming through her barred window.

Patient A (RC) D1: arrived w/uncontrolled FE; never reported before in a 14yo. In fireproof room for all's safety. Vials: B x 5 H & S x1

T1: B Potion.

PA D2: no apparent effect.

As much as Fenya could determine based on dates and her knowledge of the so-called students at Wigmore, "RC" had to be Rhys de Croia. Alongside the date, which was just over two years before, it was the only name of a Fire Elemental student here that made sense. B had to be blood, but what did H and S mean? And could B Potion mean a potion made from Rhys's blood?

It made sense, as mage blood contained the qualities and Power of the Legacist. So did other parts of a mage's body, like hair or saliva. She paused. H and S. Hair and saliva.

A Potioneer could make something out of that blood or hair and temporarily give the drinker some of the Power of another mage.

They had said they were taking her blood samples and distilling it down or transforming it some way into a potion that went into her syringe...and somehow muted her Powers—if that was even possible. But still, why did they need so much of her blood? Simply for the few potions she drank? Or were they doing something else, something nefarious with the rest of it?

Fenya scanned pages of similar treatments that made little sense to her, including a page listing what appeared to be ingredients for a potion including Rhys's blood. But she was no Potioneer, and she couldn't pretend to understand the notes. There had to be some reason that a mage would prefer blood to craft a potion. The pages after gave brief discussion to its effect on Rhys, but it mentioned very little about his Power. Instead, it mentioned something called Transference and Conveyance. Something about those words seemed familiar...but she couldn't remember.

Fenya squinted at the pages and sat up a moment to wipe at her scratchy eyes. With a glance at the window, Fenya found that the sun had slipped down toward the sea, and night was crowding the castle. No wonder it was growing harder to read.

She made it through only a few more pages before the sun sank too much for Fenya to read any longer. The moon had risen behind clouds, and she was stuck without a light to read by. Given her exhaustion, she didn't want to attempt to summon a flame to read by.

She tucked the other books into a pile at the foot of her bed and positioned herself to where the moonlight might fall if the clouds shifted. A soft, diffused light reached her, and though she squinted desperately at the journal in the darkness, she couldn't read the penciled words.

As she waited for the moonlight to strengthen, a gentle glow gave just enough light to see the objects in her room and make out that there was writing upon the pages of Henslow's journal but not enough for her to decipher individual letters or words.

She tried for another ten minutes, but finally surrendered to the darkness. She shifted in bed and stared at the window, which she could just out of from her position on the bed.

Blinking tiredly at the shard of moon, Fenya jolted as the familiar shape of a dragon in flight swooped across the night sky. Accompanying it was warm feeling of something like home.

Fang.

She sat up straight in bed.

The dragon swooped and dove, and Fenya smiled to see a slight red glow to her scales. Was that her Fire? Was it possible that the little wyvern had absorbed some of Fenya's Legacy in their blood exchange?

Fenya stood from her bed and one of the books slipped, falling toward her bare toe. She cursed before it hit, imagining Liah's angry response if she injured herself. And with a jet of Air, the book, falling straight for her small toe, practically came to a halt before somersaulting over toward the bedpost and skidding underneath the bed.

What on earth?

Fenya's heart stuttered. As it did, the dragon slid silently through the air toward Fenya's window with a little cry.

Fenya reached a hand out of the window toward her.

Fang's soft answer came this time not to her ears, but to her mind.

You're different, she sang.

Fenya gasped. "So are you," she whispered.

Your blood is different, Fang's voice answered inside Fenya's head. *It's given me my flight back.*

Fenya opened her eyes, seeking out the red form in the sky, only to find that she was inches from her. Fenya sucked in a breath and held it, but this time, it wasn't to control her Legacy, it was to gather her courage. She reached out a hand for the wyvern resting on the windowsill, and brushed a finger down the dragon's chest.

Fang shuddered under her touch. Fenya's finger burned, then a gust of air swept it away.

Fang chirruped in surprise, then as clear as day, Fenya heard her voice inside her mind.

You've gained Air, my friend.

What are you talking about? Fenya didn't bother to speak this time, except in her mind.

You are no longer just a Flame and a Dragon Speaker, you are also an Air.
What madness is this?

Fenya pulled away. *Dragon Speaker?*

It's how you could speak with me.

But...I couldn't.

You understood—and that was enough to bond. But you have gained some-thing in your blood, something that wasn't there when we became sisters.

Fenya's breath shuddered. *I don't understand.*

You have changed, is all Fang would say.

But how?

You will learn. But I think we must leave here as soon as we can. Fang ruffled her wings and turned, preparing herself to leap off the ledge. *You are not safe here. And if you are not, then I am not.*

They're...helping me.

No, they aren't, Fang answered. She spread her wings and leapt from the sill. *They are going to kill you...or else make you into a monster.*

Fenya didn't know what to answer that with, and by the time she finally found something to think in reply, Fang was as distant as the lighthouse and too far to communicate with.

"Quickly, girl, in here," Keeper Liah snapped, motioning Fenya out of her room and marching her up two flights of stairs to the top level of the castle.

"Why are we going up here?" she asked, but Liah didn't answer. It had been another two days since she had woken and begun her recovery. Two days since seeing Fang, but every day Fang communicated with her, usually right before the moon emerged. Fenya had taken to watching out her window all day until evening, and so she'd spotted almost all of the other students walking along the cliff, each distinctive by their hair, height, and sometimes the company they kept. Everyone else was allowed out.

Almost. For Bryton had been absent. Was he confined to his rooms like Fenya had been? Alone and healing? Had he taken some of her Fire as she had taken some of his Air?

A cold hand brushed her neck at the thought.

It is unnatural *what they are doing...isn't it? Like Fang said...they'll either kill me or make me into a monster. Perhaps both.*

"Come on, girl," Liah said sharply. She pointed Fenya to a room she hadn't been in before. "We've got to get a blood draw on you."

"Another?" The cold hand tightened, but Fenya forced herself into the treatment room. A small, distressed table perched in one corner.

Several journals, books, and a small stack of papers sat neatly atop one edge. Nearby them was an inkstand and quill. Tucked alongside the table was the familiar tea cart with its syringes at the ready.

Fenya sighed and took the seat near the cart. In a few minutes, the vial was full of her blood, and she scowled at it in annoyance. "Too bad you can't just leave the needle in there or something."

Liah grinned wickedly. "You don't like my creation?"

Fenya blinked. "Your creation? You made these syringes?"

"Of course. You think they'd work without a Healer's touch?"

Fenya stared at them. "I didn't give it much thought, honestly."

At Fenya's words, Liah sniffed and ripped the tourniquet off Fenya's arm so quickly that it pinched more than the injection itself. Fenya inhaled sharply but refused to give Liah the pleasure of her discomfort. Instead, she held the white cloth against her arm until the bleeding stopped, then rose to return to her rooms. But when she stepped out into the hallway and turned toward the stairs to her room, Liah stopped her.

"Wait a moment."

Fenya paused and glanced back at the keeper. "Pardon me?"

"Head to the staff lounge. You've got a visitor."

"Staff lounge? Where is that?"

Smirking, Liah tilted her head, and Fenya realized she'd focused on the wrong thing.

"I've got a visitor?" she said. "How—when—" She stopped and breathed deeply. "I didn't know people could have visitors here."

Keeper Liah's face didn't shift, but her eyes glinted, whether in annoyance or amusement, Fenya couldn't tell.

Fenya's skin bristled in irritation. "What is it?"

Keeper Liah's lips quirked. "Aren't you even going to ask who bothers to visit you?"

"It must be..." Fenya trailed off, realizing that Mama probably wouldn't care to visit, while Aunt and Uncle Verena were probably too busy in order to visit. Her stomach clenched at the joy Liah seemed to get from it. "Who is it?"

Keeper Liah's smirk grew. "You'll see."

Fenya bit back a growl. She had been all but tricked into asking and showing interest, but all the time Liah had been provoking her. There was a sadistic twist to Liah that Fenya was becoming all too acquainted with, a joy in finding someone unbalanced or in withholding information that was deeply desired. Fenya grit her teeth and strode in the direction the keeper indicated. At least no matter who visited, she would be able to visit the staff lounge. Perhaps she could steal a book or two for reading in her room. Or a journal. All the better if it held vital information... Her mind turned to Henslow's journals.

But who visited her? *It must be Mama. Perhaps she became concerned at the lack of letters from Fenya and realized the truth about Wigmore. She had come to get her. There isn't anyone else who would care, except Aunt Cali and Uncle Caius.*

Despite Fenya's resolve to remain uninterested and unhopeful, her heart thumped unevenly. She hurried down the hall, barely sparing the churning gray skies and lashing rain a glance out the window as she advanced on the staff lounge.

Her skin tingled as she entered, in almost the same way that it had when Keeper Liah had healed her in the past. Fenya cast a glance over her shoulder at the shorter woman.

"Keep going," she said flatly, though her eyes still sparked in her otherwise implacable expression.

In the hallway, Liah put a hand on Fenya's shoulder. "You'll probably want to be wearing this," she said, reaching toward Fenya's neck and pulling the chain out from beneath her dress.

Fenya inhaled slowly. "My ring?"

"Your *engagement* ring, yes," Liah replied, her eyebrow arched. "Pretty."

"Why?" she whispered, feeling as though Liah were a dragon holding out a bit of her hoard in the hopes that Fenya would fall into her trap.

But Liah's expression remained no more scrutable than an unfamiliar dragon's as Fenya removed her garnet and silver ring from her chain and slipped it onto her finger. It fit quite a bit looser than before.

"Get on inside then," Liah said.

Fenya's shoulders tightened, but she turned and pushed open the door into the staff room.

The well-dressed gentleman with his high, starched collar stuck out like a dragon in a herd of sheep. He rose from a hard wooden seat built along a wall of bookcases, his eyes lighting up at seeing her. "Miss Fenya!"

She hesitated on the threshold. "Sir Milton?"

"Don't act so surprised to see your fiancé!" He laughed as he crossed the room, arms spread as if to embrace her, but at the last moment seemed to realize she did not wish it, and offered a gloved hand instead.

Fenya struggled against her proper breeding that demanded she be polite, but allowed him to press her fingertips with his gloved hand. His eyes sparkled down at the ring on her finger.

Memories of his stealing her Fire returned to her, and she snatched her hand back abruptly. With a startled look, he withdrew his own hand, his head tilting in question. "I brought you a treat," he said, reaching a hand into his pocket and pulling out a small apple she recognized as an Avenesse Crisp. "Fresh from the branch this morning."

She stared at it. "What are you doing here?" she whispered, ignoring the proffered fruit.

"You question your fiancé's desire to visit you?" Liah said with a wry tone from behind her, where the shorter woman acted as though she hid from view to be a pestering voice in Fenya's ear.

Fenya ignored her, cheeks burning, but she held her chin high. "Why are you here, Sir Milton?"

"Why?" Sir Milton straightened and sent her a look of shock that seemed mingled with dismay at her question. "Because I couldn't stand being apart from you, of course."

Fenya's hand crawled from his touch, but she tried to hide her shudder. "You couldn't bear being apart from me? Why didn't you write then?"

Sir Milton put a hand over his heart as though she'd deeply offended him. "Write? And to where would I address it?"

"Is Wigmore not able to receive mail? They've clearly received you." Fenya bit her bottom lip to keep from speaking more.

He grinned and offered his arm, though the room was not large enough to require an escort across. Fenya ignored it. Liah nudged her in the back as though to push her toward it. Instead, Fenya stepped aside, revealing Liah's front to Milton and putting the shorter woman between them. Liah's lips curved into a smirk aimed at Fenya's discomfort.

Sir Milton's smile faltered slightly, and he cleared his throat. "Well, Wigmore doesn't typically receive visitors, no, especially ones like me. I had to work it all out with the headmaster. But, here I am."

Fenya crossed the staff room toward the window. Fully paned with leaded glass and locked against the wind, the window shook as rain lashed against it, just like she wanted to lash against Liah and her twisted desire to provoke Fenya.

"Magess Liah, if you wouldn't mind?" Sir Milton murmured.

"Of course, sir." She bobbed her head in a sort of curtsy and left the room, closing the staff door behind herself.

Fenya stiffened. *She's leaving me alone with him? How improper and defiant!* "Does the headmaster know?"

"Does the headmaster know that I am visiting?" Milton's brow furrowed, and Fenya cursed inwardly to realize she'd spoken aloud. "Of course he does. Nothing happens at Wigmore that he doesn't know about."

Fenya turned her back to the rain against the closed window. She didn't want to be alone with Milton, and she certainly didn't want to turn her back to him.

Fang, where are you? I wish you could be here.

She waited a moment, but an answer didn't come. She was probably too far away, sheltered in the cave or somewhere to avoid the rainstorm.

"How long have you been here?" she settled for asking instead, crossing her arms over her chest in a quite unladylike fashion.

"Just a day or two," he answered evasively.

She raised an eyebrow. "You don't know?"

"It depends on the weather." He smiled a mysterious smile that set Fenya's teeth on edge. "Come, sit, my dear." He patted the couch in the room, a plain but overstuffed leather couch with buttons on the back and the arms.

"Have you spoken to my mother? Do you bring anything from my aunt or uncle?" She didn't know what was wrong with her to push so— she wanted to provoke him though, to get a truthful response from him. Her body shuddered with anger, and her bracelets warmed. Her eyes drifted to them, and the delicate images ignited. Thrown off balance, having never seen them appear in real time before, Fenya couldn't help but stare at them.

"Your mother? No."

Fenya pulled her attention from the bracelets and shifted, sitting down on the window bench and shaking her long sleeves over her silver bracelets. "How is she?"

"Well, I believe."

A burst of wind rattled the window behind her.

"And my aunt and uncle?"

"Quite well. Your aunt is expecting another child, did you know?"

"No." Fenya felt something in her soften. Another cousin for her. A lump threatened in her throat. "Did she write?"

He pressed his thin lips together under his thin mustache. "I'm sorry, Fenya."

"*Miss* Fenya," she corrected with a frown. "I wasn't expecting any news. It doesn't make it any different that you're here to tell it."

"If it makes you feel better, I didn't know I would be visiting until two days ago."

"Why not?"

"The headmaster was concerned for your health. He thought it might be wise if I could come and evaluate you."

"You? Why couldn't he?"

He shrugged evasively. "We all have different strengths, my dear."

"Don't call me that," she said in annoyance. "I'm not yours yet. And you aren't answering anything I ask."

"What do you need to know?" he asked patiently. "I'm here to answer any questions. But first, please, tell me how you've found Wigmore. I'm curious, and I've been quite worried about you."

"It's..." she hesitated, glancing toward the door. "It's awful."

True concern laced his face. "Awful? What do you mean, my dear? I mean, Miss Fenya."

"I'm not...treated well here."

"My dear!" Sir Milton leaned forward, reaching a hand for her.

Fenya hesitated, but didn't draw closer. "You told me that this place would take my Fire away, Sir Milton." She allowed her pain to show on her face, allowing the tears to coat her eyes and fixing her watery gaze on her fiancé.

He pulled back his hand to place it over his heart. "I understand how difficult this must be. I know the headmaster is doing his best to heal you—to help you. Much more than your future depends on it."

More than my future? Fenya's mind raced. What was more important to one of the adults here than the students and their Legacies? The books and journals Henslow had given her jumped to the front of her mind. *It must be his journals, his project...his wife.* Fenya tried to keep her frustration and understanding from showing her face. "I've only seen the headmaster once."

"Yes, right before your major treatment, right?"

Fenya blinked. *What does Sir Milton truly know? Why is he here right now...right after my "major treatment"?*

"He's overseeing everything that's going on at Wigmore, I assure you. But he is unable to be here frequently. It's why I'm here now."

"Are you paying for this school, Sir Milton?" Fenya held her breath, wondering if he would take offense to the question.

But a proud smile lit up Milton's face. "I am not solely financing this school, Fenya, but I am a major patron, including yours."

Fenya raised a hand to her mouth. She had to keep him talking, have him confide in her, think that she agreed with whatever they were doing here. "Then you must know its future, right? And it's past. It seems a rich past full of scientific discoveries."

He beamed. "Of course. It's clear that the search for a Perfect Mage has been going on for centuries—once the first king divided his Powers and created Relic Bearers, problems ensued." Milton shook his head, a storm cloud of annoyance on his features.

Frowning, Fenya tried to follow his thoughts. *Perfect Mage? Only the First King was a complete mage, and there's no returning the relics to one joined item.*

"You know the King divided his Power into the four elements, one of which was Fire." Sir Milton motioned to Fenya. "Your ancestors were close friends and noblemen of the King's retinue."

"Yes, I'm aware," Fenya said. "But go on. I haven't heard of the Perfect Mage."

He looked shocked at his own words, as though he had been too free with them.

Fenya feigned innocence. Even if he coated his words with lies, he was telling her more than she'd learned since being at Wigmore. "What is a Perfect Mage?"

"You don't know? It's a myth," Sir Milton hurried to add, but his easy smile returned. "A myth that many people have spent their lives chasing. A silly myth, to be honest." He scoffed. "To think that people believe the relics can be rejoined."

Fenya filed away the information for another time. Perhaps to ask Henslow about. "But what does all that have to do with Wigmore? I don't understand why that myth should matter to anyone here..." She tried to inject her tone with innocent confusion.

Milton thought for a moment. "I thought it was quite obvious. You're a Flame, Miss Fenya. And a Relic Heir. Your responsibility as an Heir is critical to the treatments you receive."

A pulse of fear thrummed through Fenya's throat. "Why should they be?"

"Haven't you ever wondered at the consequence of taking away your Fire?"

She shrugged. "Of course. But I think it would be better for everyone if I lacked the ability to accidentally kill them."

Blinking in surprise, Sir Milton released a slow chuckle. He leaned forward and poured himself a cup of tea from a teapot Fenya hadn't noticed.

The tea was barely warm. She squinted at it. She felt the heat as though it still bore a connection to the flame that had warmed it. She pushed away the thought. There were fires here, including one in the staff room itself right now, a mere dozen feet away, but she still had the ability, despite her bracelets and her recent treatment, to feel the gentle remnants of fire on the tea. She eyed the teapot mistrustfully. *How strange.*

"I don't think you're truly in danger of killing anyone, Miss Fenya," he said, looking at her over his teacup.

Fenya picked at her thumbnail. "You realize the reason I'm here is because I almost killed people at Whitland?"

He tilted his head to the side in acknowledgment. "I presume you've grown since then. Matured."

Fenya pressed her lips together. "I don't think it's about maturity of mind, Sir Milton. It's about maturity of Legacy, and that remains a struggle."

"Give it some time. Trust the process, Miss Fenya." He sipped his tea. "Do you mind...if I test your Legacy?"

She inhaled sharply. "I..." She pressed her lips together. "I'm surprised you asked this time."

For a fraction of a blink, he appeared stunned, as if she had struck him, then a smile spread over his face. "I'm impressed you noticed."

"I...fainted." She frowned at him.

"Did you?" Honest surprise coated his words.

"Yes."

"So may I test you again? We'll see if you have the same response."

He can't be serious? "No, thank you," Fenya said, half expecting him to retract his request and demand that he be allowed to test her.

"Ah." His brow furrowed in disconcertion. "Ah, well, then. Um." He seemed surprisingly thrown by her response, but she didn't speak to smooth his recovery, and he pulled at his high collar as he considered his next words. "I brought you something."

"Did you?" Fenya crossed her arms, leaning back against the cool stone of the window seat.

"Indeed. Something that's been causing some problems for your mother since you turned eighteen."

Fenya blinked at him. "I... What day is it?"

A smile quirked his mouth. "Did you not celebrate?"

"No." Fenya shook her head, a strange awkwardness washing over her. "I'm eighteen?"

"Yes, as of three weeks ago."

"Oh." Fenya rubbed at a spot on her neck uncomfortably. How had she not realized? She hadn't even been considering when she might turn eighteen, she had been so distracted with the unpleasantness of being here.

"Happy birthday," he said, pulling out a small box that fit in the palm of his gloved hand.

"What—" She broke off as the jewelry box thrummed before her with a familiar Fire. Fenya gasped. "Is that the Relic?"

He smiled. "Indeed."

"*My* Relic?" She was halfway across the room before realizing it, drawn by the pulse of the box. It was different somehow. Where before it had housed Power, it had seemed distant.

"Can I...touch it?"

He laughed. "Of course. It's yours."

"But..." she hesitated. "If I wanted to surrender my Power to it...to become Ordinary...how could I? Is it possible?"

His humor faded, and his hand withdrew just enough to be noticeable. "Do you still want that?"

The Relic pulsed from within the box. "I don't know." She met his cool gaze.

"You should see whether it claims you first, Miss Fenya," he murmured, opening the box before her.

She inhaled, her eyes widening. The jewel had been reset. It no longer graced the chain of Papa's pocket watch, but was on a thick golden chain that held the gemstone securely. She had never wanted to possess something more.

"Take it," he said, holding it out to her. "It will look beautiful against your skin. I had it reset like this for you."

She reached out, then drew her hand back. "How does it work?"

"I'm not entirely sure. I've never been a Relic Bearer or an Heir."

"But I can touch it?"

"It's yours."

"I thought I couldn't touch it until twenty-one. Unless to accept my role as Relic Heir."

"You can. And there's a chance it will accept you as its Bearer today, when you touch it, now that you're eighteen."

"Is that why you brought it? To see if it would accept me?" She narrowed her eyes and stopped with her hand outstretched for it.

"No. As I said, it's been causing some problems for your mother."

"What do you mean? How can it?"

"It's got a bit of its own mind, you could say."

"What?"

"Since you left, there have been strange little fiery accidents." His brows rose in something like silent criticism.

"Fiery accidents?"

"Yes." He cleared his throat and continued holding the box on his palm out toward her. "And once you turned eighteen, this little Relic has been causing all sorts of havoc."

"Oh." A slow grin lifted the corners of her mouth.. "I guess it missed me."

"So did I," he said softly, his gaze burning into hers.

She flushed, a frown warring with the smile on her lips.

"Aren't you going to take it? It's crying out for you."

She bit her lip. *What if I do? And what if I don't? Am I ready for either response? Yes. Yes, I am.*

And carefully, she reached out a hand to grasp her Relic, picking up the amber stone between thumb and forefinger.

The touch burned, hotter than she'd ever felt fire burn before. But it also welcomed her, almost in an embrace. The gem glowed so bright she squinted, and Sir Milton raised a hand to shield his gaze.

A tendril of flame emerged from the gemstone, wrapping itself around her hand and traveling up her arm. She beamed. Without doubt, she knew that it accepted her. It claimed her.

Then the flame pulsed. Her skin burned. She gasped.

The flames brightened and burned hot, then more suddenly than they'd appeared, disappeared, leaving her eyes with haloed echoes of light.

As her vision cleared, she inspected her hands. The fire had left behind burn-like marks that wove up her arms, reminding her of flames licking at a log. She turned over her hand not grasping the Relic necklace and watched as the flames faded but didn't disappear.

"Does this mean it's accepted me?" She looked to Sir Milton, hopeful at what message this sent.

Awe made his cold eyes seem warm, or perhaps they'd been lit by the flames and had yet to fade. "I believe it does."

For the first time, a delicate tendril of hope unfurled within Fenya. Hope that she would be a suitable Relic Bearer, that she could learn control, embrace her future. She would make her father, the prior Emberheart Relic Bearer, proud. She might not be such a failure after all.

Then she met Sir Milton's gaze again and recognized the hunger there, his lust for Power, and her hope faded as quickly as it came. Even if she embraced her future as the Emberheart Relic Bearer, as soon as she married Sir Jett Milton, her claim would disappear. And some of her Power would filter into him, to be established into his male line. Would she retain any of it? Or would these flames pass to him too?

Fenya carefully unclasped the necklace and clasped it securely around her neck. She tucked the pendant, hot against her flesh, down the front of her gown. "Thank you. For bringing this. I'd like to go to my rooms now. I'm very tired."

"Of course!" He jumped up, seemingly ready to offer an arm, but she held up a hand. He stepped respectfully back, but led her to the staff lounge door a step ahead. At it, he paused in front of it and turned back to her. "I look forward to our union, Miss Fenya. I've waited a long time for a woman like you."

Fenya couldn't bring herself to look him in the eye. Instead, she curtsied and kept her gaze down, waiting for him to step aside and let her go.

He did, but reluctantly. Fenya lifted her chin and walked sedately down the hallway, past a bemused Liah, down the hall and the stairs, and into the safety of her barred prison of a room, only to be followed by Liah, who silently took out the supplies for yet another sample of her blood.

But when Liah pulled up Fenya's sleeve, an audible gasp left her lips.

"It accepted you?" she breathed, seemingly without thinking.

Fenya looked down at her arms. Raised, puffy red lines that looked like half-healed burns snaked up her arms. It had marked her. The flames hadn't disappeared, they'd sunk into her skin, branding her.

She twisted her forearms, admiring with a tingle of fear the way the flame-like burns twisted from fingertip to elbow. Would they stay?

Liah bent over her, with syringe ready. "I've never seen that before."

"Is it unusual then?"

Liah shrugged and said wryly, "I've never seen an eighteen-year-old Relic Bearer either."

The flatness of her tone made Fenya's breath catch.

The prick of the needle into her arm jolted her, never comfortable, and Liah jumped back, dropping the syringe so that it hung attached to her arm, the needle half in her flesh.

Fenya looked down to see that as her annoyance had flared, so had the burns. They flashed bright in the dim room, and Fenya couldn't help but smile a smile that quickly dimmed.

The Relic has accepted me three years early. What does that mean?

INFORMATION

Fenya woke to the sun shining into her eyes and a loud clang. She blinked scratchy eyes at Liah scowling down at the breakfast tray upon Fenya's table. That must have been the clanging she'd heard.

"Eat up. You're going out after breakfast today." Liah pushed her palms against her apron.

"To do what?" Fenya rubbed her eyes and tried to make them itch less.

"Just out," Liah said shortly and left the room without any explanation.

Alone, Fenya nibbled on a piece of soft bread and downed a few glasses of water. She still hadn't adjusted to how she felt after her newest treatment.

On the table beside Fenya's breakfast tray lay a pair of elbow-high gloves as befitting a female Fire Legacist in training. She recognized the Fire Legacy symbol embroidered on the top of the hand, a balanced, open spiral with three dots coming off it. This symbol on her gloves differed in deliberate ways, as the gloves were marked as a Fledgling Fire Legacist, or untested mage, as the line on the spiral was dashed, and there were no sparks coming from it, only dots.

Fenya looked at the locked door Liah had left through, uncertain whether this was an act of courtesy to her or one of fear. Perhaps something else to make her feel divided from the others? Others she hadn't seen since her last treatment?

With hunger pulling at her stomach, Fenya set about warming her breakfast. Her fire answered readily this morning, and she scorched the edges of the roll in her enthusiasm—or perhaps the help of her Relic. Her nearby satchel was packed with her sketchbook and Henslow's journal, but the Relic was tucked carefully down her dress and hidden from view, joined with the garnet ring she had replaced on the other chain.

As she was considering whether she had time to open Henslow's journal and decipher a few more lines, a clatter of keys in the lock and a smothered jingle as they disappeared into her pocket, Liah stomped into her room, her scowl fully in place.

"Ready?" she snapped as though Fenya had kept her waiting.

"Yes," Fenya said, jumping to her feet and slinging her satchel over her head and across her chest. She grabbed the long gloves and slid them on as she walked out of the door. In the hallway was a basket that reminded Fenya of a picnic basket. "Are we going on a picnic?"

Liah rolled her eyes. "Naturally. Because I don't have enough to do with my day."

Fenya ignored her. "Great. Can I help? Carry something?"

Liah blinked stonily at her. "No. Just follow me."

Fenya gripped her satchel strap and followed as Liah led her down the familiar hallway bordering the inside square of the castle and toward the steep spiral stairs leading directly into it from every floor of the castle.

"Who's coming with us? Henslow?" Fenya's voice echoed slightly in the enclosed stairs.

"No."

"Who then?"

"Harker. Merritt."

"That's it?" Fenya tried to hold back her grimace.

"No. Yes. Maybe."

"Who else?" Fenya pressed. "What are we doing—sheep counting again?"

"Will you shut your mouth?" Liah demanded, wheeling on her halfway down the stairs so that Fenya had to stop short or else collide into her. She grabbed for the side of the castle, free arm windmilling out to the side to keep her balance.

"I—sorry," she finally said when she regained her balance.

"What's gotten into you? Why are you so demanding?" Liah glared at her, but Fenya lifted herself up on her tiptoes in nerves and didn't answer. "You think because you get a visitor and no one else does, that you're something special? Well, you aren't. You're just as pathetic as the rest of them."

Fenya blinked. "I don't—think that."

Liah rolled her eyes again. "If you want to go outside today, stop asking questions and get down there and through that gate before I decide to close it for the week."

Fenya sucked in a breath, clasping her satchel in front of her hips. "Yes, ma'am."

Liah marched down the remaining stairs and past the squeaky gate at the bottom. Liah deposited her into the courtyard and pulled the gate shut behind her as if it personally had offended her. When it bounced back open, Liah wheeled on it and grabbed it, yanking it shut and fighting it to stay closed. As Liah marched back up the stairs, a low whistle sounded in the square behind Fenya.

She turned to find the twins standing shoulder to shoulder, staring at her.

"What did you do?" Harker asked with a saucy grin.

"Nothing," Fenya replied.

"Nice gloves," Harker added wryly.

But Merritt frowned at the door, his pock-marked forehead deeply creased in a look of concern aimed Liah's direction. "You must have done something..."

"Oh, well, I guess I asked too many questions," Fenya answered, striding over to them. "I wanted to know who was joining me today." Fenya shrugged and gripped the strap of her satchel hand over hand in front of her belly. "Is it just us? Are we free to leave?"

Harker and Merritt exchanged a glance, tilting their heads significantly at each other in silent communication.

"What's going on?" Fenya asked, annoyed with their silent communication. "Or are you going to shut me out again because you think I think I'm too good for you?"

Merritt's eyes widened, but Harker let out a bark of laughter.

"C'mon," Harker said, gripping Fenya's elbow and pushing her toward the gate. "We got somethin' to show you."

"What? Where?" *Have they found Fang?* Fenya searched Harker's face, but it was Merritt's that answered her more clearly.

His face crinkled again, as if reacting to something someone had said.

Harker shrugged, but Merritt glared at her as his sister marched them across the square and out of the gate. "Stop shoutin' at me," she demanded as they followed the path away from the castle and its rocky foundation and in the direction of the lighthouse.

"What?" Fenya asked, thinking she'd missed something.

Harker pointed at her brother. "He's shoutin' at me because he thinks I ain't listenin', when really I'm just ignorin' him."

"I don't...understand. Are we being...heard?" she mouthed the last word to Harker.

Harker rolled her eyes. "I'm going," she said aloud to Merritt.

Merritt nodded as if to say, "My point exactly."

Fenya glanced between them, but didn't speak, remembering the way Henslow hadn't spoken and how he'd written to her instead. She'd already said too much if there was an Exaudio was listening in.

Fenya remained silent as they walked across the grass and toward the cliffs. Harker veered to the left and cut across the top of the cliff, as surefooted as a mountain goat. She stopped at the edge, where the wind whistled and whipped through Fenya's loose hair. Harker grinned and flipped her braids over her shoulder again.

"So. What do you want to know?" Harker asked.

"What do you mean?" Fenya half shouted over the wind.

"I mean, there are a lot of secrets here at Wigmore you been askin' about. Whaddya wanna to know?" Harker smirked.

"Why do you want to talk to me all of a sudden?" Fenya crossed her gloved arms over her chest, reassured by the solidness of the Relic against her chest.

Harker raised one brow. "We've talked with Rhys. He...fancies you and managed to convince us to give you a try."

"Well, too bad," Fenya said, well aware of the ring still sitting on her finger underneath her gloves as Harker's words set in and heat stained her cheeks.

Merritt coughed deliberately at Fenya's rejection. "That's not exactly true, either, Harks."

Fenya caught his eye. "No?" She looked back to Harker who grinned, showing a missing incisor.

Harker gave her a look as though to say she disagreed with her brother but wouldn't say it again.

Fenya tried to shake away the thought. She was engaged. It didn't matter anyway.

Harker's smile slipped slightly, her brow furrowing.

"Will you two stop? I feel like you're just telling each other things and keeping me out of the loop. "Where is Rhys? Is he...all right?" Fenya's stomach churned uncomfortably. She wasn't sure what to think of Rhys, but something about him made him an object of pity. She wouldn't have been surprised to hear either that he had died in his sleep or jumped off the top of the castle to his death. And she couldn't tell whether to believe anything Harker told her, including the fact that Rhys fancied her.

Harker jerked her head so that her braids went flying off her shoulders and around to her back. She pointed to the path leading down to the beach, question on her face, and Merritt nodded.

"Let's go down to the beach," she said. "It's a little quieter there."

"Do we need it to be...quieter?" Fenya asked, falling behind Harker as she led the way.

"You're smarter than you act," Harker said dryly.

"Thank you," Fenya muttered primly, but the words were sucked away in a gust of wind as they half slid down the steep, rocky path.

Fenya half fell down the last quarter of the path, looking up only when her feet touched the pebbly sand of the beach.

At the bottom of the cliff, the wind was quieter, but certainly not absent. It whipped around in eddies like the distant tide swirled around the rocks that led out to the lighthouse. The light at the top was dark, but Fenya spotted a flash of red circle around the other side of the lookout. *Fang?*

I thought it was you, Fang sang back. *But who are you with? Do we trust them?*

I don't know yet, Fenya replied.

I hide then.

Good idea. Fenya might have trusted Harker and Merritt enough to go to the clifftop and beach with them, but she didn't trust them with Fang's life.

"This way," Merritt said in his soft tone, motioning Fenya along after Harker, who was halfway across the short beach.

"Where are we going?" Fenya pushed through the pebbles that tried to claim her feet. Merritt floated along as though he slid on top of glass, but Fenya's shoes glued themselves to the rocks, trying to hold her in place.

"Come on," Merritt said in answer, already almost down the beach.

Fenya hiked up her skirts and stared at her boots. "What the—?" She looked up to find Harker watching her from the end of the beach, smirking.

With a glance back at Fenya, something dawned in Merritt's face. He glared at Harker, and she shrugged in answer. The pebbles and sand relaxed around Fenya's feet, then lifted her up from the beach and pulled her along the beach by her feet.

Harker. Fenya almost shouted in the realization. Harker was playing around with her Legacy, using her Earth on the pebbles and the sand to increase or decrease the friction around her boots.

"You've had your fun now," Fenya said when the sand delivered her too quickly to Harker and Merritt, throwing her to her knees before the girl. "What did you bring me down here for?" She motioned to the lighthouse, whose rock path was half under water. "Trying to drown me against the rocks?"

"That would be too easy," Harker remarked. "We're just havin' a little fun. Since we have to be nice to you."

Fenya clenched her teeth. "Why?"

"Rhys, of course." Harker shrugged. "Come on. We only have an hour before the tide shifts. I can't do anythin' when the rocks are too far underwater."

Harker led the way, charging across the slick rocks like a surefooted goat. Merritt motioned Fenya ahead of him, and she nodded her appreciation. Perhaps if she was in the middle of the two, she'd be safer. But then, Harker could control her Legacy a lot more than Fenya had first believed. Could Merritt do the same? Her gaze scanned his cuffs for a symbol like she had on her gloves. In all her months here, she hadn't noticed any Mage Symbols. But now, there *was* something there, embroidered in the same color as his jacket, unfinished lines that suggested a quill or feather, surrounded by dashed parentheses. Was that a Fledgling Air?

She had so many questions about the other students here—if she could still call them here. Or as Henslow called them in his journal, patients. That was far more accurate.

Despite her misgivings about Harker, Fenya made it safely across the wet rocks to the lighthouse. Harker waited until Fenya reached the ledge that the lighthouse was built into and offered a hand that Fenya ignored. A shadow crossed overhead, and Fenya kept her gaze to the ground. *Fang. Stay hidden. We can't trust them.*

I am, came Fang's cheerful and slightly exasperated answer. *Friend in the lighthouse.*

Friend? What? Fenya stumbled to her knees halfway up the incline, and Harker bent down to grab her arm. Annoyed both at the other girl and herself, Fenya shook her off and clamored up the rest of the way with the use of her hands. Merritt, a few paces behind Fenya, climbed up an easier route that seemed almost to have footholds. Dusting her gloves off against each other, she glanced up at the lighthouse, but saw nothing, not even a flash of Fang's scales in the sunlight.

Fang?

No answer.

Turning away, she pressed her lips together.

Finishing his easy climb up the rock, Merritt gave her a wink. "Next time, eh?"

Fenya sighed, but her lips wanted to smile at his kindness. "Right. Should act smarter."

Harker grinned but her impatience returned almost immediately. "C'mon." She marched across the rocks to push open the door to the lighthouse.

Waves crashed against the rock foundation, spraying a fine sheen of water through the air and casting a rainbow through the air.

Fenya stepped into the lighthouse, blinking at the darkness, pausing a couple steps inside as Merritt followed and the door slammed shut.

"What are we doing in here?" Fenya's eyes were slow to adjust to the darkness inside the circular base of the lighthouse. The walls stretched high, and far above offered the only light trickling down to them. It sparkled against the glass and sent shimmers of damp light down to them standing at the base of what appeared to be a very tall, very tight spiral staircase.

"Are you coming up?" called a voice up top.

Fenya jerked her gaze up. "Who is that?"

"Rhys," Merritt said softly, motioning Fenya to the stairs. "After you."

She frowned at the twins. "Why didn't you tell me?"

Harker shrugged. "You're too nosey."

With a roll of her eyes, Fenya started for the stairs. She began at a quick pace that had her huffing after only two dozen steps. The stairs stretched on for another hundred or so steps, and she reached the top breathless and sweating.

"It's about time you got here," Rhys said amiably, peering over the railing and down the stairs.

"I didn't know you were waiting," Fenya replied. "Harker doesn't like to tell me things."

Rhys glanced to Harker. "I thought you understood the importance of this meeting, Harker."

Fenya raised a brow.

The younger girl set her mouth in a firm line, a sheen of sweat on her upper lip. "I know what you said, Rhys, but I ain't seen nothin' that tells me she'll do what you say. She's not standin' against nothin', least of all the headmaster."

"You don't really know that, Harker," Merritt said breathlessly, mounting the platform at the top to join them.

"Why should I stand up to the people trying to help us?" Fenya asked.

"It's better to die than be half of who you should be." Harker flipped her braids behind her shoulders again and shot Rhys a look of utter incredulity, rolling her eyes and shaking her head like Fenya had uttered something stupid.

"What am I doing here?" Fenya asked instead of waiting for an answer. "Rhys? Are you...all right?"

He leaned heavily against the railing, his head bowed over almost to his forearm. He nodded. "Just a...moment."

Harker went to him, lifting him up and slinging his arm around her shoulder. Merritt joined her on his other side, and they walked him over to a stone bench in the corner that was almost invisible, it was so well disguised.

The two lowered him onto the bench, and he leaned back against the stone wall, releasing a shuddering breath. His head fell back either too hard or too uncontrolled, and something on the wall crunched and shuddered.

Gasping, Fenya put a hand to her mouth. "Are you all right?"

Harker reached for him, her hands catching his head as he leaned forward, fingertips exploring the back of his skull before his own hands could reach for it. "You seem fine," she murmured, but distraction coated her words. "Did you know this was here?" Harker released him and reached for the wall behind his head, where a bit of stone had moved. "There's a secret compartment..."

Rubbing the back of his head, Rhys said, "There are secrets everywhere on this island, if you know how to look for them." He paused and inhaled a deep, shaky breath. "That wasn't the way I prefer."

Fenya smiled to herself at his humor, despite the circumstances.

Harker touched the wall, fingers exploring it until she found the right spot, pressed, and the stone moved back into place. "Nice," she said with appreciation.

Rhys shifted, groaning softly. A sheen of sweat on his forehead caught in the pale light of the tower, the sunlight reflecting off the panes of the lighthouse light and illuminating the interior as clouds shifted. Stepping to his side, Merritt seized Rhys's wrist, pressing his fingers to his pulse with a distant look.

"I told you not to come out today," Harker said, her tone surprisingly gentle.

Fenya stepped closer, but hesitated at Harker's protective glare.

Merritt set Rhys's hand down on his thigh, and sighed heavily as Rhys closed his eyes, tilted his head back again—carefully this time—and appeared to fall asleep.

"What's wrong with him?" she finally asked.

"He's been here the longest, you know," Merritt began, stepping over to stand beside her.

Rhys's tunic was too large for his emaciated frame. Maybe it had once fit him, but it didn't any longer. He could have been handsome, but instead he was devoured by the time spent on Wigmore Island.

"I know. Two, three years, right? But...should the treatments here cause...illness?" She didn't know how else to put it. The previous treatment with Bryton had left her feeling better than she had in years, completely in command of herself. Had the headmaster messed up Rhys's treatments that badly? What would happen if she were here for three years? Would she burn out? Become an Ember? A Wylde?

Merritt stared at Rhys for a long moment without answering as Harker took a handkerchief from her pocket and dabbed at his forehead, now pouring with sweat.

"It shouldn't, of course. But, as I'm sure they explained to you before you came here, there is some amount of the unknown in our treatments. They say they are trying to prevent us from becoming Wyldes." Merritt scratched at his chin absently.

Fenya shook her head. "No...Mil—I mean, I was promised that they could take my Legacy *away*."

Merritt turned on her with a startled gaze. "What?"

"What?" Harker demanded from beside Rhys. Even Rhys perked up, lifting his head off the stone wall to gape at her.

"What?" Fenya echoed. "What were you told?"

Harker laughed bitterly under her breath, Rhys exhaled and leaned back, while Merritt's lips twisted in a wry smile.

"We weren't told anything. We were kidnapped and brought here from the government facility we were at," Merritt answered.

"All of you?" She looked at Rhys, but he didn't give any answer, his eyes shut and head once again leaning against the stone.

Merritt shrugged. "A variation of the same. Few are here with their family's knowledge."

Fenya wrapped her arms around her waist, gripping the strap of her satchel tightly as if it somehow could shield her from the words she heard. "And..." She swallowed. "And Rhys has had three years of treatments, which are only making his Legacy worse?"

Merritt nodded as Harker's jaw flexed.

Harker pulled something out of her pocket that turned out to be a vial with a shiny blue liquid in it. "Take this," she said to Rhys. "I nicked it awhile ago, so it won't do enough, but it might 'elp."

"How long have you two been here?" Fenya asked Merritt.

"Fifteen months," Merritt answered. "Harks and I have been here fifteen months. We got here shortly after we turned fourteen."

She inhaled slowly and released it even slower. Her hands tingled. But she didn't feel the desire to use her Legacies, not this time. She gripped her satchel too tightly, but she didn't—couldn't—loosen her grip. "What's happened to you two in that time? If he's at this state after three years, how long do you have before you start reacting like this?"

Merritt tilted his head to the side. "It's never the same treatment for everyone. Even Harker has been treated differently from me. But then, she's Earth and I'm Air. And Rhys is Fire, like you."

"So what's the point here? If they aren't helping us lose our Legacies, and they aren't helping us control them—with the exception of a few stolen lessons from Henslow, who knows why?—the what are we all doing locked away on this island? Are they trying to slowly kill us? Perform illegal experiments on us?" She half laughed at the words, but even before they fell silent around them, Fenya knew she'd touched the truth.

"We believe so," Rhys said in a gravelly voice. "We believe they're using the bracelets to gather our excess Power—" he broke off and swallowed thickly "—using it for something."

"Our own potions..." Fenya murmured.

"More than that," Merritt said, picking up the explanation. "And so they don't want us using our Legacy and draining ourselves of Power. They use the bracelets to contain the Power within us, as each bracelet is specially crafted to contain it, and when they put the droplets of blood into the clasp, it reads our Legacies and our strength. If you're particularly Powerful—a Rank I mage or magess, perhaps—the bracelets might need to be replaced every day. At least according to Henslow."

"Has he told you this?" Fenya frowned at him.

"Some of it," Merritt answered, scratching the back of his neck. "We've learned a lot through books, actually."

Harker shot him an angry look and Merritt winced as though she'd yelled.

Fenya ignored the younger girl. "So what's the point? What are they doing with our Power?"

"Makin' potions and serums and who knows what else," Harker said. "Best we can tell. And some of us, they try to 'cure' as you say. They try to separate our Legacy from us. But they ain't been successful yet."

Swallowing thickly, Fenya twisted her gloved hands together. "Why...why would they do such a thing?"

Harker raised her brows. "To put it in someone else, maybe."

Fenya's throat went dry. Did they know about her Air? Did they realize what had just happened to her? To Bryton? Did that mean that he no longer had his Legacy? At all? Was this, as Milton said, in quest of a Perfect Mage? It seemed impossible. Chasing a myth.

"Temporarily, of course," Rhys added, breaking across Fenya's thoughts.

She pivoted her head to him. "Temporarily?"

He nodded.

"Much to the headmaster's chagrin," Harker said with a sniff. "He wants it to be permanent."

"Like...to make a Perfect Mage with?"

Harker, Merritt, and Rhys all stared at her, various degrees of shock on their faces.

Merritt recovered first. "Where did you hear about the Perfect Mage?"

Wetting her lips with the tip of her tongue, Fenya contemplated how much she should say. "Someone visited me, my...patron. And he mentioned it."

Harker's eyes narrowed. "Who visited you?"

Fenya looked to Merritt. "What *is* a Perfect Mage?"

"Best of what we can tell, from things that we've...overheard and learned through reading material, is that a Perfect Mage is someone who contains all Four Elemental Legacies inside them."

"But that's impossible," Fenya said immediately. *Milton had just mentioned rejoining the Relics, not finding someone with all four Elemental Legacies.* "People can only be born with two Elemental Legacies at the most. They might have a large range of abilities, but—"

Merritt nodded and interrupted. "Of course. We all know that. Ever since the First King separated his Complete Legacy into the Relics, the most anyone is ever born with is two Elemental Legacies. And one is always minor compared to the first. A Perfect Mage would be born with *all four* Elemental Legacies *with* near equal Power."

"It's impossible to be *born* a Perfect Mage these days," Rhys murmured. He dragged a hand across his forehead. "But I don't think that's stopping some from dreaming about it being possible to *create* one."

Dragon teeth seemed to clamp down around Fenya's throat, cutting off her air. Finally she gasped a breath, her covered hand to the base of her throat to clutch at her necklaces. "And you think—" She looked between the three of them, who watched her with bemusement, as though trying to read through her emotions and discover what she knew without her telling them.

Harker's brows continued to climb her face as she waited for Fenya to speak.

"You think that the headmaster is crafting potions and injecting us with serums that will make him an army of Perfect Magi?" Fenya's hands trembled.

The three of them exchanged glances.

"I told you she was too smart to be hanging out with Dempsey," Harker finally said, her gaze on Rhys.

Merritt sighed softly. "Yes, you're right, of course, Harks. But you don't have to be such a know-it-all."

"Hark who's talkin'." Harker put a hand on her hip as she glared at her brother.

Fenya frowned at their exchanges. "Hold on. How long have you three known about this? Or suspected it?"

The twins looked to Rhys to answer.

He inhaled deeply as if to prepare himself for answering her. "I've been here too long to be duped. The amount of things I've overheard and pieced together from simple observation... And then we have Ivy."

"Ivy?"

Once again, Harker's expression softened. "She's often ill, takes to treatments a lot like Rhys—sometimes even worse. But, like Rhys, because of that, they talk about things with her and around her that they don't think she hears."

"It helps that she's also mute," Merritt added. He motioned to Harker. "But Harks and Ivy have learned to communicate, and Harker has been teaching Ivy to read and write. The things she knows..." He shook his head in a mix of wonder and disgust.

"And the things she's had to endure," Harker added darkly.

Fenya's head swam from all this knowledge. "Why are you confiding this all in me?"

There was a pregnant pause between the three of them.

Finally, Rhys answered. "We think they're beginning to target you as a potential best candidate for this all to finally work right."

"But it's impossible." Fenya searched Rhys's golden eyes. They seemed like embers, warm and hot, as though he held a fever within himself. A fever or a fire, she wasn't quite sure which.

"It should be," Rhys agreed. "But nothing is impossible here."

"Which means that avoiding becoming the Perfect Mage shouldn't be impossible either," Fenya murmured, more to herself than them.

Three pairs of eyes fixed on her.

"What are you thinkin'?" Harker said, crossing her arms over her chest.

Words failed Fenya. "I...don't know. I...just...shouldn't we be able to fight?"

Rhys dropped his gaze to his feet, as though hope had slipped out of him. "I didn't come here willingly—and I fought hard. The fight's almost out of me." As the twins looked at him, Rhys raised his gaze again to Fenya. "That's why we hope you can help pick it up."

Fenya opened her mouth. "I—I—"

Again, three pairs of eyes stared at her.

"Why me?"

Fang screeched from the roof of the lighthouse—a warning.

Harker moved to the window and examined the view. "We should go. The tide is coming in. We're out of time."

"I'll take Rhys with me. You go first," Merritt said. "We'll follow, Harks—we shouldn't all arrive back at the castle as if we've all been together."

Fenya opened her mouth to argue, but shut it just as quickly. Harker slipped an arm around Rhys's shoulder and the twins helped him down the stairs. As they emerged into the fresh air, Fenya cast a lingering glance behind her at the catwalk. A spark of red flashed under the eaves of the lighthouse. Fang was still there then. Still safe.

Stay safe, Fang.

Fenya whispered a prayer for her as they climbed over the rocks and headed back toward the castle overlooking the sea. Whatever was happening here, Fenya had never been more certain that Fang should stay far away.

RIGHTS & GAINS

Fenya's feet carried her quickly to the castle and across an empty courtyard to the stairs. The gate squeaked obnoxiously as she slipped through, forgetting in the moment that it announced all intruders.

But the hallway was empty, and Fenya's dirty boots were the only thing making sound, except for the wind that suggested a storm. When she made the final turn from the hallway into her room, her feet stuttered to a stop.

It wasn't empty.

Her heart pounded as she took in aHeadmistress Wyn, Keeper Liah, and an unfamiliar man. Only missing were Vicar Asper and Henslow. Had the others tricked her? Had the keepers been listening all along?

Act like nothing happened. They don't know anything. Pretend you don't know anything and just go in as if they're cleaning your room.

"Don't dawdle," Liah said, motioning her into the room impatiently. "Come and meet the headmaster properly."

Fenya hesitated, glancing behind her for escape, even as she knew there was no escape from this island. Steeling herself for whatever might follow, Fenya stepped into the middle of her room.

"What's going on?" she demanded, irritated at the waver in her voice.

"Come in, come in," the unfamiliar man said with a thin smile that failed to warm his brown eyes. Though he leaned casually against the table, he still towered over Fenya in a menacing fashion.

This man...she had seen him at her treatment...but she couldn't remember any of his features. It was like staring into a sketch that had been dropped in a lake, or even the reflection of a disturbed lake and being asked to draw the face from memory. He was almost blurry around the edges, even now.

"Sit down," the headmistress said, no evidence of any smile on her face. "The headmaster and I have some things to discuss."

Headmaster? Fenya focused on him, but he was blurry around the edges.

"Am I late?" Henslow appeared at the doorway, slightly breathless. "So sorry. Had a problem with the pegasus. That animal just doesn't like me."

Keeper Liah snorted, and Henslow gave a gracious nod of his head toward her in greeting. But he shifted against the wall like he attempted invisibility before the headmaster.

Fenya hoped for a clue from Henslow, perhaps some sort of explanation or reassurance, but his stoney flatness gave nothing away.

Behind her, Keeper Liah shut the door with a snap, and Fenya's shoulders rose in a flinch.

"Sit down, Miss Fenya," the headmaster said with a smile that barely cracked his face. He pointed to her chair, which had been moved to the very center of the room.

Echoes of sitting before Magess Jolie and Mama rattled through her head as Fenya sank down upon the chair in her room and waited for someone to speak.

"Do you have any idea why we're here?" the headmaster asked.

Fenya shook her head. "Is there something wrong with me?"

His lips twitched upward, as though he found monumental but momentary amusement in her answer. "No. Not in such words."

"Then I don't understand. Are you going to try a different treatment?"

He tilted his head.

"Or do I get to go home? Am I cured?" She tried to inject hope into her tone, but it fell flat. *I hope they don't know what I just discussed with Rhys and Merritt and Harker. What if they do? What if this was all a trick of theirs to get rid of me? I don't know whether I should be happy or sad about that...out of Wigmore but back to Milton.*

The headmaster chuckled long and low. "No." He laughed again and exchanged a grin with Liah. "No, I'm afraid you're not going home anytime soon." He crossed to her with two long strides and pointed at her hands. "Would you please remove your gloves?"

Sweat broke out on her nose. *Maybe this is all about the Relic.* Reluctantly, she obeyed, removing the glove from her fingers one at a time.

"May I?" He extended his hand to her.

There was no polite way to refuse, and she offered him her naked hand.

As he lifted her wrist to his face, his warm breath rippled over her skin, and she expected his polite kiss on the back of her hand as a greeting. Instead, he stretched her arm to its longest extension, raised her wrist before his nose and scrutinized it. The Relic burns had faded since appearing, but remained clearly visible. *What is he squinting at?*

"I think I see where our treatments are going wrong," he murmured.

"Yes?" the headmistress answered, stepping to the end of the bed.

The headmaster lifted his gaze from Fenya's bracelets to her eyes, and the coldness there sent dragon ice down her spine. Then without shifting his gaze, and without warning, he wrenched the bracelets off her wrists.

She yelped at the unexpected pain as the metal glanced off her bones. "What are you doing?"

Without answering, he grabbed her other hand and ripped them off as well.

"Ah, yes, that would do it," the headmistress said. "Henslow, this is your doing."

"Ma'am?" His pale brows rose before furrowing down in question.

"You're in charge of the keepers," the headmistress began. "You should have the keepers checking their food consumption and you should be checking the security of their bracelets. These are what keep us safe and keep them from turning on us—"

"Madam," the headmaster said sharply, cutting off her tirade.

She lowered her gaze. "I'm sorry, headmaster."

"Moving on then. No treatment is going to be effective if the patient can alter the conditions." He dropped her still-throbbing hand. "I'm disappointed in you, Miss Fenya. This will require punishment." He tsked.

Her stomach clenched. "What?" Her word came out in a squeak. "But I haven't—" She broke off. If Henslow had purposefully been making them larger, perhaps he had purposefully been making other alterations to them for her to practice with her Legacies. Harker and Merritt had been coached by him in order to learn control, perhaps he had been preparing her for the same thing.

The headmaster waited, brows raised, for her to continue her denial.

She tried to search the headmaster's face, but it was still fuzzy. If she were asked to describe him, she couldn't. Was his hair auburn or brown? Blond or black? His nose long and narrow or short and wide? "I'm sorry," she finished. She wouldn't betray Henslow's trust in her or the others, even if she wasn't sure if she could trust any of them.

"Better," he murmured. "I'm taking these bracelets. We'll restructure them to fit you better. In the meantime, you'll have to go without."

Fenya leaned slightly away from him, annoyance clenching her jaw shut. The way he spoke reminded her of Mama, always shaming but never explaining. Why didn't she deserve some explanation for what they were doing to *her* body? "I want to control my Legacy," she said firmly. "I don't want any more treatments. Or any more bracelets," she added, speaking more boldly than she felt. "I don't want it taken away anymore."

The headmistress burst into laughter. Keeper Henslow's lips parted, his eyes rounding. The headmaster didn't react at all, his strangely indescribable face implacable, his motions smooth as he reached for a leather journal sitting on the tea cart.

Fenya sucked in her lower lip as she waited for his reaction.

"I'm afraid that your mother and Sir Milton have signed an agreement and that you have no choice in the matter."

"But that's not fair," she said before she could stop herself. "I'm eighteen."

He flipped open the journal, wrinkling his nose as if he had an itch on it. "Yes, well, that's the fact of the matter. You signed over your rights with your engagement to Sir Milton. He makes all the decisions on your behalf now."

Fenya's mouth dropped open. *I never should have signed that betrothal.* " want to know what you're doing to me." She clenched her fists. "I deserve to know—"

"Again, not information for you to demand. This is a government facility, and this government is at war. The information released to anyone is a need-to-know basis. You—"

"Need to know!"

"—do not need to know," he continued as if she hadn't spoken.

"But—" she began.

"If I were to tell you, you would begin to imagine results. Already, I've seen it in your responses to my questions." He scribbled something in his notebook.

"No, I haven't," she insisted.

"You, Miss Fenya, are keeping harmful secrets from me. And in the name of science, that cannot continue." He lifted his eyes from his paper, and the coldness in his eyes made her remember herself and the secrets she kept.

Headmistress Wyn's words came back to her. *We like rare things at Wigmore, Miss Verena. And Sparks are the rarest type of Fire Elementals that exist.*

She sucked in a breath. Henslow had said that she and the others were the "rarest of rare." And that it "requires stretching the limits of science."

But science? She couldn't call what he was doing that. The headmaster was killing them without care. *Trying to create a Perfect Mage. In me?* Fenya bit down on her lip, rejecting the thought. Even Bradley

Asylum would have been better than this torture. If only her pride hadn't gotten in the way—if only she hadn't decided that she was worth all this hassle of trying to save herself. Why was she here?

"Miss Fenya?"

Fenya jolted and looked around at the three adults standing before her. "What?"

"Did you hear me?" Headmistress Wyn looked severely over her glasses at Fenya.

"No, I'm sorry." Fenya twisted her hands together and tucked them between her thighs. "What did you say?"

"I asked you to pull up your sleeves."

"I..." Fenya sucked in a deep breath through her nose. "I don't want to."

"Excuse me?" Headmistress Wyn's brows flew up her high fore-head. "That's not an option, young lady."

Fenya shook her head. "I don't want to do the treatments anymore. I refuse. And if it means ending my betrothal, I will."

The headmaster straightened from where he'd been leaning against the table. "Don't force us to coerce you, Miss Fenya; I assure you that this is not your choice to make."

Throwing all caution away, Fenya looked to Henslow, begging him for some help. "Please. I don't want to. I want to learn to control myself instead. I don't want my Legacy to be taken from me anymore." Her voice cracked.

Henslow stepped forward. The headmaster and headmistress shifted to the side, allowing him to kneel before her. "Miss Fenya, I know you're frightened. But have I ever led you astray?"

She met his pale blue eyes and turned her head to the left and the right once.

"Exactly." He didn't touch her but folded his hands together and placed them between his knees. "Please trust me. I wouldn't do anything to intentionally harm you or the others here."

A breath trembled over her lips. She released her resistance in a shudder and a nod.

"Let's get that sleeve rolled up then," Henslow said, leaning forward and tugging her sleeve up.

Not looking at the headmaster or headmistress, not wanting to see their smug victory, Fenya bowed her head and fought the tears pooling on her lashes.

This time, the headmaster performed the blood draw himself, and each prick pinched more than the last. "Well, done with that." He raised the last blood to the ceiling. "Hmm. Yes. I can see the difference."

Fenya wanted to ask what he could see, but she couldn't muster enough will to do so, pained at the entire process and Milton's choices for her. What was the point of it all anymore? After she had just said to Rhys and the others that they could still fight...suddenly she understood how Rhys had been broken, how the fight had been stolen out of him.

"Sir?" Henslow asked, tucking the other four vials into the wooden stand. He accepted the last glass vial from the headmaster. Liah passed him a syringe full of a vaguely familiar dark blue serum. Henslow's gaze snagged on the vial of serum, his face tightening.

"Our newest charge has gained something, hasn't she?" The headmaster faced Fenya with the syringe and bent over her, this time reaching for her upper arm and pinching her skin together between his thumb and fingers. "What a victory."

"Gained something?" Over his shoulder, Henslow watched the headmaster inject the last syringe into Fenya's upper arm.

"Oh yes." He nearly beamed in joy. "And what a gain it is!" He held up the vial in his hand. "I think we've finally done it!"

Heart pounding, Fenya tried to swallow, but there wasn't anything in her mouth to push down. What had he discovered? What could he tell?

But the headmaster didn't answer. He carefully nestled the vial of blood into a velvet-cushioned box and shut it with reverence. He passed it to Keeper Henslow. "Take care of this, Henslow. It has been a decade in the making. And we aren't finished yet."

Henslow accepted the box with a respectful nod.

Fenya wanted to cry out, but with Henslow helping the headmaster and headmistress, there was no one to listen. She was alone and defenseless against four trained adult magi. Her tongue felt strangely captive.

"Now we can see what that little wyvern has to do with our experiments," the headmaster said. He bowed his head in feigned respect to Fenya. "I appreciate your sacrifices, young lady. You have no idea what this will one day mean to the world."

Chapter Twenty-Five

TRUTH

"So now that we've got that out of the way, why don't you tell us where we can find that little flame wyvern?"

Fenya shook her head. "No, there's no...no..." Her tongue felt thick, as though she were struggling to form the right words.

"Tell me where the dragon is, Miss Fenya," the headmaster insisted, leaning down over her. "That last injection was a poison. You'll only receive the antidote when I receive what I need from you."

"What! You wouldn't." Fenya met his gaze, hard as though she could pin him down with her hatred.

Unaffected, the headmaster waited.

She bit down harder on her lip. She could outlast him.

"Miss Fenya," he began, crouching down before her so that he was at her eye level. Despite his closeness, she still couldn't decipher the exact shade of his eyes or shape of his jaw. "Here's what will happen should you refuse me today." He waited until her eyes fixed on his. "I will wait until it's almost too late to bring you back, and then revive you."

She frowned, leaning away from him. *What is this poison going to do to me?*

"And then, should you not change your mind and reveal the information to me, I shall lock you in your room, and leave you here."

She opened her mouth to retort that she'd already experienced that prison, but he continued.

"And while you are sitting here, thinking about your decision, I shall make a short trip to the mainland." His smile, though indescribable, sent chills down her spine as she waited for his next words. "And there, I shall make a few visits. I hear that you are quite fond of your cousins. What are their names again? Zhara—"

"No!" the word broke free from her lips. "You won't touch them." She fixed him with the most hateful glare she could muster.

His smile faded, but there was victory in his eyes.

They're brown. His eyes are brown.

Blinking back burning tears, Fenya drew a deep breath and prolonged the moment where he stared into her face. She could see him now, or what part of him she could. And she would remember those eyes even if she had to sketch them a thousand times to imprint them in her memory.

"Miss Fenya?"

She blinked again, but this time her vision grew blurry, and not with tears. Her blood pulsed in her ears. The poison was taking effect then...

Fang could get away, perhaps she could speak with her before they went after her.

The choice was both impossible and inevitable. Fenya didn't doubt that the headmaster would find her cousins, and they were too young and innocent to defend themselves. But Fang...Fang had a chance. And he wouldn't harm Fang...not if he knew it would harm Fenya as well. He'd already betrayed that he would not let her die, for she and Fang were too valuable to him.

"Your time runs short."

Fenya inhaled a shaky breath and spoke with a trembling, thick tongue. "I left her on the clifftop." The words came out slow and thick. "She flies around the lighthouse...roosts in the cave at night."

"Good girl," he said, patting her hand.

She jerked it back and opened her eyes, glaring at him. "I...hate... you."

He tilted his head to the side.

"I hate...all of you." She swallowed as saliva tried to drip over her lip. "And I will exact...my revenge...upon you."

His brow rose. "Interesting." The headmaster straightened and motioned to the others in the room. "We'll go out at dusk. She should be active then." He pointed to Liah and then to Fenya. "Go ahead."

Fenya barely saw Liah as she approached with the other syringe. The needle was in her arm before she could pull away, the plunger depressed. And Fenya realized too late that it contained a sleeping potion along with the antidote.

Her eyelids drifted down, and her chin sagged to her chest. She jerked her head upright, glaring down at the injection, but the damage was done.

The medicine put her into a deep sleep, and Fenya slept hard and dreamless, waking with groggy, sleep-encrusted eyes and an aching head.

Yesterday's memories were blurry, as though she had been wandering through a fog encapsulating the island.

The island...yes. She'd gone outside...and she'd seen Merritt and Harker. And Rhys. They'd said...something. She vaguely remembered standing on the cliff, and then the lighthouse, her hair whipping in the wind. Had there been something important said? She couldn't remember.

Why can't I remember?

A groan escaped her dry, cracked lips. How long had she slept? Had it been more than the night?

The light in her room told her it was day, but it didn't tell her how far advanced the day was.

Why is yesterday a blank?

She wanted Fang.

The idea made an ache clench through her heart like a spasm.

Fang. I have to remember something about Fang. What did I do? Say?

She went through yesterday's activities again. She'd woke to break-fast, read a book, maybe sketched? And then she'd gone outside at midday...she'd talked to Harker, Merritt, and Rhys. They had told her something.

She rubbed the bridge of her nose.

Sun sparkled through the barred glass of her window, making squares of light on the opposite wall that approached the door.

She blinked slowly at the wall, her thoughts still sluggish. Maybe if she slept a little more... Just another hour or so.

Her eyes were so heavy, like lead weights had been sewn to her lashes.

She breathed softly out, letting go of the disappointment of thoughts lacking from her mind that she wanted to think, and drifted back into sleep.

Only this sleep was neither dreamless nor restful.

She dreamed she was in the air, flying, like Fang. No, she was Fang. Or with her... She could see the dragon, but she also felt as though she were the dragon. The wind rustled over the top of her wings, rippling across the bendable spikes on her back, and she used her tail to direct her flight. She dipped down, buffeting through the pockets of warm air.

Sudden and sharp, fear pulsed through her blood. Something was chasing her. The winds were too strong, tearing at her wings. Soon it would be too dangerous to continue flying, but she had to. She couldn't stop.

She aimed for the cliff of the island, went over the edge and then dove toward the water in sharp descent. With a violent twist of her body, she veered into the cave and into the blackness.

Her senses awakened to their height, and she slowed, her eyes adjusting to the darkness. A pool of light highlighted the stream of water entering the cave below her, and she cast around a glance for something to land on other than the ground, a small hole to hide in or anything of the sort. Finally, deep in the cave, she found a ledge and scrabbled onto it, her sides heaving from exertion, her heart thumping in a mixture between fear and exhaustion.

She shuffled to the far side of the ledge and faced the entrance of the cave. Maybe she could hide here, away from the wind, away from whatever it was out there.

She puffed out a breath of smoke. Her scales began to glow. She couldn't fight a large predator, and she couldn't fight wind. Even her borrowed fire couldn't do that.

A rustle. A crunch. A ripple of water.

She cocked her head.

Something...coming.

Fenya woke with a start, sitting straight up in bed, panting as though she'd been sprinting. She looked around her room, half expecting something to jump out of the shadows. But the room was empty.

She caught her breath, breathing deeply as she searched the corners of her room. It had felt so real. It had to be a dream, but... was it?

Her connection with Fang was real. Was Fang in trouble?

Fang? Are you...all right?

There was no answer. She must have been too far away to hear. Or else...could she be dead? Unconscious? Had the blood exchange not caused a life-and-death relationship after all?

Fenya rose and went to the window. Her wrists were hot and bare without the bracelets. The headmaster had never replaced them. Was their lack to blame for this dream? Was she imagining this connection? Or wishing it?

She grabbed the bars, pulling herself closer to the window, onto her tiptoes, and searching the predawn skies for that familiar speck of Fang's bright scales. She wasn't there.

She isn't there.

She closed her eyes and focused on the dragon. She tried to draw herself back into the dragon's mind, imagine the connection as strong, as if it were another thread that tied her to the dragon, more clearly than ever before. She had watched the dragon fly in front of the cliffs, try to dodge the invisible pull of her attackers. They used magic on her.

Anger burned through Fenya, and the vision wobbled.

She took a breath. *Calm down. I have to focus.*

The vision cleared. She replayed everything that had happened, pushing past the moment where she had woken, digging into her mind as though this was her own memory and not Fang's.

Fear clawed at Fenya.

The invisible forces yanked Fang out of the air and to the rocky beach. Pebbles and sand assaulted her scales, burying themselves underneath her scales and into her eyes. She screeched in anger and fear.

Pain coursed through her shoulders, ripping at the connection between her wings and her back. Searing agony. She hissed and spat, snapping and snarling.

Dragon-skinned gloves deflected her bites, and a harsh, cold rope twined around her body. Then it wrenched her off the pebbles and shoved into a dark, metal box.

Brown eyes stared through a hole at her. She snarled. Spit venom at him.

And the man laughed.

Fenya opened her eyes.

Brown eyes. He's got Fang.

She had to free her. Or else they would both die.

Chapter Twenty-Six

SEARCHING

The next morning, Fenya had been awake and poring over Henslow's books when Liah arrived with both breakfast and a new set of bracelets.

"I want to go walking," Fenya insisted to Liah as she clasped the bracelets around her wrists.

And find Fang. But she couldn't say that—Liah didn't know that Fenya knew Fang had been captured. She had to find her. Without leading anyone else to her.

"Too bad," Liah said shortly, but there was a gleam of victory in her eyes that she couldn't seem to suppress.

"Please," Fenya said. "I won't do anything. I...I just need to walk, to sketch." Her heart thudded against her sternum. She wanted Fang back, wanted her free. Why couldn't she feel her or speak to her? Where had they hidden her?

Liah sighed heavily. "You'll hurt yourself again if I don't let you, won't you?"

"Perhaps." Fenya shrugged as if it didn't matter, but her heart continued to leap as Liah decided her fate. If she couldn't walk outside the castle today, she would search the castle from top to bottom and find Fang. She had to. *What have they done to her?*

Liah shook her head in exasperation, but Fenya thought she

detected a sense of pride or admiration in the look. "There are ways to prevent you from doing that, you know."

"I'm sure there are," Fenya agreed in false calm. "But the more unhappy you make me, the less likely I am to cooperate. And the less I cooperate, and the more Power you pour into me, the less likely I am to ever see things your way."

Liah blinked as her lips formed a thin line. "Perhaps you can visit the courtyard."

Fenya narrowed her eyes, pressing her lips tight to avoid any trace of a victorious smile.

"Or the library or student lounge," Liah added.

Fenya sighed and reached for her satchel. "Fine. But tomorrow, I expect to be allowed out of the square."

And in the meantime, Fenya would search for Fang and see if there was a way out of the castle that wasn't talked about. Every castle had to have a secret exit, especially former military facilities. The library was an excellent place to start, given how rare books had once been. And the library had bricked in shelves, meaning it had been a room intended to be a library when the castle was built, and the perfect place for a secret exit.

"I'm telling the others that you aren't permitted out of the castle today," Liah said as she left. But she left the door open when she departed with her tea cart, and Fenya allowed herself to eat with the additional freedom. Wind swept through the room, rattling the bars on the window and pushing the door against the wall, but Fenya found the now-familiar wind almost comforting. It reminded her that there was something outside of Fenya's room, and even outside of the castle. Or perhaps it was just the Air that Bryton had sacrificed to her.

Hastily, Fenya finished her breakfast, having perfected the ability to melt the cheese in the middle of the bread without burning her roll anymore, with or without her bracelets, and licked her fingers clean, wiping them on her napkin before grabbing her satchel and stepping into the hallway. A quick glance into the square below showed her that no one was there. Bringing her gaze up, she found several doors across the square and one floor up open. The floor above seemed to be the boy's floor, or one of them.

Liah was nowhere in sight, providing her a rare opportunity to explore without anyone pushing her out the door. She supposed that being trapped inside the drafty castle wasn't the worst thing that she could endure today. Another treatment in the corner room came to mind. She shuddered.

This time, instead of walking directly down the spiral staircase that descended into the square, Fenya turned into it and began to climb. She didn't stop at the next floor up, but continued until she reached the very top of the castle. Though it was unlikely that Fang was kept on the roof, there might be a way out of the castle. A squeaky gate like the one at the bottom greeted her with a poor attempt to keep her on the stairs, for there was no lock.

She slipped the latch and stepped out onto a bare stone roof. The wind whistled harshly across the parapet, and a very low edge of uneven stones created a border at the top of the castle. One wrong step, and she would fall to her death. But, if she had to free Fang from the castle, she could bring her up here and let her fly away.

It had rained recently, and several large barrels collected rainwater with a funnel that disappeared into a mostly covered top, complete with a spigot on the bottom. Why they didn't just employ a Water Legacist to purify the water was beyond her understanding. And perhaps her place.

Fenya quickly explored the rest of the roof, but there was nothing of interest, not even a ladder down off the side to form an exit. The only exit here was to jump or to fly. She supposed that a pegasi or dragon could land on the roof if needed. But when she had arrived, they had brought her to the gate through the stables a short distance away. Maybe there was a ward that prevented landing atop the castle?

She took the stairs back down to the top floor. Some of the doors were locked, but the first one she opened revealed a pleasant bedroom with masculine but impersonal belongings. Fenya inhaled sharply. It had to be the headmaster's room. Or one of the male keeper's. Henslow's? The vicar was supposed to live down beside the church and library.

There was nothing personal or of interest there, and so Fenya passed through and back into the hall.

One of the bedroom's door was ajar, and Fenya found a letter on the desk addressed to "Mama" and signed from Theodore on the folded envelope. Fenya frowned, trying to remember who Theodore was. She thought he was the little boy, an Earth Elemental. But...when had she last seen him?

She reached for the letter, and when she moved it, a thin layer of dust revealed itself. The letter was sealed, or Fenya would have probed further, though she knew she shouldn't.

She left the room and continued to the next, only to find another room eerily cold and abandoned. She stood in the room for a long moment. It was nearly identical to her own, except where she'd hung a couple of her own sketches to brighten up the place. A plain pair of trousers and boots remained atop the trunk, as if waiting for a new student to come and take up residency.

But no Fang.

On the desk was an abandoned journal. She hesitated before reaching for it, but this could very well be her only chance to explore. She opened the journal and her resolve wavered. Inscribed on the first page was "Property of Bryton."

She flipped through, scanning nondescript entries of his arrival and his treatment. He wrote every day, dating back to almost seven months before. And then stopped abruptly, the day before his treatment with Fenya.

She inhaled sharply. Why hadn't he written again?

His belongings were left as though he had planned to return. A pencil on the table, his journal, his bed mussed, and a pair of socks on the floor beside it.

He's gone. They sent him home.

He wasn't coming back to claim his journal. It was probably being sent home with the rest of his belongings. A quick scan of his room showed nothing else to return though, so why had it been left behind? She hesitated for only a moment then shoved the journal into her satchel. Maybe she could read it and return it if he came back. Maybe he'd gone home for a visit. Maybe his treatment had worked.

She bit her lip and left the room, seeing nothing else of note.

The remaining rooms of the top floor were locked, which was a shame, since some of them seemed to belong to the keepers or the headmistress. What Fenya wouldn't have given in order to go through their rooms and see what secrets they hid. But then, perhaps their rooms would be as plain and uninteresting as the headmaster's.

On the floor below, Fenya found all but the common room locked. Inside the common room, a few of the boys looked up from their game of marbles.

"Hello, Miss Fenya, care to join us?" Remiel offered. "You can borrow some of my marbles."

"No, thank you, I never did well at marbles," she said. One time, she'd even set one on fire when playing with her only friend Bryn at Magess Jolie's.

"What are you doing?" Acyn asked. "Liah said you were supposed to be in here today."

She inhaled slightly and stepped inside, letting the door drift shut behind her. "Does she check on you?"

Weston shrugged. "Sometimes." He eyed her. "You goin' to stay?"

"Maybe for a little while." She took in the hopeful expressions of Acyn and Remiel. Maybe they knew something about the castle that could help her find Fang.

She sat down on the couch behind the boys and pulled out her sketchbook to start a sketch of Remiel and Acyn as they battled for the best marbles. She should have sketched all the children here, to remember them by. There behind them, she sketched Weston as he looked on, sometimes in boredom, and sometimes with curiosity as the boys exclaimed over their wins and bemoaned their losses.

"Are those enchanted marbles?" Fenya asked as one marble gave a strange flick and rolled away from the center.

Remiel nodded, a glint in his eye. "One of the best games. I brought it when I came to Wigmore. Only thing my pop gave me before I left."

Fenya considered asking another question, but then Acyn played his turn and nudged Remiel.

"C'mon, hurry up. I'm about to win."

"No, you aren't," Remiel retorted, leaning over with his shooter in hand.

Fire popped in the grate, and Fenya glanced at it in surprise. She hadn't even felt it when she walked in. The new bracelets she wore must have numbed her to the presence of it. *How strange.*

She slid her gaze around the room, looking for any spots in the wall where a door might be hidden. But, unlike most castles, this one didn't have tapestries lining the walls to warm or ornament the building. It was bare bones, with ledges made out of stone underneath the windows for people to sit on, shelves made out of the same stone the castle was made from.

Weston grabbed a book off the shelf and plopped himself down beside Fenya. "Whatcha drawing?"

Fenya nodded at the boys who were arguing over whether a marble had crossed the line or not.

He inspected her picture with a look of begrudging admiration.

"Where are your rooms?" Fenya asked as she resumed sketching. Maybe the boys knew more about the castle and where Fang might be hidden.

"Our rooms?" Weston repeated. "I'm up a level, beside Bryton." He stopped abruptly as Acyn and Remiel looked at him with wide eyes. "Or was," he finished, dropping his gaze to his lap, where the book sat unopened.

The room stayed silent for a few heartbeats, except for the crackling of the fire.

"So he's gone then?" Fenya murmured to Weston as the other boys resumed playing, Acyn's enthusiasm for the gold marble he'd captured waning.

"Yes." Weston shrugged. "We'll all be gone at some point, I suppose."

Fenya frowned. She shouldn't have asked if he was gone, but asked if he was dead. "Is he—" She broke off as the door to the lounge burst open and a gust of wind shuddered through the castle.

Acyn jumped and bumped into the marbles, and the game quickly devolved into bickering about which marbles belonged to each person.

"It was the wind!" he complained when Weston accused him of bumping the marbles on purpose. "And you know I don't have Air!"

"We were playin' for keeps!" Weston argued. "You can't take those back!"

As the boys set about sorting out the marbles and restoring peace, Fenya gave up on finishing her sketch. She'd have to reimagine the game. She poked around the room a bit, pretending to be looking at the sparse books on the shelf as she wandered.

She waved goodbye to the boys as she slipped out, closing the door behind her to remedy the wind's damage, making sure the door latched this time.

The rest of the second floor proved to be boy's bedrooms, the second level of the lookout, washrooms, and the top floor of the library, which Fenya stepped into, peering down over the iron railing that created a multi-story library. In this room were the only stained glass windows of the castle, keeping the room dry and warmer than the rest of the castle.

The shelves remained embarrassingly bare for a library, with a shelf of books tucked into the corner, and all the others empty and dusty.

She sighed as she wandered around the perimeter, inspecting the stones and checking to see if there was mortar between them to rule out a secret door. After witnessing the way the lighthouse had revealed a hidden compartment, she had no doubt that more secrets lay in the castle.

Iron steps led to the stone floor below, and Fenya repeated the process. Somewhere below, she heard a creak of a wooden floor. The church was the only room with wooden floors, connected to the library through a doorway, which might have been left open. She softened her footsteps as she walked around the perimeter of the library.

Nothing. And no hidden Fang, either.

She was beginning to think that Fang wasn't in the castle at all. At every door, she hadn't felt her presence.

Hope began to ebb away. If Fang wasn't here, wasn't in the castle—where was she? Had her vision been false? Just a nightmare?

She could hope—but then, why was Fang still silent? Fenya paused at the two-story narrow stained window and peered out the narrow clear section. The lookout jutted out in the way, blocking Fenya's view of the lighthouse and cave. She wrinkled her nose and pulled away.

The lookout jutted out toward the sea slightly, positioned on an overhang of the rock below that made it appear to be the least likely place for a secret exit from the castle. But it was attached the library.

She spent a couple of minutes silently poking around, but found nothing. Another ten minutes passed while she watched the lighthouse for Fang. By the time she gave up and returned inside, her hope was dying to embers.

Tears stung her eyes and began to slide down her cheeks. She hardly paid attention to where she was going as she buried her hands in her face and sank into a crevice beside a bookcase.

"Fenya?"

Fenya's hands fell away from her face at the soft word echoing in her ears.

"What's wrong?" Concern etched across Dempsey's handsome features. He sank down before her, for there was no room on the crevice she'd seated herself on. He didn't touch her though, ever the gentleman.

"I..." She wiped at her face. "Nothing. I mean..." Could she trust him? Whom here could she trust? She didn't know anymore. The tears threatened again.

"You can trust me," Dempsey said, as if he had heard her concerns. "I won't say anything. Cross my heart and hope to die." He drew a cross over his heart and crossed his eyes.

She smiled despite herself and sniffed. "Well, remember that dragon I made friends with? The headmaster has taken an interest in her." She squeezed her hands together.

"That little dragon?" Dempsey shook his head. "I went and left food where you said she was, but I never saw her. She's exceptional at hiding." He tilted his head at her. "How did you find her anyway?"

Fenya explained how Fang had come to the island and how she had befriended her at Whitland, then how she had helped heal her when Fang had revealed herself on the clifftop before Rhys appeared.

"Wow. That dragon must be fond of you." Dempsey shifted, still crouched before her.

She motioned to the couch in the middle of the library. "Do you want to go sit over there?"

"Oh, no, it's fine." He flashed her a smile again. "But I'm confused why the headmaster would want your dragon."

"I'm confused who told about her," Fenya answered, hardening her voice. "Did you?"

"What?" Honest shock appeared on Dempsey's face. "No! I would never betray your trust!"

She nodded. "Then it must have been Rhys."

"He knew?" Dempsey's eyebrows drew together as his eyes, full of worry, met hers. "Of course he did. He somehow finds out all the things on this island."

Fenya frowned, thinking of Ivy. Dempsey shifted from his crouch and seated himself before her so that his leg extended beside hers, brushing against the length of her leg, and flexed his toes toward himself.

"He's got some sort of connection here, I think." Dempsey rubbed the stubble on his chin. "I don't know how. Maybe he's a Telepath." He snorted. "It would make sense—the things he knows."

Suddenly aware of how alone they were and how close Dempsey sat, Fenya found focusing on his words difficult. "But can I trust him?"

"No. Nor those odd twins that he conspires with. I think they discover useful bits of information using their Legacies on the keepers."

"Is that possible? Aren't the bracelets designed to keep us from using our Legacies at all?" Fenya shifted uneasily on the window seat trying to ignore the way her skin heated at his nearness and yet he remained cool like sea water.

"I don't know. Those two are strange—and strange equals powerful here," Dempsey said.

She recoiled slightly, and he laughed.

"You're Fire—that makes you strange to me, you know?" He winked. "We're not supposed to like each other, or even get on with each other wielding opposite elements, but I don't hold your Fire against you."

This time, she couldn't stop the heat from climbing to her cheeks.

"So let me help you."

"What?"

"Let me help you find Fang. Where have you looked so far?"

"From the top down...so everywhere above here."

He blinked a few times in rapid succession, his gray eyes darkening in concern. "Oh. Well, then. We don't have much left. Have you checked the laboratory?"

"The laboratory?"

"Where the potions are made. The big ones."

"Oh. They've been locked."

"Hmm. Probably not the ground floor. The keepers often forget to lock the door behind them when they go upstairs. And I just saw Keeper Liah go in before I found you."

"That must have been who I heard down here then when I was on the top floor of the library." Fenya looked around. "Isn't the laboratory in this corner of the castle?" If her mental map was correct, the corner of the castle where the laboratories were butted up against the church and the connected library.

"Yes. That corner." Dempsey pointed to a dark corner where a door hid.

"Is that the door they don't lock?" she whispered.

Dempsey nodded. "Exactly. Let's go."

"Now?"

He offered her his hand as he stood. "Yes. Before they come and lock it. We must seize the opportunities we are given as well as making our own."

She bit her lip and hesitated for only a moment, then grabbed his hand, cool even through her glove. Her flesh burned and tingled, and she tamped down the desire to pull away. *No, I'm seizing the opportunity —whatever and wherever it might be.*

ICE AND FIRE

Dempsey pulled her into the darkest corner of the castle. The door creaked softly on its hinges, and dampness greeted Fenya's nose, along with a stench of something else. *Blood?*

Dempsey held a finger to his lips and eased the door closed behind them.

She nodded, and with her hand still in his, her eyes still damp and nose still running, followed him up the stairs. She peered down into the abyss below, and the smell of decay assaulted her nostrils. They wouldn't keep Fang down there, would they? What was even down there? As she stepped upward, a sound rose from below, the clanking of metal on metal.

A voice echoed up after it, a low curse in what sounded like a man's voice.

Dempsey tugged on her hand unexpectedly, and she stumbled against the next step, nearly falling. A soft grunt of pain escaped her lips. Dempsey paused, his hand squeezing on hers, and they both hunched over as they listened for any approaching footsteps. But the person below didn't appear to hear, and the metallic tapping resumed.

She stole a moment to catch her breath, putting her free hand on her chest. *I must be becoming unaccustomed to exercise. Or there's something odd about the air here.*

Dempsey waited for her to gain her balance this time, and she used her free hand to hold the inside wall of the spiral stairs. Together they climbed up the flight and approached the door.

Dempsey leaned against the door, pressing his ear against it. Fenya calmed her breathing, her legs shaking beneath her.

Or is it...Fang? Injured? Weak? Is that what's making me weak?

She brushed past Dempsey, pressing her palm upon the door. Could Fang be inside? She reached for the handle. The spiral stairs ended here anyway, and the only way out was back down or through the room inside.

She turned the knob and the door all but fell open. Dempsey stumbled across the threshold and tripped over a step just inside, which led down into a wooden-floored room, at least it sounded like it by the thunk of his knees hitting it.

"Are you all right?" she whispered when no one appeared at the sound. She carefully closed the door after them, cloaking them in darkness.

"Yes," he answered, but his tone was full of annoyance. He climbed to his feet and paused. "Hang on." He went to a table and grabbed something. A flick of light and Fenya felt the flash of a spark answer. She held her breath as he flicked again. This time, the match caught, and he lit the lamp, sliding the glass into place to protect its flame. She inhaled sharply.

"Oh, sorry—is this bothering you?"

She shook her head, but the new flame leapt with excitement at being born and fueled. She pushed the feeling away.

"Quick, look around." Dempsey aimed the light into the room.

"She's not here," Fenya said almost immediately.

"What? How do you know? She's small, right?"

Avoiding the treatment chair in the middle, Fenya walked around the outside of the room, which felt strange now without a treatment looming. The vacant, wooden chair glared ominously at her over the nearby tools and needles and blood-collecting bowls. She suppressed a shudder, and the flame sank down closer to the fuel in the lamp beneath it, crafting a glow that focused on Dempsey.

He had started the other way, and when they met, he stopped and shrugged. "Guess you're right. We should head up to the next floor. Maybe they wanted to keep her closer to the keepers?"

Fenya put a hand to her mouth. "What if she's in one of their rooms?"

Dempsey shrugged. "We'll get her out then."

"But the doors were locked—I've checked today already."

His lips spread into a grin. "Well, I've got a pretty nifty trick with ice I'd like to try."

She frowned. "Ice?"

"Water and cold make ice."

"Yes, but I didn't know you could control the temperature of your Water..."

His eyebrows waggled. "There are a lot of things that you don't know about me yet."

She suppressed her smile, but his eyes caught her in the darkness and solemnity came over them. His gaze skittered over her face, darting to her lips. Her heart thudded, and the little flame responded, burning low and hot.

A clattering noise in the hall broke the silence.

Fenya jumped and gripped Dempsey's arm.

The fire went out with a puff of air.

They were plunged into darkness.

"What was that?" she whispered as quietly as she could manage.

"Shh," was all he said in reply.

The door rattled, the lock engaged as the person on the other side tried to open it.

Then the sound of a key settling into the lock had Fenya scrambling back for the stairway, with Dempsey at her heels, stumbling over the step in the darkness. They stepped back into the alcove of the stairway, clinging to the wall. Dempsey, still holding the lantern, stepped in close to her, pulling her against his chest to hide her as the door shifted shut only partway. In the faint light of the stairwell, illuminated by a small window high above them, she spotted the panic on his face and the indecision of whether or not to close the door.

Fenya clung to him and focused on the door. A thread of Air... pulled through the aether...she put out a hand, grabbing the small thread with her fingers, imagining the spider web of thread through the aether, and gently pulled it toward her. *It had creaked before.* She split her concentration, creating a bubble of Air around the hinges, cushioning it, slipping threads of aether between the metal bits of the door, and the door swung slowly shut in absolute silence.

"Did you do that?" he whispered to her cheek.

Nodding, she turned into him and looked up to find their mouths were a mere inch apart. He smelled of damp earth and saltwater. As though he had bathed in the island itself. His heart beat fast against her arm. If they had been in any other situation, she could imagine their lips touching. But...

Sounds from the laboratory reached her ears. *If I muffled the squeaking hinges, could I create a buffer of aether around Dempsey and me both? Something like a shield of aether?*

The fleeting thought was interrupted by a shadow across the floor under the door.

A figure wearing trousers crossed over the room, casting several shadows between the door and floor. Fenya's heart hammered against her ribs. She stayed still, highly aware of Dempsey's breath caressing her cheek.

The shadows paused in front of the door. It shifted as though the person was listening at the other side of the door.

Fenya held her breath.

"What is he doing?" Dempsey muttered beside Fenya's cheek.

The shadow froze as though he had heard Dempsey's voice. He seemed to listen for a long moment as Dempsey gripped Fenya's forearm. In tightening his grip on Fenya, the lantern tapped against the stone wall with a chink of metal on stone.

Fenya bit her lip as Dempsey hurried to shush the ringing metal.

"Who's there?" a familiar voice called out.

Fenya couldn't suppress her gasp this time. "Rhys?"

The door swung open, and a pale bit of light scattered through the stairwell.

"Fenya?" Rhys squinted into the darkness.

"Don't," Dempsey warned, shifting to put Fenya behind him. "Don't trust him."

"I don't," Fenya answered, but she stepped toward Rhys anyway. "But he knows we're here anyway."

She squinted at the lantern, feeling the fuel on the still-warm wick, ready to bloom, and it burst into flame, startling Dempsey so that he recoiled, almost dropping the glass lantern.

"Careful," she admonished, stepping out of his arms and into the laboratory where Rhys stood.

"Did you do that?" Dempsey demanded, looking at her with wide eyes.

She lifted a shoulder.

"Fenya..." Rhys murmured from close behind her.

Dempsey raised his eyes from the lantern to Rhys, accusation darkening his gaze. "What are you doing in here?"

Rhys only met Fenya's gaze. "You are...?"

"There was just enough ember left..." Fenya said. Somehow, confessing that she was a Spark seemed too bold. Whatever additional strength she hadn't revealed yet should not be revealed at Wigmore ever.

At a rustle behind her, Dempsey's presence towered, his breath warm and damp on her neck. Or was it the lantern with warmth and he the damp? She couldn't tell with his Water so close to her Fire. They seemed to war and battle in the space between her back and Dempsey's front as his hackles rose. Rhys's eyes flickered from something within, sparking so hot that his Fire crackled in answer.

"Why are you two in here? What were you doing?" Rhys's eyes narrowed, his eyes flashing as they darted around the empty staircase behind them.

"Oh blessed berserker!" Fenya's cheeks bloomed with heat as his interpretation of their closeness came into meaning. "No—I—we were —" she stammered.

She pressed her hands to her flaming cheeks. *Fang. Nothing matters but finding Fang and getting her out. And here is the reason Fang was even captured! Standing before me, shameless.*

"Fang!" she burst out. "How could you betray me like you did, Rhys?"

He stepped back at her sudden shift. "What?"

"Fang. You told them, and they took her!" Fenya balled her fists beside her legs, advancing on him.

"I don't have the faintest clue what you're talking about," he replied, straightening at the accusation.

"Don't play dumb," Dempsey added sharply, stepping forward at full height, as though readying himself for a fight. "She told me that you're the only other one who knew."

"Miss Fenya, I promise you, I did not say anything," Rhys insisted, shooting a glare up at the taller Dempsey before focusing on Fenya again. "Maybe someone else saw you with her? But what's happened? Where is she?"

Fenya shook away the depth of his concern that she could read in his eyes flickering in the lantern light. "I don't know. But she has to be somewhere in the castle, right? And I can't find her. I've been all over the building except for the top levels of the laboratories."

He blinked and seemed to come to a decision. "Let's find her. She must be inside, right?" He frowned and tugged at his collar. "You checked below?"

"Directly below and this floor. Someone was in the basement, so we couldn't risk it."

He nodded. "Probably Asper. I think today is the day they make their potions." He rubbed his chin. "She's not on this level?"

"No." Fenya glanced at Dempsey. His face was inscrutable, though his gray eyes had gone dark, like the sky before a storm.

"Then let's go up." Without looking at Dempsey, Rhys offered his hand to Fenya, stepping back from the stairwell as Dempsey brushed past him and headed into the stairwell.

She ignored his hand. Despite his denial, she still couldn't trust him. If he hadn't done it—who else could? Who else knew? He seemed too ready with his answer. Too quick to deny and feign ignorance. She gave a quick inspection to the room she had left with Dempsey. Everything appeared the same. With a mental shrug, she slipped into the staircase and followed Dempsey up the stairs, sandwiched between the two men.

His presence hugged her, shadowing her up the stairs. Her Legacy flickered out from the embers within her. Dempsey was cold and damp before her, almost like an unpleasantly cold pond. Where behind crackled a too-hot fire, burning against her back.

At the turn in the stairs, something pull her attention back to Rhys, and his eyes clashed with hers, his face illuminated by the lantern light. She stumbled on the next step and crashed her knee into the step above, even her stolen Air unable to prevent the injury this time.

"Shh!" Rhys said, simultaneously hushing her and lifting her from the steps with strong hands on her elbows.

She glanced at him, murmuring an embarrassed thanks.

"All right?" Dempsey asked.

"Shh!" Rhys repeated with a glare at Dempsey.

"Fine." Fenya tugged herself free from Rhys's surprising strength and turned her attention to the five remaining steps. No sound came from the room, and so she picked up her skirts and tread carefully up to the landing.

The next level of the lab was empty but for a bare table stretched out in the middle of the floor, a narrow window allowing a gust of wind through it. It rustled through the room in a whistle, and Fenya followed it around the room. No Fang.

She pressed her lips together.

Dempsey stepped into the room behind her. "Do you see her?"

She shook her head, trying to suppress the tears that threatened. She inhaled a shaky breath. "Where else could she be?"

"There's another floor above us," Rhys suggested. "But it's books and things."

"How do you know?" Dempsey demanded.

Rhys rolled his eyes. "It's hardly secret knowledge—you should know too. The amount of times Henslow or Asper have gone upstairs for a reference book or a new quill during treatment? Not only that, I was around when we moved to Wigmore and they made me help carry things to the rooms." He walked absently around the edge of the room, bending down to peer into a dark space under the table. He reached under as if to check something.

"What is it?" Fenya asked.

He straightened and shook his head. "I thought there was something."

Dempsey snorted.

"Will you both be quiet?" Fenya snapped. "You're going to get us caught."

"I'm sorry, but he's full of—" Dempsey broke off as footsteps sounded above.

Fenya looked at the ceiling.

"Did you hear something below?" A muffled voice said.

"I did," came the low growl of Keeper Liah's voice.

Fenya inhaled sharply.

Grabbing her hand, Rhys yanked her toward the door, Dempsey quick at her back. Rhys gestured for both of them to leave, releasing his hold on the door just as Dempsey made his way through. With an angry glare, Dempsey let the door shut quietly, while Rhys sprinted for the stairs, Fenya following. But halfway there, Rhys reclaimed Fenya's hand and dragged her into an empty nook of the room.

"What are you—?" she gasped as he pulled at her.

"Shh!" Rhys hissed, panting softly as he groped at the wall.

She glanced over her shoulder. *Are they coming for them? Dempsey— where'd he go?*

Then something moved beside Rhys. A wall shifted. And Rhys's hand found hers again and pulled her into darkness.

Stairs materialized before them, along with a pair of slim windows on either side, but Rhys didn't pause to allow her to gather herself. He pulled her down in a spiral after him, and soon they were a floor below.

"One more flight will bring you to your floor. Do you need me to go with you?"

"My—oh!" She looked down the circular stairwell and began down as she whispered her answer. "No." She let go of his hand, and he stood for a moment on the landing, shadowed as he groped the door in the darkness. "Wait, how do I open the door...wall?"

His teeth flashed white in the darkness, and he hurried down after her. At the next landing, he reached up and felt around, then took her hand and placed it in the same spot. Under her fingertips was a small, circular item, which felt almost like a coin or a knot of a tree. He pressed her fingers into it and the wall shifted before her, sliding open with a whisper.

This must be an enchantment—just like in the lighthouse.

"Does Dempsey know about these?" she asked.

Rhys shrugged and walked her through the passageway. "I don't know. This is your floor. Go to your room. The keepers will be checking that we're all in our rooms soon. Hurry." The wall began to shift, and he stepped inside before calling back in a whisper. "And if they ask whether you were in the labs—deny—"

Fenya nodded, but the door had already shut on his words, cutting him off. She wouldn't tell, even just on Rhys. If she told on him, she told on Dempsey and herself as well. And despite not trusting Rhys, he had been the one to risk his own discovery to bring her back to her floor.

Or maybe he won't be in trouble because he was supposed to be helping the keepers. Maybe Dempsey is the one that truly on my side, trying to preserve us both by separating himself from me. I wish I knew whom to trust.

With those ominous thoughts, Fenya slid into her room just as she heard the gate at the end of the hall squeak in protest.

Lying down on her bed, trying to pretend like she'd been there for hours despite her racing heart, Fenya closed her eyes and released a tight breath.

But Liah didn't come to her room, not even to bring dinner. Fenya turned toward the wall, tucking her gloved hand under her cheek, her stomach grumbling at the passive discipline. She hadn't found Fang today, but at least she had found an ally. The only problem was that she didn't know who it was—Rhys or Dempsey.

Chapter Twenty-Eight

LIAH

The next morning, before the sun had risen, Fenya paced in her rooms, trying the lock every hour as though she thought it might miraculously unlock.

I wish I were a Metallurgist. Or Kineticist—either one could unlock the metal lock with a bit of control. But what can Fire do? Burn down the door?

And Air? I could perhaps, with Air...

As her thoughts raced alongside her feet in her rooms, her anger grew, but there remained no solid plan to find Fang.

When the tea cart came rattling down the hall, Fenya leapt toward the door, ready to pounce on Liah and demand her dragon back.

"Where is she?" Fenya demanded before Liah could fully open the door.

Liah jerked back into the hall at the question. "What's wrong with you, girl?" A furrow in her brow looked like the storm cloud brewing outside. "Back up before I call the headmistress down on you."

Fenya didn't move. "Where is my dragon?"

Liah's lips curved into a one-sided smile. "I'm sorry?"

"You know what I'm talking about. Where is she? I can't—" She stopped short, barely in time to avoid telling Liah that she couldn't feel Fang any longer. *What would Liah do if she knew I could feel Fang's presence?*

Liah pushed the teacart into the room, avoiding the stone that jutted out obnoxiously from the floor. "You'll find out soon enough."

Liah's answer sent a chill racing over Fenya's arms like cold water dousing a fire. "Why? How?"

Liah didn't answer, but made her usual circuit around the rooms.

"This is ridiculous," Fenya muttered. She turned and grabbed the door handle, pulling it open and stepping into the hallway. She wasn't going to sit around and let Liah control her with words alone again.

"I wouldn't," the keeper warned behind her.

Fenya ignored her, stepping both feet into the hallway. She wished she had a key that she could lock Liah into the room and give her a taste of her own medicine.

Her vision swam. *What is wrong with me? Oh, no... Liah's healing power. It doesn't always heal.*

As the blood drained from Fenya's head, leaving her dizzy and clutching for the wall to support herself, hands grabbed her from behind and lowered her to the floor just as the world swam, threatening to bring up whatever was left of her last meal. Her eyes fluttered closed against her will, too weak to fight.

When she opened them again, she was in a treatment room. The same one she had searched with Dempsey the day before. Liah stood in the corner with her back to her. She craned her neck the other way.

No Fang. Where is she? Where are you, Fang?

No answer.

Why don't you answer? Why can't you?

Fenya bit down on her lip to keep from groaning. Her head thudded already as though she needed water, but it was what Liah had done to her. Her Healing when pushed too far—as she had threatened—hurt. Liah hadn't even needed to touch her, had she? Fenya stared at the back of Liah's head, wariness and fear warring in her stomach.

What is this woman capable of? Could she kill me with a thought? A desire?

Suddenly every look and grin Liah had given her sent new shivers over Fenya's body.

Has Liah been thinking of ways to kill me all along? What is this place that women like this run it? There's no sympathy, no understanding. No help. If Liah is this awful—who are the headmistress and headmaster, really? And how is Milton associated with them?

"Ah, awake," Liah said in satisfaction, turning with a bloodletting bowl in her hands.

Fenya didn't even care about the bleeding now. "Where is Fang?"

"You'll find out soon enough, if you are what we think," Liah answered. "At least, we hope you will."

"What are you going to do?"

"You'll find out," Liah repeated. She set the bowl on the table to the side of Fenya's chair.

"Stop telling me that!" Fenya snapped.

"Oh, ho ho! The hatchling has teeth!" Liah laughed, putting her hands on her hips and staring down at Fenya in clear enjoyment. "The little lady, daughter of the count's daughter, Relic Heir—or should I say Relic Bearer?— has a temper after all." She winked. "It usually takes a lot less to push someone in *your* position into anger. I'm actually impressed, despite myself."

Cheeks heating, Fenya glared at the keeper. "What does that say about you that you find joy in that?"

Liah shrugged. "There's a lot about me that would scare you, girl. I spotted your weakness a mile away. I saw your fear, your lack of control when we picked you up. If it weren't for your Relic status and your... *connections*...you would never be here."

"Connections? You want to call it that?" Fenya snapped, straining against the leather bands that held her arms and legs in place, tight against the chair. "You're treating people like this—like—like animals. And I'm supposed to feel pleased? No one has even bothered to explain what you're doing to me!"

Liah sighed. "We've explained all that we are allowed to explain, *Miss* Fenya. Has no one told you that this is a government funded school? That means the Crown funds this school—and the treatments here are secret and we cannot reveal what we do."

"The...Crown?" For a moment, Fenya forgot anger and desperation to find Fang. *How on earth is the Crown connected to Wigmore?*

"Yes, you stupid girl." Liah rolled her eyes as derision dripped from her words. "The Crown. The government. The King, if you'd rather call it that. The Headmaster gains permission and funding straight from the King, and if you want to go to the King with your little Fire Relic and claim that it makes you special enough to know Crown secrets, then be my guest. I'll even take you the next time I go if you'd like."

Fenya glared at her. "You're a bully."

Liah shrugged. "And you're a fool. We each have our faults."

Footsteps crossed the floor above their heads, followed by a loud thunk as something metal hit the tabletop and muted voices trailed down the stairs.

Something metal sounded again, like a lock clicking open, and Fenya gasped as something like a friend's embrace enveloped her.

Fang!

As clear as day, Fenya felt Fang's presence. But the wyvern was weak, sad, and horribly upset.

Fenya? Fang's inner voice was soft and weak. *Is that you?*

You know my name? Yes, it's me. Are you safe?

No. They have me.

I know—you're close.

"Fang!" Fenya called out. *Can you hear me?*

Yes. You are beneath me.

Have you been there the entire time? I've been searching for you since—

No. A man kept me in his rooms. He's fed me strange things. I didn't eat them. He got angry. No. Make him stop! Please...

"What are you doing to her?" Fenya demanded. Her heart raced. *What are they doing to you, Fang?*

"Doing to whom?" Liah asked, all innocence.

Why bother to lock up a dragon? Rhys must have told them that I made Fang my Familiar.

Tears stung Fenya's eyes. Then a strange fear washed over her.

No—bad man!

Fang's voice in her head trembled, and Fenya made to bolt out of the chair, forgetting that she was strapped down.

"What are they doing?" Fenya demanded of Liah. "Why are they hurting her?"

Liah's lips quirked in interest. "Doing to whom? What are you talking about?"

"They're hurting her!" Fenya screamed, losing her patience.

Liah's brows rose. Her eyes lifted to the ceiling, where a scuffling sound bled from the floor through the ceiling and to Fenya's ears. "How can you tell?"

Fenya shifted her gaze to Liah.

Don't tell them anything, Fenya.

I'm sorry. I already told them where to find you.

That wasn't your fault—I'm not mad at you. But don't let them put any more of the evil potions in you.

Fang's soft whisper of a voice made it through the fear and anger warring within Fenya. She couldn't tell which emotion was hers and which belonged to the dragon.

Then the pain began.

Fenya bit down on her lip as burning pain ripped through her shoulder. Above her, a screech of indignant fury reached her ears, followed by a man's curse. "Dragon venom! Quick, scrape that up into a tube. Maybe it'll be useful."

Liah smiled sadistically. "What a shame. Maybe that dragon won't make it past this testing. Not all do."

Fenya gritted her teeth, focusing on Liah, grateful for the distraction from the burning sensation coursing from her shoulder down her arm and into her chest. "And how often have you done this?" she growled, pulling against her leather straps.

Liah walked to her, putting a hand on her wrist to check her pulse. Fenya fought the chair, knowing that Liah wanted her reaction, to see how she felt as the completed their treatment against Fang above her. Liah wouldn't hurt Fenya or send her to sleep as long as the treatment endured, even if Fenya wanted her to.

"Pulse racing, in such pain." Liah shut her eyes as if she felt the pain herself.

"Do you feel it when you touch someone in pain?" Fenya demanded coldly.

Liah opened her eyes and stared down directly into Fenya's. Though she didn't answer, the wince in her cheek as a surge of pain coursed through Fenya was answer enough. Fenya gasped, dropping her head forward and breaking the gaze. But when she regained control, Fenya glared at Liah, who had dropped her hand as though stung, shaking out her fingers.

"I hope it hurts you more than it hurts me."

Liah blinked once at Fenya, then the mask returned to her face. "It doesn't. I feel a fraction of your pain. Only as long as I'm touching you." She smiled thinly. "You're the one who suffers twice because of your sick connection to that dragon." She shook her head. "You're a fool to link yourself to something so weak."

"Weak?" Fenya snarled. "Fang isn't weak."

"She was weak when you found her, and she's been nothing but weak since. If you're going to create a Familiar, as you were foolish enough to do, you choose the strongest being you can in order to make yourself stronger and live longer. You don't condemn yourself to die through tying yourself forever to a young, weak dragon who will forever draw attention to herself. Don't you realize what you've done?" Liah was gaining energy now, seemingly furious at Fenya for linking herself to Fang.

What does Liah care so much? Why does it matter to her? Have I somehow ruined my treatments here?

"You've made yourself weak and given yourself a target. You'll never be able to be far from her again. This stupid little dragon. At least she is small now—but she'll keep growing. And you'll always have to be close to each other. The most you can be more than an hour's flight away from each other is perhaps two days. She's not a messenger for you, she's a chain around your neck." Liah shook her head in disgust. "So tell me, did you bind yourself to her before we left your aunt's house? Or after the dumb wyvern followed you here?"

"It doesn't matter, does it?" Fenya managed. "Apparently I'm a fool, unsuitable for your testing."

"Oh no." Liah's lips unfurled into a grin. "No, my dear, stupid girl, for you there is no hope anymore. And it's because of that dragon that you're forever linked to Wigmore now. Your foolishness has made you simply irresistible to the headmaster."

Dread coursed through Fenya that had little to do with the pain Fang was feeling and everything to do with Liah's words.

"What do you mean?" she forced through gritted teeth. She didn't want to know the answer, and she certainly didn't want Fang to suffer for it any more than she already had.

Liah chuckled as she moved to the table where an open notebook sprawled with a pencil atop it. "You show your ignorance."

Fenya gasped again as pain shot through her opposite arm. "My ignorance?" she ground out.

"Indeed. Ignorance of the power of dragon blood. It's something that the headmaster has wanted access to for ages. But dragons are difficult to coax into donating blood to our cause, and it quickly congeals. Minutes after it's taken, as a matter of fact. Ultimately, a dragon is needed at the time of treatment to go directly into a potion to stabilize it, and then that potion must go immediately into the patient. A potion with dragon blood has perhaps an hour of shelf life, unfortunately."

"Most people don't know the parameters of dragon blood use," Fenya remarked as coolly as she could, although the stinging pain continued spreading toward her fingers and heart.

Liah nodded. "But your ignorance in creating a Familiar—at even attempting to—is laughable. Did you think of what would have happened if her dragon blood was poisonous to you? Did you even pause to think? Most humans that attempt bonding if they aren't a Dragon Legacist get quite sick or even die."

"I—" Fenya broke off. She'd trusted Rhys, in the moment. And his caution had made her incautious. *Why did I trust him?* She shook her head. *No, I didn't trust him; I trusted Fang.*

Fang? Are you all right?

No answer.

Fenya tried again. *Fang? Are you all right? Are you still there?*

"Dragon blood," Liah continued, "is deeply poisonous from flame wyverns—making the fact that you've bonded with this dragon even more promising."

Liah's words tore through her attempt to contact Fang. "Promising? What do you mean?"

"For us. For Wigmore. For our purposes." Liah scratched out a note into her notebook. "It gives us hope we haven't had in so long." She sighed. "We had students we thought were promising only to have them utterly fail us. But maybe you'll be it. The student half a decade in the making. The one he's searched for."

Fenya's heart thumped awkwardly in her chest. *What is she talking about? She's rambling, and yet saying more than she's ever said to me. But what is she actually saying?*

"I'm not that unique," Fenya said when Liah seemed like she might fall silent.

"Are you kidding? A Relic Bearer who hasn't learned control? Whose parents so utterly failed them that she's lacking in the most basic control of her Fire?" Liah laughed outright. "It's like you were specially made for the headmaster's plans."

"What plans?" Fenya pressed. "I can't possibly be that important."

"And then to make yourself a Familiar—to even be able to do so." Liah scoffed as though she hadn't even heard Fenya speak. "I can't believe how perfect it is. God has delivered you into our midst and we are blessed by it. It's the Lord's blessing upon the headmaster, as Vicar Asper delights in saying."

Fenya's fingers were numb now, her head growing dim as Liah spoke. *What is happening to me? To Fang?*

Liah watched her carefully, her head tilted slightly to the side. "You're feeling it, aren't you?"

Fenya blinked slowly. "Feeling what?" she managed through a thick tongue.

"The sleeping potion they gave that dragon of yours."

"I don't...under...stand." But cold certainly settled upon her. She had made so many mistakes.

"What happens to her, Miss Fenya, happens to you." Liah stepped forward and knelt down beside Fenya. "Your most foolish act of all was binding yourself to something that could die. If she dies, you die."

"But I—" Fenya shook her head, her eyelids growing too heavy, her tongue reluctant to obey. "But I don't sleep when she sleeps."

"No. It's not like that. Normal bodily functions don't matter. You can sleep, and she can stay awake. You can be hungry, and she can be satisfied—unless dying of hunger or thirst. But if she's killed, you will die within the day. A horrible, slow, painful death."

Fenya swallowed with difficulty. "You won't kill her."

"Not tonight, no," Liah agreed, nodding casually as she touched Fenya's wrist with her cold fingers again. "But it's a very simple way to keep you under control, isn't it? Keeping your Familiar in a metal cage where you can't feel her presence...and being able to do whatever we want to her and affect you at the same time... She's altogether too valuable to do away with. She's your ball and chain, the jailor's key." Liah laughed softly. "As long as we control her, we control you."

Fenya heard Liah's words, but she couldn't respond. Her mouth simply wouldn't work properly. The gravity of what she'd done to Fang weighed on her, but she couldn't comprehend it. Her eyelids drooped and she snatched them back up, but fighting the potion was impossible.

Liah continued speaking, but Fenya lost the battle with her eyelids. And so she let the silent darkness take her.

BRYTON

F ang lived. Fenya knew because after nearly a week, she still
lived. Fenya was forced to content herself with wandering the
castle when allowed out, but found all the doors locked except
for the church, the library, and the commons.

Is everyone else locked up while I'm out? Or out counting sheep again?

She rattled a few doorknobs for good measure, especially the
staff's, an excuse ready on her tongue if the door opened, but all were
locked.

When Liah finally told her she could go outside the castle, Fenya
didn't wait to ask again or risk her freedom with an ill-timed question.

Fenya tightened her grip on her satchel as she left the castle gates
as quickly and discretely as possible. The gloves on her hands were a
necessary addition to her outfit now, hiding the flame-shaped marks
her Relic had left behind. She didn't need any additional questions
about her Legacy from anyone. As far as they knew, Fenya was just
another upperclass Legacist that was half-Wylde.

As if it heard her thoughts, the Relic pulsed against her skin.
Between it and Fang, Fenya would never again have privacy or peace.
But instead of scowling at the thought, she smiled. Fang was a friend
like she had never had. A comfort and peace with her presence. The
Relic...she still wasn't sure what it was, but it wasn't quite the burden

that she had expected. Of course, as her father had been required to do, so would she. There were special meetings in cities around Avenesse that occurred every year, and she would be forced to attend or risk being arrested. Papa had not gone to the last three, due to his failing health, but other Relic Bearers had come to visit him—to confirm the truth of his illness.

Legacy Fever had taken him in the end. She knew it happened more often with Relic Bearers, as their Legacies tended to be stronger. *Will Legacy Fever take me too? Especially now?*

Fenya's thoughts carried her toward the cave and the lighthouse, down the rocky path to the beach and toward the channel of water that ran into the cave at high tide. Turning to the cave, she stopped short to find it occupied, and not by Fang, as she had hoped, but by Rhys, Ivy, and the twins.

"What are you doing here?" Fenya asked.

"What are you doin' here?" Harker demanded at the same time.

There was a pause as they registered what the other had said, then both said together, "Walking."

Merritt and Ivy exchanged a raised brow expression.

But Rhys stepped forward in greeting. "How are you?" Concern coated his words, and his warm eyes scanned over her, like molten gold enveloping her. "You haven't been out in so long, we were concerned."

"*You* were concerned," Harker muttered from behind him, crossing her arms over her chest.

Fenya's cheeks heated at his attentions. "I...I've been fine. Trying to find Fang. Have you seen her?"

Rhys shook his head and motioned behind him to the cave without looking back. "No. I was hoping to see her here. You haven't found her yet?"

"No. I can't..." She hesitated and swallowed down the lump in her throat. "I can't feel her. Still."

"Nothing since we tried?" Rhys seemed pained at her answer.

"I..." Fenya dropped her gaze, thinking of the day after she, Dempsey and Rhys had tried to find and free Fang. "They brought me to the laboratory after we tried to find her. The next day."

Rhys's expression went from warm and concerned to stoic and guarded.

"Are you sure you didn't tell anyone about her?" she asked.

"What? No!" Rhys shook his head, his eyes crinkling in pain again. "No, I didn't say a word—even to Harker or Merritt. Not even Ivy."

Fenya glanced at the others, all who shrugged, supporting him with their silence. She narrowed her eyes at Harker, who widened her own as if in silent challenge. *I don't believe you,* Fenya thought viciously, wishing she could voice her thoughts. *She has to be lying—for Rhys. But why? What's between them? They can't be promised to each other...not with Harker only fifteen and clearly not as well-off as Rhys. And if they are, why did Harker claim that Rhys had feelings for me?*

Her gaze slid to Rhys with his pale, flushed cheeks, and her thoughts softened despite her anger at Harker.

She couldn't fault any of them much. There were only so many others here on the island, and her own fiancé was years older than her. She grimaced as her thoughts turned to the ring that remained cool against her chest in comparison to the heat of the Relic.

"How are you going to get her back?" Rhys asked.

Rhys's question reminded Fenya that he was at fault. "What?" the word came out aggressively, and Rhys paused as though she had thrown the word at him.

"How are you going to get Fang back? You can't give up." He seemed to cut short his words, his lips forming words, but he fell silent.

"I'm going to search for her," Fenya retorted with barely contained annoyance.

"I'll help—"

"I don't need your help," she interrupted. "Seeing as you got her captured in the first place."

"No—I didn't." He shook his head to emphasize his point, but his eyes were steeling over as he realized that she didn't believe his denial.

Fenya raised her eyebrows. Rhys had the audacity to look away. *That's what I thought.*

"She gotta be in the castle still," Harker said, glancing between the two of them curiously. "She ain't here."

Contemplative, Ivy's intense pale-blue gaze turned to Fenya.

"Well if she is, I can't find her." Fenya stalked deeper into the cave, hoping to see a flash of red and orange despite all evidence against her. Maybe they just had been apart too long and their connection was weak. Maybe whatever they'd done to her—chasing her around and harassing her—had weakened her. She could be curled in a corner of the cave, or trapped on a ledge afraid to fall down. *Or maybe it's not her fault, but mine. Maybe they took away our bond.*

Fang? Fenya called in her mind as she peered into the darkness of the cave. It stretched perhaps three times her height and the width of two her rooms. It shouldn't be too difficult to search. "Fang? Are you here?"

Shadows hid nothing but more shadows, small puddles of water, and a few footprints or sheep droppings.

"Fang?" she called again, hating how her voice cracked.

"She ain't here," Harker repeated with ice in her voice.

Fenya breathed deeply as the spark of anger kindled within her. *Why does Harker hate me so much? Why is she so determined to make me look foolish and feel unwelcome?*

Ignoring the younger girl, Fenya searched every corner of the cave again. The spot where they had rescued the ram was still slightly different than it had been when the ram had been caught, evidenced by the rock next to the slight mound of earth still remaining from Harker's manipulation and the way the thin trickle of water flowed around the spot now.

"You know, you could trust us," Harker said.

"Let it go, Harks," Merritt said. "She don't—doesn't—have to."

When Fenya glanced back at him, he shrugged.

"Why would you?" he added to her.

"I don't. Because of the company you keep." Fenya turned her back on the others and stared out of the cave entrance. The tide was swirling at the front, as if it was rising. How much longer did they have before getting out of the cave would require getting wet?

"Calm down," Harker said with a roll of her eyes. "I know you're hurtin' that she's gone, but none of us did nothin'. Unlike you," she muttered under her breath. But before Fenya could answer, Harker continued as if nothing had been said. "Rhys just wants to help find her for you. With you," she added when Fenya narrowed her eyes at her.

"Maybe he shouldn't be a murderer then," Fenya said, and bit down on her tongue as soon as she did. What would he do when she confronted him like this in front of everyone? But she glared at Rhys, demanding he finally answer.

Harker laughed outright as Fenya stopped, while Merritt looked confused. Ivy, implacable as ever, had only a slight furrow between her eyes.

But it was Rhys that she sought out. Rhys whose expression showed everything. Just as he had looked away before, he did the same now. Unable to even confront his own sins.

"How could you?" Fenya asked. "Did you do it on purpose or was it an accident? Did you even care?"

"What's she on about?" Harker demanded to Rhys.

"I'm talking about—"

Harker held up a hand. "I ain't gonna to talk to *you*. You're throwin' around accusations that ain't makin' sense, accusin' Rhys of doin' somethin' truly evil. I'm done with *you*."

Fenya crossed her arms and glared at Rhys, both hoping he would explain himself and hoping he couldn't. She would know who to trust if he admitted it, if he confirmed it. She would know then that Dempsey had been telling the truth all along—that he hadn't told about Fang, that he had told the truth about Rhys, and everything else, too. But if Rhys denied it, if he tried to blame Dempsey...she would be exactly where she was now, not knowing who to trust or who told about Fang.

"Hey! You're bleedin'," Harker interrupted, grabbing Rhys on the shoulder.

"What?" Rhys put a hand to his face, his fingers coming away covered in blood. He pinched the bridge of his nose as Harker pushed a white square of fabric underneath it.

From beside Rhys, Harker glared at Fenya as though she were the cause of the nosebleed.

"How long has it been bleedin'?" Harker asked Rhys with a calm tone.

"Off and on, all day," he said, his voice wavering with exhaustion.

"We need to get you back to the castle."

"Wait." Rhys looked at Fenya as he pinched his nose. "You don't understand," he began in a slightly thick, nasal tone. "It wasn't me. I was just...the last one standing."

That's all I need then.

She adjusted her satchel. "You've been lying the whole time, haven't you?" Fenya asked, her throat closing up over the words. "That's impossible to believe."

"No," he said quickly. "Please, you need to understand." He swallowed and spat out a mouthful of blood into the dark and damp ground. "Understand what it is you're talking about."

Fenya shook her head. "All those people? You...you just killed them? So Wigmore could...what? Start over?"

"I didn't kill anyone!" Rhys insisted, blood spraying slightly around him in his vehemence. "Not directly."

"Oh, then it's not supposed to matter?" Fenya spread her hands to the sky. "Just collateral damage? Like Fang?"

"Please, Fenya, just listen," he urged, reaching for her, frustration crossing his face.

But Fenya leaned away from his bloody hand and was already turning for the cave's entrance. She shouldn't have done this here, away from safety. She had been a fool to confront him. What if his excuses turned angry and he attacked her like he had Dempsey? It was a surprise he wasn't already angry and lashing out now. But he looked weary and frightened almost, like he was afraid of what she might already believe.

"I'm not going to listen to excuses," she said as she stepped past him. "If you want to tell the truth without any excuses, then I'll listen. But I won't listen to the 'I didn't do it on purpose.' None of us do things on purpose here when it comes to our Legacies, but you expect me to believe no one prevented you from killing?"

He hesitated. Harker pushed another white square of fabric at him, and he swapped out the dirty one for a clean one.

"I suppose that's all the answer I need." Fenya met his gaze, daring him to speak again.

"Wait, Fenya. You must understand that we're all victims here. None of us want what's happened, but we're all trying to survive."

She narrowed her gaze at him. "The difference between me and you and your friends is that I'm not going to survive at the cost of anyone else."

"You already have," he answered, but his voice was weak and he swayed as he stood.

"What?"

"Bryton," Merritt said in a clear, cold tone.

Harker winced. "Poor Bryton."

"May God have mercy on his soul," Rhys murmured.

Fenya's skin went cold. *Bryton? They know.*

"Amen," Merritt added.

"There ain't mercy here," Harker said in a harsh tone.

"Where is Bryton?" Fenya managed. "Is he in the sickroom? Did he go home?"

Harker didn't look at her, and Merritt scratched the back of his neck. Rhys hesitated before answering, but finally he sighed and with pain in his voice said, "We believe he's dead."

Fenya's stomach twisted. She gripped her satchel strap so hard that her fingernails bit into her palms, and she felt moisture underneath them. "Dead?" She managed to squeeze out the word through tight lips and zero air in her lungs.

"We don't have proof, of course, but...he hasn't been seen for weeks."

"Weeks," Fenya echoed. After his last journal entry. After his treatment with her. "Did he...go home? Cured?"

"Unlikely," Harker finally answered for them all. "As there's a fresh plot at the cemetery."

Fenya sucked in a breath as an invisible hand squeezed her ribs.

Dead. He's dead. No. She couldn't believe it. She couldn't make that make sense. *Why did he die when I lived? Was is me who killed him? Stealing his Legacy? Killing him?* She sank onto a rock nearby.

"So you already benefited from the lives of another, just as we all have. One falls, and they replace them as though we're sheep in the herd, bringing in a new bloodline, maybe stronger, more resistant,"

Merritt said calmly. "Though you want to be or not, we're in a game of survival of the fittest."

Fenya's cheeks heated at Merritt's accusation. "You're right. But I won't let that happen again. And I won't stay here and endure it. I'm done being someone else's pawn—including yours."

She tried to ignore the pain she could read in Rhys's eyes. Even if it hurt to think of it, he had done unspeakable things to people, all in the name of Wigmore and what it stood for. He was on their side—the people who were doing this to her, who did that to Bryton. The headmaster, Headmistress Wyn, the keepers. *All of them are committing evils against me, against them! I just didn't expect Rhys to support them.*

"We need to get you to Henslow," Harker murmured. "Come on. I'll take you back now. You can take a health potion."

Rhys's gaze locked with Fenya's above his handkerchief, his eyes reflecting a combination of reluctance and defeat. "That's probably best."

Fenya watched them go, and when she reached the entrance of the cave herself, the water lapped at her feet and wet her boots and the lower part of her dress's hem. The others were almost up off the beach already. With a scowl in their direction, she turned to the lighthouse, hoping to find Fang hiding there.

But the only thing she found were even more shadows and questions.

Chapter Thirty

THE CROWN

The pungent smell of the sea tickled Fenya's nostrils. It had become comfort the last few months, the steady constant in a world of uncertainties. She was more attuned to it since taking on Bryton's Air.

She couldn't fault the island for Wigmore's staff and their abuses. Instead, she could enjoy the smell of the sea, the screech of the gulls, and the occasional dragon flying through the air.

Wait, dragon? She raced to her window.

A dragon coach.

A dragon coach?

She grabbed hold of the window and pushed it open. It creaked and pushed back, the wind from the sea fighting her. She scowled at it, and it eased, diverting itself around the castle, pushing on the stone and directing itself up and down and out around the window.

She recoiled.

A chill ran over her skin, raising the hairs on her arms. It had been as natural as breathing to tell Air what to do. To demand that it not bother her.

Her stomach twisted uneasily at the reminders of how she'd changed since coming to Wigmore on a coach much like this one.

A dragon called through the air, screeching a gentle announcement of its own arrival. The coach, pulled by two dragons, one in front of the other, glided directly over her window and toward the roof. The underside of the carriage showed a shield painted in gold on the royal blue. The royal shield, painted in gold. Who, exactly, had just arrived? A few moments later, a gentle rumble above her head with the slightest shaking through the castle told her that the carriage had landed.

She hoped answers would come soon. The nerves gnawed on her like a hungry dragon.

The minutes ticked into hours, and Liah didn't come to deliver breakfast. Fenya's stomach growled.

Finally, hours later, the turned key in the lock, and Fenya bolted upright from her bed. She had been attempting to reread the book Henslow had left for her, and shoved it under her pillow before the door swung inward. She realized when there was a sound like Liah had walked into the door that Fenya had again used her Air without thinking about.

My Air? It's not mine. It's Bryton's. I shouldn't even have it—let alone be able to use it. Fenya bit down on her lip. *Is it because he's dead that it's stuck in me? It can't return to him? Or would it matter?*

She shook away the thought and looked up to find Liah pushing through the door and muttering under her breath about stiff hinges.

"Where's breakfast?"

The cart Liah pushed into the room was not the breakfast cart, but the treatment cart. Or rather, the pre-treatment cart. Her stomach twisted in fear that quickly mingled with loathing as the box of syringes clinked when Liah hit the bump in her floor with the cart wheel.

"No breakfast today," she said shortly, pointing at the tray. "We need to prep you for another treatment."

"No," Fenya said.

"Excuse me?" Liah turned on her, her brows raised and her hands flying to her hips. "What did you say?"

"I don't want to. I refuse." She raised her chin.

Liah narrowed her eyes. Then without a word, she rolled the cart out of the room, tucked it around the corner, shut the door and twisted the key in the lock.

Fenya's heart thumped erratically. *What am I doing?*

She didn't have to wait long to find out.

In minutes, footsteps sounded in the hallway. Fenya's heart sputtered, a flame about to go out. *What was I thinking to refuse? What are they going to do to Fang? To me? To my cousins?*

The tumblers turned in the lock, and Fenya seated herself on the edge of her bed, trying to look both poised and in control. This was simply a ballroom, a social event, a young man who had the audacity to treat her too familiarly.

But when the door swung open, Fenya's mouth fell open.

The man's lips curved into a sickly sweet smile. "Hello, my dear."

"What are you doing here?" she demanded.

Sir Milton adjusted his high starched collar. "Oh, my dear, didn't they tell you?" Innocent surprise laced his words like a truth serum laced drink at a ball. "I'm here visiting with the Crown Inspectors."

A chill slid over her body and through her bones in a way that even her Fire couldn't guard her from. "What...what do you mean? Why are the Crown Inspectors here?"

Sir Milton's smile grew as he reached for the chair. But instead of crossing the room to take the chair from its spot at the table, he narrowed his eyes at it, and it came screeching across the room to rest precisely in front of him, ready for him to sit.

Fenya shuddered at this reminder. He was a chimera who could adapt to any situation, take anyone's Legacy and use it as his own. *He could do that to me, rob me of all my Power if he wants—kill me with his Well Legacy. Is that what he's here to do? Did he hear about my refusal to cooperate?*

She swallowed thickly, waiting for his answer. "Wh—who are the Crown Inspectors, and what are they doing here at Wigmore?"

Sir Milton seated himself. "Recall, if you would, that this is a government institution. Though it's experimental, it's still under the control of the Crown. And so there must be some inspections. They, of course, want to see that their money is being wisely spent on these promising students."

Fenya's stomach twisted. "'Promising students'? You mean, promising *experiments*, don't you?"

He tilted his head with a little quirk to his lips. "You aren't an experiment, my dear."

"Might I remind you that I am not yet yours to call what you may," she said as coldly as she could manage. "But what could I possibly be except an experiment when I'm not given the freedom to make any choices regarding my 'treatments'?"

"You're under treatment. It might be a new type of treatment, but you must understand that to stop it now, while incomplete, is the worst thing we could do for everyone involved." Sir Milton leaned forward solemnly. "And that's what I hear. I hear that you dare to suggest you shall not cooperate." He crooked an eyebrow high. "Dare I remind *you* of the consequences of such a *choice*?"

Fenya held her breath, racking her brain for anything he had said regarding her refusal to cooperate at Wigmore. "You must. The only consequence I can recall is precisely what I want. And if that's the case..." She reached to her neck, separating the thicker chain of the Relic from the thin chain that held the garnet ring. She carefully removed it and held it out toward him. "I shall give this back to you in an instant, then we both can return to life before all of this."

His pale eyes sparked in annoyance. "No, *my dear*. I'll marry you right now, and all semblance of control you thought you had will disappear." He flicked his finger and the chain at her neck tightened, his Power drawing the chain of the Relic toward him. "Then you must surrender your Relic to me at my request as your legal master, and your life will end as you know it."

His touch upon the chain felt like a cold hand on her neck. She sucked in a breath, her mind going blank except for the memory of his hands leeching her Legacy away at Whitland Manor.

He stole my Fire then. And now... Whose Kinetic Legacy has he stolen to do such things?

"I know the Conveyances are working, my dear. And you know *how* I know." Sir Milton dipped his chin as he met her gaze. "But *they* will ask you, and you *will t*ell them, that the treatments are working and mention nothing of me or my Legacy."

The words held more than an instruction, but a threat. His Power washed over her in a way that felt both familiar and new. Mutely, she nodded, her skin tingling.

"And when they ask you to show them your Powers," he continued softly, "you will. Do you understand?"

"Yes." She blinked at him.

"Good." Standing, he twitched his fingers and the chair went rushing back to its place at the desk. He stepped over to her and reached out a hand expectantly.

She didn't want to give him her hand, but she couldn't resist his influence. She extended her left hand, and he took it in his, removing her glove before lifting it gently to his lips and placing a kiss on the back of it. But he didn't let go. Instead, he reached for her neck. For the briefest of moments, she wondered if he had decided to kill her. But he crooked his other finger at her neck, and the necklace with the ring unclasped itself. Without touching the ring, with only the aether, he slipped it onto her finger and smiled down at it, pleased. "This shouldn't leave your finger again."

"Yes, sir," she whispered.

He lowered his voice. "And if you dare to suggest in front of the Crown Inspectors or Wigmore staff that we had this conversation, I will make certain that the next treatment you receive will render you mute forever. And that little wyvern that you found at Whitland? It will live the rest of its life in a cage. A life which might end up painstakingly short. Do you comprehend me?"

"Yes, sir," she murmured again.

He paused as he straightened, looming over her. Then a smile crept over his face. "Good girl."

Minutes later, Liah returned, and this time, Fenya didn't bother to fight.

She didn't fight the next day, or the day after, even when Milton's influence over her wore off, and she could think clearly again. She remembered every word he spoke and kept fresh in her mind the consequence for Fang should she not cooperate. Being unable to speak with her still, after nearly two weeks, was like a part of herself was missing. Her attention lagged, drifting to Fang, even when she sketched. But sometimes, when she relaxed her mind enough and let the pencil simply flow, a picture emerged that was something she had never seen before. A strange picture through eyes that seemed not human. It wasn't until the third time it happened, when the image of a face appeared on her paper that Fenya realized it was Fang feeding her the image. Though they could not speak to one another within their minds, there still remained some connection.

The discovery warmed Fenya's heart and buoyed her spirits. It was almost possible to ignore the leeches that sucked her blood, until the image Fang sent was that of a man looming in the square opening before her, a look of evil in his eyes that instilled absolute terror and hatred in Fenya's heart.

Fenya couldn't decide whether to ball up the sketch and turn it into embers or to use it as proof of the crimes against the headmaster.

Before she decided, Liah arrived with the cart, and Fenya slapped her sketchpad shut and tucked it under her pillow.

"Time to go," Liah said shortly.

Fenya raised her brows. The last Conveyance had taken an entire week of blood draws and preparations before it was time. Now she was to be ready in a few days? She had yet to come up with any possible way of escape. Not that she hadn't tried. But without Fang's location and any clues, she couldn't very well fight. Or could she? No, that wasn't the right question. *How* could she fight?

She eyed Liah, who came with a syringe in her hands and another tube of serum in her apron pocket. By now, Fenya recognized the sleeping potion that had so subdued her at her Conveyance. The words that Milton had spoken drifted back to her. But she couldn't fully cooperate—not if it meant someone else died. She would forever be guilty of Bryton's death, but she couldn't bear to have a second die because of her. Or what if she was the one to die? Then she would be guilty of Fang's death as well. Then would the others resign themselves to a death at Wigmore for themselves? Someone had to fight.

She walked just in front of Liah to the treatment room. When she walked in, there was a tall screen in the middle of the room, shielding the farthest side from Fenya's view.

Her heart clenched in her chest. *Who is it today? Who here has Earth or Water? Pippen, Harker, Dempsey, Weston...* She tried to remember the others as her gaze darted around the room, searching for any sort of help.

"Where is Fang?" Fenya asked Liah.

Liah sighed. "Henslow is coming down with her."

Fenya opened her mouth, but Liah pointed to the chair beside the table, cutting her response off. It was the same one she had been strapped to when Bryton had been on the other side of the screen. A chill tickled her spine.

"Who is there?" Fenya started toward the screen to find out.

"No," Liah said, grabbing Fenya's wrist with a severe hand.

Fenya turned only her head, staring down at the shorter woman. "Release me," she said imperiously, and she almost flinched at her mother's voice through herself.

Liah raised her brows, but her hand loosened on Fenya's wrist.

"I have given my word," Fenya said icily. "Do you not trust me?"

"What's going on?" Henslow's voice cut through the silence that greeted her words.

Slowly, Liah released her wrist. "Nothing."

Fenya's gaze shifted to the thing held in his hand. "Is that Fang?"

Henslow nodded. "As promised." He held up the cage with some difficulty, as Fenya knew how heavy Fang was and then to include the cage, it must have been a significant weight. Fenya bent in front of the cage to inspect Fang. An amber eye glinted out of the opening and through the wire mesh. She reached a finger for her, and the wyvern purred softly, rubbing her cheek against it.

Fenya's heart clenched as anger poured through her. "Let her out," she commanded.

Henslow's smiled tightened around the corners but remained in place as though she was a petulant child demanding her way and he couldn't relent. "I'm sorry, but she'll have to stay locked in right now."

"Please?" Fenya met his pale gaze. "She looks...ill."

He inhaled slowly and peered into the cage himself. "I think she'll be fine. Given your health, she shall survive well."

"What do you mean by that?" Fenya kept her gaze on Fang, who blinked slowly.

"Miss Fenya, I ask kindly for your trust," Henslow said with a depth of honesty in his eyes that Fenya was beginning to believe despite herself. "We are doing this all for your own well being."

"Here, Keeper Liah." Henslow set down Fang's cage on a small table beside the door where Fenya would be able to see her during her time undergoing treatment.

"I already have the potion," Liah answered, pointing to the table with its array of syringes and serums.

He shook his head. "This is freshly made. We need to make certain she stays asleep, as the headmaster instructed."

"Right." Liah nodded and accepted the vial he held out. It looked a slight shade darker blue than the other two.

Fenya's heart began to pound in pure panic. She couldn't drink it. But how could she not? She had agreed to comply, or else Fang would be hurt. But if she did comply, then the person on the other side of the screen would probably die just like Bryton. *I promised I wouldn't let Wigmore take another victim.*

"I'll take the others," Henslow said. "So they don't get confused." He stepped forward and scooped up the other two, pocketing them before Liah could object.

Footsteps sounded in the stone hallway, along with low voices murmuring in a tone of suppressed excitement.

"Time to drink up," Liah said, holding the vial out toward Fenya.

Henslow stood behind the shorter woman, face inexpressive, but something in the tension of his jaw, Fenya guessed at something different.

Liah shook the vial in her hand, and Fenya barely caught her frown before it creased her face. It was different. The potion shimmered slightly in the sliver of light that cut through the room.

Fenya slipped her gaze to the cage where Fang blinked sleepily her way. They would only survive if Fenya complied today.

No matter the cost, I must drink. Willingly.

Huffing out a breath, she swiped the vial from Liah and swigged it down in one gulp. It tasted oddly like grape and mulberry.

"We must get going," Henslow said, nodding toward the screen

A LADY OF SCALES AND SMOKE

behind Fenya. "Or Miss Harker will wake before the process is complete."

Fenya couldn't breathe. *Harker? Had she just condemned them both?*

Her eyes crashed shut, her knees weakening as the potion coursed through her body.

Hands caught her on both elbows, gently carrying her back toward the table. A third set of hands caught her legs and lifted them onto the table.

The leather straps were being wrapped around her wrists. Tightening around her ankles, her thighs. She tried to open her eyes, even a slit to see the faces swimming above her. She couldn't. Then a murmur of darkness surrounded her.

She seemed to be swimming in a black sea. Her eyes were glued shut, and a thrum reverberating inside her veins. Power like she'd never known coursed through her, a frozen river released from an ice dam.

Her blood ran hot and then cold. Her Legacies mingled and coagulated. The cold of the new Power clashed with her Flames. Bonding with them, binding to her being, every inch of her body awakening to its Power.

And then something worse. The connection to the source...to Harker.

Fenya recognized the moment she took on Harker's complete Power, absorbing her entire Legacy. A solid shudder, almost like an earthquake moved through her. And suddenly there was a connection to Harker's mind that she had not even experienced with Fang. Though the girl was asleep, her mind was not inactive. A dull throb of pain coursed through it in her weak state...but it wasn't her. Merritt. He was writhing in agony, awake as he felt his twin's torture.

It was more than Fenya could bear.

Pretend, came a whisper in the back of her mind.

Merritt? She nearly gasped at his familiar voice.

If you reveal awareness, we're all lost.

She caught her nod before she moved. If they suspected, they would simply put her back asleep.

And so she did the only thing she could imagine. Eyes closed, she

321

pulled from the mingled Legacies coursing through her blood. Fire, Air, Earth...between the three of them, she could do something...

She tugged at the earth, daring it to answer her. It seemed cold, hard, unyielding. Nothing like pliable fire or air. Those were soft, easily manipulated. Earth...it was something harder to beckon, to control. But her practice with fire had trained her for this unyielding substance.

She forced her body to remain immobile, to feign sleep, while begging the earth to answer her call. On her side, fire and air pleaded with her.

And then it answered.

The floor beneath them shuddered.

"Do you feel that?"

"Is that her?"

"It's working!" a voice murmured in a thrill of excitement.

The floor shuddered and shook, and Fenya directed it toward the machinery tying her to Harker. She shifted the center of the shaking, until the machine shook so hard that it yanked the tube and needle from Fenya's arm, helped by a little tug from Air. The abrupt stop of the transfer sent a shudder through Fenya's body that ended with a jolt through her toes and scalp.

She opened her eyes and found half a dozen men crowded around her, including one that she recognized from portraits. The Elemental Regent, the Prince of Avenesse.

He locked eyes with her, somehow both amusement and admiration blending in his gaze. He nodded slightly her direction, then turned to the headmaster.

"Well done. I'd like to see the final product in a few week's time."

As the keepers bowed and curtsied to him, he walked from the room, the others following.

"What about Harker?" Fenya demanded through a drug-thick tongue. "What are you going to do about her?"

The Prince turned at the doorway and gave her a bemused look. "Who?"

"The other girl—the one you just witnessed having her Legacy stolen."

"Don't worry about her, Your Majesty," the headmaster interjected. "She has requested such treatment."

The Prince nodded. "Of course. You'll explain the situation to the girl then?"

"Yes."

"And guard her well." He slid a glance Fenya's direction. "We're entering a new era of magi. And I must prepare Avenesse for it."

Without another word, he left the laboratory as his attendants trailed behind.

Chapter Thirty-One

ANSWERS

She had failed. There was no chance of freedom now, not with the Elemental Regent personally aware of her, Wigmore's despicable experimentations, and wanting to see her fully transformed. She had hoped to approach the Crown with evidence of the acts done at Wigmore, to expose the horrid truth.

But what had happened to Harker? When she had been connected to her, awake, she had felt Harker's consciousness. Had she survived? Had she escaped Bryton's fate?

Whether she lived or not, she could not allow the final Conveyance to happen. She had to free Fang and flee Wigmore before it could happen. But how?

Her recovery from this Conveyance was quicker than any other treatment. She spent hardly a day sleeping, then returned to normal.

With her satchel over her shoulder, she tested the door as soon as she was dressed. She wanted to search for Fang, but as soon as she emerged into the hallway, Keepers Liah and Headmistress Wyn turned from their position at the end of the hall. Both expressions opened in surprise with wide eyes followed by gleam of victory spreading across their faces.

Fenya's stomach turned over, but she put her back to them and confidently strode down the hall, away from them and their victorious expressions. She didn't stop at the stairs, nor in the courtyard. She marched straight out of the gate, daring any of the keepers to stop her. But Liah watched from a second floor window of the castle, her face in shadow, and Vicar Asper watched from his ground floor doorway, a thoughtful expression playing across his sunlit face.

Fenya marched herself across the island, in the direction of the church ruins, determined to check the grounds. Today she would be looking for two tombstones, not just one.

She didn't stop until she reached the charred ruins. Its remains crouched like a beggar on the city streets, brown and crusty around the edges. Flames had evidently ravaged it, leaving scorch marks on the walls that survived the initial blast.

At the edge of the lot, before any of the grave markers behind the ruins were visible, Fenya halted and took a steadying breath. Her heart slowed back to its normal pace as she stood, the wind whistling its comfort around her.

A part of her didn't want to go on, didn't want to walk through the dilapidated iron gate to find the headstones and crude markers and see who lay here, who had died here. But finally, she forced herself forward.

The graves were around the back of the ruins, where a small path led through the scrub. The backside of the church was taller than the front, as though the explosion that brought it down was toward the front of the building. Had the person been trying to escape? Perhaps trying to avoid the explosion entirely? She imagined Rhys being there, others fleeing before him. Had he done it on purpose? Spitefully so? Or had he been simply out of control?

If she believed Dempsey, then Rhys had done it on purpose, hating the people he had been here with, desperate to get away perhaps.

"She couldn't have known about the Discerptions," a voice murmured.

"What about Bryton? She knew about him."

"Did she? Does she?"

Fenya crept closer, trying to identify the voices over the wind.

"She knew. She chose not to fight Harker's Discerption. How can you trust her?"

There was a long silence.

Then a voice that sounded like Rhys answered, "You know what I've Seen. I've told you."

"That can change. You've admitted that."

"But it hasn't. In all that has happened, there has been no change."

She neared the edge of the ruins.

"And what have you Seen about Harker?"

"I—"

"Ouch!" Fenya slapped a hand over her mouth at her exclamation at the sudden pain in her toe.

Scrambling feet against dirt and rock met her ears, and Fenya stopped, waiting for them to round the corner and confront her.

"Miss Fenya, what are you doing here?" Merritt was the first to ask. His eyes were round and dark in his pale, wind-burned face. Ivy stood behind him, face flushed from the wind, with wide, terrified blue eyes and a smudge of dirt on her nose, her cheeks bright red from the whipping wind.

"What's happened to Bryton?" Fenya asked in answer. "And why are you talking about me?"

Rhys, standing behind Merritt and Ivy, put a hand up against the crumbling building. It stood firm under his touch, but Fenya imagined how it might crumble, how Rhys had been responsible for the first explosion, and what was stopping him from doing it again?

"I'm glad you're here," Rhys said, giving her a small smile.

"Why?" Fenya asked, suspicion ebbing over her.

"What are you doing out here?" Merritt repeated. "How did you get out of the Conveyance in good health already?"

Fenya winced and looked away. *Harker.* "How is your sister? Have you seen her?"

His jaw tightened. "Not since her Conveyance."

Both of them were signing their words as they spoke them—for Ivy's sake. And Ivy's gaze flicked between their fingers and faces, scanning Fenya's now and then as well with quick and eager understanding.

Fenya shifted her weight from foot to foot. "How do you know about it? Who told you?"

"Does it matter?" he asked, but his gaze flickered in Ivy's direction.

How did she know? Fenya sent a cursory glance at Ivy, but she either didn't catch the words or meaning or was more adept at feigning indifference than Fenya. "No. I just...I wanted to know how you're getting information about me. If it's coming from someone with... connections."

Merritt gave a shrug. "I guess that's valid."

Ivy tugged on Merritt's sleeve, and when he looked at her, made quick motions with her hands, pointing at Fenya and then her own mouth.

"Yes, I agree, Ivy," Rhys said with a sigh. He turned to Fenya, stepping toward her with labored steps. "Bryton is dead."

At the admission, Fenya's eyes burned and a sense of heaviness tugged at her core. "I was afraid...of that. I'm sorry."

Rhys's gaze seemed sympathetic. "If Harker lives, then she's escaped the same fate as him, surprisingly."

Fenya bit down on her lip as he finished signing to Ivy. Should she tell them that Harker lived because Fenya stopped the Conveyance prematurely? Because she refused to let the headmaster kill again? Would they even believe her if she told them? And was she even certain Harker did live? What if they hadn't let her?

Merritt's gaze, similar to his sister's, swept over Fenya as if trying to determine something.

"Here," Rhys said, pulling a folded piece of paper out of his pocket and handed it to Fenya. "There is a lot to fill you in on," Rhys explained. "We've had to wait until Asper left for a supply run. He's an Exaudio in addition to being a Truth-Finder, and it's impossible to fill you in accurately with him around."

"But, I just saw him." Fenya gingerly held the folded paper in her gloved hand without opening it. "He's not gone."

Rhys and Merritt locked gazes.

"Oh?" Rhys asked, his tone marked with a casualness that hadn't been there before.

"Where?" Merritt said more quietly.

"At the castle, in the doorway to the chapel when I left," Fenya said.

Rhys bit down on his lip. Merritt turned from Fenya to Rhys and his gaze shifted to the younger boy's. They made a flurry of hand motions that Fenya couldn't understand.

""Have you got your dragon back yet?" Rhys asked with something like forced casualness.

Fenya rubbed at her still burning eyes. "No. I don't...know how to go about getting her back."

"It would be easiest to comply," Merritt said carefully.

She glared at him. "I can't! Not if I don't know how she's going to be treated..." Fenya tightened her arms around her waist, clutching Rhys's letter in her fist. She wanted Fang free, wanted to be able to feel her presence again. It was as if something of her was missing without the voice in her head, telling her how to act.

"Well, perhaps if you say that you will comply, they will treat her well—in my experience," Merritt added. His gaze shifted as though he meant Harker.

"You are...friends...with her?" Rhys trailed off as if afraid to say the word.

Fenya huffed out a sigh. "Yes. You were right, exchanging blood bonded us."

His eyes widened, and he raised his hands to stop her, but she shook her head and mouthed, "They already know."

"But...they've now got her trapped in something that keeps me from feeling her."

Rhys grimaced. "Probably a box made out of the same metal we wear around our wrists."

Fenya shuddered. She knew the feeling of having her magic suppressed, as though she were muted or sketched in charcoal. She couldn't bear to think of Fang completely enclosed in it. "You mentioned...Discerption. What is that? I know what a Conveyance is now, but...Discerption?"

"I can't really say." Rhys paused a few steps from her, then pointed to her satchel.

She frowned down at it.

He motioned to her as though to say, open it.

Curious, she hesitated only slightly before obeying.

Rhys pulled it open wide, peered inside for a moment, then pulled out her sketchpad and a pencil. He moved back toward Merritt, and then walked around the corner where they had been when Fenya arrived. She followed, confused but intrigued all the same. Besides, he had her sketchbook, and she couldn't leave without it.

"You asked what Discerption is," Rhys said as they stopped in the shield of the the tallest part of the ruined wall.

"Yes—I heard you say something about Harker's—"

Rhys held up a hand, stopping her, and put a finger to his lips.

"It's a dangerous process that the longtime staff have developed together. They each add a bit of their abilities to the process: the Vicar his Truth, Liah her Healing, Henslow his Potions, and Wyn and the headmaster...I don't even know. They've masterminded it together."

"Her evilness," Merritt muttered. "At least, that's what Harker says."

For once, Fenya had to agree with the other girl. "But I don't understand what it is. It's dangerous, but what does it do?"

"It severs a person's Legacy from them, forever," Rhys said softly. "Makes them Ordinary."

Fenya released a breath. "That's what I wanted when I came here."

Both of them exchanged looks.

"I was told that would be the case," she added.

"Except..." Rhys hesitated before continuing, "...except that it's being siphoned out and...*kept*...for others."

She frowned at him, but before she could reply, Merritt continued. "Remember the Perfect Mage we mentioned?"

"Yes..." *Are they trying to trap me into saying something I shouldn't? Is this all part of the headmaster's ploy so he won't have to follow through on his promises?*

"I've been doing some research in the library and...other places." Merritt's cheeks pinked, but he continued. "The First King of our country is considered the only Perfect Mage," Merritt continued. "He was rumored to have been the only one with such innate magical abilities, and he decided that no one person should have that sort of Power. So he devised a way to split his Power into several Relics. Eight or more, so the story goes. He split his Powers into the four elements, which were considered the only pure Powers. Air, Water, Earth, and

Fire." As Merritt spoke, he pointed at Ivy and himself for Air and Rhys and Fenya at Fire.

Fenya had an uncomfortable feeling that there should be another two students standing here, a Water and Earth Elemental, like Dempsey and Harker. When she'd first met Harker, Harker had been angry that she was at Wigmore, but was it anger about *her*? Or anger that there was another Fire that might replace Rhys? Was she supposed to be a Water? Had she somehow unbalanced the island by being here? *That doesn't make sense though, as Harker is Earth and Merritt is Air and...but they can communicate with one another...perhaps it was through an abundance of caution? Or an interest in Telepathy?*

"In our experience, the headmaster keeps a balance of elementals here. He's...especially looking for Relic Heirs," Rhys said. "We think that instead of bothering to combine the Relics...he is combining the Legacies within the...Relic Heir. Within...you."

A shiver ran down Fenya's spine, her heart racing it in a shudder of panic and fear. *Milton...he was friends with the headmaster...he came to Aunt and Uncle Verena's after I arrived. He was there when I lost control...came over after I burned down the cottage. Milton...associated with Wigmore. Milton... my supposed savior...willing to risk marriage to me. Had he made it worse for me all along? Did he dare—?*

The shiver was replaced by a horrible sinking feeling in her gut and the tangy taste of fear on her tongue. Bile climbed her throat. *Had he dared to burn down Whitland Cottage? Manipulated it all?*

"What is it?" Rhys asked.

Her engagement to him, forced by the cottage fire, everything.

Merritt answered slowly, his hands moving along with his words, "She's a Relic Bearer."

"You mean a Relic Heir," Rhys corrected.

Sunlight sparkled through the clouds, illuminating his pale face. He shook his head as she opened her mouth to apologize without admitting the depth of her betrayal.

"All the Relic Bearers are old," he continued. "They still live—"

"They did when you arrived here, Rhys," Merritt said shortly, turning away and running his hand through his hair to pull it out of the wind. "You've lost a lot of time here. Her father died almost a year ago now."

Shaking his head in denial, Rhys sank down on a rock, the sketchbook dangling from his hand.

"And Henslow told Ivy," Merritt added, motioning to her.

"And she told you?" Fenya darted a gaze to Ivy, not bothering to correct their assumption that she was only an Heir. Ivy knew much more than she let on, it was true. *So how much did she tell everyone about me? About Milton? And the Relic?*

Fenya put the back of her gloved hand to her mouth as another bubble of bile reached her tongue. *I might be sick.*

"She used to be a very safe confidant for anyone," Rhys agreed. "But Harker has been teaching her how to read and write. She's one of the best resources for information on this island. And in return, Ivy has taught Merritt and Harker much about their Telepathy."

Fenya exhaled through her teeth as she shook her head in wonder. "I've missed an awful lot, haven't I?"

Merritt shifted, scratching at his neck again. "I can't...feel her anymore, Miss Fenya." He looked at her warily. "But I feel you."

Tears welled on her lashes at his words, and she clenched the hand over her mouth. *He can feel me?*

"Not like her, but...different," Merritt added. The lightest brush of fine, dark hairs graced his upper lip, and she had a sudden thought of him older, no Harker to argue with him or tease him, but aging with only her memory.

"I last saw her alive," she whispered.

"If she is...she's not herself," Merritt answered, his pock-marked forehead creased with worry.

"I must leave—" Fenya began.

"Shh!" Rhys snapped, alarm racing across his face.

Fenya covered her mouth with her hand, giving him a questioning look with her eyes.

Rhys picked up the sketchbook and pencil. He scratched something onto the corner of a page and held it up to her. "If Asper is here, he can hear us all over the island."

"Why does that matter?" she said. "After all we've said?"

Rhys shot her a "why do you think?" look and lowered the sketch-pad. "We can't talk about escaping if he could be listening," he wrote.

Fenya pursed her lips. *This is too cloak-and-dagger. As though we're all playing spies—or they're playing with me. Can I trust them?*

She motioned for the sketchpad and wrote, "How do I know I can trust you?" and handed it back to Rhys. Merritt read over his shoulder and exchanged a knowing look with Rhys. He motioned for the pad and pencil, scratching onto the paper, "You can't. But Henslow is on our side. He has hidden journals all over the island and his home to prepare for giving evidence to the Crown."

Fenya bit her lip and motioned for the pencil as her thoughts churned. *The Crown? Henslow knows! Did they not realize the Crown is involved in this? Why would the two of them try to trick me and tell me this sort of information? Should I believe them? If I believe them, will I be at risk? Or will it make Dempsey a liar? And why would Henslow confide in them about the journals but not about the Crown? Students who might betray him?*

"Why are you telling me this?" she wrote and held it up for the boys to read.

"Bryton," Rhys spoke. "Harker." He tugged out a piece of paper and handed it to Merritt, along with the pencil. Then he looked to Fenya and mimed a pencil in the air.

Frowning, she dug into her satchel and handed him her backup pencil with a slight wince of regret. They were already small pencils and she would have to sharpen them again after this. There would be no way to get new ones unless she stole them from the keepers or went home.

"Because we need you to not let the final Conveyance happen," Merritt wrote and held up to her.

Fenya nodded agreement. "I feel awful about Bryton and Harker. I can't..." Tears stung her eyes, and she glanced away.

"It's not your fault. Bryton," Merritt amended.

Ivy remained stoic, her blue-eyed gaze almost condemning. But she blinked quickly, and the sunlight caught a tear, glistening brightly.

Fenya caught Merritt's eye, waiting for him to add Harker's name to that list, but he didn't, and after a moment, he turned, rubbing the back of his neck as he walked a short distance off to look down at a small stone.

Rhys's pencil scratched on the paper, and he lifted the page. "You can trust H."

Fenya shook her head. "It's not that..."

Rhys held up a finger. He wrote something else and held it up. "You've been chosen to become the Perfect Mage. We can't let it happen or they'll never let you go."

"They?" she mouthed.

"Headmaster...Wigmore," he mouthed back. He scribbled something else and held it up. "It's good you aren't a Bearer yet."

Fenya's entire body tightened at the return to this topic. "Why?"

"Can you imagine?" He laughed. "The Power?"

But Merritt was focused on her, his gaze going deep within her. *You are, aren't you?*

Fenya clenched her eyes shut as if she could drown out his voice in her head.

Tell me. It's better to know the truth.

I am.

I knew it. Merritt sighed softly, but he seemed to age in the sound. "She is, Rhys."

"What?" Rhys looked between the two. "She what?"

"She already is."

"How? She's—you're too young! It can't be!" Panic darkened his eyes. "You must be at least twenty to be the Bearer!"

Fenya motioned for the sketchpad. She quickly outlined how Sir Milton had brought the Relic, and it had accepted her. All three bent over and read it with stoic acceptance.

"How do you know it's accepted you?" Merritt wrote.

Fenya quietly peeled off the gloves that reached her elbows. The flames that had flared and faded still left marks, and Milton's ring, which she had shifted to underneath her gloves, adorned her ring finger. She pointed to her hands. "This."

"Did that happen to your father too?"

She nodded. "Only on his bicep though. I saw it only once."

"May I?" Rhys pointed to her arm.

She held out her left arm, and he took her hand, his fingers gentle and warm against her skin. Her skin tingled at his touch. His fingers brushed her engagement ring, and her cheeks burned as his fingers lingered.

"So it's true?" he murmured. His eyes flashed up to hers and burned. "You are engaged?"

She bit her lip and nodded.

He sighed softly. "It's probably for the best. But...for whom?"

She nodded again. "Not best. But forced."

His gaze hardened. "Do you feel different? With being the Relic Bearer?"

"Controlled," she murmured. "It...gave me control."

"A shame you had to come here first to find it." His hand still held hers, but the Relic scars seemed secondary now.

"Yes." She swallowed thickly. She didn't think she regretted it right now. "A...bit."

His lips quirked in a smile as he gently released her hand. "Would you consider performing me a favor?"

"What is it?"

"Don't trust...charm."

She frowned, suddenly feeling the absence of his hand, but the weight of his words had to speak of Dempsey. "Why?"

"That explains all," he said, pointing at the pocket where she'd put his letter. "But please, don't trust...him."

Fenya reached for the letter, but before she could open it, he put his hand over hers and said, "Don't. Not now. But when you're—"

She held up a hand. Something had shivered down her spine and up through her ears as though a vibration coursed through the air. She pointed at the castle and then to her ears to indicate someone was listening.

Crunching gravel reached her ear a minute later. They turned at the noise to find Dempsey. He stopped short as though surprised by them.

"What are you—" he began.

"—doing here?" Fenya finished for him. She shrugged and glanced at the others. "Just planning how to get my dragon back."

Rhys caught her eye as his lips twitched.

Ivy stared blankly at Dempsey, as Merritt nodded without missing a beat.

"And we've determined that the best way to do that is to cooperate." Fenya pursed her lips, tasting the bitterness of the words even through their lie. "I just wish I knew if she were all right."

"Did you ask the headmaster to show her to you?" Dempsey's gray gaze bounced between her and the others.

Rhys rolled his eyes. "Of course not. She's much too foolish for that," he said sarcastically. "C'mon, Merritt, Ivy, let's get away from here. The stench of idiocy is too great. Fenya, if you wish to join us and avoid...him...you're more than welcome."

Fenya stood rooted to the spot, torn between wanting to seek more information from Rhys and the others, and between talking to Dempsey who had always been more open and engaging.

"Fine," Rhys said, noting her hesitation. "Remember what I said?" He lifted the last word in a question, though it felt like more of a reminder than a question.

Fenya didn't react, but he, Ivy, and Merritt brushed past Dempsey and her without another word, Rhys placed himself between Dempsey and Ivy as though to protect her.

"He thought it suitable to warn you? Was that warning about himself?" Dempsey laughed as they disappeared on the winding trail back toward the castle.

Fenya's lips twitched downward.

Dempsey turned to her, amusement lighting his eyes. But as his gaze slid over her face, his grin faded into disappointment. "Ah. I see."

"What?" Fenya asked.

"He's trying to convince you that I'm telling lies."

Fenya shook her head. "He didn't even mention you before you showed up."

Dempsey raised an eyebrow but let it drop. "Do you really plan on rescuing Fang?"

"Of course," Fenya answered immediately.

Dempsey nodded. "Then what you need to do is figure out where they're keeping her."

"I've tried. Trust me."

He considered her. "You shouldn't be fighting them like you are."

"I'm not fighting them."

"Are you sure *they* think that?"

Fenya clenched her fists into her skirts, clenching Rhys's folded letter in her hand. "They've done anything they want to me for the entire time I've been here, and I haven't fought them. Why would you think that I have been?"

"You've been their target," he said with an edge to his tone.

"Not by choice!" Fenya retorted.

He shrugged. "But they've chosen you...and your dragon has been a part of that."

"Not her fault though—she shouldn't have to endure this treatment!"

"You shouldn't have bonded with her or it wouldn't matter," Dempsey said.

"How can you say that? She's still a living being."

He shrugged. "So was the lamb you ate this morning. As much as we might not like it, animals aren't the same as humans. They can be wonderful companions, but their lives are not equal to human lives."

She narrowed her eyes at him. "Her life matters more than most. And dragons are different."

He considered her a long moment. "Well, if that's the case, then I'll help you. We can rescue her."

Fenya hesitated, torn between what he offered and Rhys's warning. But how could she refuse the tantalizing offer set before her when it was the very thing she needed? "All right." She met his icy blue eyes. "Let's do it then."

He grinned. "Excellent. Any new information since the last time?"

"Don't you want to know what we already planned?" Fenya pulled on her abandoned glove, suddenly aware that she still exposed her scars on her left arm.

He chuckled. "If you don't know the answer to that question, then anything you've planned isn't going to help." He seated himself on a tall stone that appeared to be an old tombstone.

Fenya tried not to frown at his choice of seat. "Well, we talked about where she might be. I think she'll be in the headmaster or headmistress's rooms or in the treatment rooms."

Dempsey considered her, tilting his head. "Maybe." He scratched his lightly stubbled chin, staring thoughtfully back at the castle as Rhys and the others slowly approached the gate.

"Well? What do you think we should do?" she prompted.

"I'll investigate." He stood and brushed his hand through his hair. "If you go poking about, they'll know what you're up to. But me?" He gave one of his most charming grins. "They don't care where I go or what I do."

"I'm agreeable with that. I'll go somewhere else now and see if they follow me." For the first time, Dempsey's confidence and arrogance bothered her. With her hands in her pockets, one clutched around Rhys's letter, she hurried away as quickly as she could without seeming obvious. She found the path to the beach and the lighthouse, and instead of heading to the lighthouse, she slipped into the cave, where the tide was out and she could see anyone coming. There, she withdrew Rhys's letter and quickly read it.

Dear Miss Fenya,

You railed an accusation against me regarding the church on Wigmore, and I wish most ardently to address it, as I believe it gives you a false impression of me.

Yes, I have been at Wigmore longer than any of the others, and yes, I was on the island when the church exploded. However, I was not present and had nothing to do with it. I was, in fact, in my rooms recovering from a failed experiment. I was a few hours from death, and the headmaster had just left me to retrieve Keeper Merivale to see if I could be helped. A few minutes later, I heard an explosion and felt Fire like never before.

It was hours before the headmaster came back and told me what happened, in a rare moment of confession. Keeper Merivale had been a Well, and she absorbed too much Power from the unstable children at Wigmore. It had only taken a couple of months for her to become unstable, but since Wells are so misunderstood and their Legacies so unexplored, the risk of having her around uncontrolled, fledgling Legacists was far more dangerous than the headmaster understood. It resulted in the death of every child at Wigmore except for me, and I was considered the final lifeline to his secret project.

As such, the experimentations on me continued, with the hopes of making me a vessel that could restore the health of the headmaster's wife. Yes, it is she that he wishes to heal, and she who pulls him away from Wigmore so often. She is dying from a mixture of Legacy Fever and rare complications during pregnancy with her daughter, from what I have heard. I understand that his desire to make a Perfect Mage is in hopes of creating one mage who can heal her and restore her to life.

While I can understand his love for his wife, I cannot condone the practice. But now, I am incurably tied to his experimentation. My Legacy is volatile and uncontrollable even on the best day. When I am most drained, most tired, that is when my Legacy is safest. And that only happens when I am drugged and wearing Henslow's freshly crafted bracelets. I have no hope for my own future—but you must flee—as soon as possible.

It is imperative that you not be made into a Perfect Mage—or else I fear you will never again be safe—nor the world.

Run, Miss Fenya. Far and fast. Protect yourself and in so doing, protect us all.

- RdC

Fenya leaned against the wall of the cave, her eyes traveling up to where Fang had once roosted, her mind racing. After it had calmed, she quickly reread the letter, and then sent it up in flames, burning it to ash so that no one might discover its secrets.

Chapter Thirty-Two

AGREEMENTS

L ocked in again.

Clearly after her day exploring yesterday and getting unfettered information from the others here, the Wigmore staff were taking the Elemental Regent's warning into account. She was precious to him, and thus to them.

She paced a circle in her room, waiting for the predictable visit from Liah.

When she finally arrived, Fenya didn't wait for the keeper to enter the room, but met her at the door.

Liah held up a hand, ready to use her Healer Legacy, but Fenya stood her ground. Confidence and strength were inside her along with her new Legacies.

"I need to speak to the headmaster immediately," Fenya demanded.

Liah blinked, her hand lowering slightly. "Excuse me?"

"You heard me. Send the headmaster to my room or I will no longer subject myself to your charge. Do not test me."

Liah opened her mouth as if to argue, but Fenya's imperiousness stopped her.

Sullenness crowding over her face, Liah shut and locked the door without answer.

Fenya glared at the thick wood, irritation pulsing through her. She wanted to use her Power, blast a hole through the door and prove to them how she couldn't be contained.

I could probably do it, if I really focused. Between her Fire, Air, and now Earth, she could taste the Power available to her. The aether had never been easier to beckon to her will. Instead of giving in, she forced herself to turn away from the door, clenching her fists closed and calling the Power back into her.

Control. I have a duty to remain controlled. Especially now as a Relic Bearer. Does the Elemental Regent realize I'm a fully fledged Relic Bearer now? Does he know that my status is one of the highest among the magi now? And he's still willing to experiment on me? Upon a Relic Bearer!

How could the headmaster attempt something so foolish? And how could the fool of a prince think it acceptable to experiment on a Relic Bearer? His own ancestor appointed my family as Relic Guardians; who is he to treat me in this fashion? It goes against the very laws the Crown devised to protect the Legacies!

Anger burned through her veins.

Her angry thoughts carried her through her wait, and when the key rattled in her lock, she whirled to meet her visitors.

The door opened to reveal the headmaster flanked by the headmistress. Keeping her distance from the both of them, she narrowed her eyes at him. His face seemed as though she were looking in a reflection of water, the features constantly rippling and moving as a lake's surface, perhaps a shade of light here moving across his cheeks to make it seem larger on one side than the other. Even his skin had a mottled effect, as though the sun peered down through a dappled forest of leaves.

Could I possibly strip his aether disguise away?

"I hear you refuse to cooperate," he began with.

"No," Fenya corrected sharply. "That is *not* what I said. I said I needed to speak with you or I would no longer subject myself to her charge."

"Her?" His eyebrow seemed to rise, Fenya couldn't be quite sure.

Fenya narrowed her eyes. "I will not be subject to this school's authority if you will not respect my wishes."

He lifted his chin in response. "And what does your cooperation matter to me? I can force you."

"Perhaps. Until you remember that you are to fault for the monstrosity growing within me." She held his brown-eyed gaze, the only part of him that seemed unmoving. "Remember that you're creating a monster that one day, even you, in all your Power will struggle to control. Don't you wish me compliant and pliable then, rather than forced to act as you wish?"

He seemed to hold his breath. "Wisely spoken," he finally answered with begrudging pleasure. "Now that I can speak to you as an adult, a mage—though untested—"

"I will forever be untested now—you have made certain of that."

His brown eyes glinted. "Why so?"

"As soon as I arrive at a Year 21 Testing Exam, I shall be inspected and deemed a Feral or worse. I'll be condemned before I step through the door."

"They are not all-powerful, those Legacy Knowledge magi," the headmaster said with feigned indifference. But his strange, aether-mixed features gleamed with satisfaction, as though the knowledge that she would forever be his secret intoxicated him.

She exhaled slowly, annoyed at the way his face shifted again so that she could not read it or even describe it. "But should they catch me with even two Elemental Powers, and me a Relic Bearer, I shall be accused of experimental practices and imprisoned."

"And the Relic will be torn from you to be passed on to someone more suitable," the headmaster agreed.

"And who knows what shall happen to your masterpiece when the Relic is ceremoniously ripped away? Will all your hard work disappear? Will you ever find another one like me to replicate your hard work on crafting the Perfect Mage? Will there ever be another perfect vessel for the Perfect Mage?"

The headmaster's breath hissed through his teeth.

For the briefest of moments, Fenya thought she saw through his image, for much like Mama's when she was angered, the aether around his face shimmered and shifted, seeming to reveal a reality beneath the mask he assumed. But she blinked and it disappeared, back to the blurry edges that told her he concealed his face on purpose.

His smile tightened around the edges. "And what makes you think that's what I'm doing? Or that you are unique?"

She tilted her head to the side. "Does the Elemental Regent visit every patient? Or just the ones you hope will prove your life's work?"

His smile slid from his face as he abandoned all pretense of ignorance. "What do you want?"

"I will cooperate under the following circumstances."

He raised his brows and waited.

"You release my dragon. She will not stray far from me—she cannot —as I assume you are aware. You will keep my door unlocked—indeed, remove the lock from it entirely or move me to a room without an outside lock and bars. If you wish me to be a compliant part of this experimentation, then treat me not as a victim but as a magess of great skill."

"Great skill? And can I be sure that you have any such skill?"

Fenya narrowed her eyes. The Relic had given her understanding of her Power like nothing she had ever experienced. If only it had accepted her before the cottage fire, before coming to Wigmore, before ever meeting Sir Milton, she probably wouldn't have needed to come here at all.

With a steadying breath, she held out a hand, trying to ignore his presence and focus on her Legacies.

The moment lengthened. His lips started to curve into a smile, as though she had already failed.

Then Fire burst into flame in the midst of her palm and fixed into the image of a dragon similar to Fang in size. She looked over the flame dragon just in time to catch the shocked awe on his face.

He straightened, tension on his ever-shifting face. Something flickered between them—aether. He *was* shielding himself from her.

Smirking, she sent the dragon flying around the room, as with her other hand she called forth Harker's Earth. Bits of rock and dust from the room flew into Fenya's hand, and she purposely let some fly close to the headmaster, testing his shield. They curved around his body, racing into her hand, where she used Bryton's Air to gather them into a tight form of a Berserker dragon. It opened its mouth in a silent cry, then she sent it hurtling at the headmaster.

With an annoyed glint to his eye, but clear mastery of his skills, the headmaster waved his hand at the pebble-and-dust dragon, tearing at the ties of aether she bound it together with.

The earth shuddered under his attack, but held together, and Fenya permitted the Berserker to swerve around his head, whirling in the air with the flame dragon until she allowed both dragons to entwine and the flames to burn away the earth. With Bryton's Air, she hurried the smoke and ashes away through the window to drift down onto the sea.

As the remainder of the Power faded away into the aether, Fenya couldn't miss the look of satisfaction and smugness in the headmaster's eyes. Her victory turned sour, like she'd feasted on too many sweets and would be sick.

I did too much. Showed off.

"It is what we knew you were capable of," the headmaster said finally, his voice trembling with excitement. "But I'm afraid we have uses for the dragon that require her presence in the castle."

Fenya's body went stiff. "That's not—"

"I'm afraid you won't have a choice. I will allow you to wander freely among the island. However, the dragon will stay confined. I must have *some* way to ensure that you don't go back on your word."

The blood drained from her head down into her hands. They tingled with her desire to raise her hands and summon back her newfound Powers, but this time to fight.

"I assume we have an accord?"

"I don't—" she broke off. He had taken her bargaining chip from her, prevented her from victory. Any control she thought she had, he was taking from her.

"As I thought. Either you agree, or—"

"I agree." Fenya lifted her chin, pleased to see him start back as if her words and interruption had startled him. "I will comply, as long as you show Fang to me morning and evening. I must confirm her health."

"You can tell her health through—"

"I will confirm her health by personal sight and touch, Headmaster," Fenya said calmly. "Or we do *not* have an agreement. And I will become the monster that others already fear."

He studied her with his dark brown gaze for a long, contemplative moment. Then with a nod her direction, he turned on his heel and strode out of the door.

"One more thing," Fenya said. "I presume that Harker lives? Unlike Bryton?"

He paused, his hand on the door and looked over his shoulder at her. "Yes."

"Good. Will she recover?"

His eyes narrowed slightly as though determining how to answer her. "She lives. That is all I can offer."

As it swung closed, she heard him say to those in the hallway, "Her door will always remain unlocked from now on. Put thicker bracelets on her, double the if necessary. And the dragon is to be displayed to her at breakfast and dinner. And if she does not comply with treatments...the dragon will have its scales ripped from its back one by one and bled to within a breath of life until she does."

Fenya sucked in a sharp breath.

The headmaster didn't wait for a reply but his boots made a confident, unhurried retreat down the castle hall.

Fenya steadied herself. She would comply. But only so long as was necessary to secure Fang's freedom. *And I will make absolutely certain that I will find and free Fang before the final Conveyance.*

Chapter Thirty-Three

HENSLOW

An hour later, Fenya stared at the sketchbook in front of her. The notes she and Rhys had written to each other had been forgotten in the day's events, but now she had to destroy them. It was good practice anyway. She summoned her flames and directed it at the writing. From there, the nature of the flame took over, burning the lines of Rhys and Merritt's writing. She made the flames burn only the graphite, telling it to leave the paper itself alone, and watched the flames devour it happily.

When the graphite ran out, the flame ached in sorrow, as though it could feel its impending death. She took pity on it and allowed it to revive, feeding it on the paper itself. It flashed and churned with appreciation, and she let it burn until the words that they had exchanged and the paper used for it, was nothing but ash. But she called back her Fire, and calling it to her palm, she cradled it for a moment to say a thank you and a simple goodbye before closing her fist over it. She smiled in thought. How her relationship with fire had changed.

Footsteps in the hallway sounded, and Fenya quickly brushed away the ash with a flick of her finger and Bryton's Air, wincing in guilt as she did. But the Air took it out of the window, the fastest way to cover her actions that she could think of, and there, the aether swallowed it.

There was a pause of the footsteps right outside her door, then a knock.

She blinked. Knock? Who would knock?

But she rose, cast a glance back at her desk to check the state of her room, then crossed to answer it.

On the other side was Keeper Henslow, looking nervously over his shoulder as she held the door.

"May I come in?" he murmured.

She opened the door wider, allowing him to shuffle in. She didn't close the door, but stood beside it and watched as he strode to the far side of the room, peered out of the window and seemed to steel himself for something.

He turned and spoke in a normal tone, "I wished to check on your bracelets. How are they doing?"

She held up her wrists. She didn't even feel the effect of the bracelets anymore, which the headmistress had insisted on being replaced multiple times since accusing Henslow of failure. They were nearly invisible to her now, just decorations. "They're fine. I feel... fine."

"Good, good." Henslow reached into his pocket and pulled out a folded piece of paper just like Rhys's. He glanced at the door, and Fenya shut it with a flick of her wrist.

Looking startled, Henslow paused before he gave a lopsided smile. "I came to check on you before my departure."

She frowned. "Departure?"

He pointed at the letter in her hand, indicating for her to open it. "Yes, I have a few errands that must be completed on the mainland."

She unfolded the letter as he spoke and began to skim it. *Dear Miss Fenya, I write in the hopes of communicating secretly to you outside of listening ears. I must tell you that you are unsafe here and must leave as soon as possible. It is worth the risk to your life to leave with or without the dragon. If you must leave without the dragon, then do so, and I will make it my life's work to free her and bring her back to you. If you do not leave immediately, you will suffer a third Conveyance, and this will make you a prisoner to the headmaster, even more so than you are.*

I leave for the next day or two, and in that time, you must leave. There will be one pegasus left, and you must steal it from the stalls underneath the castle. That will hopefully prevent the staff from following immediately.

When you get to the mainland, go immediately to your uncle and ask him to contact Mage de Croia. Rhys is his nephew, and was kidnapped to be experimented on. I regret my role in all of this, and I cannot apologize enough for what I have done to you and the others.

Before you leave, check the secret spot in the lighthouse tower, for I have a stack of papers that I cannot go to right now, and they will help support your claims to your uncle and Mage de Croia. Go fast and far—and keep these papers safe. - H.W.

Slowly, Fenya raised her eyes to Keeper Henslow. He had watched her out of the corner of his eye while he bustled around the room tidying up and keeping a running commentary of how well she had been doing after this treatment.

She gave him a questioning look, pointing to the letter.

"Any other complaints?"

"No...well..." She couldn't come up with a safe way of asking any questions, and it didn't seem likely that they could scribble notes to each other.

"Will that be all then for today?" he asked rather formally.

"I..."

Henslow shook his head slowly back and forth and pointed to her bracelets.

"I'm not sure about my bracelets," she said slowly. "They might be...full."

"Oh? Let's take another look." Henslow rattled her bracelets on her wrists, seeming to make a show of inspecting them. "Ah, you're right, full again, I see. Let's replace those."

She squinted at him, but he nodded as if he reassured an uncertain child.

"There we are," he said, pressing something small into the palm of her hand. "That should do it to get you through the evening."

She looked into her palm to see a small metal key in her palm. Her heart thudded unevenly in her chest. Henslow was a Metallurgist. *He made me a key. It's bound to work...isn't it? But where?*

"I think with that adjustment, everything will line up quite nicely.

There is a storm coming in tonight, you know," he added casually. "Which is why I'm in a bit of a hurry. I haven't been able to get to all my chores before leaving... I stashed quite a few things in the bowels of the castle, to be honest." He winked, but there was urgency in it, not humor.

Fenya gave an uncertain little laugh, as it seemed the most natural thing to do. "Are you sure you're going to be quite well in avoiding the storm?"

He chuckled, though it sounded strained. "Of course, there's nothing to be worried about for me. Or for you. The storm will probably surround Wigmore tonight, but you should be quite safe in your room, and I shall be quite safe as I'll leave early enough to beat it to the mainland. The wards are intended to protect us all."

"How long is it to the mainland?"

He considered her a moment, then conspiratorially lowered his voice as if they were speaking in a room full of others. "I shouldn't tell you this, but what harm can it do? It's only an hour's flight on our pegasi. They are quite intelligent animals, did you know?"

She raised her brows. "Are they?"

"Indeed. They can be told where to go and take you there."

"An address?" she asked in surprise.

"Yes, the more intelligent ones. The least intelligent will get you to the street, at least."

"Impressive," Fenya murmured. *Why is he telling me all this? Except to aid in my escape?* She considered him as he stood before her, fiddling with one of her old bracelets. "How do you know so much about pegasi?"

His lips curved into an absent smile. "Knowledge has always been an intense pastime of mine."

She smiled ruefully. "I've never enjoyed academia."

"It's not for all, but I used to find intense joy in obtaining knowledge that others didn't even know possible."

Used to? She wanted to ask, but fear of the Exaudio kept her quiet.

"Is that what brought you here?"

"Indeed." He seemed pleased that she connected his knowledge to his current position, but regret simmered in his eyes, a coal searching for fuel, for heat, for some sort of extension of life.

What he learned here—did here—must have tainted his desire for knowledge. And to be as trapped as I am? Sympathy washed over Fenya as she internalized his undeniable regret. *Regret will steal his life away. I can't permit it the chance to destroy me. I must leave here, as he tells me. I must trust him.*

"Good evening, then, Miss Fenya. I trust the new bracelets will tide you over until my return." He bowed his head, and pressed a book into her hands that she hadn't even seen him take.

When she glanced down to the book in her hand, it was the one he had given her when she arrived, the one with the hidden journal inside. "Do you—" she began, but the only answer was a click of her door shutting, and his shoes soft on the stone hallway. *Will I see him again?*

Not much later, a saddled gray pegasus carried Henslow away from Wigmore, slicing across the afternoon sun while the pegasus's wings glittered silver. She had an uneasy sense that he would never return. All too soon, the pair became a speck against the sky. So her window faced the mainland. That was why she had seen the Elemental Regent's carriage arrive.

Her stomach writhed with nerves. He had said to go tonight or tomorrow... *But I can't be ready—not without Fang! And I don't even know where she's being kept. Even though he said he would bring her to me...what if he can't?*

Tears stung as her throat burned with unshed emotion at the hopelessness before her. *Stop. I must think straight. There will be enough time for crying later, if all fails. And if it doesn't—then this is a waste of time and energy.*

Wait...Henslow had said the bowels of the castle. What else is there? Perhaps Fang was waiting for her even now.

Henslow had said a storm was arriving before nightfall, which was in less than three hours. Which meant that she had no time to lose.

Chapter Thirty-Four

SEEN

She turned and reached for her satchel, ready to stash all her belongings when there was a brush against her door and it flew open.

Rhys stepped inside, pulling the door closed behind him. Urgency claimed his pale features.

"Wha—?" she opened her mouth to ask what was wrong, but at his alarmed expression trailed off, and he darted for her, putting his fingers to her mouth with a shake of his head. His fingers burned hot against her lips. Staring into his amber eyes, she was suddenly aware of how intimate his gesture was.

He raised a finger from his other hand to his lips for silence, then with a long blink, his gaze went distant for several seconds. Blinking several times, Rhys gaze returned to her, and he slowly removed his hand. He mimed writing onto his palm. Still silent, she went to her desk and pulled out a small stack of writing paper and a pencil she'd left on the desk.

He bent over and wrote quickly, *I Saw you leaving soon, under a storm. Tonight?*

Her eyes widened. *He really does have Sight.* She swallowed and nodded slowly.

He turned to the paper. *Good. Go now if you can. I will find and release Fang.*

She shook her head and held out her hand for the pencil. *I need Fang before I go. She goes with me or I don't go.*

He sighed and huffed, shaking his head urgently. *No. I promise, I'll release her.*

I can't take that chance, she scribbled back.

He raised his eyes to the ceiling and took a deep breath.

I talked to H. He said I should leave before the storm hits. She hesitated. *Come with me?*

Rhys's gaze lingered on the last three words. His eyes stuttered back as though he read them again. Rolling his bottom lip between his teeth, he slowly raised his gaze to hers.

You're to be married, he finally wrote back. *I will ruin your reputation to go with you alone.*

Numbly, Fenya stared at the words. He was right. But...she couldn't possibly marry Milton now. He was involved in this deceit, in this horrible school—deeply involved. For her to marry him was to consent to her treatment at Wigmore. Rhys's cheeks burned hot with fever. She slowly wrote her reply.

I won't marry him. He's involved in this. I can't.

Staring at the words, Rhys released a long, slow breath. Then he wrote, *Good.*

Her heart thumped harder.

Couldn't you See that I wouldn't?

I don't See everything I want to, was his response.

She hesitated. *You wanted to See my future?*

He wet his cracked lips as though he wanted to speak, instead he bent back over the page. *I want to See a future with you.* He paused to show her the words. Then bent over them again. *And I do. But it's not complete. I can't control what I See, not always.*

Fenya's heart stuttered against her ribs.

You See a future with me? What does that mean?

You ARE my future, one way or another. I've always Seen that to be true. Since I first brushed your hand. But I wanted you to trust me, not feel obligated to a future I couldn't prove. He lifted his golden gaze to hers, and a fire shimmered within.

As her heart thumped unevenly, she could only gape at him, not knowing what to think. What about Dempsey? Ivy? Harker? Merritt? What about any of the others? Were they in her future too? Or was he talking about a romantic relationship? All she could manage to write, *How?*

His lips quirked. *I See us living in a little cottage in the countryside. Fang's there. You're beautiful, confident, and Powerful. You have purpose. Strength.*

She read his words, her heart slowing nearly to a stop. "And?" she whispered.

And I know that I love you.

She crossed the distance between them and pressed her lips to his. His dry, cracked lips parted in surprise, and she kissed him more fiercely. She distantly recognized the sound of the pencil hitting the floor and a crumpling sound as he gripped her waist with one hand and the back of her head with the other. He buried his hand in her hair, tilting her head and deepening the kiss.

Then as suddenly as their lips met, he broke them apart. She caught her breath, sucking in a desperate need for oxygen and recognizing a sudden flare in his body temperature. He closed his eyes, his fingers tightening.

He's losing control.

She moved her hands from his shoulders to cup his face. "It's all right," she whispered. "Breathe slowly."

His eyes clenched shut. "My bracelets."

She glanced at them and had to still the gasp that wanted to cross her lips. The bracelets glowed red, then orange. The heat—his Fire—burned her face from where she stood, gripping his face in her hands.

She reached into the aether for the Fire, calling to the burning metal as though they were flames. Maybe she could do something to help him, soothe his Fire, take it away, upon herself.

He was Powerful. As soon as she touched his flames, his Legacy, she knew that he could have once overpowered her own. But now, these were flames without control, hurting, searching for someone to guide them. Searching for a leader, a king...

She tried to coax them into her control, much like she had coaxed Fang out of the metal trap. But they didn't want to respond, they liked their freedom to burn. They were like a wild dragon. Wylde...perhaps Feral. But for Rhys's desperation to do the right thing. She had chosen correctly. She could trust him.

A sound escaped Rhys as though he were being burned. But a Flame couldn't burn—how—?

She redoubled her focus on the bracelets. They attacked him within, invisible flames enveloped him, wrapping the bracelets and burning them hotter than she'd ever felt before. She tugged on the flames, pulling when they resisted. And after a moment's hesitation, they burst free from whatever kept them and leapt for her.

She caught them as though someone had tossed her a flaming fireball. She held them in her hands, calming them the same way she might a raging toddler.

When they stilled, they faded, dying away into invisible embers in her hands, and then into her flesh as water disappeared through sand.

She opened her eyes to Rhys watching her, his bracelets no longer red, but silver again.

"Does it hurt?" she whispered.

"I was going to ask you that," he replied, his eyes shining with admiration. "When did you learn that?"

She flushed. "I've been practicing." She wanted to say more, but the idea of an Exaudio listening stilled her tongue.

Panting softly, like he was recovering from a sprint, he nodded with a half smile. "Keep doing so. You'll need it."

A shimmer of unease wriggled in her gut as she considered his words. He said he was a Seer. Could she trust what he Saw? She had so many questions—how did it work, how certain was what he Saw? And could they channel it somehow, together, with what she could do now?

But before she could determine how to ask, Rhys stumbled to his knees.

"What happened? Are you ill?" She clutched at him, worry overwhelming her as she knelt before him.

He clenched his eyes closed as a groan escaped him. His face drained of color. "I need...my room. Henslow."

"He's gone..." Fenya whispered.

Rhys wrenched his eyes open, panic dimming them.

"Healer?" she asked, not wanting to say Liah's name.

His motions uneven, his head shook jerkily from side to side. "My rooms. Please."

Fenya nodded and slipped an arm under his.

As soon as she returned him to his rooms, bringing him to his bed, Rhys reached for a small triangular flask holding a deep blue liquid potion from his bedside table. He downed half of it in one gulp, and the color ebbed back into his cheeks. He tilted the rest down his throat and nearly missed the table in putting the flask back on the table.

Fenya helped him lay down as his eyes drifted shut. He was ill. How could he be so ill? What was wrong with him? *Legacy Fever?*

He lay on his bed, his eyes closed, as his breathing slowly calmed and became regular. He had fallen asleep.

She turned. She would find Fang and come back for him. Something grabbed her wrist. She barely bit back her shriek of surprise but found only his hand gripping her, his eyes open and filled with panic.

"What?" she leaned toward him.

"Leave—now," he rasped. "Alone if you must. I promise to release Fang. I will."

She bit her lip, her heart swelling.

"Take...on my desk..." Rhys managed. "Letter for my uncle. When you go."

Gently, she disentangled his hand from her wrist and put it back on his chest. She pulled the blanket up to his chin, tucking it under his shoulders gently. She paused for a moment, thinking of the way she had tucked her father in just over a year before, and emotion swelled up inside her. *She would see Rhys again. He had Seen it.*

She brushed his cheek with her hand and hesitated before leaning over and pressing her lips to his clammy forehead.

"I'll try," she said, but she knew that she wouldn't dare leave Fang behind. It was like she had lost a limb simply not being able to feel her.

She couldn't leave Fang on this cursed island, in the control of the headmaster. Still, she took the folded letter from his desk and tucked it into her pocket.

Rhys's breathing was stable now, but his eyelids appearing too heavy to raise. When she looked back from his door, he was sleeping soundly, his cheeks with normal color, but his muscles twitching in dream.

She closed Rhys's door behind her with a soft click, only to turn and find Dempsey standing at the end, eyes narrowed.

She flinched guiltily, her cheeks flushing. He'd just seen her leave a boy's room—not only that, but the one boy here at Wigmore he appeared to loathe. She raised her chin high and strode toward him.

"What are you doing on this level?" he asked as she neared.

She shrugged, thinking of all that she had done this morning. Talking practical treason against Wigmore, escaping, kissing a boy. Her cheeks heated.

"Ah," Dempsey said, seeming to read her thoughts.

"What?" she asked quickly.

He tilted his head, his lips pursing and eyebrow rising in a way that said he could read her feelings on her face. "I wondered when he'd enchant you."

"What are you talking about?"

He shook his head, breathing deeply. "It's happened before, you know." He considered her a moment, then shook his head again, more firmly this time, as though talking himself out of saying something.

"What?" Fenya insisted. What did he think he had to say about Rhys that she didn't want to hear?

"You won't listen," Dempsey said, walking away from Rhys's room. "They never do."

She frowned and followed, annoyed at his closed-mouth attitude just when she asked for more. Mama had done that. "Why would you assume that?"

He stopped as if honestly surprised, one hand on the stairway to the square. "Because I've lost. You've fallen for him. You've chosen him."

She blinked in confusion. "I'm not blindly choosing anyone, Dempsey. I choose what I do with my eyes open."

A small smile playing on his lips, he tilted his head in sympathetic appreciation. "I know; I like that about you. You try to make up your mind with the information you've gathered. I've always admired you... Fenya," he added softly. "But you're choosing to believe someone so unstable he can't even stand the treatments here. He's too weak for you."

Thoughtfully, she considered him and the depth of his words. "What if I don't need someone to be strong for me?"

"But how will he support you? You'd be better off marrying that fiancé of yours than someone who spends half his life in bed."

She set her jaw at his words. He was speaking just like Mama would. Everything depended on her future, her well-being, her wealth. Mama's words were in his mouth, as though she could have said them herself, and the worst thing was that he was right. Rhys was weak and weaker every day. Was he ill or did he indulge in it? She couldn't very well tell him to stop—he wasn't faking after the Fire she'd calmed from his veins. "I don't need someone to support me."

He raised his eyebrows. "What job could a Relic Bearer get that would support anyone?"

Fenya narrowed her eyes. "There's sure to be something." *But a female Relic Bearer, no less? Odds are stacked against me.*

A distant boom sounded. Thunder. She glanced at the window. "The storm..."

He narrowed his eyes. "You...you're going, aren't you?"

She hesitated, but that was all the answer he needed.

"Then let me go with you."

"I..." Fenya hesitated. He was more dependable than Rhys, at least in terms of stable Power. But could she trust him? She never really knew.

"We must leave quickly though." He motioned toward the stairs.

"I need to find Fang."

"I'll help you find her."

Fenya hesitated and glanced back at Rhys's door. She half hoped that he would hear and open the door, tell her what to do. But this was her decision now, a decision that even Henslow had recognized as hers to make. And Rhys's visions...they suggested that she was capable of making the right choices, wasn't she? Either she trusted Dempsey and brought him with her now or...she would have to trust him more to stay quiet if she left without him.

"All right," she murmured. *But we'll come back,* she added silently, not wanting anything overheard.

The sky darkened over the open square, and both Fenya and Dempsey glanced its way.

He tilted his head as if he suppressed a shudder. "We have to go now," he whispered.

She nodded. It was time. Henslow had said she had to go to the basement and everything would be there. She slipped her hand into her pocket, touching the key that he had given her. It would help her. She had to trust him.

"This way," she murmured, taking his hand and pulling him toward the corner stairs that led down to the basement laboratory and the under-the-castle stable entrance.

At the door, she cast a glance back to Dempsey, skimming over his face. There was something there, a storm brewing in his blue-gray eyes just like the storm that approached the island. Could he feel it with his Water? Something stirred in her, perhaps Bryton's Air?

She grabbed his hand and tugged Dempsey down with her. They disappeared into the darkness and descended toward the ground. She stumbled at the bottom but caught herself as Dempsey's arms went around her and steadied her. She nodded, but when he didn't let go, she whispered that she wasn't injured.

It's too dark in here. With a huff, she willed her Fire into existence. A marble-sized ball of flame burst out upon her palm. Dempsey's expression shimmered in the light, like a rabbit caught in the light of a fire.

"You're a Spark?" he exclaimed.

A strong sense of foreboding clenched Fenya's gut. But it was too late. *I forgot.* She had already revealed her Spark nature to the headmaster, hadn't she? No wonder he had been so victorious. She had given him so much in her determination to prove herself.

She had to strike forward now.

Her foot hit the steps to the basement laboratory, and she sent her light on ahead of her, freeing it from her palm. She had to concentrate just slightly more to let it go free from her skin, allowing it to hover in the air in front. She used Air to push it out from her, gently letting it float two feet ahead as though she had buffeted herself with a bubble.

As her lower foot hit the bottom step, relief flooded through Fenya short and fast, with fear on its heels.

The box. Fang's box.

She leapt for it, bumping into the fireball and sending it sputtering and skittering across the room.

With a quiet curse, she steadied the flame and pushed around it to let it hover in the middle of the room as she crossed to the box.

"Fang?" she whispered. "Fang?" She scrambled for the key in her pocket, pulling it out and slipping it into the lock. She stifled a sob as she twisted it. *Why isn't it working?* She was so close to Fang that her fingers burned.

"Here, let me help," Dempsey said, nudging her clumsy hands aside and seizing the key from her. He moved toward the cage with key in hand.

"I didn't think you'd *both* be here," came a calm voice.

Fenya whirled, gasping to see Keeper Liah standing in the darkest corner of the room.

Then she reacted almost without thought, rocketing the fireball her way.

Liah darted out of its path, shock on her face shown in the fireball's path. "How dare you!" She raised her hands, and Fenya called for her Fire. The fireball grew to a blinding light, but then something happened.

Fenya's vision began to blacken, her strength ebbing. What was happening? *Liah.*

Stumbling back, Fenya tried to fight Liah's distant touch. If she used the Air, if she forced away Liah's hand... She focused on pushing Air toward Liah's hand, pushing it out of alignment with her body. The aether shimmered between them.

Fenya gasped, not realizing she hadn't been able to breathe. But she couldn't stop fighting now. She redoubled her effort, calling back the flames that had sputtered. The room burst again into light. From inside the cage, a weak screech distracted her.

Fang.

With a shriek, Liah stumbled backward as Fenya's Fire surged toward her. Fenya glanced at the cage to see the key in the lock, half turned. If only she could get Fang out, she could flee into the door just beyond and mount the pegasus and they could escape...it was all within her grasp. Liah couldn't kill her.

Liah was cowering against the wall, hands up against the flames that raged in front of her. Even Dempsey seemed afraid, cringing backward from the heat that, to Fenya, felt like Aunt Cali's loving embrace.

Fenya kept one hand up, pushing the flames toward Keeper Liah, and extended the other toward the cage. Her fingers fumbled with the lock. She nearly had it!

Then something cold washed over her from the back. She wobbled, her eyelids fluttering, and then she crumpled. She thought that maybe she landed in Dempsey's arms. Or maybe it was just atop his lifeless body.

Chapter Thirty-Five

WATER

S
he was having a very strange day.

She remembered waking up and going down to breakfast at Aunt Cali's. Mama was there, glowering, like usual. But then someone entered the room, and Mama's glower turned to a glow.

Mountains of mouth-watering pastries filled with jams and custards crowded the table. But when she went to lift a Duskberry Tart to her mouth, she couldn't. Her strength was gone. Exhaustion weighed her arm down. Try as she might, she couldn't lift even the smallest pastry to her mouth.

Her stomach growled as her mouth watered.

Someone shook her shoulder.

"Miss Verena, wake up."

She just wanted to sleep. She was exhausted. Her eyes couldn't open. Wouldn't.

"Wake up, Miss Verena, we don't have much time."

That voice though. Persistent, kind, worried.

She opened her mouth, but it was so dry that her lips stuck together. She tried dampening them with her tongue only to find her tongue too dry to offer any relief. She was a lake consumed by fire, dried and evaporated of all moisture.

She tried to speak, her eyes still refusing to open. She couldn't speak to ask for water, but she felt it nearby. She pulled at it, and heard something clatter.

"What? Water? Oh, yes." He shuffled quietly around her in the room, she heard liquid being poured into a cup, then it was pressed against her lips. "Here, water."

She drank greedily, allowing the icy water to caress her lips in a lingering embrace. The water was pure, unaltered, against her tongue. Nothing had been put in it. She gulped water so quickly that it poured over her cheeks and chin.

"Slowly, there's plenty," he murmured. As he spoke, he rustled around. She tried to open her eyes again—why wouldn't they open?

Then something wet and warm pressed against one eye with gentle pressure, loosening the lids. Then against the other.

She pried her eyes open, blinking against the darkness and the feel of thick eyelashes.

Henslow stood above her and gave her a tight smile. "Better?"

"What...happened?" She didn't know what else to ask.

Henslow placed the cup and cloth aside and turned his attention to her wrists, rubbing them. "How do you feel?"

"I...I don't know." She realized her wrists were free from both bracelets and chains. *When did he untie me? Why is he here? Isn't he supposed to be on the mainland?*

Henslow bent over her ankles then and tugged the straps against them. The pressure mounted, then released. "Slowly now." He leaned her forward and helped her sit up, turning her toward him so that she could throw her legs over the edge of the table. "We must act fast, Miss Fenya."

"What happened?" She searched Henslow's face, but he wouldn't meet her eye. "Please, tell me. It didn't—"

He half turned away as if to check on something.

She inhaled sharply. Dempsey lay on the table, unmoving. Dread and horror washed over her as her memories came flooding back. Being in the basement and confronted by Liah. Her trying to free Fang. Pushing Liah back with her Fire. Fenya struggling to control the Power that had surged through her, and then feeling something dark and oppressive over her.

Water. She sat up straighter and stared at the water jug. Water. She had *sensed* water. Not just felt it splash her face and cover her tongue, but she had sensed it before it had touched her. Her eyes closed in horror. *He'll never leave me alone now. I've failed.*

"Here, drink." Henslow held a vial of lavender-colored potion toward her.

"What is it?" She knew she could trust him, but that table...the table of the headmaster's supplies, tossed over and crumpled and used up, was the farthest thing from trustworthy she could think of. Bloody rags and used syringes littered the surface, bracelets—her bracelets— abandoned in an open box lined with velvet and stained with blood. *Where are the others? Why is Henslow alone with us?*

"It's a healing and strength potion," Henslow said, drawing her attention away from the wreckage. "It will restore your strength just enough to get you out of here." He pressed the vial into her hand and popped the cork out of the top. "Quickly now. You don't have much time. They'll be back any moment."

"What—?" she began to ask but he lifted her hand toward her mouth, encouraging her to drink it fast. She gulped it down. It tasted slightly of berries, with a crisp freshness almost as though they had been warmed in the sun. Even as she swallowed it, her eyes opened more widely, her body felt awake and refreshed from her bones outward.

"I'm afraid it won't do much for your...Legacies, but it should at least physically renew you," Henslow said in his slow, deep voice. He glanced over her shoulder in the direction of the door. "You must hurry."

"But Dempsey..."

"Yes, I'll assist him now that you've drank the potion."

"Is there another for him?"

"Yes, he'll need more, I'm afraid." Sorrow creased Henslow's forehead as he released Fenya and shifted to the bed of Dempsey, which was exactly like hers except that, she realized as Henslow went to the young man's bedside...

He hadn't been tied down. At least, not like her. From her table were chains six centimeters wide and a quarter as thick, made to snap together. But his...there were only thick straps of leather that buckled together to hold him in place.

"What happened to us?" Fenya didn't realize she'd spoken until Henslow answered, putting a hand on Dempsey's forehead as he had on hers, and then another on his wrist to check his pulse.

"He's been Discerped, Miss Fenya. And in so doing, Conveyed his Power to you." Henslow lifted his gaze from his task alongside Dempsey and met her gaze for the first time. "And a partial reversal, a sharing of your...perfection...was attempted."

As her eyes widened, her mouth went tight at the thought. The headmaster had attempted to share her Legacy, her ungodly, unnatural Powers with Dempsey? "But...why?"

"There is great pressure from the Crown, and urgency to prove Wigmore's abilities and salvage the work done here."

"The prince is eager to have this work?" Fenya leaned back against the table, shock stealing her strength from her legs. "I don't under-stand...why?"

"Can't you imagine the Power?" Henslow shook his head and shifted the screen so that Dempsey's face became visible as he tended to him. "The King is ill—very ill—and the Prince is desperate to heal him, not quite ready to give up his life of leisure and claim his title."

"But why did the headmaster...and you...?" she trailed off, not sure how to ask the question.

"You have read the journals, Miss Fenya. We both have had similar losses in our lives," Henslow answered grimly, pressing a potion upon Dempsey's lips. "And there was a time when I would have given my own life to save another's. But that has not been possible for many years now, yet I remain trapped in this attempt to manipulate natural life."

"And did he..." Fenya motioned at Dempsey. "Did he survive?"

"I feel a pulse, and he should respond, with enough time."

Time? They had little of that. But her sluggish mind was reviving, was awakening to the very real, eminent danger they were all in. Henslow was back—he had come back to Wigmore at risk to himself, and Dempsey was drained of both Legacy and strength. And she? Everything she fought against had happened.

Fenya nodded, more to herself than anything. "Help him then."

Henslow hadn't waited for permission, but pried open Dempsey's mouth and trickled the first potion down his mouth. "It is no longer safe for any of us if you stay. He is determined..."

"Determined for what?"

"I've explained it all in my correspondence. I've written and posted letters to people I trust over the past few months, in code. His act will not remain secret forever. I am finished being a part of it now."

As Fenya nodded, a thought occurred to her. "Why can we talk freely here, now?"

His jaw flexed as he clasped a second vial, the first not having produced any effect on Dempsey. His hands trembled. "We cannot, except that Asper is gone at the moment." He darted an uncomfortable look at the door and then at Fenya. "He is the Exaudio, and his fiancée, Wyn, is the one he reports to daily."

"Fiancée?" Fenya's mouth fell open.

Henslow's expression turned grim. "Yes. And they are deeply invested in Wigmore's success, I assure you. Should you succeed tonight, and reveal the truth about Wigmore, they will be forced to go into hiding."

"And should I fail?" Fenya murmured, gaze slipping to Dempsey, his face pale and still as death.

Henslow's hand paused in tilting the remaining half of the vial's contents down Dempsey's throat. "Then all of Avenesse will be consumed by Wigmore's...success." His mouth twisted on the last word.

A successful Wigmore was anything but that for them...for her.

Fenya closed her eyes. Her body hummed tensely. "How has it all come to this?"

"You were made for a time like this, my dear. Do not allow doubts and insecurities to plague you. You have been equipped for success tonight, not failure."

Fenya inhaled deeply, and her body trembled in response, the marks on her wrists brightening to a deep red of a birthmark. Her Fire, Bryton's Air, Harker's Earth...and there it was, Dempsey's Water. But there was more than that, as she felt with Harker's...a sense of knowledge of other's thoughts, a stronger understanding or impulse of what people knew, or what they thought. Bryton...had he had a second Legacy as well? And Dempsey? Could she feel them inside her? That was a question for another time, another place.

"Miss Fenya?" Henslow murmured. "Could you be so kind as to untie Mr. Dempsey?"

"What? Oh, yes!" She flew into action, her earlier sluggishness and exhaustion gone thanks to Henslow's potion. She raced to Dempsey's wrists and unlatched the first. Her stomach churned at the way she had succumbed to this treatment, at the willingness she had offered, like a lamb to the slaughter. She was no longer a lamb though, no longer a sheep, but a dragon. She was transformed—and not because of what they had poured into her, but because of what they had taken from her. She blinked back tears of frustrated anger. They'd taken her innocence. Her trust. She wouldn't be such a fool to trust a stranger again. Or anyone. With what she knew now, she knew that the world was not the world she had imagined it. The headmaster had shown her that.

Please don't be dead, she couldn't help but silently beg as she stared at the young man she had come to know. *Even he with all his faults, didn't deserve this.* But his chest rose and fell, if not steadily, at least sporadically.

Appeased, she slipped the strap from Dempsey's second wrist, gently rubbing the red mark away from his skin, but in that moment as she shifted her attention to his ankles and before she moved to those straps, his fingers closed around her wrist and trapped her in place. Gasping in surprise, she met Dempsey's gaze. His head hadn't moved but his eyes were open and staring at her, an expression of pain and betrayal on his face.

"Why?" he asked through cracked, dry lips.

Fenya wet her lips as though it could help his and swallowed. "Water, Henslow. Please."

"Of course."

Dempsey's expression didn't change, and he tightened his grip on her.

She inhaled. "I didn't do this. I didn't want this, Dempsey."

He sighed and closed his eyes as though to argue with her took too much strength. But his hand relaxed, and Fenya tugged herself free.

A distant noise had Fenya's hand pausing and meeting Henslow's wide eyes over Dempsey's body.

"Miss Fenya, you must go. Now."

"What? Not without you—"

"Yes, without. Take the remaining pegasus in the stables—Fang awaits you there—and—"

"What about you?"

"I must stay," he said serenely. "You might consider injuring me first, to make my loyalty look unwavering."

"I—I can't!" she exclaimed, covering her mouth with her hand.

"Remember what I said before?"

"What?" Her attention slipped to Dempsey, who groaned on the table.

"What to gather from the location?" Henslow said with urgency.

Biting her lip, she nodded, fear rolling over her in waves. Her body lurched in its fear, violent trembles that made her feel like she was going to dry heave or pass out.

Henslow stepped up to her, grasping her hands in his. "My dear, I hope and pray my daughters will be like you one day—strong and courageous. You were made for this time, remember that. No matter what happens to me, you were made to make these wrongs right."

"How?"

"As we discussed. Use your resources, your mind, your Power, your Legacies. I have complete faith in you." Henslow gave her a fatherly smile.

"It's vital that you do so now. As we discussed."

"Yes."

"Then go. Unless you plan on fighting me?" His eyes twinkled sadly.

"I...I can't." She wilted before him.

His face fell into something like understanding and pity. "Then I won't ask."

Fenya inhaled sharply, looked at the door and then at Dempsey, who gave a tired nod and murmured, "Go."

"My satchel..." Fenya murmured. "Where is it? I had it with me—"

369

Henslow pointed to a table in the corner, where her leather bag sat as silent witness.

Her mouth felt unusually dry; she couldn't swallow past the lump in her throat. *What if Henslow doesn't survive? What if I can't make anyone believe me about the experiments at Wigmore? What if no one bothers to return and save them? What if I don't make it to the mainland?*

Her gaze lingered on the pair of men watching her settle the satchel strap across her chest, wishing she could somehow make everything right this moment. But she couldn't. She gave a half wave of goodbye and turned.

If I can't make anyone believe me and come back with me, then I come back alone.

She hurried down the steps as quietly as she could, one hand on the wall, the other out before her. She didn't dare summon her Fire and chance giving herself away through some sliver of light escaping the laboratory doors.

Her heart was the loudest thing there, pounding in her ears. She raced for the door and reached out a hand.

Once in the basement laboratory, Fenya tiptoed through the door into the lower stable.

Energy lamps lit the walls, safe lighting for the pegasus that looked up from its extra-large stall with a cage going all around the top portion. The lamps cast a dim light around half the room, putting the stall in shadows, fully prepared for the night as the pegasus munched its hay. It had to be a male by the size of it, for she guessed the animal would tower over her if she stood beside it.

Her hands shook as she stepped forward, momentarily ignoring the giant animal that blinked with mild interest at her.

Fang? Are you in here?

There was the barest flutter of an answer in Fenya's mind. A curious poke, like something she had first felt when she hadn't realized what it was like to have Fang speak in her mind.

"Fang?" she whispered aloud. "It's me. Can you hear me?"

A weak squawk sounded from a dark corner of the room. Fenya flew toward it.

The key! Fenya's heart squeezed in panic. Had the key been taken before the Conveyance? She patted her dress pocket and relief flooded through her. It was still there. Somehow...but she wasn't going to guess how or why. Perhaps Henslow had replaced it from Dempsey's hand, or else crafted a new one. He thought of everything, it seemed.

She pulled the key from her pocket as she went, fumbling it in her haste and dropping it. It clattered across the room and into a shadow of a corner.

"Dragon dung!" she whispered to the still air.

The pegasus snorted his disapproval of her language.

Fenya jumped at the sound, but Fang's reassuring amusement rippled over her mind, soothing her slightly.

Crouching in the dark corner, Fenya tried to spy the metal key in the dim light.

After a harried minute of fruitless, furious searching, where Fang made mews of encouragement and impatience from her locked cage, Fenya clenched her fists together and sparks flew from her fingernails.

What am I doing? Use my Fire! It's already light in here, for shattered relic's sake!

With a snap of her fingers, she summoned the Fire ready within her. It had never been so easy to call it. Never. Her heart fluttered in fear. She had never expected it to be this easy—to have the Fire before her energize her rather than drain her. It filled her with something like more Fire...it made her want to make it larger, bigger, give it life.

Or maybe I'm going crazy...slipping into Legacy Fever after all that's happened.

She closed her heart against the feeling, but she couldn't close herself to the fright it gave her.

Control.

She wasn't sure if it was Fang's voice or her own in her head that reminded her. But she was supposed to control it, not allow it to control her. She had to remember that.

She spotted the key on the ground and scooped it into her hand. As quickly as she could, she moved to Fang's cage and unlocked it. This time, it unlocked easily, and the cage sprang open.

"Fenya."

Fenya leapt in front of the cage, protecting Fang from the person who spoke her name. She raised her fire again, sending it toward the voice, illuminating Dempsey's face. He flinched back from the Fire, eyes going wide, raising his hands against her attack. She closed her fist, and the Fire blinked away.

"What are you doing here?" she demanded in a hiss. "You're supposed to be with Henslow."

"It didn't go right," he said. "I can't stay here. You must take me with you."

"What?" Unease gnawed at her stomach. "What didn't go right?"

He shook his head, shaking off her question. "They took my Legacy," he said, casting a quick glance over his shoulder at the door, then pointed to the pegasus. "There's only one pegasus here. I can support your claim." He pulled up his sleeves and showed his arms, scarred by needle marks and half-healed cuts.

She winced. *I agreed to take him with me before. If I leave him behind—* She bit her lip. *He's heard too much.*

"Let's go. Hurry. I have to stop by the lighthouse." She turned and scooped Fang out of the cage. The dragon was half limp, weakened from her time in the cage and the treatment of the headmaster. She pulled Fang against her chest, wrapping her shawl around the animal and tying it into a sling to keep Fang against her chest. Fang mewed in something like appreciation, warming against her chest.

You're different again. The thought appeared in Fenya's head, and Fenya stared down at the dragon's yellow eyes.

I know, Fenya replied after a long pause.

Dempsey hadn't hesitated, but moved toward the tack in the corner of the room. He picked up a large saddle and stepped into the pegasus's stall. The top of his head hardly came up halfway to the pegasus's back. How was he supposed to saddle the animal? How were they supposed to ride and control it?

But Dempsey confidently approached the animal, nudging him into a position against the wall of the stall, then he ducked under the animal's neck with the saddle, reappeared on the other side and quickly saddled the beast. In moments, he had bridled it and led the pegasus from the stall. A gust of wind rippled through the entrance of the cave, and Fenya's gaze shifted. The animal didn't seem to mind his presence or even bother with him.

"Come," Dempsey said. He'd led the pegasus up to a mounting block, the several steps up which brought Dempsey to just peering over the saddle. "I'll help you up." He swung up into the saddle and gazed expectantly at her.

Fenya hesitated. She hadn't planned on leaving with Dempsey, of all people. She still wasn't certain if she could trust him. But her fingers tingled. She had taken his Legacy. Not on purpose—she had fought not to—but it had still happened. *I owe him safety from Wigmore, at the least.* If it wasn't such a risk, if they had more than one animal—a sole animal who couldn't pull the carriage alone—then she would go upstairs and get everyone from their beds and leave together. But all she could do was go now and return. And it was better to leave with someone else, wasn't it? As he said, he could support her claims. She would be easy to ignore, but to come with another—a young man who had seen more?

"Come on, please," Dempsey said, glancing at the door. "They could be coming any moment."

I don't trust him. Fang's voice whispered in her mind.

I don't...I don't think I do either. But what else can I do?

Try to get him to leave, Fang answered. *Should I bite him?*

Fenya fought back a smile. Outside, the wind howled past the castle.

"I think there's another storm coming, Fenya, we have to go!" Dempsey held out his hand.

Making her choice, Fenya crossed to the mounting block. Skirt fisted in one hand, the other clutching Fang against her chest like a babe, she climbed it. Dempsey grabbed her hand, leaning forward so she could mount behind him. The saddle was only a one-person saddle, and she slipped halfway off the wide back of the pegasus as he side-stepped at her mounting.

"Hold on," Dempsey said, then nudged the animal forward.

The pegasus required two kicks before snorting and stepping his overlarge hooves toward the opening of the deep cave.

He clattered on the flat stone ground, annoyed clops that echoed in the cave. Could they hear it above? Fenya clutched Dempsey's waist.

As they neared the exit of the cave, the spray of water from waves crashing below touched her face. It seemed to seek her out, cling to her. She shuddered as her Fire crackled in annoyance.

What the— Water. Dempsey's Water.

Her hand trembled, the one around Dempsey's waist, and the one gripping Fang to her chest, not trusting her knot in her shawl for the weakened dragon. Her mind raced. Henslow had warned her against delaying. And he had been there when she woke, urging her to leave. Who was she to trust? Dempsey was here, Henslow had sent him down. She had to trust them. Had to act even if they weren't trustworthy.

"Go to the lighthouse first," Fenya said in Dempsey's ear.

"The lighthouse?" he questioned, twisting in the saddle to look at her.

"Yes, please. Just land on the beach or the rocks if you can, and then I'll run in and back down."

"As you wish," he murmured, nudging the pegasus off the cliff.

The animal spread his wings, but within the confines of the cave, he couldn't quite stretch them wide open.

Fenya's breath caught as she spotted the rocks below them. Her hand tightened around Dempsey's waist, her legs gripping the sides of the animal. She wished she were in the saddle. She tightened her hand on Fang. She couldn't let her fall.

The pegasus leapt off the cave's edge and plummeted down.

Chapter Thirty-Six

THE LIGHTHOUSE

Fenya closed her eyes, failing to breathe as the pegasus fell from the cave's entrance.

But his wings caught the wind, and a shudder went through the animal as his wings pumped and the beast lifted them higher into the air as Dempsey guided him toward the lighthouse.

"On the rocks?" he yelled back at her.

She nodded, then realized that he couldn't see her with his attention forward. "Yes, if possible!"

"The tide is coming in, it looks like, but I'll try." He maneuvered the pegasus down toward the large string of rocks the lighthouse was built on. The pegasus clattered against them with his cloven hooves, but couldn't gain purchase and kicked off again.

"He won't land!" Dempsey called back at her. "I'll have to drop you on the beach."

Fenya's stomach lurched as the pegasus veered off over the water at Dempsey's command. This time, the pegasus landed on the beach, gentler than Fenya thought he would, but she wasted no time in scrambling down from the animal, sliding so quickly from his back that she stumbled to her knees on the ground. Fang spilled out, a mewling screech of annoyance from her lips.

Watch it! she called in Fenya's head.

"Sorry, sorry!" Fenya forgot to speak in her head. She scooped the dragon back up in her hands, and Fang nestled against her neck as Fenya clutched her to her chest. Warmth flooded through her as Fenya started hurrying toward the cave and the channel of water that separated her from the rocky strip to the lighthouse.

The channel across the cave was dark and foreboding, and thoughts of nightmarish creatures living in the deeper flow raced through her mind, but Fenya didn't have a choice. She waded across it, her boots squelching in the mud. She reached the middle, the water high against her thighs, as waves crashed over her, colliding into her hip. Fang squirmed against her neck, warming her despite the stiff wind that blew icy water against her face.

She gasped in shock as a large spray of water enveloped her face.

What are you doing? Use your Legacies, silly, Fang admonished.

Fenya almost laughed in surprise. *How could I forget? Because I shouldn't have the Water Legacy, that's why.*

You do now, Fang said firmly in her mind. *And whether you wanted it or not, now you can control water. Use your Power. Embrace it. Or it will devour you from the inside out.*

How do you know these things? Fenya pushed at the little wyvern.

I haven't always lived a lonely life. I know other dragons, and dragons know Legacies.

They do?

We know it because we are a part of them.

Fenya's foot collided with a rock under the water. She winced, but pulled her attention back to the conversation in her head. *What does that mean? Dragons are a part of Legacies?*

Fang's presence was calming the panic that climbed up her throat. She was several lengths away from the edge of the water still, but the conversation had carried her through her fear. She couldn't even see where it ended in the darkness.

Dragons are observant creatures, so we know all about humans. We might not know everything about human Legacies, but we know enough. And I can feel you and your Legacies like my own.

A low glow brightened the dimness. Fenya blinked, and Fang began to gleam. Her scales glowed.

"What are you doing?" she whispered to the dragon.

Fang stretched her wings. *I feel better. Stronger. You shared Power with me.*

How? I didn't—

Just your touch. It's enough to heal me. I feel as though I could fight a full-sized wyvern now.

Fenya grinned.

Let me go. Before I glow too bright or take too much from you.

Realizing she still gripped Fang as tightly as she could against her chest, Fenya released her.

Not so fast! Fang's annoyance bled through as Fenya attempted to correct herself and caught at the dragon, razor-sharp talons scratching through Fenya's finger as she clutched for anything to keep the wyvern from falling into the churning water below.

Easy, Fang admonished. But she kicked off Fenya's now-throbbing hand, spreading her wings and rocketing into the air with a moon-like glow.

Watching, Fenya took a deep breath, calming herself. She couldn't panic now. Fang would survive. It wasn't possible to come so far and fail. If she failed tonight...chances were she would end up chained to the wall in her room. Or dead because she would refuse to accept that future for herself. Even though she wished the headmaster were willing to kill her instead of a life of being locked up, Fenya believed him—he would not dare endanger his prized possession of a Perfect Mage. Everything he had designed Wigmore for now rested on her. But Henslow's words returned to her, how he had attempted to reverse the process, drawing her Legacies out of her and into Dempsey. He wasn't trying to create one Perfect Mage, but many. Or perhaps her refusal to comply had made him attempt to Discerp her Legacies into Dempsey, a more pliable subject.

There's no possibility of returning to Wigmore's control. Fenya dragged herself forward. She pulled her feet out of the squelching sand. One more step, then one more. Just keep going. *Don't use a Legacy unless necessary. I have to preserve my strength for whatever may come.*

Fang had swept herself off into the air, toward the lighthouse, calling silent encouragement in Fenya's head to keep going. *I'll check the lighthouse as much as I can.*

Keep an eye on the pegasus and Dempsey.

Yes, Fang agreed. *Can't trust him.*

Abruptly, the water went from thigh-deep to ankle deep, and Fenya fell forward onto her knees and hands, gasping as the water lapped at her feet as though she were a fish that escaped its grasp, an ungainly flop against the sand.

She pushed herself to her feet and picked up her sopping skirts, racing across the beach to the lighthouse up on the rocks. Water lashed at the rocks, spurting at Fenya's boots as she slipped across the rocks to the base of the lighthouse.

Reaching the door, she fell against it in relief, twisting the handle. She'd never been so grateful for a door to open.

She slammed it behind her as though someone were after her and raced up the stairs. Panting, she raced to the top and to the corner of the turret. She ran her hands over the edges of the bricks. *There, a little bump, like what Rhys showed me in the castle.* She pushed it and a spring popped, opening a little door. Instead of being empty like when Rhys had accidentally discovered it, inside lay two journals atop a rectangular box.

Opening the box, Fenya found a stack of papers inside. Setting the journals on the bend, Fenya squinted at the papers inside the box, but the moon filtering into the lighthouse was too dark to read anything by. She snapped the box shut again and stuffed it into her satchel.

A door squeaked far below her.

Fenya froze, then slowly reached for the journals.

That hadn't sounded like the base door to the lighthouse. She crept over to the stairs and peeked over the railing, heart thumping in her ears. *Who else is here?*

Fenya held her breath, all too aware of the way she became instantly visible with her head over the railing. Someone was on the stairs. They stepped out of whatever room they had been in and stood on one of the landings, a dark shadow standing in place.

Fenya cursed herself. *How could I assume no one ever stays in the light-*

house? A lighthouse often has an attendant. Why did Henslow send me here if he knew that? God, please don't let that person hear me.

Stay away, Fang. Especially if you still glow.

Fang's answering voice didn't come, and Fenya inhaled shallowly. Could she hear her? Was she truly alone, in this moment? Henslow's journals were heavy in her blood and saltwater-soaked hands. Sand from the beach had stuck in her wound. She fought to keep still, the burning itch of her wound suddenly unbearable.

The shadow shifted slowly, almost too minutely to make out the movement, and Fenya drew in an equally slow breath, trying to calm her heart.

The shadow stayed still and quiet.

Fenya's heart might as well be jumping out of her chest. *Where is Dempsey? And how am I going to get out of the lighthouse to meet him if someone is standing on the stairs, blocking my only exit?*

He'd have to come to the top, she realized with a prick of fear. But she'd have to reveal herself in order to do so—and how would she climb from the lighthouse railing to the pegasus without falling?

She swallowed, her mouth suddenly dry. She didn't like heights. And where was Fang?

Fang? Where are you?

Still no answer.

The shadowed figure remained motionless, and Fenya followed suit. She couldn't reveal herself until the pegasus and Dempsey arrived.

The moments lengthened. Her heart slowed to a steady, though rapid beat. Her hands ached, both with injury and Power.

Then something moved to Fenya's right. Anticipating danger, Fenya flinched away, scratching a foot across the landing and sucking in a sharp breath. The sound crashed in the stillness, echoing through the narrow chamber of the lighthouse.

Something had fallen near Fenya, but no one stood there. *Milton? And his stolen Telekineses? No—why would he be here?* Fenya leaned over the railing, cursing silently as she tried to identify her opponent.

The shadowed figure was racing up the steps, feet light but determined, a skirt billowing around their legs. *Liah? Wyn? It doesn't matter!*

Abandoning her thoughts, Fenya raced for the outer catwalk of the lighthouse, gripping Henslow's box tight as she scanned the sky, desperate to see a dark spot moving across the sky—but nothing came.

Where are you, Dempsey? She wanted to scream for him, but didn't want to give herself away more than she already had.

She ran for the opposite side of the catwalk, hoping to buy herself time, but it was too late, for a woman came racing up before she could make it.

"You!" Headmistress Wyn burst out from the door at the top, an expression of devious delight on her features. "I don't usually get a chance like this..."

Fenya faced her, clenching her fists. "You aren't getting a chance at all."

"No?" Wyn laughed. "I think so. And this time, you're alone. You don't have that miserable dragon to save you."

"Miserable?" Fenya's fists tightened. "The only miserable beings here on this island are the adults."

"You know nothing—understand nothing!" Wyn's laugh contained a hysterical tinge. "Wait, you—!"

At the change in Wyn's tone, Fenya followed her gaze to her hand. Henslow's journals.

"You thieving little glimmerdrake!" Without warning, Wyn lunged at Fenya.

Fenya dodged the other direction, hitting the railing to the outer edge of the catwalk. Her mind whirled as half her body faced the waves crashing many stories below.

Something tugged at her hand, a soft, deliberate touch.

Fenya fought the Power, grasping the journals tighter in her hand. "No!" she shouted as Headmistress Wyn growled and renewed her attempt to use her Legacy on the item. The leather slipped to the tips of her fingers before Fenya shouted, and Wyn's grasp on the journals dropped as though the touch had been severed.

Fenya clenched the books against her chest with a gasp.

Wyn jumped forward, her hands stretched out in front of her as though she were going to strangle Fenya.

Dashing to the side at the last moment, Fenya left Wyn grasping at the railing to avoid falling and stretching her hand toward the lighthouse like she used her powers to bring herself back into balance.

Fenya raced for the stairs only to have the gate slam shut just before she arrived, narrowly missing her fingers. She collided stomach-first into it, and breathless, nearly toppled headfirst over the gate and down the spiral stairs. She scrambled for the rails with her free hand, determined to hold onto the box with her other.

Deliberately slow footsteps advanced. "You'll give that to me if I have to rip it from your hands, you thief." Headmistress Wyn stood behind her, her face alight in the reflection of the lighthouse's energy flame. "You Legacy-addled traitor. We gave you everything. More than you could ever realize."

Stomach still smarting from the impact of the iron gate, Fenya gasped in large breaths, clutching Henslow's journals to her stomach. But at Wyn's last words, Fenya gave a short laugh and straightened, ignoring the pain in her ribs. "You're right."

"Why are you laughing?" Wyn demanded. "You—you have nothing to laugh about."

Too pained to continue laughing, Fenya allowed her smile to grow. "I do. You see, you're right. You gave me everything. So you *can't* kill me. Even if you physically could, you can't...yet. Because the headmaster wants my Power—*me*—too badly. *I* am his prize—the very thing you're threatening—and if you kill me, then there's no way he can claim it. He doesn't know why it worked with me—and finding another like me is impossible."

Headmistress Wyn hissed at her like a startled wyvern. "He'd forgive me," she said, but her voice wavered, betraying her worry.

"No." Fenya steadied herself on her feet. "He wouldn't."

Behind Wyn, the door to the lighthouse swung in the breeze, and the pegasus darted across the sky, Dempsey aboard.

It was time to leave.

Chapter Thirty-Seven

PERFECT

Fenya's fingers tingled, advancing up her arms as though electrified. Was Wyn doing something to her? Her vision blackened around the edges. Fenya squeezed her eyes shut briefly to shake the feeling. *Calm. Remain calm.*

She took a deep breath and refocused on the headmistress.

"He would forgive me," she was saying. "You don't know him. You just know *of* him. But he is the most powerful mage in the world—stronger than you. If he were to be tested, he would be beyond a Rank I Order I mage."

"Even now?" Fenya tried to appear unaffected by Wyn's attack, arching a brow high in skepticism.

Fury flitted across Wyn's features. "How dare you—"

But when the older woman broke off, attempting to find the words to finish her insult, Fenya understood that her words had struck a chord deep inside the headmistress.

Outside, the sky was darkening. The storm approached. She felt it. She felt the water, the air, the movement of the clouds. The earth tingled with anticipation. Electricity primed for lightning...for Fire.

Wyn was still sputtering her defense to Fenya's insult of the headmaster.

"You don't have a defense," Fenya realized aloud, cutting across her words. "He's told you not to hurt me."

The headmistress snapped her mouth shut only to raise her lip in a sneer. "It's no matter. I'll tell him that I did everything I could, but that with your...your...clear *excess* of Power as a Perfect Mage, there was nothing I could do." Her eyes danced with delight. "I'm not a Healer, after all. And he trusts me."

Fenya shivered at the casual way in which she spoke. Wyn clearly had done things like this before, not hesitating to hurt, maim, or perhaps even kill. Fenya had to do something, had to distract her somehow, get out of here without letting Wyn have Henslow's documents.

"Are you only Kinetic?" Fenya heard the words come out of her mouth, not knowing what made her ask that question. Perhaps if she just kept the headmistress talking, she could edge over to the railing and Dempsey could position the pegasus.

The headmistress laughed, low and long, a sound that echoed in the lighthouse's tower. "I don't need a Legacy to make someone obey me. Though mine can help," she added as an afterthought, tilting her head at Fenya in way that suggested the headmistress was trying to choose the best way to make her obey.

Fenya glanced around the lighthouse. Except for a waist-high railing to keep someone from falling, the catwalk was barren.

Behind her the gate still dug into her lower spine. *The gate.* One of the only things up here that willingly moved, though undoubtedly the headmistress could move more with her Legacy.

Before Fenya could move, the gate propelled her forward, and she crashed into the railing across the catwalk, her lower ribs hitting hard and her upper body flinging itself over the top of the railing.

Fenya grunted.

Don't drop the journals! If anything matters, it's them.

Without her hands to stop her fall, Fenya's body began a slow tip over the railing.

No no no!

Helplessly, Fenya began to fall, clutching the books to her chest with one hand while she scrambled for purchase with the other.

The headmistress screeched in fury.

The journals moved in her arms, and Fenya clutched it tighter.

Wyn was fighting her for it.

She lurched toward the railing as Wyn let her grip go, and Fenya's feet left the ground.

She screamed.

Then there was a tug on her foot. No, her boot. Almost as if a hand had grabbed her by the ankle, but she didn't feel fingers.

With a wrench that left Fenya gasping and feeling as though her insides had been scrambled, she was suddenly slammed back into the catwalk floor.

"I'll be having a talk with Griff about those bracelets," the headmistress muttered, striding over to Fenya as she lay sprawled, gasping for breath and trying to assess her injuries.

Her body ached, her ribs and back where she'd been bent over the railing, and her hip had slammed into the catwalk floor. Even her hands and wrists ached. Had she broken something?

She rolled onto her back, bending her wrists at the same time. *The journals!*

Fenya's eyes shot around the room, then she pushed herself up with a gasp, only to see the headmistress standing there with Henslow's books in her hand.

"No!" Fenya cried.

The headmistress smiled over the box at Fenya. "Yes. I'm afraid you haven't won as you might have believed."

Fenya scrambled to her knees, ignoring the pain coursing through her, her thoughts on one thing. "Give them back."

Wyn scoffed in disbelief. "Do you think that will work? You are Powerless in manipulation." She motioned to Fenya's bracelets. "And I? I am a Rank I Order 2 magess. I *am* Power."

And to prove it, she flicked her wrist and Fenya rose into the air by her feet. The wind whistled around her, wrapping her braided hair around her throat like a rope. Fenya screamed as the rocks flashed below her.

Stop it, Fenya! she thought, mentally trying to slap herself. *I can over-*

power her—but how? Find my center, breathe slowly. Wyn can't control my body, just what I'm wearing.

Even as she spun in a circle over the distant rocks, waiting for Wyn to act, she ignored the woman chattering something on the catwalk, letting her words disappear into the air.

Then she crashed down, down—and thumped onto the catwalk again with a groan. The rotating aether light flashed in her eyes.

"Unfortunately, you are right. He doesn't want me to kill you—yet," the headmistress said from a few feet away. "Though I'd love to, in all honesty."

"When have you ever been honest?" Fenya rolled onto her back to gauge the impact of her words, pleased to find annoyance written on the older woman's face.

I cannot let her win. What will make this woman stop?

Fenya pushed herself upright with a groan. Her elbow ached. "I won't stop fighting. You'll have to kill me."

Come back, Dempsey. Where are you? Fang?

The headmistress shook her head. "Those bracelets might stop me for the moment, but they stop you more. And there are ways of stopping you without killing you. That's what he thinks. He made a mistake...chose the wrong one. It's his weakness, if you ask me. She's already paid for that mistake. Or maybe she did it on purpose to protect him..."

Fenya had to keep her talking. "I don't know what you mean. Why would he want to keep me alive? I'd tell people what he's done. Protect who? Dempsey?"

"No, no, you wouldn't be able to," the headmistress said absently, opening the first of Henslow's journals with a little frown creasing her forehead.

Fenya bit her lip. If she burned them, she would destroy Henslow's papers, the very proof he risked his life for in letting her go. Did Wyn even know it was Henslow's? And then there, above Wyn's head, was a ray of hope. Dempsey waved to her, motioning her out to the railing toward him. He was mouthing something. *Jump?*

Her stomach squirmed at the thought as fear took hold.

But his presence offered hope, the only courage and resolve that she needed. She drew a deep breath, but the headmistress was slowing down in her movement through the book, anger flickering across her face in tense wrinkles. "I know what the headmaster is getting out of this, but what do you get?" She tossed out the words, hoping to distract her.

Headmistress Wyn lifted her gaze from the journal and narrowed it at Fenya. "I never liked you. Too perceptive. Too quiet. The quiet ones are the smart ones, I told him. I told him he was playing with more than fire with you." She laughed at her own joke.

Fenya ignored the laugh, fighting for control in the midst of the wind buffeting them, of the headmistress's words a waterfall around her.

"Yes, it's perfect, isn't it?" Headmistress Wyn was saying conversationally, the journal forgotten. "Beautiful irony."

Fenya tuned out the words, hearing only bits and parts of sentences.

"All this time he's thinking that he does this for himself... And truly he does it for us all. Think of the people whose Legacies we could absorb. Of Legacies that we could use. For all purposes. Even wholesome ones," she added, with a half motion to Fenya, who jolted back to awareness at the attention.

"He convinced the King that his intentions were wholesome, didn't he?" Fenya said amiably. "That the headmaster is trying to help the Crown." Fenya almost scoffed.

"The Elemental Regent, of course...of course. But even if the King had doubts, the need outweighs the risks. To protect our country by Discerption of Power from evil magi." She paused to chuckle softly and turn the box over in her hands. "Of course, if this ability ever reaches the King, it would only be Discerption. He's still perfecting that, you know? But the King...he's got troubles of his own that this might fix. The mad king and all that."

Fenya blinked in alarm. Henslow had spoken of healing the King. To considering Discerping him? That had to be high treason. What would that do to the country? The perception of their strength? To the ailing king himself?

"But this ability—it has potential to save lives." The headmistress's eyes snapped to Fenya with a dark glare. "And you—you're going to make all this worthless if you escape. You'll be as guilty as him if you do."

As fury roiled inside her, Fenya knew what her mistake had been. She had been thinking about her own risk, about her own future—but what of the other's stolen Powers? She had a responsibility to speak for them all: Rhys, Bryton, Harker, and Dempsey...all of them. They all had suffered—some more than her.

"You could have wealth beyond your dreams, Miss Fenya. You could be the very delight of this nation—the possibility to end our war, to equip our people as magi of never-before seen Power, returning the rulers of the throne to full Power like it should be." The headmistress seemed to be talking herself into something, and Fenya had a terrifying idea that it was to end her.

Fenya let the headmistress's words trickle over her as she breathed in slowly, calming the storm raging inside her. With one hand hidden behind her back, Fenya drew her flames into that arm and down into her flame marks. It burned, but she coaxed the Power out of her heart, up to her arm, then down through her aching elbow and her own resistance. She understood how it worked now. It was a part of her, a part of her soul, of her wants, of her desires. She wanted nothing more than her flames in this moment though. No other flame could compare. She drew that Power into her palm, centered it there, prepared it like kindling ready for the spark.

Only she *was* the Spark.

"Yes, you'll ruin it all. I have to kill you, you see. It must be done." Headmistress Wyn shook her head, her lips twisted in something like false sadness. "We'll have to find another...with the Crown's approval, that won't be too difficult."

Her eyes fixed on the headmistress. *Yes. I am a Spark. And she will feel my burn.*

Fenya moved her hand to her front and grinned as the headmistress' eyes widened in shock.

"How—how?" she stammered. "Without a flame, with the bracelets?—you are a Spark!"

Did the headmaster not tell her? Fenya bolted to her feet as carefully as she could. "I suppose you aren't as trusted as you think then. The headmaster has known for some time." The flames licked the air above her hand, several balls of orange fire that she'd coaxed out of herself. She was filled with it—with Power. But she wasn't accustomed to wielding so much aether at once, and already she felt herself fading. The health potion would not provide energy forever, and her body had suffered much today. She had to work fast.

"No, Headmistress, I won't let you win. You thought you were breaking me, but you were teaching me how to burn. And now you will see what you have done." Fenya hurled the flames, dashing the ball against Wyn's chest.

Or at least, that was what she had tried to do. But the headmistress was fast. She threw herself out of the way, somehow, and the flames hit the side of the aether light behind her. Fenya fought for control, calling it back to her as the headmistress grinned. Letting the fire skitter for several seconds, Fenya rapidly drew the aether around her in a shield, preparing for Wyn's attack.

"You have no hope against me, girl." Wyn's hands were loose and ready, one holding the journals off to the side, the other up and ready to defend herself.

Fenya's gaze darted around the top of the top of the lighthouse again. Nothing here. Nothing except the light, the gate down, and the catwalk...but first, she needed the journals back. Wyn's gaze flicked down. Fenya directed the flame at Wyn again, forcing her to step to the side, and Fenya dropped to her feet at the same time, shielding herself with her bracelets.

Wyn released a cry of fury and threw her hand toward Fenya, but she hadn't expected the shield of the bracelets combined with Fenya's own aether protection.

Dempsey and the pegasus were almost upon them. She could trust him. She knew she could now.

At least enough to get away from here.

Her stomach clenched. Her ball of flames constricted.

I have to trust him—I have no other choice.

Concentrating on breaking through the shields around Fenya, Wyn grunted.

Fenya dug deep, pulling and pushing more Power across the barrier of her bracelets. Her flames grew again, and Fenya threw it at Wyn's hand with the journals.

Screeching like an owl in flight, the woman dropped them, scalded by Fenya's flames.

They fell and opened on the floor as they slid toward the gap underneath the gate and the stairs.

It was going to go over.

Fenya's breath caught just before she leapt for it.

One book reached the edge—and Fenya's fingers closed over it. Then the other book skittered to a halt a foot behind her, and she grabbed for it.

A tug on her boots.

Fenya writhed, holding the journals tight against her chest with one hand, calling her flames and thrusting them toward the headmistress again.

The pressure on her feet released, and Fenya scrambled upright. She twisted to see Dempsey approaching the railing, close enough to spot the concern on his face. She shoved the journals into her satchel and took another glance behind to see Wyn approaching, murder written on her face.

Fenya scaled the railing, didn't pause for even a heartbeat, and jumped.

Chapter Thirty-Eight

FALLING

The wind whistled past Fenya's ears and ripped into her hair as she fell.

She stretched her hands for the pegasus, but she'd misjudged in her haste to escape the headmistress.

Her fingers brushed the tip of the pegasus's feathered wings as Dempsey hauled back on its reins and stopped it midair.

"Fenya!" Dempsey screamed.

She twisted in the air, locking eyes with him as she fell.

A scream bubbled to her lips, but her mouth refused to open, to make a sound.

The time in the air seemed eternal, the water a gaping mouth beneath her that roared as it waited for her to sate its appetite. She couldn't call for her Legacies, couldn't summon them or even beg them to save her.

She searched for the rocks, trying to twist mid-air in order to avoid them, but the surf was too high, hiding the large rocks the lighthouse warned against.

She was falling directly onto them.

And this time, she couldn't depend on Keeper Liah to heal her injuries.

Fenya closed her eyes just before she hit.

As the icy water enveloped her, Fenya waited for the rocks to claim her, for darkness to engulf her. But water closed over her head, and there was no pain.

The waves pulled at her, an unforgiving force that yanked and shoved.

Her feet hit the ground, soft and rocky both, and her skin shivered like the very water rippled off her. She pushed for the surface and kicked. Her skirts swirled in the currents, pulling her different directions, tugging her back toward the sandy ground. Fenya opened her eyes, but closed them at the burn, unable to see in the stinging salt and sand swirling around her.

A deep blaze kindled in her lungs. She kicked for the surface. When had she sunk so far?

She fought the surf as it tugged one way and then the next, ripping at her gown, pulling her back a foot for every half foot she gained. Panicking, she called for her Legacy.

Her Legacy rumbled, but Fire hated Water.

The sea yanked at her, trying to pull her back. She sank farther toward the bottom.

Her lungs ached.

She opened her eyes again, searching for light, for air.

She couldn't hold her breath any longer. She was supposed to be a Perfect Mage now—how could she die in the Aether Sea like this?

Her shoulder collided with something hard, and her lungs forgot they were underwater. She sucked in water, choking and fighting for the surface. The headmistress could not win.

But the surf pulled her farther out to sea. Her head bobbed along the surface, then an invisible tide tugged her back, pulling her away from the shore.

Her lungs burned. She wouldn't be able to save herself. Her Fire warred with Water, a battle within her that raged like bickering siblings. Her feet couldn't find the sandy bottom anymore. She kept sinking...lower and lower...

A nudge touched her bottom. She craned around with the last of her energy. A dragon.

An Aether Leviathan nosed her legs, pushing her up from the bottom with gentle guidance.

Fenya barely refrained from a sharp inhale, a drink of seawater, before her head broke the surface.

Treading water, she coughed and hacked out water before the waves could pull her under again. The support from underneath had faded away. Had she imagined it?

Spitting out the burning seawater, Fenya looked around for Dempsey. She needed help. She needed her Legacy. Fenya fought the waves, but they were too strong. Then something called to her.

A trickle of Fire crept through her, and this time, it felt like cold, flowing Water instead of hot, bubbling lava. She couldn't summon it. Not in Water, dampened like this.

Still, she called to it, summoning it, demanding it, then coaxing it.

Help me. Please.

Nothing answered.

Then the waves replied, gentling their touch on her, cradling her instead of thrashing her. Rocking her like an infant in a mother's arms. And the Air, it welcomed her, pushing the water out of her gown and lightening her as the water pushed upward, pushing her skirts with her so they didn't yank her down. She bobbed to the surface this time, and the waves curled around her.

She looked up to see Dempsey circling the pegasus around the lighthouse, craning his head around the animal's wings to look down at the sea.

Fenya gasped for air and it rushed into her lungs, filling them to capacity.

Water. Dempsey was Water. Water, the opposite of Fire. Is it to be controlled the same? With gentle coaxing? Or does it answer to force?

The current pushed her toward a cluster of waves, and Fenya realized it was one of the rocks surrounding the lighthouse peninsula. She reached for it, expecting to collide into it, but instead it welcomed her gently. She dragged herself onto it, pulling her sodden skirts up after herself. The water almost pulled itself out of her gown and even her shoes, returning itself to the sea with only the barest scratch of salt against her skin.

She coughed again, clearing her lungs, and inhaled fresh, dry air in relief.

Dempsey brought the pegasus close and pulled it to a hovering stop beside her. "Climb on!"

Fenya shifted on the rock as the pegasus neared. The flapping of the animal's wings nearly slapped her face as the beast hovered beside her and the rock. She ducked and allowed the wings in front of her. How was she supposed to manage this?

Dempsey angled the animal so that its haunches lined up with Fenya as she stood on the rock. "Come on!" He reached for her hand and kicked his foot out of the stirrup. She shoved her foot into the stirrup, hitched up her skirts, and threw her leg over the animal's back, clutching Dempsey from behind.

"Go!" she shouted.

"You contemptible little miscreants!" the headmistress screamed from the lighthouse deck.

With a shudder as Dempsey wheeled the pegasus around in the air, Fenya looked to Wyn.

"I will make sure you wish you were never born!"

"About sixteen years too late on that," Dempsey called over his shoulder at her, a crooked grin on his lips.

Trembling and panting, Fenya clung to his back. Dempsey's attention shifted to her.

"What were you thinking?" Dempsey demanded. "You nearly died!"

"I had to get away. It felt like the safest way at the time." Fenya gripped Dempsey's tunic with cramping hands, the back of the pegasus slick with the spray from the sea's waves. The smooth feathers sticking out of its back made her slip on its haunches like water slipped off a dragon's scales. "You took your time in getting there. I nearly lost everything before you arrived."

Dempsey cast a quick grin over his shoulder. "I got there, didn't I? And just in the nick of time."

She trembled all over from a mix of adrenaline and cold. Cold? She jolted at the realization. She'd used her Power—a lot of it. She couldn't quite comprehend the coldness of the surrounding air. It must have been the water. Perhaps salt water had a worse effect than fresh water. Her teeth knocked against each other.

"We've m-m-must get away—and back soon. We were supposed to be out of here without anyone knowing."

"Then why didn't you end her? Incapacitate her?"

"She's Powerful!" Fenya replied through her chattering teeth. "More than I thought. She—she's trained, too. Well trained."

"Well now—" He stopped speaking, half looking back at her in confusion.

"What?"

"The reins!" Dempsey leaned back against Fenya. "They just—"

The right rein was taut, pulling harshly against the pegasus's mouth so that his neck arched toward the lighthouse. She twisted on the back of the pegasus. The headmistress stood on the catwalk, her hand outstretched toward them as they made their way from her.

"It's her!" Fenya said. "The headmistress. She's using her Telekinesis!"

Dempsey twisted to glance at the lighthouse, with the closest thing to fear she'd ever seen on his face taking residence. "From there? How?"

"I told you—she's Powerful! We have to get farther away. She can still use her Legacy." Fenya clutched Dempsey, then felt the familiar tug on her feet. "She'll go for your boots next—something to pull us off the pegasus if she can't bring us back alive."

The pegasus was careening through the air, turning so fast that Fenya and Dempsey slipped the opposite direction. She clutched him tightly, gripping the smooth, slippery back of the pegasus with her knees. Dempsey, still pulling hard against the left rein, was like a stone in the saddle.

"She's bringing us back!" Fenya cried. "Do something!"

Dempsey fought against the headmistress's control. "What? She's got the bit—the entire bridle in her control!"

"Then cut it! Take it off!"

"How will we control it?" Dempsey demanded.

"Who cares? If we don't get away from her now, we never will."

"Right." Dempsey leaned forward. "Hold onto me. Just in case I slip."

Dempsey stood in the stirrups and leaned up, stretching for the animal's head. He grabbed hold of the pegasus's ear and held tight. They dipped in the air, and Fenya fought back a scream of terror. A quick glance down at the ocean showed a large shadow under the water. Her skin prickled. A leviathan? Waiting to help or hinder?

The pegasus raised its head, fighting the grasp on his ear. Dempsey fought with it briefly, then slid his hand up under the headstall on the bridle and slipped it off over the animal's spiked ears.

The bridle went flying through the air, the headmistress's grasp no longer holding the pegasus.

Fenya let out a low sigh of relief. Even if she worked on the saddle, it didn't have the same controlling nature as a bridle. "Hurry, get him redirected to the mainland."

Dempsey sank back into the saddle, his body shaking. He looked paler than before, as though he hadn't expected such a struggle.

Fenya's satchel thumped against her leg and the back of the pegasus, and she snatched it up, clutching it between them. The pegasus swerved away from the lighthouse again, and Fenya's heart leaped against her ribcage, as if it wanted to escape her body. Fang. *Fang, where are you?*

I'm here. The little wyvern bobbed along on the mainland side of the pegasus, watching their progress but staying clear of the larger flying animal. *I'm sorry—I couldn't help you earlier.*

It's fine. You couldn't have done anything. Fenya aimed a smile at her companion. *I'm glad you stayed safe.*

Dempsey gripped the pegasus's lower mane, the only part of the animal that seemed more horselike, keeping his legs tight against the body of the animal. Fenya remembered suddenly what Henslow had said--that pegasi were intelligent animals.

"Did you tell the pegasus where to take us?" she managed, pulling some of Dempsey's heat toward her.

"What?"

"Henslow said you can tell them where to take you and they'll take you."

"Tell it then," he said.

Where do we go? Fenya's thoughts projected themselves automatically to Fang.

To the dragon warriors, was Fang's answer.

"Yes!" Fenya said aloud. "Pegasus, take us to...to...the Elite Dragon Squad headquarters for the border of Virellia."

Dempsey tensed under her grip, as though he hadn't realized how serious this was until her spoken words. The pegasus continued on his path, as though he either hadn't heard her instructions or had already been heading that direction.

"I think we're safe," Dempsey ventured a few seconds later. "I don't feel her pull anymore."

"I don't know how far her reach is." Fenya gave a nervous glance back. Though the adrenaline of the chase had given her some energy, her fingers were numb, her hands trembling as she gripped Dempsey.

"Are you well?" Dempsey glanced over his shoulder at her. "You're white."

She gritted her teeth together. "I'm...fine. Just get us to land. I don't want to fall in the water again."

"Of course." Dempsey leaned forward over the pegasus's neck as if by shifting his weight forward he could encourage him to go faster. "I'll get you there—I promise."

Something tugged at Fenya's shoulder. She gasped.

"She can still reach us!" Fenya cried. "She's going after my satchel!"

"Hold onto it!" Dempsey instructed as he kicked the pegasus in the sides. The beast flattened his ears and tossed his head but his wings churned faster.

Fenya let go of Dempsey with one hand and grabbed at the satchel strap. Wyn would not get it from her.

The force continued to pull at the strap, and Fenya yelped as it stretched to its breaking point. As the pegasus's wings continued to carry them toward the mainland, it seemed as though the strap was caught on something in the air, like a nail in a log. It was going to break.

Headmistress Wyn would get Henslow's materials.

Fenya shifted her grip, holding the satchel around its middle and pulling it toward her chest. Her fingers slipped over the wet leather, but she refused to loosen her hold.

She's so powerful. The strap stretched; it thinned before Fenya's eyes.

Another yank on the bag, and the strap snapped. Fenya gasped, her heart twisting in her chest. Her numb fingers were weakening. *A shield!*

"No, no no." She took her other hand off Dempsey, leaning back and grappling for the bag with both hands. She couldn't lose it.

Fenya closed her eyes, feeling for the ripple in the aether across her satchel. Henslow's box of journals and papers was all she had to prove that she was telling the truth.

The idea of Wyn stealing it made her cheeks heat. Power awakened in Fenya, and her skin rippled with sudden heat only to be doused by cold and followed by a feeling as though she were encased with sand. Then the aether rippled over her skin, shaking the feeling away. And when she opened her eyes, the satchel was calm and quiet in her hands.

"Are you still there?" Dempsey asked, drawing her attention back.

"Where else would I be?" she murmured.

"I thought she sucked you away for a moment..."

She gave a weak chuckle, suddenly drained and flushed. Her hands shook, and she prayed that Wyn couldn't reach them any longer.

After several long minutes of silence, where there was no more pull from Wyn and the lighthouse was a small pin on the rocky outcrop of Wigmore Island, Fenya allowed her shoulders to relax and pressed a cheek against Dempsey's back. They probably had an hour's flight before the mainland, if she remembered correctly. *If I fall asleep, will I fall to the sea?* The thought made her keep her eyes open.

"When's the last time you've been to the mainland?" she asked to keep herself awake.

"Last month. I went to Linthorne with the headmaster."

"So you know the way to the EDS Headquarters?" she started.

Then his words sank in.

Chapter Thirty-Nine

ORPHAN

Fenya jolted at the pronouncement. *He traveled to the mainland last month. With the headmaster. How? Why?*

She couldn't decide how to respond. Finally, she just settled for saying, "What did you say?"

"Oh, no." He huffed a long-suffering sigh. "Right, I shouldn't have said that."

"Well...let's begin with why you went to the mainland."

"I was helping get supplies."

"Why?" Fenya's heart beat rapidly, making her head almost swim with faintness.

"Uh." Dempsey scratched the back of his neck, which seemed hotter than usual. "Well, the headmaster...he's sort of...my guardian. I'm an orphan."

Fenya didn't speak.

"Are you still there?" Dempsey asked, his voice filled with wry amusement, even over the buffeting of the wind around them.

"Where would I go?" she answered curtly. Regardless of what she said or what she thought, she was captive on the back of a pegasus with Dempsey, a young man whose full name she didn't even know.

"Fenya?" Dempsey half turned to look at her. At the sight of her, his expression fell, disappointment darkening his eyes. "Of course. I should have known that you wouldn't believe me. Wouldn't trust an orphan."

His words jerked Fenya out of her shock. "Trust an *orphan*? I don't care about that, Dempsey. I'm half orphaned already—as good as orphaned anyway. What I care about—" She bit her lip and took a deep breath. "I care if you're truthful with me. And I don't think you ever have been."

"Truthful?" Dempsey twisted in the saddle to search her face. "I am truthful."

"Are you? What about the stories you've told me about Rhys?" She put iron in her words, her questions pouring out. "Are those truth? Or are they what you want me to believe so that I'll trust you and not him? What about why you were the last one to have your Legacy Conveyed to me? What makes *you* so special that you go to the mainland with your guardian?" She spat all the questions at him, finally free to ask.

Dempsey faced forward again, but not before she saw how his face turned contemplative more than angry. "You don't know... I didn't... Rhys is...not friendly to orphans. Nor to me. He's always been just short of cruel to me. He's a snob of the worst sort."

"Rhys? Cruel?" Fenya shook her head, but stopped herself short. *I am alone on a pegasus that he controls, over an ocean where he could push me off and fly away. I can't offend him.* They were just discussing this, no one needed to be offended. "I...I've never seen him be cruel without cause."

Dempsey shrugged. "I wouldn't expect you to believe an orphan. Besides, I don't know where I was before the headmaster's. I have no past worth speaking of, and my orphanage makes me ineligible for—"

"Stop it," Fenya said. "Stop it now. Even though you're an orphan, you're the only one who has a problem with it. I've said nothing—ever —to indicate that there is something shameful about orphans. You can't control that any more than I can control the death of my father. Am I somehow less because I don't have a father?"

"No, of course not."

"Well, how about if I tell you that I no longer have a home?" she added.

He shook his head.

"There are things we cannot control, and why should we be penalized for them?" Fenya clutched the satchel tighter with one hand and Dempsey with the other as the pegasus wobbled in the air, catching a draft.

"We shouldn't, I agree. Tell that to Mr. Rhys de Croia."

"Listen, he of all people should know that we don't choose what we are. If you just told him how he made you feel—"

"There's no talking to him. He doesn't listen."

"And how do you know his surname?" Fenya frowned. *There must be more to this story, more than what Dempsey says.* "Tell me more about how you ended up at Wigmore then. I thought it was Rhys who had been here the longest, but if you were living with the headmaster..."

He shrugged. "I was at his home."

"Where's that?" she asked.

He laughed. "I couldn't tell you without consequence."

Fenya stared at the approaching land over Dempsey's shoulder and between the pegasus's ears. "What's your family name?"

"What?" Dempsey stiffened.

"I mean, your surname. What is it?"

"I...I don't know."

"You don't know? You really don't remember your life before you were orphaned? You haven't been told anything?"

"No."

She was quiet. Had his memory been stolen, perhaps? She'd heard of Legacies that permitted the stealing of memories. It was illegal to do so, but the headmaster had done things more illegal than that. "And your Legacies...they developed right away?"

Dempsey's ribs expanded under her touch. "No. Not exactly, not right away. At least, I don't think so."

"When?"

"When what?"

"When did they develop then?"

"Well, I'm not sure... I was at the headmaster's from the time I was twelve until seventeen."

"And you are now eighteen..."

"Yes."

"So...you have no memories of your time before the headmaster, and your Legacy wasn't developed until...?"

"I'm not entirely sure. It came on one night, suddenly. Perhaps when I was thirteen?" Dempsey stretched his neck to the side. "It was abrupt...almost overnight. I just remember having a bad dream. Something about my parents, I think. And then I suddenly had this achingly awful ability to control Water."

A shiver ran through Fenya's veins. *This entire story is odd. What if the headmaster took him in only to experiment on him? Could his cruelty possibly extend so far to steal children and experiment on them in his own home? Yes. Yes, it does, if he could do what he's done to me and the others...*

"Why did the headmaster take you in?" she ventured, clamping down on her thoughts.

"I don't know. I think maybe I was a long-lost relative, or something."

"Did you ever ask him?"

"Yes. But he never answered me. Told me I'd have to wait."

She frowned again. "Is he married?"

"Yes."

"What does he do?"

Dempsey shook his head. "I don't know. He's a gentleman."

She scoffed at the ironic response

"I think he's involved with the military, perhaps. Or some sort of something that uses rank." Dempsey pointed ahead. "Land."

Fenya followed his finger. *Thank you, Lord. I've never been so relieved to see land.*

But the distraction didn't keep her attention for long, despite her relief. What Dempsey shared was concerning. "So you think he's a military man? Why?"

"Because I've heard him called by military titles before."

"Which one?"

"Colonel? Lieutenant?" Dempsey shrugged. "Does it matter?"

"It might. Especially when we're trying to have the military believe us and come rescue the rest of them at Wigmore."

"I can't..." Dempsey trailed off, staring straight ahead. "I can't help you with that, Fenya."

"What?"

Dempsey was silent. The land loomed closer and closer. It had been closer than she'd thought when it first appeared, for the mist from the storm had shrouded it until they were almost upon the shore.

Fenya squinted to see if there were buildings or people below, but it was rocky at one end and smooth on the other. She gripped Dempsey around the middle and brought the satchel tight to her. She expected to keep flying over the land, but he leaned forward, aiming the pegasus for the ground.

"What are you doing?" she demanded, leaning forward to speak into his ear. "We need to go to the EDS. Immediately."

Dempsey pointed his finger down at the pegasus. "He needs a rest. We'll start again after he's watered."

The pegasus felt perfectly capable and healthy underneath Fenya, but she wasn't experienced with pegasi, and how could one tell whether it needed a break?

They had to have been flying for at least an hour by now, and the battle with Wyn had taken a lot of out her, perhaps it had exhausted the pegasus too. The landing on this beach was much smoother than Fenya had anticipated, and there was only a slight, jarring bump as all four feet hit the ground almost at once.

But glancing around, Fenya saw why the landing was unnecessary. There was no fresh water here. Pegasi were like horses and dragons, they needed fresh water. The only exceptions were sea kelpie and sea dragons. She opened her mouth to point this out to Dempsey, but he had already slid off the pegasus and was stretching his back.

Stay on the pegasus.

Fenya jolted. *Fang? Where are you?*

Stay on the pegasus.

But where are you?

This time, Fang didn't answer. Fenya covertly inspected the beach before she slipped herself forward into the saddle and tried to act as though nothing was out of the ordinary, but that she'd rather simply remain aboard.

Dempsey wandered a short distance away, peering into the pools the tide had left behind in the sand.

The pegasus pawed the ground and leaned his head down to sniff at the earth, then violently shook his head, a shudder racing all down his back.

Fenya readjusted her skirts. She patted the animal's neck. She smoothed his rough hair. Dempsey remained staring into a nearby tide pool. She bent forward to inspect the pegasus's mane. It was coarser and thicker than any hair that a horse had, while only a few inches long and standing straight into the air. Some pegasi had feathers on their faces, looking more bird than horse, while others even had scales. She wondered absently whether they were more dragon or horse...maybe bird?

"Do you care to dismount?" Dempsey motioned to the beach, his head tilted curiously at her. "Nice night for a beach walk."

She shook her head. "I'd rather just stay up." She glanced up at the sky. "We should get going. We need to get to the EDS base."

Dempsey cocked his head at her. "You're so easy to read."

She frowned. "What?"

"You'll have to fix that if you ever intend on deceiving the headmaster."

Her frown deepened so that her forehead crinkled. "I don't want to *deceive* him, I just want to stop him from doing what he's doing." Anger curdled inside her. "There's no excuse for experimenting on children and killing them all for the sake of a stupid—stupid myth."

Dempsey raised his brows. "But is it?"

"Is it what?" she snapped.

"Is it a myth?" he asked so quietly that Fenya almost didn't hear him.

He knows. Fang's sing-songy voice whispered in her head.

Fenya hesitated, glancing down at the pegasus. She had no way to control him if they took to the air again. She put a hand on his side and he turned, eyeing her with surprising intelligence. *Could he just understand me? Do you understand me?*

The animal snorted and tossed his head into the air. But unlike with Fang, she didn't hear a voice in her head, just a certain knowledge of understanding.

"It might be less myth than we thought..." Dempsey continued.

"Of course it's a myth," Fenya answered, stroking the pegasus's neck gently.

"Why are you so certain?" he pushed.

"The First King forever split the Legacies into four Elemental Powers. From there they were made into Relics and passed out to the trustworthy families in the First King's service. You know that history—even as an orphan, you must have learned it." She half winced at her mention of him as an orphan, knowing how touchy he was about it, but she pushed on. "How could it ever be possible to reverse such a permanent decision? That's why the First King did it. He knew how dangerous the idea of an all-powerful mage was. How treacherous just the idea was. The headmaster—your guardian—is committing treason under the King's nose." She scoffed. "With the Elemental Regent's permission!" She swept an angry hand at the hair that whipped around her face. "It's worth running to the King about—not just the Elite Dragon Squad. To reveal to the public."

"It was supposed to be shared." Dempsey kicked at a rock, muttering as if to himself.

"What?" she asked slowly. "What was supposed to be shared?"

"Nothing." He shook his head but turned his back to her.

Her heart pounded violently in her throat. *He knew. He knew all along.*

Betrayal washed over her. "Were you...did you know? About the experiment?"

He didn't face her, but she thought his shoulders tensed.

It was all the answer she needed. "You did. And you wanted it for yourself?" Her mind whirled at his betrayal. "You as good as killed Bryton. You robbed Harker of her Legacy—"

"And now I've lost my own!" He whirled on her, anger coloring his face, his fists clenched in fury at his sides. "It was supposed to be shared with me!"

The air around them stilled, but Dempsey did not—could not.

He swung a fist her direction, anger in every motion. "*Your* Legacies were supposed to be shared with *me*! I waited *years* for this—just like him—working alongside him—waiting—and now you've got *everything* I waited for! You're the mistake—and I was supposed to gain the reward. Now it's all messed up because Henslow, that Legacy-rotted traitor threw it all away—for the sake of a Legacy-addled half-trained Spark who never deserved anything she's gotten." He kicked a large rock on the beach, but it didn't move, and his face wrinkled in pain, adding to his fury.

Fenya's stomach knotted at the fury in his words, both wanting him to continue and hating every word he said. He had deceived her far more than she could have ever believed, if he hated her so much. But still, she couldn't turn her back on him. He had acted out of deception himself perhaps.

Fenya slid from the pegasus's back, putting a hand on his neck and silently asking him to stay put.

What are you doing? Fang's voice screeched in her head.

What had his guardian said to him? What lies was he told? Did he know better?

Any sparkless fool would know better.

But look at what he was given growing up, Fang. He was alone, orphaned...in pain...confused... What chance did he have to learn right from wrong?

Fenya approached Dempsey from behind, but stopped a meter away. "Henslow...he did what he thought right. What he *knew* right."

"He doesn't know the whole story," Dempsey muttered, glaring darkly at the waves as they crashed against the rocky beach a dozen paces away. "And if he does, then he's more awful than I believe."

Fenya's forehead creased. "What do you mean? What's the whole story?"

Dempsey shook his head and crouched down, poking at the rock that he'd kicked. It was half covered in sand from the departed surf. He dragged a finger across the sand, leaving a line. "My mother...the headmaster's wife, I mean...my adoptive mother...she's very ill."

"I'm sorry," Fenya said, feeling his heartbreak.

He ignored her. "After she had her babies, her daughter, something happened to her Legacy. It wasn't Legacy Fever, at least that's what the

Healers said. But something made it so that she couldn't be around anyone, even her daughter. Especially her daughter."

"To lose your parents and then see your adoptive mother suffer... that must be difficult. But some ailments can't—and shouldn't—be healed."

He hung his head, drawing shapes in the sand and shaking off his finger when the sand clumped too much. "She's the only mother I can remember. She's too young to die."

Fenya bit her lip, but she stepped up and crouched down beside him. "You know I lost my father to Legacy Fever. He hung on for years, but it eventually took him. Thankfully not before he could say his goodbyes. But no one lives forever. And no one should. Who are we to question the time we are to die?"

He turned his head to her so slowly that she felt it like a storm coming. "That's what people always say when they don't care."

She caught her breath. "That's not true. I do care about you, Dempsey."

"But you don't care if she dies. And that's the same thing." He gripped a handful of sand so tightly that it spilled out of his fingers.

"Of course I care, Dempsey. Every life is precious."

"Even mine?"

"Of course!"

"Even the headmaster's?"

Fenya hesitated. "I'm sure he's done some things worthy of redemption. He clearly loves his family deeply. If he were to channel his knowledge and skills into good for example—"

Dempsey rose so fast that Fenya toppled backward, expecting attack. Her hands tingled in surprise but stilled just as quickly as he offered her a hand.

"Then we ride to save his wife. You're the only hope she has now. What's done is done—but you can still save her."

Fenya opened her mouth to protest. She couldn't heal anyone. She didn't even know what abilities she had, let alone how to do the intricate work of healing someone so ill and near death.

But he was gripping her hand with such firmness and hope that she couldn't find it in her to destroy his hopes.

"All right," she whispered. "We'll see what we can do." She swallowed as he began to pull her up and toward the pegasus who stamped a foot impatiently in the sand. "But *after* we rescue the others."

He stopped and turned to stare at her, still holding onto her. "After?"

"Of course, after," she said calmly. "Time matters most for them. If the headmaster had enough time to experiment on us to find a Perfect Mage, then we have enough time to rescue the others from his grasp."

He stared at her a long moment, clearly thinking through her logic. "All right," he finally agreed.

"Please let me go, Dempsey," she said with forced calm, trying to tug her hand gently from his.

"No—you'll try to trick me." He pulled on her wrist, dragging her toward the pegasus.

"If you want me to help you, you must let me go." Fenya dug her heels into the sand.

"Why? Do you really think I can trust you? I've lost everything to you—including my own Legacy. Both of them," he added aside under his breath.

"Both?" she asked calmly. "What lesser Legacy were you blessed with?"

He gave her a withering glare. "You should know." He yanked her forward. "Get up."

She hesitated. She was more powerful than him, but exhaustion had crept in. "I...I'm tired."

"You can't stop," Dempsey told her, pushing her against the pegasus.

"Why not? You don't want me to stop him." She tried to fight him, but he was stronger than her, and her limbs felt heavy. *I have to keep him calm, happy—appeased somehow.* She allowed him to help her into the saddle, this time putting her in front.

Fang snorted in her head. *Don't be cinder-welp or you're going to be burned.*

Fenya ignored the dragon's warning as Dempsey continued. He stepped to the pegasus and removed the animal's chest strap, twisting it into something resembling a halter and slipping it over the animal's head. He pointed to Fenya's satchel. "Give me the strap."

"What?"

"Do you want to control the pegasus or not?"

Reluctantly, Fenya untied the strap from her satchel and gave it to him. She would need to control the pegasus to get to the EDS safely, but the items within her satchel were invaluable to proving the truth.

"Fine. But I'm staying in front to guide him."

"I don't care. We're going to save my mother one way or another." Dempsey snorted. "I don't want the headmaster to stop like you do. I want him to keep going. But I want to prove that I am worth being a part of it."

A chill settled over Fenya, shaking her from her shoulders to her toes. The pegasus shuddered underneath her, his ears flicking back at them. "So you think that all this experimentation should happen?"

"Yes!" he said vehemently as he mounted the pegasus behind her. "It can save lives!"

"And take them," Fenya returned, clutching her satchel to her stomach and grabbing the makeshift reins. "Well, I think you know by now that I disagree."

Dempsey chuckled dryly. "I can see that."

"You're going to let me return and free them?"

"Of course." He shrugged. "If I can return you to the headmaster after all this, then I'll gain even more trust than ever before."

Fenya's stomach knotted tighter. Something was very very wrong in Dempsey's mind. "I'm sorry you've suffered so. You don't deserve it."

"You don't know that," he said darkly, and kicked the pegasus's sides so that the animal bolted forward and took to the air.

Chapter Forty

THE EDS

The pegasus kept trying to curve back in the direction of Wigmore, but Fenya forced him inland with the reins and her legs. Telling him again where to go, she relaxed as he settled into his flight north. Every time she peeked back over her shoulder, her stomach squirmed. It would be easy for Dempsey to simply push her off mid-flight and her to plummet to her death.

You should have left him behind, came Fang's voice in her head. *Traitors get torn apart in my world.*

Well, I'm not a dragon, Fenya replied firmly. *He can be redeemed. He's just...misguided. Who's to say I wouldn't have made the same choice if I were raised in his life?*

Fang made a sound in Fenya's head like a scoff.

Fenya bit back a smile, but the humor quickly left her. She remembered Mage Balderik telling her something about the location of his squad. It was located in a small town near the northern border of Avenesse. But she couldn't recall the name... What if the pegasus really didn't know where to go? What happened if they got lost?

Fenya bit the inside of her lip, worry racing through her faster than the pegasus's wings flapped.

What if Mage Balderik wasn't there when she arrived? She had to find him and convince him to launch a rescue mission. With Wyn knowing they were gone, time was impossibly short to rescue the others. It would be harder to convince complete strangers that she spoke the truth.

Her thoughts made her press the pegasus faster with her mind. He caught her urgency and deepened the strokes of his wings.

The minutes ticked by, the sun sank low, a fading moon emerged, and the silence between them lengthened and turned awkward. Fenya wished she could confide in Dempsey—wished that they were in this together. But it felt too much like an enemy behind her, one she could not outrun, for she brought the enemy into her inner circle with her. What would Balderik say?

She mentally shook herself. Balderik would be able to defend himself against a newly Discerped teen. Her stomach twisted in dismay.

He was Ordinary now, wasn't he?

His Discerption was her fault.

Which he wanted, a little voice reminded her. *He walked in under his own power and lay down to be Discerped. He helped bring me there. What had he been thinking?*

Despite herself, her sorrow swelled for him. He was misguided just like the headmaster to think that more Legacies would solve any of his problems. Legacies couldn't solve everything—it couldn't prevent death, couldn't bring anyone back. And even in the case of the illegal and unimaginable Necromancy, it couldn't bring someone back fully into life. Once a person had crossed into death, death kept them. There could be no bringing them back.

As her mind churned, Fenya kept the pegasus on its route toward Highmere EDS. All she could think was to get to them, to bring them back to Wigmore and save her friends.

She worried on her lip.

At night, many larger dragons went hunting. The trees below seemed suddenly treacherous, not a friendly forest, but a den of danger.

Already the pegasus aimed himself around the forest, but they couldn't waste any more time. They wouldn't be able to see where to land in the dark, and they had to reach the EDS before total darkness.

Pegasi didn't care for dragons, and she had no bridle on the animal any longer.

Fang? Help us keep an eye out for dragons, will you?

Already am, Fang's cheerful reply came.

Thank you. Fenya focused her attention on the landscape ahead, searching for the wide-open arena space that a dragon facility usually required. Dragons liked cover, so it was likely at the base of a hill or mountain or even clifftop, but training would require flat area for groundwork.

It was almost exactly when she spotted it with its aether fires burning in a circle around the arena, that Dempsey leaned forward and yanked one makeshift rein from Fenya's fingers.

"Hey!" she cried out.

What is it? Fang's voice answered immediately.

"Stop, Dempsey!"

Dempsey continued to pull, twisting behind her, pushing her away from him so she grabbed for the pegasus's mane to keep herself aboard. The pegasus veered sharply away from the forest ahead.

"Give me the reins!" Righting herself, Fenya grabbed for the makeshift reins, her heart hammering. If she hadn't been in the saddle with her feet in the stirrups, she would have fallen.

He ignored her, wrapping his arms around her waist and pulling harder.

The pegasus yielded to the pressure, despite the lack of bit.

Fenya reached for the other rein, pulling on it, trying to even out the animal. She pressed her hand against the animal's skin. *Please, listen to me. Take us down to the EDS.*

Under the confused direction, the pegasus wavered in the sky, dipping precariously toward Dempsey's rein.

"Stop! You're going to send us to our deaths!"

"I don't think so," he replied, a wry grin on his lips.

Despite her fear, she twisted to look at him.

He swept his gaze over her. "You have no idea what you are, Fenya," he whispered so quietly that she more read his words than heard them.

A shudder raced a chill down her spine.

"I may not know *what* I am now, but I know *who* I am," she answered solemnly. "And I'm not going to save myself at the expense of others."

He met her gaze, searching her face.

Out of the corner of her eye, she saw a flash of red.

"Land your beast by order of the Crown!" cried a rider atop a crimson berserker.

Fenya reached for the other rein to obey.

"No!" Dempsey said, his eyes wide and voice strained with terror.

"We must," she said through gritted teeth. This wasn't how she wanted to meet the Dragon Riders.

She aimed the pegasus for the ground, tilting forward and putting her hands at the base of his neck as she'd seen Dempsey do.

"No, we have to run for it!"

"Run for it?" She was torn between a laugh and a cry at his desperation. "That's certain death, Dempsey!"

He gripped her upper arm. "Don't tell them. Don't tell them anything—not about you. We'll get the headmaster to release them all —after you save my mother."

Fenya didn't need his warning to know that she couldn't tell the EDS everything, especially what had been done to her. Telling about Dempsey losing his Legacy was a risk in itself, but to dare to try and convince skilled magi that she had gained Legacies while he had lost them? They would consider her insane, and she would lose all credibility. Or if they believed her, they might consider her complicit and arrest her for illegal experimentation.

"Don't tell them, don't tell them," Dempsey repeated in a whisper into her ear as the ground neared. The berserker followed them, and as the ground neared, two Moon Dragons flew out from either side, their scales practically disappearing into the night sky.

Clearly she'd crossed a border into controlled airspace.

The pegasus spooked, his head flying up in fear at being surrounded by the three dragons. Chain link reins led to a metal ring through their noses which led back to a frightening saddle of spikes, leather, chains, and weapons.

As her pegasus hit the ground before the EDS gates, he threw up his head, rearing into the air as the dragons closed rank.

A thrill of fear went through her.

"Dismount and keep your hands where they can be seen," said a man with his face covered by a pale blue mask.

Fenya's spine shuddered. "I'm here for help—"

"Identify yourself." The man with his face covered was dressed in the blue uniform hemmed with ice-blue piping and silver buttons. A pin with a taloned claw shone on his collar, reflecting the aether lights that surrounded the arena.

"Get off," Fenya murmured to Dempsey behind her. She couldn't move until he did, but he was stiff and solid behind her. Fenya raised her hands to show her innocence. "I am Fenya Verena, and I was a student at Wigmore Academy. I beg you to listen to what I have to say—"

"Dismount!" a second soldier commanded, but the first held up his hand.

Fenya kept her hands raised. "Please," she begged. "I need you to listen—"

"Miss Fenya Verena?" the first man said.

She paused and found his pale gaze vaguely familiar. "Yes."

"Fenya Verena, daughter to Magess Seraphina Verena?"

Dempsey flinched in surprise behind her.

The man's mouth remained opened in surprise. His leather helmet shielded his face, and the short, white feathers on the top looked as though the tips had been dipped in blood.

"Yes. What—who are you? Do you know my mother?"

The man pulled off helmet to reveal a distantly familiar face.

She frowned, for there was something about it she recognized but couldn't place. "Who—who are you?"

"I am Flight Lieutenant Jaromir Balderik. My brother has met you. He is in charge of this regiment. Let me take you to him."

"Please!" Fenya exclaimed. "I need his help—urgently."

He turned his beast, which was easily twice the size of the pegasus, in the direction of a tall fence ahead of them that Fenya had hardly noticed. Now she took in her surroundings, the fence was easily a dozen feet high, blocking the view, and lined with razor-sharp spikes on the top.

Lieutenant Balderik raised his hand to his mouth and a shrill whistle comprising a complicated tune rang out.

In answer, the fence's large gates that spanned a width large enough to fit half a dozen of his dragons, swung open to less than the halfway mark. He soldiered through with the pegasus following as though on a leash, both Dempsey and Fenya still aboard. The Moon Dragons all but herded him inside.

She felt almost like a prisoner. Almost like she would be marched back to a place just like Wigmore and locked up.

We are here for help, Fang's voice said. *They will not treat us like prisoners.*

Fang, they're helping—calm down.

Fang bristled though; Fenya could almost feel her scales rippling from her back.

Stay out of it. Stay safe. If you can go get help if we need it, do so.

Help? What could I do to get help?

Fenya chewed on her lip. *You have to know some dragons, right?*

And what might they do? Fang's voice didn't seem rude, but honestly confused.

Destroy Wigmore, and bring the others to freedom. Fenya's pegasus halted under her with a skid of his hooves against the soft sandy pebbles of the arena.

"Dismount," said a voice at the pegasus's shoulder.

Fenya found Lieutenant Balderik at her knee.

Behind her, Dempsey sat frozen, staring at her with unfocused shock.

Fenya quickly made a decision. He hadn't asked, but told. It was an instruction. She had to keep him on her side and willing to listen. She immediately threw her right leg over the neck of the beast and slid down the shoulder of the pegasus.

"Penrose, keep close." Lieutenant Balderik glanced at Dempsey, but spoke to another soldier.

Fenya waved him away. "He's a bit shocked. I promise you, we have no weapons. He doesn't even have a Legacy."

Lieutenant Balderik frowned sharpened his way.

"I mean, he cannot control his Legacy, it's so weak now," she hurried to add.

Lieutenant Balderik glanced at her and back at Dempsey. Fenya stepped toward him.

The other dragons and officers had formed a small circle around the pegasus, but Fenya spoke loudly. "Where is your brother? Captain Havardur Balderik? I must get him to go with me back to Wigmore immediately."

"What?" Lieutenant Balderik's forehead deepened.

"What is going on out here, Lieutenant?" came a deep, calm, and controlled voice.

Fenya whirled to find Captain Balderik striding across the arena, three steps ahead of a half dozen dragon riders on foot.

Fenya turned and raced for him. He didn't slow his forward motion, but stepped fully forward to meet her.

"Miss Verena. How unexpected. What has happened?"

"Wigmore," Fenya panted. "It's all a front."

"Excuse me?" he tilted his chin slightly to the side in an attempt to understand.

"Wigmore. It's...it's all about experimenting on the students there."

"Miss Verena..." Captain Balderik reached a hand for her, and she gripped his forearms with her hands.

"You must believe me, please. We have no time to waste."

"Please slow down, I don't understand. You must start at the beginning."

Fenya took a deep breath and tried to calm herself. Then she began at her invitation to Wigmore by Milton, the engagement, and the briefest version of the dangers the others at Wigmore faced. As she spoke, the earlier animation in Colonel Balderik's face drained away, leaving his expression tight and focused.

"So you can see how we have to go now—"

Captain Balderik stepped back from Fenya and she broke off. He motioned to one of the men behind him and murmured something that she couldn't hear.

Fenya bit her lip. "Please, Captain, we have to go back."

"Sir, it could be a trap. How can we trust her? If even half of what she says is true, this could be an attack."

"Yes, Sergeant Marlowe, I agree."

Fenya's hands went cold. "I'm not— Sir, I'm not false. I promise you that this is true. Every word. Dempsey can confirm—the experiments—"

Captain Balderik held up a hand. "Just a moment, Miss Verena. There's someone here whom I believe needs to hear certain aspects of your testimony."

"There...there is?" Fenya's stomach squirmed. Out of the corner of her eye, she saw a flash of red-orange and shook her head. *Stay away, Fang.*

The dragon blurred off toward the stands where she perched herself half behind a piece of the architecture that hide most of her.

"Come with me," Captain Balderik said. He motioned to his brother and nodded at Dempsey, where he sat on the pegasus. "Watch him while I question Miss Verena."

Before she could object, the soldiers fell into place around her and Captain Balderik motioned her forward. She went with him, heading toward the arena arches, and as she passed underneath it, she glanced back to see Dempsey staring after her, his gray eyes dark and storming, curiosity mingling with distrust.

She bit her lip and looked away. She must speak carefully, so as not to get him in trouble. But...what if trouble was the thing he deserved? The very right thing to put him on the right path?

What would they do to him if she told the full truth? She glanced at Balderik. Would he dare to believe her if she told the entire truth? Was he ready for something so awful? Was she?

Captain Balderik led Fenya through the covered arched pathway toward a doorway at the end of the walk. He only gave her the tiniest of glances before striding through and expecting her to follow. She shivered. While he was still as kind as he had been at the ball at Whitland, there was an authority he possessed now that make her tremble.

She followed him through the doorway without question, the other soldiers filing in behind her.

They paused inside a high ceilinged room with a rack of weapons on the wall at the other end. A padlock secured them at the end, perhaps to keep a Metallurgist or Animationist from being able to wield them without permission.

Captain Balderik nodded toward one of his men, who strode across the dirt floor and disappeared through a heavy wooden door with a snarling berserker emblazoned on the front of it in copper.

As the door slammed shut behind him, Fenya eyed the rest of the room, her gaze faltering at what she saw. On that wall was a richly crafted mural of dragons and men fighting alongside each other. They fought against men and three headed beasts. She inspected it, momentarily distracted from her wait. The artistry was beautiful, a true work of art.

The door opened behind her and she started, pulling her attention away.

To her shock, Mage de Croia walked in, the annoyance on his face melting into confusion as his eyes fell on her. "Miss Verena...? What is the meaning of this, Captain? Miss Verena, you are supposed to be at Wigmore."

She glanced to Captain Balderik. "Yes, sir, I am. I was, I mean. But I escaped."

He raised his brows and darted a seeking glance to Balderik. "Escaped?"

When no one stopped her, Fenya gave him the shortest version of her situation as she could. "Wigmore is not a proper boarding school, Mage. It's a school of abuse and nothing more than a prison. And I believe a young man related to you is also there. Rhys."

Mage de Croia's eyes widened as the blood drained from his face. "Impossible."

She shook her head and withdrew Rhys's letter from her satchel. "I didn't think I would see you," she continued to Mage de Croia, "but Rhys told me that if I escaped, to give you this."

He hesitantly reached out a hand but plucked it from her fingers and sliced it open. She watched him read, watching the play of emotions chasing each other across his face.

With outrage, Mage de Croia's hand flexed as he finished reading, crumpling one side of the paper. "This is impossible! Have you written your mother?"

"I couldn't," she explained. "Letters out were never sent—or replies never delivered." She motioned toward his hands. "Or else your nephew would have written you long ago. He's almost given up hope."

He frowned. "This seems almost impossible to believe."

Her heart constricted. "I...I am telling the truth. I've embellished nothing."

No, you've not told enough truth, came Fang's voice in her head. *You haven't told them the worst.*

Why would they believe me?

Why wouldn't they?

If they don't believe this, that we were simply abused and imprisoned, they how could they believe experimentation and Discerption and Conveyance?

Tears pooled in her eyes, and she had to blink them away as she stared at the circle of men surrounding her. Some faces were impossible to read, others contemplative, while some gazes seemed hard and disbelieving.

"You see my dilemma, Mage de Croia. Your nephew is believed there, the boy we've long been searching for. However, to forge ahead as planned with other children and their safety to consider..."

"Not to mention that we know nothing of the genuineness of the girl standing before us," came a soldier's voice from behind.

"Quiet," snapped Lieutenant Balderik.

Captain Balderik held up a hand to his brother. "No. Sergeant Marlowe is not wrong." He fixed Fenya with a questioning stare. "She could be a Shifter giving us a complicated and yet believable story in order to trap us."

Fenya's face drained of blood as she turned to address the soldier who had spoken. He was the one who seemed hard but seemed like he could be softer in the right circumstance. How could she evoke those circumstances, though? He seemed determined to hate her. "I promise I speak truth—I am no Shifter."

"I'm afraid we need proof," Marlowe demanded, his dark eyes cold and piercing. She imagined that in a different setting, she could see his eyes warm and even be tender toward one. But at the moment, they were only demanding.

"How can I prove myself?" she responded immediately.

Mage de Croia looked between Fenya and Captain Balderik again. "Uh..." he began, clearly searching for an idea to make her prove it.

"Can you tell me what your Legacy is?" Captain Balderik interjected.

Fenya tilted her head to the side and a little smile flicked up one side of her lips. Anyone from her aunt and uncle's would know that she was a Fire Legacist and Relic Heir. "I can show you, how about that?"

"I'm not sure—" Mage de Croia began, but another voice cut in.

"That's best," Captain Balderik said in his deep, calm voice. "Shifters cannot impersonate another's Legacy, just their appearance."

Mage de Croia opened his mouth to protest, but Fenya was already putting out a palm. *I'm sure he thinks I'm going to burn us all down after what he's seen from me before.*

She pulled off her gloves and tucked them into her dress pocket, thankful that her sleeves covered her arms to the wrist anyway. Closing her eyes and blocking out the critical faces around her, she summoned her Fire. It came easily this time, twin flames popping into existence in her palms.

A gasp went around the circle, including a curse from Mage de Croia.

He never knew I was a Spark, she realized. She opened her eyes to find his mouth agape, eyes fixed on the flames.

Vaguely she felt Fang's presence outside the arena, some distance away.

"Well, Miss Verena, that's sufficient to prove your Legacy," Captain Balderik said wryly.

Show them fire dragons, Fang whispered in her head.

Fenya grinned. *Why not?* With a thought and a twist of her hands, she called the flames toward her, pigeon-sized dragons, one a wyvern and the other a berserker taking shape in her palms. She focused on the one on the left, twisting it into blue flames, while the other she turned to a deep red. She directed them to fly around herself, careful not to direct them at the soldiers, but to curve their flames around her. She trusted them. For the first time, she trusted herself.

Still, the nearest soldier leapt back with a curse.

Captain Balderik's gaze had turned slightly amused, his lips pinching together as if to keep from smirking.

Figuring she had done enough to prove herself, Fenya summoned the dragons back to her palms, shrinking as they came, where she let them perch for a moment before closing her fists and sending them back to where they'd come from—wherever that was—the aether she supposed.

A puff of smoke in each hand was all that was left when she raised her gaze to the men standing in a wider circle around her now. Some exchanged wary glances with each other across their circle, their stances no longer relaxed and indifferent, but stiff and suspecting. How had her proof turned them against her?

Because you're Powerful, my dear human, Fang's voice answered her unvoiced thought. *People will always fear Power.*

She worried on her lip.

"Well, Mage de Croia?" Captain Balderik asked. "Do you confirm that she is who she claims to be?"

Mage de Croia nodded in affirmation, a little smirk on his face. "She is certainly Miss Verena. And she's learned some new tricks, if I must say so."

"Then you will allow me to help you?" Fenya asked immediately. "I must return to Wigmore and free the others. I can help you—show you where to go."

"No!" Mage de Croia said immediately, joined by the voices of other soldiers.

Captain Balderik held up a hand, asking for silence.

"You don't know where you're going, do you? Or what you're flying into." Fenya dared to meet the gaze of every soldier in the circle around her, finishing by landing on Mage de Croia, whose anxious expression trumped their worry.

Sergeant Marlowe jutted out his chin for a moment and looked off somewhere above her head before meeting her gaze again, as if swallowing his pride. "No. But you're familiar with it?"

"Yes."

"And you remember how to get back?"

"I've made it this far already, haven't I?" she said with a thin smile. "And I would love to show you the way. I'm ready for a fight. I left the headmistress there recovering from her fight with me." At the thought, she remembered Henslow's box. "Oh! I have proof of what they're doing to us—"

Captain Balderik raised his hand yet again. "Miss Verena, please save that for later. If you speak truth, every moment matters. You are familiar with the island? And the school?"

She swallowed. "Yes."

"You can give us directions then?" Marlowe asked.

"I'm going with you." She glanced around at the men.

"No, we aren't taking you back in there—" began the hot-headed soldier.

Fire sparked inside her. "I'm going back—I promised!"

"Just a moment, please," Captain Balderik said, holding up a hand. "Calm yourself, Miss Verena."

Marlowe narrowed his eyes, but fell silent.

"We could use some direction—and if your Powers are what you showed us, then we could use your help as well." He motioned to her hands and bent his head and added with a lowered voice, "And as I see evidence of your Relic acceptance, I have an idea that you have much more...ability...than you showed us."

Her cheeks heated as she fought the urge to hide her hands behind her back. "Yes, you see truth."

Behind Captain Balderik, the cold-faced soldier's eyes narrowed and focused on Fenya's exposed hands as if he, too, noticed her marks and wondered at their meaning. She pulled her gloves back on, tucking their ends underneath her sleeves.

"It's settled then," Captain Balderik confirmed. "She flies with us."

"You can't!" Mage de Croia burst out.

She blinked at him in surprise.

He sputtered out an addition. "If something happened to you, how would I ever explain to your...your mother..." He trailed off as she smiled wryly.

"Lady Magess Seraphina Verena would probably be quite content to not have to care for a daughter like me. She might even be relieved to pass the Relic to another family." Fenya smiled a little too broadly. "Though it's true—Aunt Cali might be disappointed in you if you left me behind."

He grimaced and raked his fingers through his thick brown hair. "Fine. Only because you've seemed to gain some control...all of a sudden." He narrowed his eyes at her.

"It wasn't all of a sudden," Fenya said softly. "It's Fang."

Mage de Croia frowned. "Who—?"

But commotion outside interrupted de Croia, and as one, the circle of soldiers whirled while surrounding Fenya and Mage de Croia. She faced the door a beat after the soldiers, taking a half step back as the soldiers who had been left outside came bursting in through the door.

"Captain! He's gone." One of the soldiers cried, the doorway framing him with a bright blur of light.

"What?" Captain Balderik leapt toward him, crossing the room in a handful of great strides.

He hurried out of the hall, and Fenya was quick to follow.

As soon as she emerged into the arena, it was clear what the soldiers meant. The pegasus was high in the air, making a straight path back in the direction they had come.

"Go after him!" Captain Balderik barked. "Bring him back."

"We must go—quickly," Fenya urged, grabbing the captain's elbow with clutching fingers. "Before he can warn them."

"Yes," he agreed, peering down at her with concern in his blue eyes. "I'd like you to ride with me, Miss Verena, that way you can guide me directly to the island."

"Yes," Fenya agreed. "I must."

And without any further delay, even as Captain Balderik barked orders at two soldiers to go after Dempsey on the pegasus, to catch up with the rest of them later, Fenya wasted no time in following the captain to his Berserker and mounting up behind him.

The dragon spread his wings, crouched and rolled his weight back on his haunches.

"Hold on!" Captain Balderik called back to her.

She clutched his waist, sandwiching the satchel between them, realizing she hadn't even opened it to prove the atrocities at Wigmore. All it had taken was two familiar faces and a letter from Rhys.

She closed her eyes and sent up a prayer. *Please let him be alive. Let what he's Seen come true.*

Chapter Forty-One

THE STAIRCASE

F enya pointed Captain Balderik toward Wigmore Island, her hands trembling on his leather breastplate.

Fang, are you following?

Of course, came the immediate answer. *And far away from these monster dragons. I'll meet you there.*

Unease squirmed in Fenya's stomach. *Stay safe, Fang. I'd rather you stay here, alive, then come with me and suffer.*

I won't stay behind, I belong with you, Fang insisted. *Now stop talking— I need to concentrate on trailing you. Despite what you might think, these dragons are excellent at concealing the purpose and direction of their flight.*

Good thing you know where we're going, Fenya retorted.

In answer, all she got was a snort.

What felt like minutes later, the island of Wigmore came into view. She pointed over Balderik's shoulder at the lighthouse, the aether light barely peeking through the low clouds. "That's the lighthouse. You can land on top of the castle though, another bit ahead. It will be the most tactically surprising, coming down from the rooftop."

"There's access from the roof to the rest of the castle?" he called back at her.

"Yes! I've gone all over the castle." She described the route from the rooftop to the staff's rooms and the laboratory.

When she was done, he made a motion to the rider to his right and then to the one on his left. Fenya twisted to watch as the riders repeated the motions to the others behind them until each had confirmed the message.

The dragons curved as one around the southern end of the island, rising into the clouds as they set themselves up for a landing. They pierced through the clouds and down upon the rooftop of the castle, their feet surprisingly soft against the stone. Captain Balderik threw himself from the dragon's back without a second to waste, ripping his belt from her fingers with surprising ease. As she had already described the castle to Balderik, he knew exactly where to go and directed his feet toward the steps descending into the castle.

The other soldiers bounded off their dragons with a speed that shot energy through Fenya as they left her behind. Balderik's dragon was already back on his feet and craning his head back as if annoyed at her presence.

Fenya half slid and half fell from the dragon's back to stumble after the soldiers, none of whom waited for her. Heart thudding against her ribs, she followed the brush of leather boots shuffling over the floor as they cleared the first level of the castle in near silence.

At the exit to the stairs, she hesitated. Rhys was on the floor below —she had to get to him, warn him. What if they frightened him and Rhys lost control? While she might be able to control the Fire, he could injure himself or someone else first. But could she control his flames if they were truly out of control—if they spread? She would have to. For everyone's sake.

Darting a glance after the soldiers, she made her decision.

She took the stairs two at a time, half leaping down the final six steps only to find that half the soldiers had descended before her. They made their way through room by room, but she raced past them to arrive at Rhys's door the same time as Sergeant Penrose. He was already turning the knob when she stopped short on his heels. But her panic was for naught, as he opened the door to an empty room.

A curse slipped out from him. "They knew," he growled and turned on her.

She took a half step back, tripping over an uneven stone in the floor.

Eyes flashing, Mage Penrose descended on her. "This was a trap—wasn't it?"

"No! I promise." Panic rose in her, and she cast around for someone, for a sign, for anything to help her explain herself. "I escaped—and I promised them I would come back. Dempsey—I don't know if he managed to warn them, but I don't know how he could have—"

"You're a liar," Penrose said. "A two-faced fraud who tried to trap us, I should have warned the captain, demanded that we investigate you further, wait before rushing into such a stupid—"

As her heart skittered in its cage, a hissing sound accompanied by flapping wings sounded behind her. Fang flew at Penrose's face, and he yelped in surprise before she grabbed for the dragon and missed. *No! Don't attack him!*

"That's enough," came a deep, calm voice from the hallway.

After a quick swoop near enough to blind, Fang swerved away and passed Penrose to perch in Rhys's window. Fenya raised her chin at the captain's reproof of his own man, but Penrose didn't take his eyes off Fang, who remained crouched in Rhys's window with her fangs bared. Fenya smothered her grin.

"In case you've forgotten, Penrose, there is a certain amount of truth I can Discern. Miss Verena is telling the truth, as far as she is able."

Sucking in a sharp breath, Penrose aimed a glare at her before tempering it to meet his superior's gaze.

"Now get down and clear the rest of the building," Captain Balderik said coldly. "We'll discuss this later."

Fenya's hands tingled. When she looked down, she found them glowing through her gloves as though lit by embers.

"Yes, sir," Penrose said, and disappeared past them both out into the hallway.

"I'm sorry," Fenya hastened to say.

"For what?" Captain Balderik asked as if there were no rush.

"For whatever we don't find," Fenya answered after a moment's thought.

He shook his head with a small tilt to his lips. "You could not foresee this."

She ducked her head in a nod. *I couldn't foresee it...but Rhys might have. Why didn't he tell me? Maybe he couldn't. Or never Saw it.*

Captain Balderik moved as if to step away, then paused, raising a hand to the window where Fang perched.

"She's your Familiar?"

Her breath caught.

Lie to him, Fang demanded.

I... Fenya hesitated.

Balderik tilted his head, a look of suspicion crossing his features.

And then she felt it. His Discernment Legacy, pressing upon her skull. Fear flooded through her, and she shook her head, resisting his touch with an aether push.

A sharp breath from Balderik, and shock crossed his face before he could bury it.

She could nearly read his thoughts as his shock turned to curiosity, his head tilted and brows slightly furrowed. But he didn't speak for a long moment.

He knows, Fang said flatly.

I think you're right.

He dipped his head and put a hand to his heart. "I apologize for pressing. In times of stress, I...I can overstep my bounds. And there is much riding on this."

Fenya blinked in surprise. "I...that's all right. Thank you."

He stepped away and was halfway through the doorway when he paused and looked back at her. "Miss Verena, please understand that you are safe with me—now or in the future. Whatever might be."

She bit the inside of her lower lip, her mind racing through what he might know. Then she nodded her thanks.

His footsteps disappeared, sounding off down the hallway and down the stairs, but she stood in Rhys's room for several long moments, her fingers traveling over his desk. She saw the scorch marks he had left in his lack of control, and when she focused on it, felt the pressure of a "fire-proofed" room. But now...just to see if she could, she made a flame appear in her palm. It was reluctant, but it was there, solid, reassuring. Familiar.

She wandered back into the now empty hallway, echoing the soldier's steps with dragging feet. After all this, and they were too late? Where had they all gone?

But no, she wouldn't give up hope now—she couldn't. Not until every room and every crevice was searched. They could be in the church or in the basement stables, in the lighthouse or the cave—they had to be somewhere. Perhaps even an underground bunker.

Yet an hour later, after employing Fang's help in searching the island, it was obvious that they had all gone.

Someone had warned them.

"No one left in the castle," came an echoing voice from the courtyard below. "They must have been informed or had an escape route."

Captain Balderik's low voice answered in a murmur she couldn't decipher. From the inner hallway railing, Fenya peered down into the courtyard, disoriented as the sight of the two soldiers and a green dragon standing where until recently the other so-called students had stood.

"Search again," Captain Balderik said. "We must make certain there is no one hiding."

"Perhaps, sir, we should ask the girl if she knows of any hiding spots."

"Yes, I will," said Balderik, his tone cold with warning.

Fenya bristled, but her anger quickly dissipated. Hiding spots? The cave, the bowels of the castle, the lighthouse, the staircase—

She blinked. The staircase. Rhys knew of it. Perhaps—maybe if they'd had some warning?

She turned on her heel and raced for it.

She fled past a soldier, Fang flapping along behind her.

What is it? Fang was asking.

The staircase! The secret staircase. What if someone is hiding after all?

Do you think so? Fang sounded less optimistic.

Worth a try.

Fenya stopped short at the wall, her eyes searching hungrily for the hidden mechanism.

As her fingers fell over it and pushed it in, the soldier, who had followed, gave an audible gasp. "What is this?"

She didn't glance back. "A secret staircase I just remembered. I doubt anyone is in here—it just connects the floors. But..."

"Wise to check," Sergeant Marlowe murmured, falling in behind her as the door slid open and the dark cylindrical staircase came into view, barely lit by the moon outside.

Her heart sank. It was empty.

She crossed inside and peered into the darkest corners, flanked by the soldier behind her. She glanced up the stairs at the empty landing.

But as she stood, about to admit defeat, she heard the faintest scratching.

Do you hear that? Fenya asked Fang.

I do. Fang swept down the stairs, silently. *She's here!*

Fenya nearly fell down the stairs at the excitement in Fang's voice. *Who?* she sent back when she was halfway down.

The girl who gave you her powers.

Harker? Fenya's heart leapt and then plummeted. Would Harker even speak to her? Would she want to be rescued? Was it even a rescue?

Fenya refused to let herself think any more, racing down the steps to where Fang hopped along the ground toward Harker, nudging her elbow with her nose.

"Harker?" Fenya whispered. "Harker, are you all right?"

"Do you know this girl?" Marlowe asked, his gaze darting between Harker and the rest of the staircase.

"Yes, she—she's another resident here at Wigmore," Fenya answered, taking Harker's cold wrist in her warm hand. "She's freezing. She needs a Healer." She looked up at the soldier. "Do you have a Healer in your ranks?"

"I—we—"

"Soldier!" she snapped. "This girl desperately needs a Healer right now—can you find your Healer?"

"Yes, of course." Still clearly on edge, he turned and started up the stairs. "Wait—how do I open the door?"

Fenya bit back a retort. "Never mind. Help me with her. We'll take her with us."

"Right." Marlowe returned, peered around as if evaluating the best way to handle the situation, then squatted down and lifted Harker as though she were nothing but a featherbed.

Fenya led the way to the next exit, palpating the wall until she found the knobby rock that she pressed in. The door creaked almost silently open, and she found herself face to face with Soldier Penrose, his hands raised defensively and skin shimmering amongst the aether.

Fenya froze, lifting her hands in a show of innocence. "It's just me and Soldier Marlowe. And a victim of the headmaster's."

"Come out," he growled his command.

Fenya slowly emerged, followed by the Marlowe.

"Where did you find her?" Penrose demanded.

"In the hidden staircase," Fenya answered as the tension slowly eased from Penrose's frame.

"It's all right, Penrose," Marlowe said. "But we need to get her to Breslau. She's ill."

"Right." Penrose flexed his fists, the aether shimmer between them fading. "Yes, Breslau..."

"Go get him, Penrose!" Marlowe snapped, finally losing patience when the man continued to stand in place.

"Oh! Yes. Yes, of course." Penrose snapped a salute at Marlowe and disappeared down the stairs, where Fenya could only presume the squad had all convened in the dining hall as they briefed the captain on their findings. Or lack of.

His expression tight, Marlowe shifted Harker in his arms. "Let's take her into the laboratory. Get the door," he commanded Fenya.

As Harker's head lolled against his shoulder, exposing her throat, Fenya's heart twinged. She wanted to ask if she would be all right, but he couldn't possibly know. So she led him to the laboratory, her stomach clenching with every step. Returning to the room where Harker's Legacies had been taken from her, where Dempsey had willingly betrayed her, hoping for her own Legacies in return. And poor Bryton. She would never forgive herself.

She marched into the lab and shuddered at the sight of the table.

She didn't want to put Harker on it. She couldn't. Her feet stopped and refused to obey her command to move.

Marlowe walked past her, not noticing her hesitation, and slid Harker upon the flat table.

The leather arm straps flopped down from the table to hang off the corners, and Fenya clenched her teeth. She wanted to rip them off the table. Destroy the table so that no one else could be hurt on it.

"Stay here with her," Marlowe commanded. "I'm going to see if I can expedite Breslau."

Fenya forced her feet to move, and she sidled up to the table as Marlowe's booted feet echoed across the hallway.

Harker's face was soft and gentle in her unconsciousness.

"Oh, Harker...what happened?" she whispered to the younger girl. Fenya hesitantly put a finger to Harker's wrist again. She didn't move. But there was a pulse. A faint, unsteady pulse, but a pulse nonetheless.

What had Dempsey said? That a Perfect Mage could have all Legacies? Just like the First King.

A shudder worked its way down Fenya's spine. She couldn't be like the First King. She didn't feel that Powerful. She didn't feel special. She felt...uncomfortable...even wrong. As though her body didn't belong to her, as though she were constantly humming, aware of almost everything around her.

As she stared at Harker, feeling her pulse thrum softly through her fingertips, Fenya also heard the footsteps of Marlowe all the way down below. She concentrated and another set of footsteps joined them.

"You said you found her in a secret stairwell? How?" came the voice of Healer Breslau.

"No, Miss Verena found her. She knew about the stairwell and willingly took me in. We found the girl together."

"And she's unconscious?"

Fenya tuned out the rest of the conversation, turning her attention to another floor on the castle. She scanned the rooms, imagining traveling down it as though she were an invisible Fang. There was Captain Balderik walking up to the rooftop, presumably to check on the dragons and continue his check of the building. If she extended her hearing beyond the castle, it was harder, but possible. There were sheep huddling together in the night, terrified tiny breaths and sounds as they tried to be brave at the scent of predatory dragons in the air.

She tuned out the wind and the birds. People. That was what she wanted to hear. Were there any people outside of the castle? Hiding? Where would they hide?

The church ruins. The lighthouse. The cave. The stable.

She flew her mind toward those places, one by one. She searched every crevice, her own eyes closed, but she could almost see it in her mind as she searched. She felt as though she were a bat, identifying objects by echolocation.

And when she finished searching the island, she pulled her mind back to herself, both thrilled and disappointed.

She opened her eyes to find Captain Balderik standing in the room beside her, herself a few paces away from where she remembered standing last, beside Harker, and yet she stood at the narrow window to the laboratory, facing the island.

"Anything of interest out there, Miss Verena?" Captain Balderik asked mildly.

Fenya darted a glance over her shoulder, where Healer Breslau was working on Harker, his eyes closed, hands on her temples, deep in concentration. She doubted, like her experience just now, that he could hear anything but Harker's heartbeat and body speaking to him as he worked the delicate healing process.

"What do you know?" she asked Captain Balderik, meeting his pale blue eyes straight on this time.

His lips twitched, but not in pleasure. It seemed an expression of deepest disgust and sorrow. "We have been aware of the events here for some time—shortly after your departure for Wigmore. Indeed, it was your recruitment that tipped the scales of our knowledge. But we have not known the location, nor the extent."

She inhaled slowly and held it, holding it against the pulse of anger. Why didn't they try harder? "What did you think they were doing?"

"We've known they were trying to create a cure for unstable Legacies—as that has been what they've told the Crown. That, indeed, is why the Crown bothered to fund them, given the King's long illness." Captain Balderik spread a hand toward the castle as if to say that it explained much of their delay. "However, it's become clear, as parents and families have lost touch with their children—Mage de Croia being a prime example—that what is happening here is not exactly transparent. I would be most interested in hearing of your experience."

She shook her head before he even finished. "I can't."

"Miss Verena—"

"You don't understand." Panic rose in Fenya's throat, and she felt the telltale tingle of her hands warning her that she was near to losing control. "I can't. If I tell you what happened—if anyone were to know —I would never be safe. He will hunt me until he finds me."

"I can help you, Miss Verena."

She tilted her head to the side. "I don't think anyone can hide from him. Not forever."

"Do you know whom you face?" he asked.

"Do you mean if I know his name? No. We just called him the headmaster. But I know enough to know that he's not going to let me go easily—not after what he's done to me." Fenya paused. "Wait. The headmistress, when I fought her at the lighthouse..." She looked that direction as though searching for an answer. "She called him something...but I can't remember." She frowned as she thought of her ride with Dempsey and her talk with Wyn. "He might be...a gentleman. Or in the military, according to Dempsey. His name begins with a G, I believe."

"First or surname?"

She shook her head. "I don't know."

Captain Balderik cocked an eyebrow up slightly. "What has he done, Miss Verena?"

Fenya couldn't say it. Even though she wanted to share with him, she simply couldn't. But if she were a Perfect Mage, perhaps then she could show him without stating it. She could hear all over the island, so perhaps she could hear his thoughts or Discern if he were speaking truth. But she didn't know how to use it. Didn't even know how to feel about using it. High ranking magi all too often turned evil. They were tainted by their Power, or so the sayings went. But how much was too much? She had more Legacies than she'd ever heard of—and unnaturally made. She was a monster. A monster who deserved whatever fate she received.

"Miss Verena?" Captain Balderik's gentle voice prodded her out of her self pity.

His image was blurry, and she realized she was silently crying. She dashed away the tears from her face, rubbing at her eyelashes. "I'm sorry," she hastened to say.

"No, Miss Verena. It is I who must apologize. I wish I did not have to press you for particulars now, not when your friend is prone on a table and her future uncertain. I understand your pain. I do," he added after a beat where she slid her glance to him.

"I believe you," she said. He was a soldier, after all.

Harker moaned in pain. Fenya started for her before she remembered herself, catching Balderik's hand as it flinched toward her to stop her movement.

"She's fine," he said. "It's part of the process."

The Healer's face clenched in concentration, as though he were deciphering a book written in a language that perplexed him and required his entire focus.

Fenya joined him in staring at Harker, willing her to wake. If she tried hard enough, maybe she could do what Dempsey had already requested of her...heal. Despite no training and no experience...she thought she felt Harper's blood from here.

The Healer glanced her way, a new crease to his forehead, and then, with meaning, jerked his gaze to Captain Balderik.

"Perhaps we should step outside and give him peace to work," Balderik suggested softly. He offered his elbow to Fenya. "Will you?"

Fenya hesitated as Harker gasped again, her body arching and lungs rattling.

What would Harker think? Would she be offended if she woke without Fenya here? If she knew that Fenya had been here and left her? But no, Harker wouldn't care. Harker would probably prefer Fenya be absent.

She turned, and ignoring Balderik's offered elbow, preceded him out of the lab. As she reached the first door in the hallway, Fang glided silently through the courtyard window, carefully avoiding the rock frame and settled heavily on Fenya's shoulder.

Ow, Fenya thought as her talons dug through her cloak.

Sorry. Misjudged. There was a cheeky tone to her words though, reassuring Fenya.

"A Spark, a Familiar...an Exaudio," Captain Balderik murmured he quickened his step to walk beside her down the hall. "I wager you didn't have all those abilities when you arrived at Wigmore. What else are you now?"

Fenya's breath caught, her amusement at Fang's cheekiness evaporating. "I was always a Spark, Captain. Which is why I came here. I wouldn't have gotten into nearly as much trouble if I couldn't have made the fires that plagued me. But I came here hoping to *lose* my Legacy, Captain," she said firmly. "Others came to learn control. And others, it would appear, came with the intention of gaining...Legacies."

"And what did you get then?" Though his tone was casual, Fenya felt the weight of her answer looming. What she told him would determine her future. If he deemed her a threat to society, to the world, she would be putting her own life at risk. If anyone overheard them, they could reveal her secret to a number of people who would take her for their own purposes. She would never be safe.

"Everything except what I wanted," she finally answered. "Everything that I feared."

"Miss Verena?" Balderik asked.

Without another word to him, Fenya sped up and raced down the hallway as fast as she could without running. Tears made her vision blur.

"Miss Verena?" she heard again behind her.

"Let her go," answered another voice. "We've searched the grounds; she's safe."

Chapter Forty-Two

LIBRARY

Fenya continued all the way down the hallway and turned the corner, walking until she found herself in the library. She wasn't quite sure what had brought her there. Her father had always sought solace in his books and the church, and here was both, though she trusted neither right now. She had Henslow's journals and papers in her satchel, a rope strap she stole from the laboratory replacing the strap she's given to the pegasus's improvised reins, and the rope bit into her shoulder as her satchel thumped against her hip in its comforting way.

At least I didn't lose the proof Henslow entrusted me with. Yet she couldn't help but feel as though she had already failed. She hadn't shared his information with anyone yet, and only Harker had been found here, and not in good health.

At odds with her roiling emotions, the double story library was quiet and peaceful. Just outside, the waves crashed against the cliff below, every attack on the rock, a jolt to her system.

A sob caught in her throat. She had risked everything by leaving only to come back to nothing. To failure. She had failed. Her mother was right—everything she touched was bound to fail.

She choked back a sob, afraid someone was going to follow her into the library and find her completely broken down. But she couldn't do it anymore. The terror of the day, the fear confronting Wyn, the desperation of the return...only to be met by utter failure all overwhelmed. She couldn't catch her breath.

What's wrong? Fang's voice slipped into her head. *Why so sad? Why the wet face?*

Fenya curled the wyvern into her arms, hugging the little animal against her chest, unable to formulate an answer or an explanation of her tears in her mind. Instead, she clutched the dragon to her chest and sank to the floor, leaning against the lower part of the wall underneath the windowsill seat as the tears cascaded against each other down her cheeks.

Why are you sad? What's wrong? Fang persisted.

She couldn't answer, so Fang instead nuzzled her neck, licking her cheeks with a sandpaper, cat-like tongue.

Sometime later, the tears had ebbed, and though her eyes burned as though Fang had licked them too, sense had returned. She wasn't the same girl that she'd been when she'd arrived at Wigmore.

The window above her was dark, and the pale shadow of a slivered moon slipped through the window. She had spent too long in the library bemoaning her fate. She might have done something to find the others in this time.

She leaned her head back and sighed deeply. Fang was curled in her lap with a soft glow to her scales and snoring softly.

Fenya closed her eyes and slowed her breathing. The familiar silence of the castle enveloped her. Then a scratching reached her ears, like that of a rat.

Fenya opened her eyes. *What was that sound? Another student?*

Abruptly, Fang's snores stopped. She pried open one eye, her head cocking sideways just enough to show that she was awake and listening. The spikes on her spine crept up. *Human...familiar...wrong...*

Tailbone aching from the extended time on the floor and leaning against the stone wall under the window, Fenya forced herself to remain still and listened. *It's probably Captain Balderik or his men.*

In the library?

Searching everywhere... she answered. *For clues. Evidence. That I'm telling the truth.*

Fang's spikes lowered halfway. *Evidence. What is that?*

Evidence is...proof. Something to show that what is said is right. Fenya shrugged. Sometimes it was easy to forget that Fang was young and not human. Her voice was always so human in her mind, so natural. They understood each other more than anyone else could through their bond. But still, words were hard.

And humans want this...evidence? Fang asked.

Yes. Of course. We want to know that we're making the right choices. That's what Henslow's journals are supposed to be to the authorities.

Hmm. I think we need to find evidence that this person is doing what we think then.

Fenya's lips twitched at the idea. Fang was right.

Then let's go see what they're up to.

She quietly lifted herself to her feet, twisting to set Fang on the windowsill as she dragged her reluctant, sleep-stinging legs out from under them both.

As silently as possible, she crept around the railing portioned of the library, trying to identify where the sound was coming from in the echo of the cavernous room.

At the end of the stacks, A young soldier dressed in charcoal gray with scarlet piping and a matching scarlet sash around his waist stood with his back toward her, pulling notebooks and papers off the bookshelf, opening them and dropping them on the ground as if there wasn't anything worth keeping in them.

"What are you looking for?" Fenya asked.

The man flinched, his shoulders tensing, but he kept his back to her. Without answer, he ran his fingers over the spines of several notebooks on the shelf, then swept a hand across them, and a heap of notebooks and papers crashed to the floor.

Fenya started forward but something made her feet hesitate, and instead she clung to the shadows.

There's something odd going on...

Fang, still upstairs, hissed in her mind. *He's here.*

Fenya inhaled. *Who?*

Him. The one who hurt me.

Fenya narrowed her eyes at the man. He was dressed in the Sergeant's uniform like Marlowe, but what was he doing? And why wasn't he answering her? She couldn't see more than his profile, and she inched closer, still clinging to the shadows, to get a better look. "I asked you a question," she said shortly.

This time, Marlowe paused and half-glanced over his shoulder.

A shiver of dread washed over Fenya. The man standing in front of her looked exactly like Marlowe, but there was something off about him. *What is it?*

"What are you looking for?" she repeated, attempting to be firm and conceal the growing pit in her stomach.

"Nothing of your concern," he answered gruffly. His voice wasn't right. Sergeant Marlowe had a smooth tone, and this one...it was thrown somehow. She let her gaze travel over him. His clothing, now that she scrutinized them, seemed different somehow. Wrong. As though a shimmer covered them, like the haze from a hot surface.

"Face me or I call for the captain," Fenya said solemnly. "I don't believe you are who you appear to be." She was already drawing her fire to defend or attack when the man slowly rotated to face her. Seeing him fully, Fenya saw the differences in him that she hadn't been able to tell with his back turned. She gasped and all fight went out of her.

He seemed infinitely more tired, with a darkness in his eyes that she hadn't noticed before. His eyes, they were different. Where Marlowe had pale brown eyes, these man's eyes were dark brown with glints of gold. Where Marlowe had a warmth that could be seen in his gaze, there was no warmness here. Nothing but a darkness swirling in confusion.

The man before her frowned in apparent concern. "Are you all right...miss?"

It's him, Fang said in her mind as she screeched aloud and swooped around Fenya's head. *Run. Run. We must run.*

Fenya's hands tingled even as her body went ice cold. She stared at him, and as she did, the aether swam between them. For a moment, she thought she glimpsed the true image underneath his façade, but then something collided with her shoulders as though he had physically shoved her.

He's a Shifter! Fang cried in her head.

The man before her cocked his head and smiled. "I would have let you go if it weren't for that infernal dragon."

Fenya tried to summon her flames, but they felt cold, as though she were doused with icy water.

"What is it?" The man's smile twitched. "Can't believe what you're seeing?"

"How did you—" She broke off and glanced out the door, expecting Captain Balderik or the true Marlowe to appear.

"Don't worry, we won't be interrupted." The man, the fake Marlowe...the headmaster, smiled sinisterly. "I've got a few tricks up my sleeve, you see?"

As if the icy water that encased her had been engulfed in a frigid wind, Fenya's limbs froze. "Captain!" she screamed.

The headmaster winced at the noise, but he only made a dismissive shake of his head. "My dear, Miss Verena, no one can hear us. I've used a few potions on myself and enchanted the surrounding room, you see? Had you not entered before me, you would not be able to enter at all. So fortuitous it was that you chose this location to weep."

She stiffened, her hatred for him growing. She pushed it away to focus on him and their surroundings. He'd enchanted the room—that meant it could be broken. Could she break the enchantment? Or even see it?

If she focused on the edges of the room, the aether was shimmering like a thin veil blocking access to the room. If she could see it —did that mean others could too? Fenya raised her chin in what she hoped was defiance. "And what do you think you're going to accomplish by enchanting the room around us?"

"Oh, just a little bit of privacy to have a conversation in."

"What could you possibly have to say to me?"

"Quite a bit, if you weren't aware. In fact, we haven't gotten to speak much all year, and here we are, about to embark on a big change of scenery." The headmaster kept his voice neutral, but it sent shivers down Fenya's spine.

"Are we?" she managed. *Fang, where are you?*

Up here. I don't trust him. You need to go.

I know. But only if you're safe. I can't risk you being taken again.

"Oh yes, I don't think I'll be able to come back here, not now that the EDS knows about it." The headmaster casually picked up another notebook and flipped through it, his nose wrinkling slightly in distaste. It ended up in the same pile as the others as his feet.

"What are you looking for?" she asked.

Fang, see if you can go and get help. This is the chance to arrest him and make him pay for all he's done.

Yes, yes, Fang nearly sang in her head. *Make him pay.*

The headmaster glanced up at the ceiling, where Fang fluttered on the second floor. His lips curved slightly, as though he knew something Fenya didn't. Mage Marlowe could speak to dragons, couldn't he? Could the headmaster speak to them as he was Shifted into Marlowe's appearance? It couldn't be, even the EDS had said so...but then...she also wouldn't have believed that she could permanently absorb the Legacies of another. What if he had a potion that allowed him to control Fang now? He'd taken blood, perhaps more from Fang. Despite Liah's words about dragon blood not being long lived outside of the body, perhaps the headmaster had determined some way to preserve it.

Her throat closed over at the thought. "You deserve to be punished for what you've done," she burst out.

The headmaster fixed her with a pleasantly surprised look. "Do I?"

"Yes." She forced the nerves away. "You killed Bryton. You stole Harker's Legacy. You experimented on God knows how many children —and you think that's acceptable?"

"They are a small cost to the greater good," he replied with a shrug. "What do I care for a few Wyldes? Of them all, you are the one with value. The one that worked. Science requires sacrifice. And sacrifice is worth it."

"Not when you're not the one sacrificing—you're the only one who benefits!" Fenya returned, her anger flaring as her fists clenched.

"Now, now, that's not true," he answered mildly. "You've seen some benefit, I believe."

"It's not a benefit to be forced into thieving."

"Thieving? Oh, you mean your additional Legacies. Well, you should know that your gift was intended to be shared—"

"Yes, I know! Dempsey told me."

The headmaster's eyebrows rose. "Did he now? Interesting."

"He's angry that I stopped it." She bit her lip to keep from sharing more.

"You—" His forehead creased and a darkness came over his face. "I suspected as much. How?"

"Why would I tell you? You've done nothing but use everything against me in ways I don't want. I tell you to take my Legacy and you pour more into me like I'm some vessel to fill until it bursts. Is that your goal? To make me explode? Make me into a weapon?"

"A weapon, a tool, a mage of unimaginable, unheard-of-before Power...any of those things. Have you no idea what's going on in the world, Miss Verena?"

She bit back a huff of annoyance. "I know some. I knew what was happening before I came here. But you kept us isolated—no doubt intentionally."

His expression was impassive as he let fall another notebook. "We wouldn't want to create undue fear."

"Undue fear?" Fenya bristled and she felt her flames answering. "You struck fear into everyone here—for no reason other than control."

"Control is important. Can you imagine if I didn't have Dempsey helping me coerce you into compliance? Whispering sweet nothings into your ears so that you trusted him enough to follow him into the keeper's hands? I would have failed again. And you, being the Relic Bearer you are..." His lips curved into a smile.

"What does that have to do with anything?"

"Oh, you know so much and yet understand so little." He sighed. "It's almost a delight to educate you." He picked up another journal and opened it, flipping through with his gaze on the pages as he spoke. "Relics are the most valuable Legacy items in our world. If we lose the Relics, there's a belief that we would lose our Legacies. We must guard them carefully—which means that until you produce an heir of your bloodline, no one can touch you, for there is no Heir within your line."

"I thought the Crown could reassign it."

He tilted his head at her. "They won't. They haven't."

"They could." Despite her brave words, Fenya shivered, and something deeper tingled in her hands. *If they won't, the Relic will have to die with me. I couldn't risk passing these stolen Legacies to a future child. What danger would they be in all their life?*

"But to my delight, I've found myths regarding the Perfect Mage. And that's what led me to you, eventually. You see," he said as he dropped the journal to the floor and picked up another from the shelf, "you might not have heard that the Relics call to one another. Now that you are a Bearer and not an Heir, you will undoubtedly realize it, the more you go out into the world. But there are ten Relics in the world, ten families touched by this burden."

Fenya tried to hide her frown. She'd always been taught that there were only eight. Two for each of the elements. What additional two did he know of? Had he dared to create two more? But no...he had said ten families.

His eyes gleamed as he looked at Fenya. "The smart ones have hidden their Relics. Hidden themselves. But it wasn't until your father died, leaving you the Emberheart Fire Heir, a set of circumstances that lent themselves perfectly to my plans. And imagine my delight when I learned the Relic hadn't been properly passed on before your father's death. But that you were left unguided." He grinned. "It was too good to ignore. And I was right. Your Power was unchecked and unexpected. And that Fire was what I needed to bind other Legacies to your core." He considered the journal in his hands and tucked it into the front of his jacket, then reached for another.

"Why did it work on me and not on Rhys?" Fenya asked. "Because of the Relic?"

"Perhaps. But perhaps not." He pursed his lips and turned several pages in the journal before continuing. He took so long that she wondered if he were going to speak again. "I only have theories about that. And while science is built on theories, they must be proven." With sudden violence, he threw the journal in his hands across the room so that it collided with the opposite bookshelf.

Fenya flinched.

He's angry, Fang said to her from her perch across the library. She hissed as if to emphasize her point.

I know. Did you tell the soldiers?

I can't get out. The room is enchanted against me, too. We're all trapped here until it's broken.

Fenya shivered. *I have to alert the soldiers. But how?*

Silently, with as little movement as possible, she reached for the aether around them. She imagined herself transported the way she had inspected the island earlier, as though she were a dragon flying through the air, invisible. This time though, she sought the soldiers.

And with half her mind on the soldiers, and half on the headmaster before her, Fenya kept him talking. "Why do you care about the science so much? It's cruel what you're doing."

He huffed. "You don't understand."

"But I do. I understand that you don't care about anyone but yourself. Why adopt Dempsey if you hate him enough to ruin him in such a way? You've stripped him of his Legacy—made him an Ordinary—stolen his chances from him—do you even care?"

"Care? About that tepid trickle of Water? About that drain on my coffers? Who wants Water when Fire is offered? *You* were who I needed. You, the Relic Bearer. The Heir to the Emberheart Fire Relic, a Relic that goes seven hundred years back to the First King—the true mage. Dempsey? I don't need him anymore—I hardly ever needed him. I only used him for *you.* That was his only—surprise—use. He's a worthless boy who happened to have a mediocre Water Legacy. And you, Oh you! You arrived a broken little girl who only wanted to obey. So desperate for her mother's love that she never realized her own self worth—never realized that she had far more Power than anything her mother might ever imagine! Ignored by her jealous mother, orphaned by her proud father, out of control, desperate to do anything to make herself worthy..." His gold-flecked eyes alit as he advanced on her. "Tell me I'm wrong, Miss Verena. Tell me that when I first saw you at Magess Jolie's that you weren't a scared little Relic Heir who would have sold her soul in order to avoid her future responsibility as Relic Bearer."

Fenya gasped. "At Magess Jolie's? You—were there?"

He wiped a hand over his mouth. "Of course! I've been watching all the Relic Heirs for *years*." He shook his head as though disappointed in himself. But he motioned to his body. "You can see I have ways of disguising myself. And methods of removing large numbers of people in a short amount of time," he added as an afterthought.

She narrowed her eyes, feeling repulsed. "How? Legacies you've stolen from others?"

He chuckled. "No, of course not. I am an Energy Mage, after all."

She shook her head. "There's no such thing."

He chuckled. "You haven't been summoned to a Bearer's Tribune yet. But you'll see. There are not just four elements."

"And...Energy Magi can Shift? I find it difficult to believe they've gone so far unknown to the general population." Fenya rebalanced herself on her feet, leaning away from his nearness, distracted from the conversation. "Even the Church of the Aether denies Energy Magi exist at all."

"Of course they do, of course. We can't share all secrets with the masses. But there is a potion." He turned his attention back to the books and yanked out three leather notebooks in one large hand. "The problem is that I don't know where he put it before fleeing!" He cursed and threw the largest notebook across the room. It sailed away from him and skidded across the stone floor before landing at the leg of a wooden table.

Her body tensed, the telltale ripple of aether skimming over her hands. *Control. Control.* She focused again on her invisible search, reaching for the commons where she thought the soldiers might be spending the night. Were they wondering where she had gone? Were they watching? Had they really let her go, trusting in their search? They, too, had underestimated the headmaster. She entered the commons and found three of the soldiers sitting together, poring over a map on the table between them.

The headmaster ripped another notebook out of the shelf and wrenched it open. "I remember it...I know his writing...where are they?"

"Whose?" Fenya asked on impulse. Her heart thudded. Henslow's notebooks were in her satchel. She sent her invisible self into the table of the soldiers. Napkins rustled. They were eating. One's mouth moved, drawing the attention of the others to the movement.

"Henslow had his little secret spots, I know," the headmaster continued as though she hadn't spoken. "But the lighthouse was empty, the stable revealed nothing... Curse him to the Netherworld!" he exploded.

Fenya flinched, taking a half-step back, her attention on the soldiers wavering.

"I will find him. And I'll kill him for stealing my secrets."

"*Your* secrets?" Fenya challenged, putting an expression of skepticism on her face. The other half of her attention pulled at the soldier's map. She swept it up with Air and sent it spiraling out of their reach.

"I don't think you actually did much when it came down to it," she told the headmaster. "Nothing except show up and watch the children you experimented on die." Her heart raced throughout her body at her own words. They were vehement, strong, powerful, and utterly provoking. It was poking a dragon in the eye and praying that she wasn't immediately vaporized.

She spun the map higher in the air, but a soldier lunged for it and caught one corner. She gave a mental tug on the map and felt the map's corner separate.

At first Fenya thought the headmaster hadn't heard her words, for he continued flipping through the notebook in his hands, but then his hand clenched and the notebook slammed shut. He turned to her, his eyes flat and dark. "One thing I hate is ungrateful brats like you. I've given you everything. I've given you *life* that no other will experience. And you accuse me of doing nothing? None of this would have been done without my knowledge—without me putting together the most forward-thinking Potioneer, the most talented Metallurgist, and the most skilled Healer here together on Wigmore. They never would have dared to attempt anything so brazen alone. And they never would have had the combined intelligence to do so. *I* am what made this work—I am who told them to do what they did—and they betrayed me!" He roared the last words, chucking the notebook at her head so that she flinched, but instead of ducking, she raised her hands and stopped it a foot away from herself.

She gasped silently at her mistake, at revealing exactly what control she had over a Legacy that she hadn't been gifted. How could she be so foolish?

He chuckled, his face going so quickly from fury to amusement that confusion washed over her. "I knew it worked. I just couldn't have pictured how well and how quickly you would master it."

It was awe. Awe on his face.

And what was more—*she* had awed him.

She buffeted the map closer to the library door. She hoped the soldiers were following, realizing something.

"You're truly a Perfect Mage—nothing can stop you now, don't you understand?" His eyes gleamed with satisfaction, with unwavering belief of what he had created. "You must realize that there is no place for you in this world now—no one can undo what I have done to you. No one can understand you. They will only ever fear you. Your place is with me."

The truth of his words sent icy fear draining Fire from her as though glacial water had extinguished it. *He's right, just like Dempsey warned me not to tell the soldiers. I'll never be safe if anyone else knows, if anyone else ever learns that I am a...a Perfect Mage...I will be forced into hiding. Forever.*

A shudder vibrated down her spine.

"Perfection. Utter perfection," he admired in such a tone that shivers raced over her skin.

Her thoughts jolted as something hit the Shield she had put around herself. In her distraction, the headmaster had reached for her, snatching at her wrist, but her Shield, put there to protect her from the book he'd flung, remained in the aether, silent and invisible between them. Though if she focused on it, she could see the barest shimmer of aether between them, threaded together in a criss-cross that blocked out everything but sound and sight.

The headmaster jerked back his hand at the Shield, rubbing his fingertips as though it had shocked him.

"One day, you'll see it." His lips curved into a smile. "You'll see that you belong with me. I've made you fit for nothing else."

"I would rather live the life of a hermit before I let you use me.

Before I succumb to your wishes," she declared, putting all her hurt of everything that had happened to her at Wigmore and the suffering of the others into her words. "I will stop you." She raised her hands, preparing to call her Fire.

But his eyes glinted as though her flames were caught inside him. "I hope you try that, my dear. For the best way—"

"Stop where you are!" came a forbidding voice at the door.

Chapter Forty-Three

CHOICES

"Miss Verena, this way!" Captain Balderik was at the door, his hand raised and sword unsheathed in the other.

Keeping half her attention on her Shield between herself and the headmaster, Fenya shook her head. "This ends now. I won't let you harm another child." She called her flames, and they answered, burning through her arms, cutting along the marks on her arms, burning through the gloves that protected them from view.

"What the—" Marlowe's true voice spoke behind her.

Fenya formed her Fire into spheres in her palms, ready to fly his way. But how could she stop him from Shifting or Transporting—if he still could? Or would he race to a dragon and attempt to fly away?

She wouldn't be the first to maim, despite his sins. If Balderik and the EDS could capture the headmaster, they could interrogate him, find out where the others were—she could maybe still save them. She just had to delay him, capture him.

"Put out your hands, sir," Balderik was saying.

The headmaster turned to Balderik with something like amused shame. He seemed to see potential wasted, a failure of the deepest kind. "You don't know who you're up against."

Fenya gritted her teeth, fighting back her nerves. If she used anything but her natural Fire, she would expose herself to Balderik and the true Marlowe. She already risked much in keeping her Shield in place, especially not knowing the Legacies of the others.

As he twisted in the spot, Fenya reached for him, innately. In some inexplicable way, her body knew what to do. She extended her Shield, interrupting his reach for whatever aether he was grasping at.

He roared as if in pain, and his body Shifted. She gasped as his face morphed, changing from Marlowe's image to an unfamiliar one—with the same gold-flecked brown eyes as before. They burned in fury and anger, pain and fear. Then a flash of blue light came from his hands, not at Fenya, but aimed behind her. She turned, her concentration wavering, turning at a yell behind her of pain.

"Marlowe!" Balderik's word split the air in a crush of fear and fury, and Fenya's heart lurched.

"No!" another voice shouted. "Stop!"

Marlowe stood rooted to the spot, his eyes wide in shock as his limbs went still. Fenya gasped. Ice crept up from the floor, freezing him to the ground. His every limb was unmoving, unmovable. Only his eyes flicked back and forth, absorbing the scene in front of him.

Balderik's yells had summoned others within earshot, and they thundered down the hallway now, boots heavy with urgency.

She whirled toward the headmaster just in time to see him disappear through a secret door in the back of the library. The door instantly began closing. She flew after him, probing for the entrance, when the sounds of panic behind her sank in.

Balderik was barking instructions, telling Healer Breslau to attend to Marlowe as he crashed into the area beside Fenya. "How do we follow?" he demanded.

"I—I don't know!" She ran her hands along the spot she thought the headmaster had touched when he'd gone crashing into the wall. "Somewhere here!"

She scraped her hands once again over the wall as Balderik did the same. Their hands collided at the corner, and both realized at the same time where the latch was.

"Balderik!" came a cry from behind. "He's not going to make it— not without a second Healer!"

Balderik looked back while still probing the corner of the wall, pressing down on the lodged lever that had to be the mechanism to open the door. Fenya added her weight to the spot, dragging at it, willing it to move.

Abruptly, it released, and the door flung open so quickly that both nearly fell through. Down below she thought she could hear scrabbling of disappearing footsteps.

Balderik hesitated on the spot, warring desires written on his face. Save his soldier or follow the one who had cursed him?

Fenya met his gaze, her foot already halfway through the opening to the tunnel. She was going to stop him—she had to. Before he did this to who knew how many others.

Then she felt Balderik's hand on her elbow.

She turned, question and confusion rising within her.

"I don't want to ask but—" Pain raked across his face. "Would you?" his voice cracked, and he hastily cleared his throat. "We won't have time to get him back to the mainland, and we only have one Healer here."

Fenya looked below, then back at Marlowe. Ice nearly eclipsed his entire body already. Did he know what he was asking? To give up her own pursuit of the man who had so tortured her and her friends?

Just as she had seen the battle on his face, he saw hers. "Please," he murmured. "I promise you, I will track this man down, but please— he's my friend as well as soldier."

Fenya barely bit back the roar of frustration inside her. *I can't deny his request.* The man who had believed her, who had saved her, whom she had chosen to trust.

The dark tunnel loomed before her, a hole which disappeared into who knew where, a passage to find the headmaster and eliminate him once and for all. If she turned away now, would she ever find him again?

Her gaze stuck on the torment on his face. But he didn't ask again. And that was all it took.

With a feral growl, she pushed herself away from the door and ran at Marlowe, yelling back over her shoulder, "You'd best go quickly then —for if I find him, I will *not* spare him."

She skidded to a halt in front of Marlowe, where the ice crept up his neck, toward his jaw.

Breslau gave her a barest glance, hopelessness in his gaze amidst his concentration. "If it reaches his brain, he'll die."

Fenya took a deep, steadying breath. "I think I can help."

"Then help!" he growled, pain lacing his words.

His desperation was clear. If she didn't help, Marlowe would die. Healer Breslau could not keep it from spreading. His concentration was focused on healing, and it was clear that his energy was fading, for the ice moved faster, reaching Marlowe's lower lip and advancing.

She didn't dare admit that she had no idea what she was doing, but the desperation on both Balderik's and the Healer's face was enough to inform her that it didn't matter how much or little she knew—if she could do anything to turn the tide, it might be enough.

She put her hands close to Marlowe's heart. His eyes locked on hers, and a tear glistened as it ebbed from the corner of his eye. As it trailed out, it froze only a small finger's width from where it began. He didn't have long.

Fenya closed her eyes, needing to focus. The pained breathing of the Healer filled the air, but she focused on Marlowe. His breathing was labored, small, hardly possible as the ice on his skin burrowed deeper within his body.

She took her attention from the Healer's breathing and from Marlowe's. Instead, she focused on the ice that crept into his body, centimeter by centimeter. It was growing dangerously close to his heart, his center, she realized with alarm. It wasn't his brain that she needed to save, but his heart.

She reached for it, imagining how she might draw it from his body without further damaging him. Already it touched his ears, crept down his biceps and toward his fingers. What it touched, it tainted. It was more than ice—it was poison, corrupting everything it touched.

She probed it more, as though palpating an injured bone. And then she felt Healer Breslau's attempts. She felt what he was doing, paused to watch it. Aether from without Marlowe was entering through the Healer's acts. And something else...a life force...his own energy. He held the heels of the poison, dragging at it as though he could physically hold it back.

But Fenya saw something more. She cast a net of aether over Marlowe's body, tracing the tendrils of the poison toward his very center. It would not be satisfied to be pulled away, it would fight... But she would try.

She hesitated. *What has he done to him? What is this poison?*

Fenya called out her Legacies, drawing her Healing out by some innate knowledge she didn't understand. All she knew was that she could do it—and she should. His life was not to be forfeit because of her. No more lives would be if she had anything to say about it. She concentrated, probing the poison. It had to be drawn out. But Healer Breslau's attempts showed that to pull it back wasn't enough. The only way to stop it was...to draw it into her. If she had been a lesser mage, she wouldn't have attempted it. And she didn't blame Breslau for not trying.

She set to work, slowly drawing the poisoned ice into her own hands, tendrils of ice drawn through the aether that she dissolved in the air. She pulled the ice from his cheeks, his nose, following it down his throat into his torso, working painstakingly. Every pull on the aether cost her energy. Sweat broke out on her forehead and nose, her heart racing at the effort.

Then she spotted his Legacy, in the center of his heart, a steady glow of blue, pulsing softly as though a heartbeat. It was beautiful. It looked as though it might be his very soul, nestled inside his heart, the very center of his being. She almost gasped, watching its tender flame quiver and shrink as the poisonous ice neared.

And she suddenly understood exactly what the poison had been designed to do.

It wanted to quench not only his mortal life but his Legacy. That was the cost of it all, the headmaster's ultimate cost. Legacy valued more than life.

A shiver ran over her, raising the hairs on her arms despite the sweat on her brow. *How could he? He was cruel—cruel to steal another man's Legacy in such a fashion. But then, would Marlowe want life without his Legacy?*

To be deprived of it, to rip it from him—was it not better to die?

It's better to die than be half of who you should be. Harker's words trembled in Fenya's mind.

And it would be worse yet to see that half in someone else, Fenya added to herself as guilt tore at her attention.

Concentrate! This command came from Fang, whose presence Fenya had almost forgotten.

Fenya yanked her attention from the pulsing glow in Marlowe's heart. It was fading the longer she watched, fluttering in panic like that of a bird caught in a snare. If left too long, the bird would be strangled in the net and all life snuffed out.

It's time to show who you are, Fang told her firmly. *No fear, just action.*

The ice had slowed to a glacial crawl, already at the tips of her fingers where she held her hands an inch from Marlowe's ribs. It hesitated in its quest for his heart, stopped, then reached for her Power. But the gap between them seemed too much for the poison to leap, and it began its slow crawl back toward his heart, the core of his Legacy. She fought for it, and it slowed again, but she couldn't turn it back.

Help me! she heard in her mind, a desperate scream.

She nearly stumbled forward out of her trance, opening her eyes to lock them with Marlowe's gaze. There she read the plea that had been a thought so clearly in her head a moment before.

His Strength Legacy was too weak. If the poison reached that blue flame within him, both life and Legacy would be snuffed out. Despite his Power, and Fenya could feel how very great it was, the poison was stronger. But it shrank from her because...

Dread washed over her in the perfection of the headmaster's attack.

Her Legacy was more. She could snuff out the poison, she felt it in her bones, her Fire ready to consume it. If she put her Legacy into Marlowe though—he would burn from the inside out. And yet, *she* could consume it. The only cost was Marlowe's Legacy.

She understood then what choice the headmaster had forced upon her. He knew her better than she thought he did. He saw her desire to save those from him, and he'd burdened her with this choice. The headmaster was making her choose to Discerp Marlowe.

The choice was clear: Marlowe's life or his Legacy.

Save me, came the plea again.

"At the cost of your Legacy?" Her words broke the silence in the room.

YES. Came the silent answer. *I have a family—wife—children.*

"All right," Fenya whispered her answer. And she closed her eyes, knowing somehow without question the headmaster had not underestimated her after all. Again the choice, again the decision to sacrifice Legacy or life.

She hated him. She did not think she could hate any person any more than she hated him.

She crashed her hands against Marlowe's chest where they met ice that burned hotter than the hottest fire. But Power burned within her. The ice collided with her skin, and she gasped, tilting her head back in the shock.

And she called for it.

The ice stopped, hesitated between the Legacy in Marlowe's core and what she taunted it with.

Come to me, she thought to it, redoubling her efforts.

It sought her then, ripping through her skin with the unrelenting force of a tempest breaking upon the sea.

She screamed as it came for her, coursing through her veins, racing for heart as though it had only waited for permission.

No! She slammed her teeth shut, and the jarring sensation shocked her back to herself. Groaning, she met the poisoned ice with her Legacies. Her Fire was only one that roared forth to meet the ice. Air swept it together as Water cleansed it and Earth filtered it. And as the poisoned ice flowed in, pushed from behind as Marlowe's body sagged forward in relief, caught by Breslau, Fenya felt her Legacy meet it as a canyon absorbed a flash flood.

Her body convulsed, but she didn't fall. Her hands clenched and released, her every muscle tightening as the silent battle raged within her. But even as she knew her Power was more, that it would win, darkness threatened. Could she still get Legacy Fever with her Power being what it was now? She didn't know, but this would reveal all.

As her Fire consumed the last of the poisoned ice, a gasp rattled her bones as her Legacies chased ice through them. A gasp rattled out of her mouth with a whoosh of frozen breath chased by flames.

A shout of surprise rang out in the library, and then Fenya fell in a heap, her head crashing against the stone floor and blackness greeted her.

Chapter Forty-Four

LEAVING

When Fenya woke, she was in the library.

For a moment, her heart leapt to her throat, and she wanted to jolt up, panicked to find herself still at Wigmore. Then memories crashed against her skull, each a throb that gave more than physical pain. The worst headache of her life clawed at the back of her skull.

Headmaster disguised as Marlowe. The ice attack on real Marlowe. Headmaster's flight. Balderik begging Fenya to save Marlowe. Balderik giving chase. And her desperate act to save Marlowe's life. Had she succeeded?

For several minutes, she stared at the library ceiling, allowing the memories to assault her, worse than the pain that coursed through her.

Finally, she pushed herself up slowly, waiting as the room whirled around her and nausea threatened. With a rub of her head, she found dried blood there. Her Legacy—had she come out as unscathed as she thought? She probed within herself, feeling the familiar burn of her Fire, and the less familiar trickle of Water, breath of Air, and the unmoving stone of Earth.

A sigh of relief escaped her even as she shook her head at herself. She had once only had Fire—what gave her the right to worry about the loss of her other Legacies? Her *stolen* Legacies?

Her hands clutched the edge of something soft. She wasn't on the floor then.

She turned to the right. She lay on a cot, and the Healer lay on a second a short distance away. Just beyond him, on a third cot, lay Harker, covered in a blanket, on her side with her knees tucked up to her chest, sleeping like a child. She watched her for several quiet moments, counting the times her chest moved in and out, her face peaceful and twitching.

She was alive, at least. *But was Balderik successful?*

In the fireplace, a fire burned steadily, warming the room and heating her like a wool blanket.

She turned the other way and her breath stuttered. There lay Marlowe, his face still, arms crossed on his chest.

"No," she whispered.

"Miss Verena?" a voice said.

She stumbled out of her bed to Marlowe's cot. "No, is he—"

With a ragged snore, he inhaled and exhaled in a deep breath, and then shifted.

A gasp of relief and a deep laughter bubbled out of her. "I thought —" She looked around her, giddy in her relief.

"Miss Verena?" came the question again.

She pushed her hands over her mouth to silence herself and sank onto the floor in front of Marlowe's cot.

Mage de Croia approached with question and concern chasing each other across his face.

"Are you well?" He bent in front of her.

She motioned weakly to Marlowe, grateful that her weakness came from relief, not Legacy Fever or exhaustion. "I thought...for a moment...I thought...I had failed. I thought...he was dead."

A small smile tugged at Mage de Croia's mouth. He offered his hand to her. "Are you well?"

"Yes, I...I feel strong as before." She touched her head where it still throbbed. "Except for this."

He tilted his head in agreement. "You took quite a fall from what I hear."

She reached out to take his still offered hand and paused at the sight of her bare arms. The sleeves of her dress were singed off to her elbows, revealing her Relic scars. They were brighter than before, but their image had changed somehow.

"Miss Verena?" Mage de Croia prodded, moving his hand slightly.

I can look at my arms later. She shook away her thoughts and put her hand in Mage de Croia's.

He assisted her to her feet and tucked her hand into his elbow to better support her.

"What happened to the headmaster? Did the captain get him?" she asked.

Mage de Croia held a finger to his lips and then pointed around them to the sleeping forms, leading her toward the fireplace. "No," he answered quietly as they walked. "The dragon-cursed shadow of a man escaped with hardly a sign. Balderik and his men searched for several hours with no luck. They scoured both sky and earth..." He sighed heavily, the answer clearly a burden to him as it was to her.

He led her the short distance to a few chairs in front of the fire, in which a couple of soldiers slumped in them, dozing. "Are you cold?" he asked in a voice hardly above a whisper.

She smiled wryly and answered at the same level. "I don't get cold."

"Ah, right. You're like my nephew—Rhys. He never truly gets cold either. Always has a fire within him."

"In more than one way," she agreed softly. She motioned to the door. "Shall we walk outside, so as not to wake them?"

"Yes."

They walked from the library and through the courtyard in silence, only his motion toward the gate expressing his question of whether they should go or stay. Taking the lead, she briskly guided them out of the imposing castle. She had never wanted to return to this prison, and yet the island itself was a respite from the cold stone that had too long been her jail.

Her strength resuming in the fresh air, caressed by the damp salt of the sea. As the fire in the library had invigorated her, so the wet air did the same. She paused, dropping Mage de Croia's arm, then leaned down and did the most unladylike thing she could imagine: she removed her boots and let her feet touch the earth.

She stood, abandoning the shoes on a dry rock and strode for the clifftop.

"Careful, Miss Fenya!" Mage de Croia called out, stopping far from the cliff's edge.

But she pushed on, confident of her Air's support and her Earth under foot.

Toes gripping the edge, she stopped, spreading out her arms, and leaned her head back to the heavens.

The wind yanked her hair out of its braid and whipped it away from her face, drying the tears on her face with a strict caress.

Breathing deeply, she lowered her gaze to the waters churning below. The high tide covered the rocks on the path to the lighthouse almost completely. The lighthouse still glinted through the morning light coming up from the sea before them. The rich saltiness of the sea assaulted her nostrils on the wind, heavy with the previous storm.

The scene between her and Headmistress Wyn flashed back across her mind culminating in her desperate jump from the top. It looked smaller now. Both the tide's storm-swelled height and the distance made it seem as though it could have been a safe leap. But Dempsey had rescued her from the surf, despite all odds. *Where is he? Did he go back home—wherever that is? I should have gotten more information from him, where home is...anything to help find him now.*

As she surveyed the sea crashing on the base of the lighthouse, Fang leapt from the top of the lighthouse, curving gracefully away. The wyvern arced through the sky, flying behind her before landing gently on her shoulder and butting her head against her cheek with concern and affection.

Better? she asked in Fenya's head.

Yes, where were you?

If dragons could shrug, Fang did. *I thought it best to hide from the headmaster, as you said. If he got me, you would come for me. And you...you're strong now.*

I'm glad you're safe.

You didn't need my help—you have enough Power in you to kill five men and still remain standing.

Fenya laughed aloud. *No I don't,* she told Fang.

Yes, you do. Trust me. The little wyvern tilted her head at Fenya, her golden eye gleaming.

I do?

Yes. Fang fell silent, reassuring Fenya with her steady presence and the murmur of her heart near her ear.

Mage de Croia crept up closer beside her and gave Fenya a slanted, sidelong consideration while she searched the top of the lighthouse. "What can you tell me of him—how...how was he when you left him?"

Tugged from her private conversation with Fang, Fenya flinched at the question she had long been expecting. Should she tell him the entire truth or shield him from the worst?

Tell him the truth—he needs to know, Fang advised.

"He...was not well, to be honest," she finally said, trusting Fang.

It was Mage de Croia's turn to flinch at her words. But his shoulders dipped into a deep slump that bespoke his pain. "I was afraid to hear that. Dare I ask... Can you tell me more?"

Fenya considered the man before her. To want information and not have it was a terrible thing, especially when so long awaited. It was, in her mind, worse than knowing nothing or knowing part. "Rhys's Legacy is nearing a Wylde state, I think. He is only safe, in his mind, when he has the headmaster's controlling bracelets fully charged on his wrists."

Mage de Croia inhaled a slow breath. "I see."

"Rhys is...frightened. Deeply, deeply frightened of what he might become." She absently stroked Fang's chest with a finger. "What he has already become."

"I see," Mage de Croia repeated through his exhale.

"He feels forever tied to the headmaster...fearful to be without working bracelets." She brushed a lock of hair from her face and idly realized that the wind had calmed. "He told me to go and come back for him—he wouldn't come with me. I don't know that even if I had returned, he would have gone with me willingly."

Mage de Croia swiped at his face, brushing back his hair but also dragging a sleeve across his eyes in a quick manner that Fenya knew he hoped remained invisible to her.

"He is in great pain and fear of becoming a complete Wylde."

He clenched his eyes shut as he held a tight fist to his mouth as though to keep in a sob unsuitable for her ears.

Fenya had hardly realized until his quiet, desperate sounds to regain control, that she had diverted the Air around them, protecting them in a sort of silent bubble out of the direct wind. It was too much work to divert the entirety of the breeze without conscious effort, but she was surprised to find herself doing it unconsciously. She would have to be careful indeed to avoid detection from a Legacy Knowledge Mage.

She averted her eyes from his pain. She had shed too many tears already over her mistakes—she was going to rectify them now. The time to sit on them and meditate over them was over. But she gave him his moments to regain his control, pretending not to notice the hiccups he forced down and the tears that wetted his lashes.

"Have you heard any more about Harker? Is she well?" Fenya finally asked. "I saw her...asleep..."

"The girl? She's no worse and not much better," he admitted, his voice rough. "She's clearly been through something traumatic. Once awake, she refused to speak."

"Refused?"

"Or was unable, either way; she said nothing."

Fenya bit her lip. "And what will happen to her?"

Mage de Croia lifted a shoulder. "She will go to her family, if we can find them."

"She has no family."

"Then to whomever will take her. She's underage, so an orphanage, perhaps."

"No," Fenya said decisively. "She'll come with me."

"With you?"

"I'll bring her home with me—she cannot go to an orphanage; it will be the worst place for her. She will lose all control—be sent to an asylum within a day."

"What does she have to control anymore?"

"Her life," Fenya said fiercely. "Her future?" She shook her head as he began to apologize. "It doesn't matter. I don't trust that the headmaster thought of everything and properly severed her Legacy completely. Besides..." She trailed off, biting down on her lip as she faced the truth. "It was my fault that Harker lived."

"Your...fault?" Mage de Croia shook his head, confusion knitting his brow. "What do you mean?"

She tugged at a loose piece of skin on her bottom lip. "I stopped the transfer early. It's my fault she lived—but I couldn't let her die like Bryton."

Only when Mage de Croia touched her gently on the shoulder did she realize that tears again slipped down her cheeks. "You did the right thing. Even if the results weren't what you could have anticipated, you did the right thing."

"Even if *she* suffers for it?" Fenya blinked at the blurry lighthouse. Fang butted her head against Fenya's cheek.

Don't cry.

"Yes, even then. Suffering is an unavoidable part of life. And the more one suffers, the more one appreciates life."

Fenya swiped at her eyes. "I don't know that I agree with that, but at least she lives. That's the only solace I can take. And I'll use my entire life to pay it back, if I have to."

Mage de Croia met her steely gaze and considered her for a long moment before nodding. "Then let me help. I will give you the funds to provide for her. Whether it be alongside you or in an orphanage or asylum, or wherever the path may lead."

She inhaled softly, having not thought of what he said before. "I thank you. I hope that I will not need it, but..." She sighed. "Life may not provide for me."

He offered his hand as one might to another man.

With a slight twist to her lips, she shook it.

"Shall we return?" he asked, turning toward the castle.

With a deep breath, Fenya took his proffered arm.

MOTHER

T he depths of another night put Wigmore in an unsettling
state of stillness that gave Fenya a deep sense of unease. Too
much was unsolved, uncertain. Although eager to leave this
prison, she faced yet another night upon the island. Captain Balderik
wanted to search out the island's secrets with his men while they gave
Marlowe and Harker another day to recover before making the flight
inland.

She couldn't blame him. After all, there was the cave, the lighthouse, the stables, the church ruined, and numerous nooks and cran-
nies that information or people could hide. They couldn't leave until
they knew for sure the others had gone.

Midday, a pair of dragons arrived, and upon them two men: a
soldier and Mage Caius Verena.

"Uncle!" Fenya exclaimed in surprise when he dismounted from a
burgundy Common Wyvern.

He raced to her and pulled her into his arms like her father might
have done. "I thought you were dead for certain, Fenya!" he exclaimed.
He cupped her face in his hands. "My dear, I'm so very amazed to see
you again." Tears spilled over his lashes, and Fenya pulled back in
surprise.

"Uncle, I—" Emotion swelled in her and she had to blink back her own tears. Then she abandoned her attempts at control and buried her face in his chest. "I'm relieved to see you as well."

"Are you well?" He held her at arm's length suddenly, taking her in with his rich, deep blue eyes that reminded her vividly of her dear father's. "My dear? I'm shocked to find you looking so...unharmed." His cheeks were damp as were his palms as he cupped her face in his hands again. "I'm so sorry."

She frowned at him. "For what, Uncle?"

He blinked rapidly, but his tears overtook him and dripped down his nose as he gazed down at her. "It's all my fault—I pushed your mother into sending you here. I told her it was the best thing for you —I was certain it would help you control yourself—and then Milton wanted to marry you, and it seemed the perfect solution—but then—"

"I'm sorry—" Fenya suddenly blurted out, remembering abruptly that she had never told him the truth.

"*You're* sorry? Whatever for?" he asked, startled out of his train of thought.

"You were right to send me here." The words burst from her mouth in a rush. "I burned down the cottage. I couldn't control it. It's all my fault, and I'm so sorry. The fires—it wasn't the maid's fault, it was all mine. And she's ruined because of it!" She buried her face in her hands.

"Oh my sweet, sweet niece, I know." He patted her shoulder. "My dear, we've known from the beginning."

She gaped at him, her mouth moving like a gasping fish. "You knew? And you let her suffer for my sins?"

Alarmed, he drew back and shook his head. "Of course not! Outwardly, we had to accuse her in order to protect you."

"But her livelihood!"

"She is well cared for." Uncle Caius squeezed her shoulder. "I promise you. She has been given a promotion in a friend's house and is most trusted."

Tears of relief brimmed on Fenya's lower lashes.

"I'm sorry we couldn't tell you. We couldn't risk you telling your mother." Uncle Caius grimaced as if he had said too much.

Realization spread over her. "Oh." She paused as the reality of what he said sank in. "Where is she? Mama?" Fenya looked behind her uncle, and for a brief moment, she thought her deepest desire was manifesting before her. "Mama?" she whispered.

"You will not stop me, sir!" commanded a female voice imperiously. "Where is she?"

Fenya smiled.

"Cali!" Uncle Caius gasped. "What are you doing here?"

Fenya abandoned her reserve and raced for Aunt Cali, and as she ran, Aunt Cali spotted her, and the older woman picked up her skirts, racing for Fenya.

Fenya collided with her, wrapping her arms around her neck and barely holding back her sobs. But as Aunt Cali smoothed her hair and rocked her back and forth in her arms as one might rock a babe. Her aunt's hard stomach pressed against Fenya's in the intensity of her hug. Milton had spoke the truth—she was with child again.

"I want to leave here," Fenya sobbed.

"I know. We'll take you off here immediately," Aunt Cali said.

"Actually, ma'am, if you don't mind...may I speak to Miss Verena before she departs?" Captain Balderik's calm voice had an immediate calming effect on Fenya. She glanced at him, more aware than ever of how she had just lost utter control in front of anyone nearby, such as half the soldiers she'd stood beside and begged to come with because she wouldn't act like such a fool.

Aunt Cali shot daggers at Captain Balderik. "No, she will leave."

But Fenya shook her head, even as she dragged her hands across her eyes and discretely wiped her nose. She must look like a half-crazed woman. "Of course. Of course you can. Just...a moment."

Captain Balderik stepped back, averting his eyes from her discomfort. "You may meet me beside the fire in the common room."

"Yes, of course."

Aunt Cali faced her as he moved away. Uncle Caius moved beside his wife, putting a protective hand on her stomach and talking low to her so even Fenya couldn't hear. She shook her head, fire in her gaze.

Mage de Croia approached him almost silently, bending toward his ear to speak. After another comment to his wife, Uncle Caius led Mage de Croia toward the castle as well.

Fenya paused though, drinking in the presence of her aunt.

"Darling, there's no requirement for your involvement in anything more." Aunt Cali clutched Fenya's hands in hers. "You know that, don't you?"

Fenya nodded, her earlier panic and emotion having faded. "Yes. I... I'm sorry. I lost my head."

"No, you...you've been through too much for your age." Aunt Cali gripped her hands tightly as if she could impress comfort upon her with the pressure.

She bit her lip, forcing away the thoughts that wanted to come back. "There are things I need to do though. Things to say...to discover."

Aunt Cali frowned maternally. "Dear, there's nothing you need to do. You simply need to rest and recover."

Fenya removed her gloves and pulled up her sleeves, spreading her palms before her aunt, fully displaying the scars that marked her. "No. I'm afraid that's not true, Aunt Cali. Not anymore."

Aunt Cali gasped softly and took her arm gently in her own. "What happened? When did this happen? How—?"

Fenya smiled wryly, allowing Aunt Cali to rotate her wrist and inspect the scars as she wanted. "When the Relic was sent here."

"The Relic—?" Her mouth turned into a perfect "O" shape.

Fenya frowned. "Didn't you know?"

Aunt Cali covered her mouth with her hand for a moment then resumed her inspection of Fenya's wrists and forearms, her mouth now in a thin line. "No. We didn't." After several seconds of silence, she finally dropped Fenya's hands and met her gaze. "Well it's done now, isn't it?"

"Yes, it is."

"You're right, my dear. There is much to discuss that can no longer be hidden from you." She tucked Fenya's arm into hers. "Come. There is no time to waste then. And no time like the present."

Bemused, Fenya allowed herself to be led into the common room, where three men waited for them.

Captain Balderik stood beside the fire, staring moodily into the flames, and Mage de Croia paced in the middle of the room, while

Uncle Caius sat in a chair before the fire with his head tilted back against the headrest.

Balderik spotted her and straightened.

Aunt Cali dropped Fenya's arm and went to her husband, putting her hand on his shoulder and leaning down to speak into his ear. His bloodshot eyes widened and he darted a glance to Fenya's face only to fall immediately to her arms, exposed now with their flame-shaped burns.

"Miss Verena, Magess Verena," Captain Balderik greeted them both properly.

Fenya waved away his protocol. "Captain, what is it you wished to speak to me about?"

He looked discreetly in the direction of her aunt and uncle in question, but Fenya smiled wryly.

"You can speak freely, sir. I think we all are in this together now."

His lips thinned slightly, but he bowed his head in agreement. "Yes, Miss Verena. And that is my concern."

A sense of dread threatened deep in her belly at his confession. "Go on."

"You are in grave danger of this man pursuing you, given what he has done to you and what he has invested in you." He paused, his gaze again encompassing the room.

"Go on," she said. "I trust every person in this room. And if one of your men is listening nearby, I would hope you can speak freely in front of them as well."

"Absolutely," he agreed. "I would have it no other way."

"Then speak freely," she repeated. "And when you're finished, I have many questions."

"Yes, miss." He motioned to the vacant chair beside her uncle, but she shook her head. "Well, given the circumstances, and your status as the Relic Bearer now, I believe that the headmaster, as you call him, will pursue you wherever you go. You are more of a target now than ever before, given your status and your relative unknown."

She nodded. "I understand that as a newly accepted Relic Bearer, I must present myself to King Alaric?"

Captain Balderik dipped his head in agreement. "Not at present. At present, you must introduce yourself to his son, the Elemental Regent."

"Prince Lucien?" Fenya sucked in a sharp breath as the man's image flashed before her. She weaved in her spot and drifted idly over to the still empty chair to sink down in horror.

"My dear, you're pale! Are you well?" Aunt Cali was at her side in seconds, Uncle Caius moving to rise.

"Why the prince?" Fenya asked, locking gazes with Balderik.

"It's not well known yet, but the King is deathly ill and his son is standing in his place. It's believed that it might be a form of Legacy Madness."

"But I..." Fenya's dread continued to grow as she trailed off and gathered herself. Knowledge was power. She needed to keep as much knowledge to herself as she could, while sharing what was needed to help her find the headmaster and stop him. "I see. And how long do I have before I must report to his court?"

"That depends. When did the Relic accept you?"

She shook her head. "When Sir Milton brought it to me. I don't know of the date."

"Hmm."

"I must ask if you're aware..." Fenya hesitated, then pushed forward, "of the Prince Regent's involvement in Wigmore?"

Captain Balderik studied her for a long moment, and Fenya was aware of the exchange of glances between her aunt and uncle. Finally he answered, "Yes. And therein lies the problem, Miss Verena. If you present yourself to him, you reveal your location to him, you could endanger yourself more than being a Relic Bearer warrants. We do not know how far his corruption goes."

She sighed and gazed down at her forearms. The flame-shaped burns traveled up her forearms like tattoos, reaching toward her elbows. They were darker now, almost like a birthmark, but they also had changed slightly, as though the flames crystalized at the tips. It was difficult to describe the change she had seen, but somehow, when she looked at them, they appeared to encompass all four elements. But not the fifth... "The Relics are more trouble than they're worth," she murmured.

"Dearest, can you tell me...you've clearly communicated something to the others here, but what has the headmaster done to you?" Aunt Cali began.

The fire danced merrily in the grate, happily devouring its fuel. Whereas once it would have driven her mad to be this close to it without manipulating it, now it was calm, as though the fact that she contained the Relic, was tied to it, bound to the flames forever, made them rest easy. She knew she could enrage them or calm them with a flick of her fingers or even a thought. She could form them into shapes and beckon them from nothing. She could make them destroy this very castle. And now, as the Relic Bearer, she had a responsibility to all the country.

Quickly, distantly, Fenya heard herself explain what the headmaster had done. When she finished, ending at the moment that the headmaster escaped, she looked again to Balderik. "How is Marlowe?"

"He is alive. He will live."

She narrowed her eyes at him, reading beyond what he said. "He has no Legacy does he?"

Balderik released a sigh. "No, he does not."

"I stole it from him. Like the headmaster stole it from others." She shook her head. "He is despicable. He has made *me* despicable—a monster." Her voice broke.

"You saved him!" Aunt Cali said fiercely. "Any reasonable man or woman would rather live a life as an Ordinary rather than have no life to live at all!"

"I'm a monster." Fenya shook her head. She had once believed that too, but was it true?

"You are not," Aunt Cali knelt in front of her, and Fenya realized she'd spoken aloud. "You are not a monster. You saved a life and that was at great cost—to you and him. You did not know whether your identity and newfound Power was safe with anyone here and yet you risked everything to save someone you hardly knew. Fenya, you're a heroine, not a villain." She took Fenya's hands in hers. "And though you might have more Power now than you ever wanted or anyone thought possible—" Aunt Cali broke off and swallowed thickly. "It's how you choose to go forward that makes the difference. And what you plan to do about it."

Fenya met her aunt's gaze. She already knew what she was going to do about, she thought. But she turned to Uncle Caius. "Uncle...there are things I need to know about being the Relic Bearer. You were alarmed when I said that it had claimed me, and seeing my arms. What makes you so alarmed for me?"

He shrugged and glanced at Balderik. "As the good captain said— you must expose yourself now. There is no escaping the responsibilities that come knocking now. It's unusual for a woman to be the Relic Bearer, and there has never been one so young. That will, unfortunately, mark you as a Bearer stronger than expected. Perhaps stronger than seen before. And there will be interest. Some might want to study you, investigate you. Marry you. Some won't leave you be." He twisted his hands together on his knees. "I'm afraid that until you're legally an adult, your aunt and I can shield you and attempt to protect you, if your mother would allow, but after that...the King can summon you to court at a moment's notice. And it is treason to refuse."

Fenya rolled her lip between her teeth. Then a small smile started on her lips. "Well he can't summon me if he can't find me."

Aunt Cali shot an alarmed look at her husband. "Dearest, there are magi who are training in tracking down runaways and—" She broke off as Fenya raised her brows.

"I don't think they've tried to track down someone like me, Aunt Cali."

Aunt Cali straightened. "No. I believe you're right." She stepped back to Uncle Caius and took his hand in hers. "Then we stand behind you. Whatever you choose, we will support you."

"I know what must happen," Fenya said, turning her attention to Mage de Croia, who had stopped his pacing to stand against a bookcase. "We must find your nephew and the other students. I cannot rest until they are all safe and protected for the rest of their lives. And to do that, we must find the headmaster. I'm certain that he's not abandoned his task and will only hurt others if left to his own desires."

"I agree," came a quiet voice from behind the chairs.

Fenya leapt to her feet and whirled at Harker's voice. "Harker!

You're awake?" She hurried over to the smaller girl, wanting to pull her into her arms, but hesitating, remembering belatedly that they had never been friendly and Harker's expression was bemused at best.

"Yes, I...I'm alive. Still." Her lips twisted bitterly. "And I've heard enough to know that he has my brother still."

Fenya's heart stilled. "Yes. As well as Rhys and the others. You and I are the only two to escape."

Harker's bitterness intensified as she limped over toward the chair as though her every muscle ached. Just as she reached its side, she collapsed, her back arching backward and her arms thrashing against the armchair.

"Harker!" Fenya raced forward, ignoring the others and taking the girl's wrist in her hands. Under her skin, aether rippled as a riptide, a million tugs pulling against one another.

Without hesitating, Fenya pulled at the pulsing flares of Power, drawing them out of Harker's body and into her own. Her body snatched them up, absorbing the aether with little shocks that had her flinching with their strength.

When the last pop of Power sparked and faded, Fenya opened her eyes to find Harker limp against the back of the chair, her body limp and eyes filled with twisted wonder.

Fenya didn't speak, but slowly released Harker's wrist. Her hands still stung, and as she looked at them, there were blisters over her palms that disappeared under her skin. Harker shifted, sitting up and watching them disappear with disbelief.

The room was silent but for the crackling of the fire in the grate.

Finally, Harker spoke again, sitting forward and adjusting herself with more ease than before. "What a pair we are. One Powerless and would-be Feral, the other a magess of ne'er before seen Power."

"Hopefully never *seen* Power," Fenya corrected quietly. "I never wanted anything but to *lose* my Fire, Harker, because of how much pain I caused with it. But if I can do good with it—if I can ease your pain or make any of this right, I will."

Harker's hard gaze collided with Fenya's, but this time, Fenya didn't feel the desire to back down. Instead, she outlasted the younger girl's glare, and something like respect simmered there.

"Well, I'm useless now," Harker said. "But I still want my brother back. And I'll do anything—go to the ends of the earth—to get him out of Griffin's grasp."

The fire snapped violently in the grate as Fenya blinked at her, her body going still. "Griffin?"

Harker slowly wet her dry lips and leaned forward, her hands shaking violently. "It's time you know what I know."

Epilogue

Fenya ambled through the Ashmere Wood by Whitland at the height of their autumn colors, musing on all that had happened over the summer months.

After three nights spent on Wigmore Island with the soldiers, Fenya and her aunt and uncle had finally been able to leave with an escort most of the way to Whitland Manor. At the nearest EDS quarters, they all had landed with the EDS soldiers, and a carriage was called for the family and Harker. Trailing discreetly behind it, Captain Balderik had personally escorted them home.

Since then, Harker had made slow progress in her recovery, but most days were a delicate dance in avoiding her triggers. She did best when alone, or with only Fenya, who could calm her outbursts. Their relationship, too, had improved. Aunt Cali and Fenya provided her with books for her education, partly distraction, partly out of her own desire to learn. But often they walked together in the woods, and Harker and Fenya stayed together in the rebuilt cottage beside the lake.

There, they often analyzed the texts available to them, Henslow's journals and papers, Bryton's journal, and Theodore's letter home, which she had taken before leaving Wigmore for the last time. She'd also taken Bryton's jar of marbles, which sat on her bedside table, both silent witness and painful memory.

Fenya had not seen Mama since before leaving for Wigmore. But a letter had arrived soon after her return to Whitland Manor, not from Mama but from Sir Milton. She had read it so often that she had memorized it.

Dear Miss Verena,

It has come to my attention through multiple sources that you have not completed the required full term at Wigmore. As a result, I am releasing you from our engagement. If you would like, you may return my ring to me at the following address, or you might keep it as a reminder of the cost of broken promises. I also wish to inform you that I have married. While you were at Wigmore, Seraphina was a comfort in my isolation. We have been wed for a month now and are expecting a child the beginning of next year. It would please us both greatly if you were to visit.

JM

Fenya had responded only with the return of his ring. She had no desire to keep it as a bauble, as she knew she would never wear it again. Indeed, just looking at garnets reminded her of the hateful ring and all the imprisonment it held.

Most days she chose not to think of Mama or Milton at all. Her mind and energy was aimed at a far more productive task: tracking down Griffin. But day after day of searching local parishes, Legacy registrars, and all other documents she could find, only failure after failure greeted her.

She had accepted the failure at Wigmore. After all, there had always been a chance she would fail the moment she left with Dempsey. It didn't make the failure bite less. It festered like an untreated dragon bite, aching and painful at the very thought. And it burned all the worse for Dempsey's betrayal. A young man she had thought was true and honest, a friend, someone suffering the very same thing as she was...to be so betrayed... When she closed her eyes at night, his was the first face she saw. It was only moments before Griffin and Rhys replaced them. To be followed by all those she had failed to save.

Bitter dragon blood.

That's what it tasted like.

At least according to Fang.

Fenya sighed and paused to stare at a bush where a few green and white fairy dragons were creeping into the middle. As she watched the amber-hued bush the dragons played within, the dragons shifted their scale colors to match the foliage. Once upon a time she would pull out her sketchbook and watch them for hours, sketching every angle she could as quickly as possible.

Now...her sketching was single-minded. She sketched the headmaster, Griffin, over and over, in every form she could remember, adding notes from Harker's memory. Often they pored over her sketches together, and Fenya made slight changes based on one or the other's recollections.

Harker had told of overhearing the headmaster called Griffin by some of the staff. She had confessed that Ivy had known so much more than she had ever been able to communicate, and that Harker had been actively trying to teach Ivy her letters and writing so that she could communicate more clearly. But what Harker had been able to glean from the mute Ivy with her powerful Exaudio Legacy had been that the headmaster had plans for them that stretched far beyond Wigmore. And that Wigmore wasn't the only experimental school he had created.

The thought made her stomach roll and clench in panic. To think of others...children and even adults being experimented on, unable to fight him. Children she had never met, perhaps bound by the very bracelets she had broken free from. But not everyone had the Power to do so, especially to control it. And what if he had different experimentations? What if different schools used different methods of control over the students? The cruelties were endless, and they chased each other through her mind, keeping her awake at night.

Within weeks, she would be obligated to send notice to the Crown that her Relic had properly claimed her as its Bearer and she would be required to come at the King or Prince's summons within a few months.

If they can find me.

She allowed herself a small, wry smile as she kicked at a pile of autumn leaves. She fully intended to post the letter and leave, revealing to no one where she went. She was already planning it out. She would go into hiding, traveling frequently, and disguising her appearance. She would go by another name, using falsified documents or true documents like the ones she had been searching for evidence of Griffin.

The only difficulty was Harker and her lingering, unpredictable remnants of Legacy. It was rapidly turning Wylde, and Fenya had no idea what the future held outside an asylum. Harker pressed Fenya to resort to when her days were especially difficult. But to send her to such a place...Fenya would rather die. She would keep Harker with her as long as she could, keep her safe with her presence. Protect her—one way or another, with Mage de Croia's help.

The trees rustled and a stick cracked, and Fenya halted, searching the skies and scanning the forest path. Automatically, she sent out her Legacies, searching for life nearby. She heard the wind with sudden clarity, but she ignored those sounds and focused on the stick.

Then a smile came to her lips. "Hello, Harker," she said softly.

Harker sighed and emerged from the brush a short distance away. "I followed you a good half mile that time."

"Yes, I was deep in thoughts." She shook her head as the younger girl, now dressed in proper clothing, with her hair bound up into a braided crown like a young lady, came forward. It had become a game of Harker's to try and evade the staff and follow Fenya out into the woods as she escaped with her notebook and satchel, her only constant companions.

Fang sang a low note from the trees. *I spotted her when she left the house.*

I'm sure you did. You two are conspiring against me.

Fang made a sound like a chuckle in answer, then flapped away to harass the fairy dragons in a bush ahead.

Harker was barely recognizable now in the clothes Aunt Cali had provided. A plentiful wardrobe had appeared for Harker within a week at Whitland, and Aunt Cali became a surrogate mother, treating her as well or better than she treated Fenya. The earthy colors chosen for her dresses and ember-crop jacket flattered her dark hair and complexion. She glowed in good health, despite her volatile Legacy which almost daily exploded and sent her into a "seizure" as Healer Elric called it. Fenya rarely strayed far from her, unless Cali's private Healer was present at the house. But Harker had decided she didn't like him and didn't trust him. Fenya had yet to meet him, as she did not want to risk her aunt or uncle's safety if there were any suspicion of Fenya at their home. So she evaded him, escaping to the woods before he arrived, staying out late, and returning long after his horses had carried him away. Fang always helped her keep an eye out for the Healer and his departure. She'd learned that they could communicate up to two miles away, which came in most useful.

"How are you feeling today?" Fenya asked as Harker fell into step beside her.

Harker shrugged and stooped to pick up a smooth rock on the path. "Well enough. No seizures today. Healer Elric's new potion has been workin'—working," she corrected her accent before Fenya could, then added, "So far."

Fenya nodded in approval. "That's good. Hopeful, right?"

Harker shot her a dark look. "Hope's for people who haven't been burned."

The cynicism stung, but only because it was true. How could Fenya dare to hope when everything had been taken, and the one who knew what had been done was lost in the aether?

"I can't stay here forever," Harker said bluntly. "I endanger your aunt and uncle. Their children. The more unstable I become, the worse it'll get. Like Elric said—it's only a matter of time before I go fully Wylde."

Fenya drew a deep, steadying breath. It did nothing to stop the sting behind her eyes. "I know what he said. But I can't leave you at the nearest asylum and—"

"Why not?" Harker released a humorless laugh. "I'm fully capable of givin' 'em plenty o' trouble."

Fenya tilted her head in answer, a reluctant smile tugging at her lips. Despite all her suffering, Harker had lost neither her cynicism nor her wicked humor. It had taken Fenya time to appreciate her biting humor, but now she couldn't imagine life without it. "Still. Griffin will investigate every asylum. If you're tracked there, he'll find you."

"And if he finds me," Harker said grimly, "he'll find you. And that would be the end of all Avenesse—and maybe beyond."

Fenya shrugged and said in opposing lightness, "At least the end of me."

Harker stopped short, grasping Fenya's arm. "Don't joke about that. If we lose you—" her voice caught. "You're the only one who can stop him."

"Please don't put that on me." Fenya closed her eyes.

Harker's grip tightened. "I didn't—*he* did."

The way she spoke sent chills down Fenya's spine. Panic and resolve warred in Harker's face. Fenya understood. Merritt was still with him. And if Fenya was the only one who was Powerful—and stable—enough to track Griffin down, then she was Harker's only hope. To deny the burden Griffin had put upon her, denied Harker any chance of seeing her brother again. Before Harker did end up in an asylum for all the wrong reasons. Or tracked down by some crazed bounty hunters who brought Wyldes to the Crown for coin.

"You know," Fenya murmured, "I still hope. I hope we find Griffin —and Rhys and Merritt and Ivy and the others." Her mouth twitched. "I have to keep hoping—it's all I have left. Because I won't rest until I find them. I can't get any rest until then. And let's be honest—I could use some real rest."

Harker smirked. "As could I. It's been weeks since I've had a full night's sleep."

Fenya glanced away, tormented by the faces that haunted her dreams and the memories of Harker's screams—past and present. If she didn't hear them in her nightmares, she heard them echoing through the walls beside her bed.

One thing was certain: Griffin would haunt them until she found him.

"What are we going to do then?" Fenya asked. "Because we could both use some rest."

Harker slid her arm into Fenya's. "I'd say we start plotting our revenge."

Fenya's lips curved into a similar smirk. "We've waited long enough."

"Then one thing's certain," Harker said.

"And what's that?"

"Griffin had better beware. Because I've got some rather creative ideas brewing"

Fenya's laugh startled the bush of fairy dragons beside her, and they burst out with a furious twitter of sparkling scales. One snagged itself on the bush, flailing about until Harker plucked it from the stick. She held it out, and it caught the light sparkling through the treetops.

"Look—a dragon scale." Harker held it aloft between thumb and forefinger, offering it to Fenya, but Fenya shook her head.

"Keep it. It's supposed to be good luck." She winked at her now friend. "And let's face it—you need more luck than I do."

Harker snorted, then tucked the scale into a small pocket at her waist. "Ain't that the truth."

Fenya linked her arm through Harker's and aimed them back at the house, praying—just this once— that luck would stay on their side.

Would You Leave A Review?

Did you enjoy this book? If so, please don't be shy about telling a friend—or leaving a review. Or both!

Indie authors thrive because of readers like you. Reviews truly make a difference: they help retailers decide which books to promote, help other readers know what to expect, and help stories like this one find their way into the right hands.

Your review does not need to be long or polished. A rating and a few honest words—what you liked, what didn't work for you, what stood out—are more than enough. High or low, glowing or critical, I value every review deeply. Whether it's three words or three hundred, each one matters to me.

Thank you, from the bottom of my heart, for reading *A Lady of Scales and Smoke* and for supporting independent authors.

To leave a review, simply scan the QR code below and select "Leave a review" on the book's page.

With gratitude,

Kelsie

Below are the review links and QR codes for your convenience. Reviews on multiple sites are deeply appreciated.

Amazon

https://bit.ly/ALady

Goodreads

https://bit.ly/GR-alady

Bookbub:

https://bit.ly/3YpieP3

Don't Like Leaving Reviews?

Other Ways You Can Help

If you enjoyed this book and would like to support it further, here are a few other meaningful ways—only if you wish:

• **Share a mention of the book on social media.**

You don't need to tag me, but sharing it with your community helps it find the right readers.

• **Give the book as a gift.**

Buying a copy for a friend, book club, or fellow reader is a wonderful way to support any book.

• **Recommend it in person or in reading groups.**

A thoughtful word-of-mouth recommendation is incredibly powerful.

• **Request it at your local library or indie bookstore (or both).**

Reader requests often influence what libraries and shops choose to carry.

• **Add the book to your reading lists or favorites.**

On platforms like Goodreads or StoryGraph, even a simple add helps visibility.

• Include it in a reading wrap-up or TBR post.

Whether on social media, a blog, or a newsletter, these mentions matter.

Thank you for every bit of support—whether large or small. Each one helps more than you know.

About the Author

Kelsie Engen grew up in North Pole, Alaska, where long, snowy winters fostered a lifelong love of reading and storytelling. Today, she writes fantasy inspired by classic literature, fairy tales, and the quiet tension between light and darkness.

She still lives in Alaska with her husband, children, cats, and dog—who provide endless joy and just enough distraction to slow the writing of her next book (though she wouldn't trade it for anything). When she's not writing or editing, she can usually be found escaping the cold by disappearing into magical, uncharted worlds.

To stay up to date on new releases, behind-the-scenes peeks, and other bookish shenanigans, sign up for her newsletter at **www.Kelsie-EngenAuthor.com**. She can also be reached at **scriptor.librorum@gmail.com**

Where to find her online:
- Instagram: @KelsieEngen
- Facebook: KelsieEngenAuthor
- Pinterest: KEngenAuthor

Website: www.KelsieEngenAuthor.com

Also by Kelsie Engen

Find all my books at my website:

www.kelsieengenauthor.com/buy-my-books

WORKS BY KELSIE ENGEN

- SERIES:
  - The Canens Chronicles
  - A Canens Chronicles Short Story
  - A Seven Kingdoms Faery Tale
- STANDALONES:
  - Spurn the Moon
  - Finding Home
  - Bernadette & the Stranger

Scan me

https://bit.ly/worksbykelsieengen.

Or scan the QR code above for the links to all stores.

www.ingramcontent.com/pod-product-compliance
Lightning Source LLC
Chambersburg PA
CBHW051056030726
47504CB00006B/1646